You and Me and Us

You and Me and Us

A Novel

Alison Hammer

WM

WILLIAM MORROW

An Imprint of HarperCollinsPublishers

P.S.™ is a trademark of HarperCollins Publishers.

YOU AND ME AND US. Copyright © 2020 by Alison Hammer. All rights reserved. Printed in the United States of America. No part of this book may be used or reproduced in any manner whatsoever without written permission except in the case of brief quotations embodied in critical articles and reviews. For information, address HarperCollins Publishers, 195 Broadway, New York, NY 10007.

HarperCollins books may be purchased for educational, business, or sales promotional use. For information, please email the Special Markets Department at SPsales@harpercollins.com.

FIRST EDITION

Designed by Diahann Sturge

Library of Congress Cataloging-in-Publication Data has been applied for.

ISBN 978-0-06-293485-7
ISBN 978-0-06-299386-1 (hardcover library edition)

20 21 22 23 24   LSC   10 9 8 7 6 5 4 3 2 1

To Kathy, Randy and Elizabeth,
my original "Us"

You and Me and Us

Chapter One
Alexis

It's dark outside by the time I finally look up from my computer—so much for being home early. I check my phone to see just how late it is: 11:10. So close to the lucky minute I've been wishing on since I was old enough to tell time. I wait for it, keeping my unblinking eyes on the screen until it hits 11:11.

Even though it's silly to waste a wish on something I get to do every night, I wish I were home in bed with Tommy, not sitting in the ergonomic chair designed to be so comfortable that I forget I'm going on fourteen hours at my desk. I love my job, I remind myself.

My eyes find Tommy's smiling face in the silver frame on my cluttered desk, his arms wrapped around our daughter at her eighth-grade graduation last summer. I linger on CeCe's face, a younger version of my own, partially hidden by the thick black glasses she insists are "totally on-trend." I missed seeing her cross the stage in her cap and gown by minutes thanks to a creative presentation that ran late, but I made it in time to take the picture.

An incoming email dings and my focus shifts back to my computer like one of Pavlov's dogs. Another Google Alert, their frequency increasing at the speed of Monica's fame, which unfortunately has been gaining momentum in the past year.

Setting up a Google Alert for Tommy's ex-wife wasn't exactly my proudest moment, but I couldn't know she was out there and not know what she was up to. With CeCe's acting obsession, it's a small miracle she hasn't figured out that it isn't a coincidence the semifamous actress shares her last name.

The information is out there if she'd ever google it. Or asked. But CeCe would never think to ask if either of us had been married before. The only conversation about marriage in our house is centered around the fact that her dad and I never took that "till death do us part" step.

I'm the one who's resisted all these years; we'd be an old married couple by now if it were up to Tommy. But he didn't grow up in a house like mine, with parents that were married in name alone. There was no love between them, and that was not the kind of relationship I wanted to model ours after.

I glance back at the email and consider deleting it unread, but curiosity gets the best of me. Lately the alerts have been full of sightings around L.A., pictures of Monica on the arm of a dozen different celebrity bachelors. I keep hoping one of them will stick so she can take someone else's name, but no such luck yet. I open the email to see what the devil is up to now.

"*Netflix's* The Seasiders *adds Monica Whistler to its cast.*"

"You've got to be kidding me," I accidentally say out loud.

Becky, my best friend and business partner, peers over the giant monitor where she's making the fourth round of revisions to an ad for Dox Pharmacy, our biggest client. "What's up, buttercup?"

"Nothing," I mutter, too tired to explain that not only did Monica land another big role, but she'll be filming all summer in Destin, Florida.

Of all the beaches in all the world, Destin is *our* beach. It's where Tommy grew up, where he and I first met as kids, spending every summer together until the year I turned twelve and stopped going to my grandmother's beach house. It's where we reconnected twenty years later, fell in love, and had the *oops* that turned into CeCe. We still go down there as often as we can, just not as often as Tommy would like.

It's a small miracle we don't have a trip planned this summer—CeCe's too excited about a theater camp here in Atlanta, and I pretty much had to say goodbye to that much time off when I opened my own ad agency three years ago. But still. I cringe at the thought of Monica going back to the beach where she left Tommy with a broken heart and a condo full of modern furniture that was as hideous as it was uncomfortable.

I stand to stretch and start gathering my things. Now that my concentration has been broken, I might as well get some sleep.

"You going home?" Becky asks, running a hand through her signature pink hair. She looks as tired as I feel.

"Yeah, I should have left hours ago—Tommy had something he wanted to talk to me about."

"Everything okay?"

I shrug through a yawn. "Probably just something about CeCe."

3

"She still upset about that party?"

"And a million other things," I say, yawning again. "See you tomorrow."

My shoes echo on the industrial floor as I drag myself through our trendy office space. I doubt Tommy will be awake when I get home, which is probably for the best since I'm too tired to talk about anything tonight.

Some days it's harder than others to remind myself that this is the life I fought to live. The reward for standing up against every chauvinist who told me that women don't make it far in the advertising industry because they have kids. They probably would have been right about me if it hadn't been for Tommy.

"DADDY, HAVE YOU seen my purple tank?"

I step into the hallway between our bedrooms and answer CeCe. "I think it's down in the laundry room."

"Daddy?" she asks again, and I wonder if I said the words out loud or just thought them.

"It's in the laundry room," Tommy echoes. "Still in the dryer, I bet."

He coughs the deep cough he's had for a few weeks now. The long hours I've been putting in are taking a toll on him, too. I'm about to remind him he should make an appointment to get a Z-Pak or something, when CeCe steps between us, scowling in my direction before making a dramatic exit.

As much as I want to remind her she has me to thank for buying her the tank top in the first place, I don't. And not just because I can feel Tommy watching, waiting to critique my reaction. Sometimes it stinks living with a shrink.

"If you say it's just a stage I'll scream," I tell him.

"You came in late last night," he says, wisely changing the subject.

I yawn, as if realizing just how little I slept could make me even more tired. "This project will be over soon."

"And then the next one will start," Tommy says. I want to defend myself and say that's not fair, but he's right. "Don't forget CeCe is making a special dinner for us tonight."

"I won't forget," I promise.

Tommy smiles and kisses the bridge of my nose before pulling me in for a hug. I love the way we still fit perfectly together after all these years. I wrap my arms around him, breathing in the scent of the herbal shampoo he uses even though there hasn't been any hair on his head in more than two decades.

Sometimes it's hard to reconcile this strong and sturdy forty-eight-year-old man with little Tommy Whistler, the chubby boy from my childhood who stuttered when he spoke, quietly observing the world with one blue eye and one brown.

I tilt my head to give him a kiss, a silent thank-you for being everything he is. He's the one who holds our family, and our life, together. If it weren't for him always being there for CeCe, my guilt over putting in the hours it takes to run an agency would be crippling.

"Get a room." CeCe squeezes past us into her bedroom, purple tank top in hand, and slams the door in our faces.

I parrot her tone: "We don't need a room, we got a house."

"You're not helping," Tommy says.

I'm about to tell him I was trying to be funny when my phone chirps a warning alarm. It's almost time to go and I'm nowhere near ready. He frowns as I slip out of his arms.

"I'm not avoiding anything," I tell him before he has a chance to say otherwise. "I just have to get ready for work."

He follows me into the bathroom, watching as I put a serum on my face that costs more than a month of lattes. "You wanted to talk about something?" I ask, remembering the email he sent yesterday afternoon.

Before he can answer, my phone starts quacking—the tone Becky programmed for her calls. "Sorry." I'm saying that word a lot lately.

Tommy heads downstairs to make our princess's lunch while I talk to Becky about an early morning client request and speed through my blush-bronzer-eye-shadow-lip routine. He's a better mom than I'd ever dream of being. Not that I ever dreamed of being a mom.

I find him in the kitchen for a quick kiss goodbye.

"Don't forget dinner tonight," Tommy says. "Six-thirty."

"I won't," I promise. "I'll even set an alarm to remind me."

On my way out, I call up to tell CeCe to have a good day. I pause, waiting for a response I know isn't coming. One day she'll be old enough to appreciate how hard I work to give her the life she takes for granted. One day.

Chapter Two

CeCe

I wish you and Mom would get a divorce." I toss my backpack on the floor and lift myself onto the kitchen counter in my usual spot. I thought about it all day at school, how much better things would be if it were just Dad and me. Mom's barely ever here anyway.

"Never going to happen," Dad says. "Feet off the counter."

"Why not?" I unfold my legs, letting them swing below me.

"Well, for starters, we can't get divorced if we aren't legally married."

"You don't have to remind me I'm a bastard."

"But you're such a cute bastard." He leans over to ruffle my hair, then coughs a loud cough that sounds like it hurts. He clears his throat. "Hand me a glass?"

I grab one from the cupboard and Dad fills it from the tap, even though water from the fridge is colder and better. "Pretty much everyone I know has divorced parents," I tell him.

"That's sad," he says before taking a long sip.

"No, it's not." I push my glasses back up my nose. I hate it when they fall down when I'm trying to make a point. "It's kinda cool, actually—they get two houses, and their parents pretty much buy them whatever they want to let them know they still love them."

"You're lucky your parents don't need to buy you anything to show how much we love you, or each other." He plants a sloppy, wet kiss on my cheek that I wipe away.

"I'd be luckier if it was just you and me."

Dad shakes his head and I know I should let it go. But I'm sick of letting everything go. All the little things, like when Mom has to cancel our mother-daughter manicures, and the big things, like when she postponed shopping for my first bra so many times that Dad eventually had to take me. He stood outside while a saleslady went in the dressing room with me. Her hands were freezing, and her breath smelled like garlic. It was awful, but I let it go.

"She doesn't even like being a mom."

"That's not fair," Dad says in his shrink voice.

"But it's fair she always chooses work over me? Like my ballet recital in third grade? Or my thirteenth birthday? Graduation last year?"

Mom had been super annoying, making a huge deal about what a big milestone graduating from middle school was, and then I looked out from the stage to see Dad sitting next to an empty chair. The only empty seat in the whole auditorium.

"I don't remember the ballet thing, but she got to your graduation as soon as she could, and we celebrated your birthday last year for a full week."

"You always take her side."

"I have two sides—one for each of you." He turns around

and looks over his shoulder. His smile fades when he sees I'm not amused. "Got everything you need to make dinner?"

"Yeah," I say, trying not to sound too excited. This gourmet dinner is part of my plan—when Mom or Dad says something about how grown-up and mature I am, I'm going to ask them again about Liam's party this weekend. If they trust me, it shouldn't matter whether or not his parents are going to be there.

"Perfect," Dad says. "I've got another patient in five minutes, and after that I'm all yours until my last patient at eight."

"West Coaster?" I ask.

"Doctor-patient confidentiality." He moves his hand across his mouth as though he's zipping his lips shut.

"I don't get what the big deal is, it's not like I'll ever meet this person."

"You're just like your mother."

"Take that back." I lower my voice so he knows I mean it. We may look alike with our boring brown hair, hazel eyes, and our noses that are a little too big for our faces, but I am nothing like my mother.

"*Oh, Cecelia,*" he sings. "*You're breaking my heart.*"

"Yeah, yeah. And I'm shaking your confidence daily." I roll my eyes as he kisses my forehead before going into his office, helping strangers on the Internet while his only daughter is dealing with major life problems on her own.

I wish there was a way I could make him understand this isn't just any party. And Liam Donnelly isn't just any boy.

Chapter Three

Alexis

Sorry I'm late," I call as I open the front door at a quarter till nine. "Emergency at work."

The door to Tommy's office is closed, which means he's videoconferencing with a patient somewhere in the world.

"Dinner smells amazing!" My mouth is watering and I'm glad I only had one slice of pizza at the office.

"It *was* amazing," CeCe says from the living room. "Two hours ago."

I forgive the saltiness in her voice since I am almost three hours late. "Everything's a fire drill with this new client." I walk into the living room and find her curled up in her usual spot on the couch. "I'm sorry I'm so late."

"You already said that." CeCe turns the volume up on whatever cooking competition show she's watching. I step closer and rest my hand on her shoulder, but she jerks away and stomps upstairs without finding out which chef won.

Before scavenging the kitchen for leftovers, I turn off the

TV and walk back down the hallway toward Tommy's office. The low murmur of his voice is comforting even though I can't hear what he's saying. I lean my head against the door, willing time to move faster so his session will be over and he can cheer me up.

If he finds me out here he'll think I'm trying to eavesdrop again, so I wander back to the kitchen, where I find a mess that's even scarier than the floor in my half of the bedroom closet.

Every pot and pan has been used and discarded, lying on the stove or next to the sink. I accept my punishment and start cleaning. The water is almost too hot, but it feels good. The harder I move the scraper back and forth, the more tension leaves my body. This must be why people like working out.

I'm so focused I don't hear Tommy walk up behind me. I startle when I hear him cough.

"I'm sorry," I say for the thousandth time, turning around to face him. He offers a weak smile and reaches behind me to turn off the water. "You're not mad at me, too, are you?"

"I'm not mad," he says, although his tone implies otherwise.

"Don't say you're disappointed." I turn back toward the sink.

"Your daughter made something special tonight, she wanted to impress you."

"Was it good?"

"Still is, I bet. We left you a plate in the fridge."

Sure enough, there's a foil-wrapped plate sitting on the first shelf. "I honestly don't get why she cares I wasn't here, she clearly hates me."

"She doesn't hate you, she's a teenager."

"I tried to apologize, but she wouldn't listen."

"She was hurt—which she wouldn't be if she didn't love you."

"I guess." I sigh. "Eat dinner with me?"

Tommy pours two glasses of wine while I snap a picture of the plate. I have to admit, it looks like something I'd order in a restaurant. There's some kind of whitefish, sautéed spinach, and a few tiny roasted potatoes, purple, of course. I find an Instagram filter that makes it look even better and tag CeCe in the caption: *My daughter, the chef. @WhistlerGurl. #ProudMom #Delicious #ILY.*

Sad that it's easier to tell the world I love my daughter in a hashtag than it is for me to say it to her face.

Tommy sets the glasses down and sits in his usual chair, across from mine and next to CeCe's. "So there was an emergency at work?"

"You don't want to hear about it." I fork a piece of fish. Even cold, it's good. Really good. "The new chief marketing officer at Dox Pharmacy keeps dangling the business in front of us like a damn carrot. His requests are ridiculous, like he's trying to see how high we'll jump."

"And you keep jumping."

"There's no other choice. We can't lose that account—I have seventeen employees counting on me."

"They're not the only ones."

Ouch. I reach for my wine and take a big sip. When that doesn't help me feel better, I try to find comfort and understanding in Tommy's eyes. "I'm trying."

"You have to try harder."

The edge in his voice catches me off guard. I like it better when he's soft and supportive, but I know he's right. He shouldn't have to handle everything around here. And I can't even make it home in time to have dinner or a conversation. "You wanted to talk about something last night?"

He shakes his head and takes a sip of his wine. "It can wait, I'm too tired. Wasn't an easy day here, either."

"Bad patient?" I raise my eyebrow in jest. Trying to get him to spill details about the strangers he counsels is one of my favorite games to play even though I never win.

"Not bad, but there was one really tough one. This guy just got a terminal diagnosis."

"Cancer?"

Tommy nods. "It's bad. So bad he's thinking about not doing any treatment."

"Does he have a family?"

Tommy nods again.

"Then he has to fight it," I tell him. "For his family, if not for himself."

"You really think so?" Tommy asks. He looks exhausted. I wish he would talk to me about these things more often. It can't be healthy to try to carry so many people's problems alone.

"Don't you?"

"Maybe he doesn't want to put his family through a long illness when it's going to end all the same." Tommy runs his hands over his head, smoothing hair that isn't there anymore. "I'm honestly not sure. You weren't there when my mom was sick. The treatment was worse than the breast cancer—three years of chemo and radiation and surgery, then more chemo and more radiation. She kept fighting past the point her life was worth fighting for, and in the end all that pain and suffering was for nothing."

I reach out and take his hand in mine. I hate that I wasn't there for him when he was losing his mom, almost as much as I hate that Monica was. If I had known, I'd like to think I would have come back sooner. So much happened in the twenty years I was gone, time we'll never get back.

Picking up my fork again, I dredge a baby potato through the lemon butter sauce. "Our daughter is a pretty stellar chef."

"She's pretty great all around." Tommy's eyes light up the way they always do when he talks about CeCe. "She made a pretty good case over the dinner about going to that party this weekend."

"Not that again." I stab the last bite of fish.

"So that's a no?"

"Not if the parents aren't going to be there." I drain the rest of my wine. "And by the way, thanks for making me the bad guy."

"You know I've always had a thing for the bad girls," Tommy says, smiling with his whole face. Those dimples still get me every time. His foot finds mine beneath the table. "What do you say we leave the dishes for tomorrow and go to bed early?"

"That's the best idea I've heard all day," I agree, as he stands and walks around the table toward me.

He pulls me up and folds me into his arms, kissing me like we haven't seen each other in days, not hours. Breathless, I step back and look at him looking at me with hungry eyes.

He keeps his hands on my waist as I lead the way upstairs, as if even a step apart would be too far.

Before I turn off the bedroom lights, I glance down at my phone. There's a notification from Instagram that @Whistler Gurl liked my photo.

Chapter Four

CeCe

The music is so loud Sofia practically has to yell for me to hear. "I can't believe we're really here."

I shrug as if it's not a big deal, even though it's the biggest deal—and the biggest lie I've ever told my dad.

"My fair Juliet!" Heads turn and it feels like there's a spotlight on me as Liam slides off the kitchen island where he was perched above a group of girls. I almost died when Mrs. Katz announced that the two of us would be playing the leads in the spring play. "I didn't think you were going to make it," Liam says.

"I'm not officially here," I say, grateful Sofia had the idea for me to spend the night at her house. It almost didn't work since I'd already told Dad her parents were letting her go, but I covered it up by saying she didn't want to go without me. I told him it was a best-friend thing and he actually bought it. One benefit of having a workaholic mom: if she were home, she would've seen right through my lie.

Liam gives me a hug and I breathe in the woodsy scent of his cologne. He shifts, leaving one arm draped heavily on my shoulder. "Want a beer?"

I hesitate, but Sofia answers for us both. "We'd love one."

I've had a crush on Liam Donnelly for the last four years, from the moment I spotted him on the first day of middle school. As an eighth grader, he was up onstage at orientation with all the other club presidents, telling my entire class about the drama club. But it felt like he was just talking to me. I signed up, of course, and got to spend an hour every Thursday after school in a room with Liam doing acting exercises and improv games. But the spring play was the first time we'd be onstage, playing opposite each other.

"Great party," I tell him as he hands us both our beers.

"It is now that you're here." He smiles a crooked smile, and a flock of butterflies take flight in my stomach.

"Bella just got here," Sofia says, even though Bella was the first one we saw when we walked in. "I'm going to say hi."

I mouth a silent thank-you in her direction. When I turn back, Liam is looking at me and I'm seriously worried I might turn into a puddle. I glance away, down at the red Solo cup in my hands. The foam has gone down a bit, so I take a sip and try not to gag. I don't understand why people like beer.

"I love this song," I say because I can't think of anything else. Liam and I have had tons of conversations before, but they're always about something specific, usually related to drama club. I need a script for this sort of thing.

"Then let's dance." Liam grabs my free hand and leads me into the living room where the couches have been pushed back against the wall to create a makeshift dance floor.

I take another sip and attempt to keep rhythm with my

hips. I'm not a good dancer when choreography isn't involved. But then his hand is on my waist and we're swaying
in sync with the music and each other. His skin feels warm
beneath the faded T-shirt that's so soft I wish I could wrap
myself up in it, and when his chocolate-brown eyes focus on
mine, I don't look away.

Liam and I keep dancing through the next three songs,
getting a little closer with each one. I bite my lip in anticipation when a slow song starts to play. I push my glasses up and
smile, my eyes meeting his.

"I'm going to get us some more beer," he says.

I try not to look disappointed, but the place where his
hand used to be feels empty. I look stupid standing there
alone, so I make my way to the edge of the room, trying
not to stare at the couple making out right there in front of
everybody. The guy's hands are literally in the back pockets
of the girl's jeans and his tongue is most definitely in her
mouth. I didn't think it was possible to be so grossed out and
jealous at the same time.

Liam finds me leaning against the fireplace. "Your beer,
m'lady."

Feeling a little braver now, I finish almost half of the glass
in one gulp.

"Shall we?" He nods toward the dance floor. The slow song
is still playing, but it's got to be close to the end. He reaches
for my beer, but I stop him, taking another big sip first.

Liam nods his approval and I hiccup before handing it
over. He leaves our cups on the fireplace mantel and leads me
to the dance floor.

We're swaying back and forth, and I'm on the edge of feeling lost in the moment, when my stupid glasses start slipping

down my nose. I squinch my face, hoping they'll go back up on their own so we don't have to stop dancing, not even for a second.

Liam must notice, because he takes a hand off my waist to push them back up for me. "You're cute," he says.

"So are you." I feel my cheeks turning red, but I'm not sure if it's from the beer or because he's looking at me like I'm the only girl in the room.

The song stops playing and another slow one starts. A playlist faux pas, but I'm grateful for the mistake. I step a little closer, he holds my waist a little tighter, and I try to memorize this moment so I can remember it for the rest of my life.

He bends down and I try not to shiver as his lips brush against my ear. "I'm glad you're my Juliet."

"I'm glad you're my Romeo."

"We should probably start practicing for that final scene."

The kiss happens in the middle of the play, but I don't correct him. It's the only part I've been worrying about—if I look like I don't know what I'm doing, everyone will find out that I'm probably the only girl in ninth grade who hasn't been kissed. Sofia's the only one who knows my secret. And Beau, but he doesn't count since he doesn't go to our school, or even live in the same state.

"Mrs. Katz said we were just going to pretend."

"She said we *could* pretend, or we could really kiss if we wanted to." Liam leans back a little and I look up at him. I'm trying really hard to look at his eyes and not his lips, *but his lips*.

"Don't you want to?" He tucks a strand of hair behind my ear.

I look away for a second, but when I glance back up, Liam is leaning toward me. I can't believe this is about to happen.

I hope Sofia is seeing this. Actually, maybe it's better if she doesn't in case I don't do it right. I hope I do it right. His eyes are closed and he's getting closer. My heart is beating faster than the music. And then—

"Cecelia!"

No, no, no. Please, no.

"Cecelia," my dad says again. "In the car. Now."

I drop my arms from around Liam's neck and step back. The whole room has gone silent except for the whispers. This can't be happening.

"Say goodbye, Cecelia."

To my social life.

Chapter Five

Alexis

I can't believe she lied to us," Tommy says as he joins me outside, letting the front door fall closed behind him.

"I can't believe you fell for it."

He gives me a sideways glance as he sits beside me on the front porch swing, my favorite part of this old house. I lean over and kiss his neck. "There's no way in hell Sofia would give up going to the party of the year just because CeCe wasn't allowed to go."

"But they're best friends."

"Even best friends have to draw the line somewhere." I put my hand on his leg, hoping my touch comforts him. Thanks to my parents, I learned early in life that it's easy to be let down when your expectations of people are too high.

"Was it really the party of the year?"

"Oh yeah," I say. "I mean, a party at Liam Donnelly's is already pretty awesome, but a party at Liam Donnelly's when his parents are out of town?"

"What's the big deal about this kid?"

"He's a junior, and she's a freshman with a crush." I smile, happy to be the one with an inside scoop for once. Our regular mani-pedi dates have become somewhat less regular, but last week as CeCe and I got our fingers and toes pampered, it was "Liam this" and "Liam that" and "Liam said."

"Interesting," Tommy says. "Did I tell you they were slow dancing when I walked in?"

"How slow?"

He shakes his head. "Real slow."

"Show me." I stand and reach for Tommy's hand. He resists at first, but eventually gives in like he always does. I put my arms around his neck and he brings his hands to my waist. "Were they standing like this?"

"A little closer."

"Like this?" I take a step toward him and start swaying even though there isn't any music and the neighbors might be watching.

"Like that," Tommy says with a sigh.

I sigh, too, but mine is a happy one, because there's no place I'd rather be than here with him, slow dancing under the moonlight. We should dance more often; the last time might have been at Jack and Blake's wedding last fall. Too long ago.

I start humming "It Had to Be You," the song we declared as ours. He joins in and I'm standing in the arms of the man I love, wondering if life can get any better than this. "I love you," I whisper into his neck.

"Then will you marry me?"

"Never." I smile, resting my head on his chest. "But thank you for asking."

Tommy laughs and the vibrations pass through his body

into mine. But then the laugh becomes a fit of coughs and I pull back. "You should see a doctor about that cough."

"I have," he says, catching his breath.

"Did he give you a Z-Pak?" Tommy's eyes meet mine for a second, but he quickly looks away and I get a weird feeling in the pit of my stomach. "Babe?"

"There's something we need to talk about."

Every cell in my body is suddenly standing at full attention. "Should I sit down for this?"

"Maybe we both should."

He takes my hands in his and keeps holding them as we sit back down on the swing. The swing where I curl up with a novel on lazy Sunday mornings while Tommy reads the paper or does a crossword puzzle. The swing where I rocked CeCe to sleep when she was a baby. The swing where Tommy and I sometimes sit with a glass of wine, talking about our days and trying to solve the problems of the world.

I tighten my grip on his hand. "You're scaring me."

"I'm scared, too."

But Tommy doesn't get scared.

I hold my breath. When he starts to speak, my world stops.

THE NEXT THIRTY minutes are the longest and slowest of my life. His words bounce around my head, refusing to stick: *Small cell lung cancer. Stage 4. It's not good.*

"Lex?" he says my name as if it's a lifeline, and I realize I haven't said a word.

"How could this happen? You're too young."

"And too good-looking," he says, trying and failing to lighten the mood.

"Why didn't you tell me something was wrong? I thought it was just a bad cough."

"The cough was just one symptom," Tommy explains. "There were others, a little chest pain, shortness of breath. I didn't want to worry you until there was something to worry about."

Either he's a better actor than CeCe, or I've been oblivious. But he didn't say anything—I would have heard him; I would have noticed something was wrong. *How long has he been pretending everything is okay?*

"How long have you known?" I ask.

"They did a CT scan and a needle biopsy last week, but I didn't get the results until Wednesday."

"You had a biopsy? How the hell did I miss that?" I feel myself starting to hyperventilate so I focus on breathing, inhaling and exhaling with purpose.

"You were in New York for that big Dox presentation. I knew it was an important meeting."

"Not more important than you," I insist.

Tommy takes my hand and brings it gently to his mouth, forgiving me for what I didn't know, what I didn't do. "You needed your head in the game so you could impress that new bigwig. If you knew . . ." He stops and looks down at me, and I wish I could read his mind the way he always manages to read mine.

"If I knew, I would have been there." I take my hand back and rest it in my lap, playing with a loose thread on the hem of my shirt. "You shouldn't have had to go through that alone."

"The whole thing took less than an hour, I was fine. Well, not that fine in hindsight."

I shake my head. I would be furious with him if I wasn't so scared. I should have been with him, to hold his hand, to wait, to be nervous, to try to stay hopeful. He should have told me.

"Why didn't you tell me as soon as you knew?"

"I tried," Tommy says, and I feel sick to my stomach. The email. He said he'd wanted to talk. "But honestly, I didn't try that hard." There's a raspiness to his voice I haven't noticed before. I should have noticed. "I think I just needed to come to terms with it on my own first. I knew you'd have questions, and I wanted to have the answers."

I need more than answers. I need to know that he's going to be okay; he has to be okay.

"I want to talk to your doctor."

"I have an appointment Monday to get a second opinion. But he's going to say the same thing the first one did."

"And what exactly was that?" I need him to say it again.

"It's lung cancer, small cell. Stage 4B."

"How many letters are there?" I knew about the numbers, but I didn't know there were letters.

"Just two."

A and B. My heart sinks.

"It means the cancer has spread outside my chest," Tommy explains in his shrink voice.

"Spread? Where? How much?"

"Pretty much everywhere. Lymph nodes. Liver. They even found a few spots in my bones."

Our conversation the other night flashes in my mind. "Your patient. You never tell me about your patients."

24

He turns his face away from me and lowers his head.

"But you said . . ." I can't finish the sentence.

Tommy looks at me with those eyes—one blue, one brown—that see right through me. They look sadder than I've ever seen them before.

"We're going to fight this." My voice is shaky, which I know makes me sound uncertain, so I say it again. "We are going to fight this."

He squeezes my hand.

"Say it." I need to hear him say the words.

"Lex."

"Say we're going to fight this."

"It's too late," Tommy says. "The doctor may not use those words, but he'll tell us the treatment would be tough. I'll lose my hair." I narrow my eyes at him. This is not the time for jokes.

"We're going to fight this," I say again, with more conviction this time.

Tommy's face falls. "This is why I didn't tell you before I made my own mind up; I knew you'd try to convince me. But the treatment wouldn't just be hard on me, it would be hard on all of us. And chances are it won't work."

"But there's a chance it will."

"It won't. And I'm not going to put you or CeCe through what I went through with my mom. The false hope, the pain and suffering." His voice cracks with emotion. "I won't do that to you."

"What am I supposed to say to that?"

"I don't know," Tommy says, soft as a whisper. He turns and looks at me, his eyes pleading. "That you'll stay with me, that you're not going anywhere?"

ALISON HAMMER

His desperation is palpable, and my heart is suddenly in my throat. How could he think for a second that I would leave?

I swing myself around so I'm facing him, one leg on each side, careful not to put too much weight on him. "Of course I'm not going anywhere," I tell him. "I love you."

I kiss his neck on the left and then the right. I kiss his cheeks, where silent tears have started to fall. I kiss his mouth hungrily, as if I can make it all better. He kisses me back, but it feels like an apology so I pull away.

"If you love me, you'll fight to stay with me," I plead.

"It's not that simple."

"Of course it is. If you love me, if you love our daughter, if you love our life, you'll fight to keep living it. You are not your mother; medicine has gotten so much more advanced since she was sick."

"Shhh." He brings a finger to my lips. I hadn't realized I'd raised my voice. "I'm not ready for CeCe to know. And we don't have to solve everything tonight."

"Like hell we don't." I slide off him and lean against the porch railing. I look into the Shulmans' house across the street. Their lights are on and the drapes are open, so I can see Jenna and Corey in their living room, playing a game with their boys, Micah and Brett. Never in my life have I wanted so badly to trade lives with somebody, anybody else.

My legs buckle, but Tommy's there to catch me. He holds me up, his hands wrapped around my waist. His touch, which usually calms me, has the opposite effect tonight. Neither of us says anything as we sit back down on the swing.

"Let's go to bed," he eventually says. "We can talk more tomorrow."

"You don't get to control this," I tell him, my voice sharper

26

than I intended. "And you're the one who says we should never go to bed angry."

"Please don't be angry with me."

"Please don't give up on me. On you. On us."

He sighs. "You don't understand."

"Then make me." I grasp his hands, as if he could explain it through osmosis. "In what world wouldn't you want as much time with us as you can get?"

"Even if I fight it, the doctor says I have six months, tops."

"And if you don't?"

"Two to three."

I inhale sharply and hold my breath, afraid I might throw up. Neither scenario gives us enough time.

Tommy turns my face toward his so I'm looking him in the eye. "If chemo or radiation could give me a few more years with you and Ceese, I'd do it in a heartbeat. But we're talking months either way. And I want them to be good ones."

TWENTY MINUTES LATER, my tears have dried, leaving salty tracks on my cheeks, but I'm nowhere closer to understanding. Tommy is staring straight ahead, not speaking. I don't want to fight; I just want him to.

"I don't know how else I can say it to make you understand. It's quality over quantity," he says, slipping into his shrink voice. "I'd rather have fewer good days than more miserable ones, when I'd be too sick to make the best of them."

"But what if—"

"There are no 'what if's."

"You don't know everything, Tommy Whistler." I'm aware

that my voice is getting louder again, but I can't help it. "Doctors are wrong all the time; they might be wrong."

I lean back into the swing, trying to catch my breath again. It's like someone stole all the oxygen and I can't breathe. I can't do this. Tommy puts his arm around me, rubbing circles on my back. The repetitive motion and the weight of his hand help calm me. I don't want it to, but it does.

"I'm not giving up on this," I warn him. "I'm going to try to change your mind."

"I know." He pulls me closer so I can rest my head on his shoulder. The weight and unfairness of it all settles over me like a fog.

"How did this happen? You look so healthy."

"Why, thank you," Tommy says with a smile in his voice, but I don't let his charm distract me. I need to find the logic in this, but there isn't any, it doesn't make sense.

"You don't even smoke."

"Twenty percent of people with lung cancer never smoked."

I sit back up so I can look him in the eye. "Please don't quote statistics at me."

"Not even the one where people who tell their spouses they have less than six months to live have a hundred percent chance of getting laid that night?"

"Don't try to make this a joke, it's not funny."

"It's my cancer, I can joke if I want to," he teases. "Wasn't that a Patty Duke song?"

"Lesley Gore," I correct him. " 'It's my party and I'll cry if I want to.' "

"Please don't cry anymore," Tommy says. "I don't want to remember your face all red and splotchy."

I elbow his side and he bends forward, making a dreadful

sound. I jump up, causing the swing to sway in my wake. I steady it, afraid I accidentally hurt him. "I'm so sorry, are you okay?"

Tommy's shoulders start to shake, and my stomach drops to my knees. When I realize he's laughing, I step back and cross my arms. "I am so mad at you."

He looks up at me with that smile and those dimples and I realize I love him so much it hurts. I cringe when his laughter turns into another coughing fit.

"What can I do?" I plead.

"You can forgive me," he says, his voice strained.

"There's nothing to forgive." I reach for his hand, and we let ourselves back inside, where Tommy turns off the front porch light and locks the door as if it's any other night. But it isn't any other night. This is the night that will forever divide the before and the after.

When tomorrow comes, I'll find a way to convince him we have to fight this. But tonight, I just want to close my eyes and drown myself in him, to forget everything except us. I want to pull him as close as he can get, until he's a part of me. The best part of me.

I catch a sob in my throat and he silences me with a kiss. There's no apology in this one. It's more urgent, as if he's already trying to make up for the lifetime of kisses he won't be here to give or receive. I taste the salt of tears; I'm just not sure if they're his or they're mine.

Chapter Six

Alexis

Nothing at the office has changed in the two days I've been out, but everything feels different. My eyes keep drifting to the stack of Tommy's love notes on the corner of my desk. I want to read them all over and over again, memorizing each word.

I should have called in sick for another day, but Tommy seemed desperate for things to feel normal—and my being home, hanging on his every move, is as far from normal as we could get. But being away from him is killing me, because every minute I'm not with him is one less minute we'll have together.

"What do you think, sugarplum?" Becky asks, using another of her rotating nicknames.

"Sorry, what?" I say.

Becky gives me a look that is full of frustration and concern. I should have known better than to try to pretend everything is okay when it so clearly isn't. "You, come with me," she says in a tone normally reserved for whatever poor Tinder guy she's about to break up with.

Knowing I don't have a choice, I follow her out of the office we share and through the open space where our employees are trying not to stare. I feel like a kid being led down a hallway to the principal's office. At least there will be alcohol where she's taking me.

MOE, OUR FAVORITE bartender at Rí Rá, the Irish pub across the street from our office, waves hello when we walk in. "Early lunch?"

"We're not eating," Becky says. "Just drinking."

Moe nods and smiles, opting out of our usual chitchat.

"Now talk," Becky says, as we seat ourselves at our usual table in the back room.

"What?" I ask, knowing full well my coy act isn't going to work on her.

"Something is clearly going on with you. Is it your parents? It can't be you and Tommy—that man is crazy about you, all those love notes . . ."

I reach into my pocket for the note I found tucked inside the visor of my car this morning. I unfold it and hand it over to Becky.

"*I love you more today than yesterday, and I'll love you more tomorrow than today,*" Becky reads out loud. "Where does he come up with this stuff?"

"Google." I smile before I can stop myself.

"You're kidding?"

"It started as a joke. He said it was too hard to compete

with a copywriter, so he started to Google love notes and quotes and song lyrics."

"All these years, you had me thinking he was a closet poet."

Adina, one of our usual waitresses, comes over with two beers—a Guinness for Becky and an Allagash White for me. "On the house," she says. "Moe's treat."

Becky thanks her, then lifts her beer toward mine. We clink glasses, but I set mine down without taking a sip.

"Shit, you're not pregnant, are you?"

"What? No, it's not that." I take a big sip to prove I'm not lying.

"And CeCe's not pregnant?"

"Oh god, no."

"Then what's got you so down, lovey?" Becky says. She reaches across the table and puts her hand on top of mine. "I can't help if I don't know what's going on."

"You can't help," I tell her. "No one can."

"I can try?"

I pull my hand from under hers and take a long sip of my beer. It feels good going down, so I take another. "Tommy's sick." I briefly make eye contact before looking back down at my glass. "Sick-sick."

"But he's going to be okay?"

I lift the glass to take another sip, but my hand is shaking so hard the beer spills down my chin. Suddenly, Becky is on my side of the table, folding me into a hug. As much as I want to find comfort in her arms and let her tell me everything is going to be okay, I know it isn't and it won't be. I stiffen like a statue, turned to stone in her awkward embrace.

"You guys ready for another?" Adina asks, rounding the corner. She retreats without waiting for an answer.

"So, what is it?" Becky asks, her arms still around me.

"Lung cancer." She pulls back, studying my face. "It's bad. We got a second opinion that confirms it."

Monday morning we sat in a waiting room for almost two hours to get less than ten minutes with the oncologist. I shivered as soon as we walked into his office, and not just because the AC was blasting. There was something about the stark white walls and the hard vinyl chairs that made it all feel hopeless. I sat there, afraid to move as the doctor shuffled the thick stack of papers in Tommy's file, barely making eye contact. As if our grief were contagious.

"Shit. Is he going to do chemo?"

I shake my head.

"Radiation?"

When I don't respond, Becky asks, "Then what? Something experimental?"

I shake my head again, remembering how angry Tommy got on the way home when I brought up a clinical trial I'd found online. He shut me down before the words were out of my mouth, and I lost it, screaming at him for giving up so easily, for not telling me sooner, for making me live in a world without him for even a minute longer than I had to. I yelled until my throat was raw, but Tommy just kept driving, looking straight ahead until he pulled into the driveway.

He turned the car off and looked at me with the saddest eyes I've ever seen. He looked so hurt and alone that I wanted to take it all back even though I still meant every word.

"Babe?" Becky asks, bringing me back to the moment.

"He's not fighting it."

"What do you mean, he isn't going to fight?"

I look up to see her eyes shimmering with tears. "He says

he's choosing quality of life over quantity. They gave him a bunch of prescriptions for comfort care—things that will make him feel better, but nothing that'll cure him."

"He isn't even going to try?" Becky's voice wavers and the heavy stone is back in the pit of my stomach. I take a deep breath, and when that doesn't help me feel any better, I take another sip.

"What are you going to do?" Becky asks.

"Whatever it takes to change his mind," I say.

"How?"

I shrug. I haven't gotten that far in my plan, but I figure I've made a career of persuading strangers and influencing their behavior, so I should be able to convince the person I love most in this world that life is worth living. I shiver at the thought of life without him. I won't let it come to that. I can't.

Becky finishes the last of her beer and signals for another round. "I used to hook up with an oncologist. If he'll take my call, I can ask him to help."

I laugh for the first time since Friday night, but I don't say no. It feels good to feel something that isn't sadness or anger. "If one of your old 'swipe rights' can help save Tommy, I'll marry the guy for you!"

"I'm pretty sure he was already married," Becky admits. I shake my head, not wanting to know more details. "And if you're going to marry anyone, it should be Tommy."

"You sound just like him."

Becky smiles. "For a man who hasn't given up on trying to get you down the aisle after all these years, I'm surprised he's giving up so easily on this."

"You and me both." Adina drops off our second round and

I raise my full glass toward Becky before taking a sip. "The irony of it all is that both our mothers are to blame—his for taking the fight out of him, and mine for ruining my idea of marriage."

"Maybe you can use this to your advantage," Becky says. I recognize the timbre of her voice, a tell for when she's about to share what she thinks is a brilliant idea. "Say you'll marry him if and only if he gets treatment."

"Tried it."

Becky slouches back in her chair. "What does he want to do, then? Sit at home and wait to die?"

The word "die" knocks the wind out of me, but I recover with the help of another sip. "Not exactly."

When Tommy told me how he wants to spend the little time he has left, my heart and my jaw dropped. On one hand, it made sense. Destin is his home; he only moved away from the white sand beaches and emerald-green water to be with me. On the other hand, it can't be a coincidence that Monica will be there, too. I don't think they've been in touch, but it's not like I monitor his texts or emails like we do with CeCe.

I look up at Becky's face, waiting for me to answer. "He wants us all to go back to Destin for the summer," I tell her. "Until . . ." I can't finish the sentence.

She nods, twirling a strand of pink hair around her finger in her signature thinking move, probably worrying about how she'll be able to handle everything going on at work on her own. That was the reason I gave Tommy when I told him we couldn't go.

"Don't worry," I tell her. "We aren't going to go."

"Why not?"

"What do you mean, why not? For starters, if you recall—

you and I own an advertising agency that might be losing our biggest client if the new CMO has his way."

"You can work anywhere as long as there's Wi-Fi," Becky says. "And if something big comes up, you can always drive back up for a day or two."

I shake my head even though she isn't wrong. I've done it before.

When CeCe was in elementary school, she and Tommy would spend most of the summer in Destin, and I'd come down for long weekends as often as I could. The year she was eight, I'd planned a two-week trip down there, the most time I'd ever taken off work. Of course, I ended up having to drive back for a few days because of some big client meeting.

I don't even remember what the meeting was for, I just remember how I rationalized it—that I had to prove to my boss that I took the job just as seriously as my male counterparts. And of course, I always thought back to the advice my dad gave me before I started my first real job that included paid time off. He told me never to be gone long enough for them to realize they didn't need me. He was the ultimate businessman and he trained me to think like a businesswoman. Not a woman balancing her career and her family.

"I know I can, but I don't want to."

Becky furrows her eyebrows, trying to make sense out of the pieces I know don't fit together. But I can't tell her the truth, that I can't stand the thought of running into Monica. Or worse, having Tommy run into her. Or, god forbid, CeCe.

"Going down to Destin just isn't realistic," I try to explain. "His doctors are all here, and we already paid for CeCe's theater camp. She's been looking forward to it all year."

Becky sighs and nods in agreement. "How is the bean taking everything?"

"She doesn't know yet."

Becky coughs, choking midsip.

"I'm pretty sure she knows something is going on, but she has no idea what."

"When are you going to tell her?"

I shrug. "I don't want to think about that right now."

"Finally, something I can help with."

Now I'm the one to raise an eyebrow.

"The best way to avoid thinking about something is to drink about it instead. Adina!" she calls out. "Another round, por favor!"

Chapter Seven

CeCe

I open the front door to find Mom standing on the other side, trying to get her key in the lock. She glances up, looking like a mess in one of the shapeless shirts she usually wears just around the house. Her eyes look sad even though she's laughing.

"What is wrong with you?" I ask. I could hear her banging around from the kitchen, where I was trying to memorize my lines. She's been acting off all week—but just because something is clearly going wrong at work doesn't mean we should have to suffer at home.

"You saved my life," Mom slurs as she falls inside, throwing her arms around me. Her weight is heavy on my shoulders and she reeks of beer.

"Are you drunk?" I shrug her off me and she stumbles back, giggling as she balances herself against the wall.

"Maybe just a little?" she whispers loudly, as if she just noticed we're standing outside Dad's closed office door.

"You're wasted."

She shrugs and stumbles past me, heading toward the kitchen. I follow a few steps behind, a little worried she might fall. If she does, I'll have to break the one rule I've never broken and interrupt Dad when he's counseling one of his online patients. But it'll be her fault—she is not a small woman and I doubt I'd be able to pick her up on my own.

"Careful," I say as she falls into her chair at the kitchen table. What kind of mother comes home out-of-her-mind drunk before it's even dark outside? I glance at the clock on the microwave—it's 4:35. Thank god Dad will be out of his session soon. She's his responsibility, not mine.

"I can do this; I'll be fine on my own." Mom's slurring her words together so I don't fully understand. "The two of us, we'll be fine."

"What are you talking about?" I ask, sounding more like the parent than the child, which is totally screwed up.

She rests her head on her hands and hiccups. "Water."

I get a glass from the cabinet and fill it with the cold filtered water from the fridge and set it down in front of her. She hiccups again. "Thank you," she says before taking a sip. "You love me, don't you?"

"Not when you're like this."

Mom closes her eyes and nods. I almost feel bad for a second that I may have hurt her feelings, but this is not how a mother is supposed to act.

"You didn't drive home, did you?" I ask, fully assuming the role of parent.

"Uber," she says, hiccuping again.

At least she was semismart about it.

Her glass is almost empty, so I fill it up again. When I turn back, her eyes are fluttering closed like she's about to fall asleep—right there at the kitchen table where we eat dinner, where I do my homework, where I'm supposed to be memorizing lines for a play she clearly doesn't care about.

"You should go to bed," I tell her.

She mumbles in agreement, so I grab her arm and attempt to pull her up. She resists, but I'm younger, I'm stronger, and I'm sober.

I take a step back and steady myself, giving her arm a big yank. She finally stands up and drapes her arm around my shoulder. The two of us walk slow and steady like we're tied together in a three-legged race. We're rounding the corner of the living room toward the stairs when the door to Dad's office flies open.

"What in the world?"

"Hi, baby." Mom lifts her head up, but it wobbles around like her neck isn't really supporting it. "Everything's fine."

"I've got this," Dad says, taking over just as Mom lets out a disgusting man-size belch.

"Gross." I step away and brush her germs off my shoulder.

Dad lifts her up, holding her like a baby in his arms. A big, drunk baby. It looks like it's taking a lot of effort to carry her up the stairs, so I stay at the bottom in case he needs help.

"Don't leave me," I hear Mom say before he turns into their room. The door closes, but I can still hear the sound of her crying.

There's a weird feeling in the pit of my stomach, and for a second, I'm scared that something is really wrong. Mom's never done anything like this before. I try to think back to all the incoherent things she was mumbling about. Then all of a sudden, it's so obvious.

I smile and head back into the kitchen. Maybe wishes do come true. Because I heard her, clear as day. She said, "Don't leave me." There's no other explanation—Mom and Dad are getting a divorce. Or breaking up, since they aren't officially married.

Now I just have to decide how I'm going to let all this play out. If I let Dad know that I know, I could catch him off guard. Which could be good. Or it might make him mad. And if he's mad, then I won't be able to take full advantage.

When Sofia's parents told her they were getting divorced, she practically had a meltdown. She locked herself in her room until her dad promised to put his credit card on an Uber account so she could go back and forth between their houses whenever she wanted.

Lauren got her mom to take her on a trip to Paris. I don't remember how she pulled it off, something about being worried that she and her mom wouldn't be as close since they weren't going to be living in the same house all the time.

Come to think about it, not having to live in a house with my mom would be even better than a trip to Paris. I could tell the judge how Mom came home drunk today. The courts would never leave an innocent child with a woman who did that sort of thing.

I hear Dad's cough getting closer, so I push my script aside and get him a glass of water—no time like the present to show him things will be okay when it's just the two of us. I can help take care of him, probably better than Mom does. She's so focused on her stupid agency, it's like her employees mean more to her than we do. She'll have plenty of time to spend with them once Dad and I move out.

On second thought, Mom should be the one to move out.

She can get an apartment and Dad and I can stay at the house. It makes more sense since his office is here, and so is all my stuff.

"Whoa, careful." Dad reaches over my shoulder to turn off the faucet. The water is overflowing, pouring out of the glass like the fountain at Piedmont Park.

"Sorry, I was distracted."

"Understandable," he says, before coughing again. I hand him the glass of water and he gives me a sad smile before taking a sip. "That must have been scary, seeing your mom like that."

"Whatever." I shrug it off, remembering too late that I was supposed to make it seem like a bigger deal so I'm not lying when I tell the divorce judge about it.

"Your mom's got a lot going on," he says, making excuses for her like he always does. Sometimes I wonder what he sees in her. At least he's finally come to his senses; we'll be better off without her.

I lift myself up on the counter and watch as he tries to act normal and pretend nothing is wrong. I know I decided not to steal his thunder and let him break the news, but I don't think I can wait. And with Mom being passed out drunk upstairs, there might not be a better time to go in for the full-custody kill.

"I know," I tell him.

"What do you know?" Dad asks, raising an eyebrow.

"I know what's going on."

Dad takes a step back and sits down at the kitchen table. He looks tired and sad. "Oh, kiddo," he says. "I wanted to be the one to tell you."

"It's okay," I say, trying to keep my voice upbeat. "I already told you—most of my friends' parents are divorced. As long as you can get full custody, it'll be fine."

"Full custody?"

"Or whatever it's called. Mom can move out and you and I can stay here." Dad takes a deep breath, which starts him coughing again. I hop off the counter and bring him the glass of water he left by the sink. "You've said it yourself: I'm grown-up for my age. I can help take care of you."

"Oh, Cecelia," he says.

"Yeah, yeah. I'm breaking your heart."

"Sit down with me." He reaches for my hand and pulls me closer until I'm sitting in his lap, the way I used to when I was little. "Your mom and I aren't getting divorced."

"I know you're not officially married."

"It's not that."

My stomach feels weird, the way it does for a second right before I go onstage. I stand up and turn around so I can look him in the face. "But I heard her. Mom said, 'Don't leave me.'"

"She did," Dad says, his voice eerily quiet.

"Where are you going?" I pull my chair out and sit down so our knees are almost touching. "Daddy?"

He reaches over and takes my hands in his. They're shaking, and so is his right leg. "I'm sick, baby girl." He coughs again as if he's making a point.

"But you'll get better," I tell him. "You'll go to the doctor."

He looks down at the floor and squeezes my hands. When he looks back up, I can see the truth in his eyes, shining with tears that are about to fall.

I've never seen my dad cry before. I don't want to see him cry.

"I have to go." My legs wobble beneath me as I stand up.

43

I take a careful step, like I'm made of glass and the smallest wrong move could shatter me into a million tiny pieces that he'll never be able to put back together. "I should go check on Mom."

I keep walking out of the room, away from his sad eyes. He doesn't stop me.

Upstairs, I close the door and collapse on my bed. The tears start falling before my head even hits the pillow. My shoulders start to shake and a loud noise comes out of my mouth that I've never heard before. My heart is racing, my stomach aches, and my breath is fogging up my glasses, but I don't care enough to wipe them off.

I don't hear my door open, but I feel the bed shift as Dad sits down beside me.

"It's okay," he lies. "It's going to be okay."

Chapter Eight

Alexis

The sound of a jackhammer wakes me before I'm ready to get up. Everything hurts. The roof of my mouth is drier than a desert and my tongue feels thick, like it's coated with sandpaper.

There's no need to call in sick today now that Becky knows what's going on—it was her idea for me to take another few days off. I flip the pillow over to the cool side and try to fall back asleep when I realize the offensive noise is inside my head.

In the hallway, I hear CeCe banging around, getting ready for school. I'm not sure if it's my imagination or my current state, but it sounds louder than normal.

"Keep it down, please," Tommy whispers loudly. His normal shrink voice is soft and quiet, but whenever he tries to whisper, he fails miserably. "Your mom is still sleeping."

"So, what, she gets rewarded for being drunk?" CeCe's voice gets louder with every word. "You're the one who's sick, but she gets to stay home from work? And I have to go to school?"

My stomach turns—I hope I didn't let it slip last night that he was sick.

"I said keep it down." Tommy raises his voice, clearly forgetting he was trying not to wake me.

"It's not fair."

I strain to hear his reply, but I can't. Either they really are whispering now, or more likely, Tommy is using one of his shrink moves and not saying anything at all.

"Do you want to stay home from school today?" he finally asks. "I'll be working, but you can hang out with your mom."

Now it's CeCe's turn to not say anything. I picture the scowl on her face, causing her thick black glasses to slide down her nose, making her even angrier. The image makes me smile until I realize Tommy used the thought of spending time with me to make school look like the better option.

"Well?" I hear Tommy say.

"It's not like I can just miss rehearsal after school," she says in defeat.

"I think that's a smart decision," Tommy says, again in his shrink-voice. "I'm going to make breakfast, come down if you want to join me."

Nailed it. I burrow deeper under the covers and close my eyes again. Since I'm not going into the office, I can spend the day doing more research on treatment options. I saw an ad the other day for a drug, Keytruda. It's only for non–small cell lung cancer, but I figure it's worth a shot to do some digging. Maybe the pharmaceutical company is working on a similar drug for the small cell kind?

I roll over and reach for my phone, which is miraculously in its usual spot, plugged in on the nightstand. I google "cure for small cell lung cancer."

The first few results are ads for the clinic at Emory University where Tommy's oncologist works. But halfway down the page, there's a link to a blog by a stage 4 cancer survivor who beat the odds thanks to homeopathic remedies.

I tap the link and hold my breath as the page loads. I have to read the woman's story twice to make sure I didn't misunderstand. But the beautiful truth is there, written in black-and-white: her doctor told her there was no hope, but eleven years later, she's still cancer-free after going to a clinic in Mexico that used natural remedies. She went from stage 4 to a zero, so it is possible.

For the next ten minutes, I continue down the rabbit hole, reading patient testimonials, choosing to ignore the "results may vary" and "not approved by the FDA" warnings. The site doesn't go into detail of what the treatments entail, but the author lists a few by name. I reach for the notepad and pen on my nightstand and jot down the phrases to research individually: hyperthermia ("local whole body heat"), sono-dynamic therapy, oxygen treatments, enzyme therapy.

Another quick Google search locates the clinic I'm pretty sure she's talking about. It's in Tijuana, less than half an hour from the San Diego airport. My pulse quickens as I read about their philosophy, how important the patient's attitude is and how they see fewer patients in order to provide the highest level of individual care.

I've got to get Tommy into this program. As I fill out the form for more information, a plan starts to formulate.

It'll be a compromise. Shrinks love compromise, it's like part of their code of conduct. Tommy will get to spend the summer at the beach like he wanted, just a different beach, one near a clinic that can save his life so we can go back to

Destin for years to come, long after Monica's stupid show has wrapped. It's the best of both worlds.

I'm so relieved to be feeling hope instead of despair that when I hear the bedroom door slowly open, I forget that I shouldn't look quite so happy.

"Morning," he says, slightly suspicious. "You look like you're feeling better."

"Just happy to see you," I say. "CeCe left for school?"

Tommy nods and leans against the doorframe. He looks exhausted.

I hesitate before asking the next question, afraid to hear the answer. "I didn't tell her, did I?"

Tommy shakes his head, and I feel more relieved than I have the right to be. "I told her," he says.

I know better than to ask how it went, so I pat the bed beside me instead. Tommy gives me a small smile and walks closer. His eyes graze across the page where my scribbled notes and plans are outlined. He frowns and I quickly turn over the notepad before reaching for his hand.

"I have a patient in half an hour," he says, lifting the covers and sliding underneath.

"I'll take all the time I can get." I curl into his side and throw my arm around him, letting my head rise and fall with his breaths, which I try not to notice are shorter than they should be. I should have noticed; why didn't I pay more attention? If I had, if I'd made him go to the doctor sooner, then maybe it wouldn't be too late.

As if the universe wants to make the point loud and clear, Tommy coughs and I can hear the rattle echo in his chest. The sound hurts my heart, so I lift my head, away from what's trying to destroy him from the inside out, and focus on his lips instead. I drink him in, tasting the coffee on his tongue.

Tommy's hands slip underneath the pajama top I don't remember putting on last night. His fingers feel cool on my back and I don't want to wait any longer. I want his hands, his skin, his lips, on every part of me.

Knowing we don't have much time to waste, I sit up and slip the shirt over my head before doing the same to his. I hesitate for a second too long, my eyes lingering on his chest, imagining the tumors hiding beneath the surface. Tommy notices and takes charge, flipping me over so I'm lying on my back. I smile before pulling him down to me. Lying beneath him, with his weight holding me down, I feel safer than I have since our lives turned upside down.

Tommy's touch is both gentle and firm. I wrap my arms around him, holding him as close as I can. I relinquish all control and let him show me that he's still very much alive.

AFTERWARD, AS WE lie together, Tommy kisses the top of my head. "I would have told you sooner if I knew it meant I'd keep getting lucky."

"You have to stop making a joke of this. It's not funny."

"Of course it isn't." He kisses my forehead, then my cheek, and then my neck. "It's just my coping mechanism."

"I love it when you talk shrinky to me."

"You hate it," Tommy says, propping himself up on his arm. "Promise you won't start lying to me, you'll stay real."

"I promise." And from this moment forward, I will. He

doesn't need to know that I didn't tell him the real reason I don't want to go to Destin.

He lowers himself for one more kiss before rolling over to get his shirt. I watch him, so strong both physically and emotionally. I'm ashamed to admit what he's too polite to say, that I've failed him the past few days.

"I'm sorry."

"For what?" He sits back down on the bed beside me.

"For everything. The way I've been acting—you're the one who's sick, and here I am, falling apart."

"It's okay," he says, forgiving me too easily.

"It's not. But starting today, I'm back," I tell him. "I'm here, just let me know what I can do. What can I do?"

"You can be here, loving me."

"Done. What else?"

"You can try to understand . . ." I know the words aren't easy to find, so I reach up and rest my hand on his cheek. "I know you don't agree with me, but you can try to understand my decision."

I bite my lip. That's the one thing I don't know if I can do. I look past him to where the notepad sits, full of hope.

"And you can reconsider going to Destin."

The other one thing I don't know if I can do.

As quickly as it disappeared, the tension I've been carrying around for days is back, making itself at home across my shoulders and down to my toes. Anything else I would do for him. Anything.

I don't really think Tommy has a clue that Monica is back in Destin. Not that it would matter much to him if he did; he doesn't have as much to lose. I'm not exactly jealous of her anymore. I don't doubt for a second that he loves me. But I also know better than to underestimate the attraction to a beautiful woman and the power of fame.

And CeCe. The town's just too small, and it's too risky. If she finds out, she'll think Monica is the reason I haven't wanted her to pursue acting. But that's not all of it. I've been on the other side of the casting couch, seeing over a hundred girls audition for a part that only one girl will get. The part that ninety-nine girls won't. Being a teenager is hard enough without willingly putting yourself out there for people to reject you.

Plus, it wouldn't be fair leaving Becky alone to handle everything back here. I made a commitment to her when we went out on our own to open the agency. She would have been happy to go on working for someone else, but she believed in me and my dream of opening up a woman-owned agency that could compete with the old boys' clubs. I convinced her to walk away from a steady paycheck, from our 401k match and insurance plans we didn't have to think or worry about.

"I just want one more summer," he says, trying his best to convince me. I know he hates being landlocked in Atlanta, that he would never have moved so far away from the ocean if my career hadn't kept me here.

I reach for the notepad. I guess now is as good a time as any to bring it up.

"What if I gave you the beach? An even better beach. In Mexico." Tommy looks confused. "I found this clinic in Tijuana, they have natural cures, things like—"

"No."

51

"But—"

"Goddammit, Lexie. Don't make this harder than it already is."

The words I want to say are caught in my throat—why can't he see that's the opposite of what I'm trying to do?

"I've got a patient."

He turns and goes without kissing me goodbye, leaving me with a sinking feeling that I'm a horrible, selfish person who doesn't deserve him.

Chapter Nine

CeCe

Earth to CeCe," Sofia says, putting her lunch tray down at our usual table. "Did you hear me? I said my life is over."

"Sorry, what?"

Sofia sits down next to me in a huff. "It's like you're not even here half the time."

She isn't wrong. Since I found out last week, it's like there's a dark cloud following me. It's literally impossible to think of anything other than what's happening at home, especially when there are reminders everywhere. Anytime someone coughs or even says the word "dad," my heart drops.

"Hello?" Sofia says again.

"Sorry, what's going on?"

I stop listening before she even starts to talk, focusing instead on my brown paper lunch bag. Inside, I find a tightly wrapped tinfoil package. I unwrap it slowly, like a present, revealing a sliced baguette with fresh mozzarella, sliced Roma tomatoes, and torn pieces of basil. *Well done, Dad.* His pairing skills could use some work, considering the bag of Cheetos along with it, but he's come a long way since I got him watching Food Network with me.

A note falls out of the napkin, surprising me even though I knew there would be one in there somewhere. There always is. I unfold the paper and read his familiar handwriting, this one lyrics from a song by a band he and Mom like.

> *"If I had wings and I could fly,*
> *Well, I'd still walk with you."*
> —Sister Hazel

I fold the note and tuck it in my pocket so I won't forget to add it to the others in the shoeboxes under my bed. Just a few weeks ago, I was thinking that it might be time to start another box. Now, I'll be happy if there will be enough notes, enough time, to fill the current one.

"Can you believe it?" Sofia shakes her head.

"No, I can't," I say, hoping I can jump back into the conversation without it being obvious I zoned out again. Lauren and Bella have joined our table, so hopefully it will be easier to get by without paying attention—or worse, having to talk about what's going on with me.

Sofia's the only one I told about my dad, and I swore her to secrecy. I don't want my friends acting strange around me; it's already been weird enough at home. Mom went from being like a sleepwalking stranger to a super-peppy cheerleader overnight, trying to act like everything is going to be okay when we all know it won't be.

"My dad told me I'm grounded for the rest of the school year," Sofia says as if it's the worst thing in the world. It feels like a million years ago that I thought being grounded was the worst thing that could happen to me. I was so stupid.

"Parents suck," I hear Liam say from behind me. He takes the empty chair next to mine and turns it around before sitting backward in it. "How's my fair Juliet?"

I can't help but blush even though I'm pretty sure he's just acting like he likes me because of the play. A junior like him would never really be interested in a freshman like me.

"Ready for rehearsal tonight?" he asks, smiling that crooked smile.

Tonight's the night we're rehearsing the scene with the kiss. I haven't fully decided if we should just pretend or really go for it like Liam wants to.

"Ready as I'll ever be." I smile and take an awkwardly small bite of my sandwich.

"I hope there isn't garlic in there," Liam whispers. He stands up to join his regular table, but before he goes, he gives my glasses a little push back up my nose. I'd been so distracted by his warm breath tickling my ear that I hadn't noticed they'd fallen.

"You are so lucky," Lauren says as soon as he's out of earshot.

The luckiest. The voice in my head is full of sarcasm, but I can't blame Lauren since she and most everyone else don't know I'm probably the unluckiest girl in the world right now.

But then I glance up and see Sofia giving Lauren a look that screams *shut up.* And then Lauren stares at me, her wide eyes a dead giveaway. I look around the table and realize every single one of them is watching me with the same sad eyes. *Stupid Sofia.* And stupid me for trusting her.

I push my chair back so fast, the metal legs squeak offensively loud against the floor. I've got to get away from their stupid sympathy. I keep my eyes on the ground, stuffing my uneaten lunch in the trash can as I walk by, making a beeline for the double doors.

There are still thirty-five minutes before the next class starts, and we're only allowed to be in the cafeteria or the library during lunch. Since I can't go back to the cafeteria, I head toward the library. But the thought of being in that quiet room makes my head want to explode.

Instead, I turn left down the hallway, hoping the door to the theater will be unlocked. I take a deep breath and turn the handle. Sure enough, the door gives. I look behind me, and the coast is miraculously clear, so I slip inside before someone catches me.

The room is dark with nothing but the ghost light shining in the middle of the stage. I start slowly down the aisle, my steps getting quicker with the incline. I choose a row far back enough that the light doesn't reach me if anyone were to open the door and look inside. The velvet of the chair feels soft against my legs, and I rub the cushion as if it were a teddy bear.

I wish I could stay in here all day. Skipping a few classes would certainly be better than the way Mom handled the news. Maybe I should just get drunk like she did. I didn't like the taste of beer at Liam's party, but I liked the way it made me feel—light and happy, like I didn't have a care in the world.

Although I didn't really have a care in the world back then.

The door to the theater opens and light floods the room. I sink lower in the chair, hoping whoever it is will go away.

No such luck.

I hear steps, slow and steady as they come down the aisle.

They're getting closer. My eyes have adjusted to the lack of light and I see a tall, slender shadow stop at the end of my row. The shadow walks closer, and I recognize the woodsy smell of his cologne.

I sit back up. "You scared me."

"How'd you know it was me?" Liam asks, walking down the row toward me.

"I smelled you." It's easier to talk to him when I don't have to worry about getting lost in those deep brown eyes.

"Do I smell?" He sniffs and I imagine him dropping his head to smell his collar.

"It's good," I assure him. "Your cologne."

"Curve for Men," he says. "My sister got it for me."

I nod, forgetting it's dark enough that he probably can't see.

Liam takes another step toward me, feeling for the seat. He sits down and lifts the armrest between us. "Now you can smell me even better."

My stomach does a little flip; I'm doubly nervous now that he's sitting so close. "Is that what you came in here for?"

"I saw you run out of the cafeteria."

"I didn't run," I say, defending myself.

"You looked upset. You weren't in the library, so I figured you might be in here."

"Am I that predictable?" I ask, flattered he would worry about me. Maybe he really does like me.

"I just assumed you wanted to get a head start for practicing our scene?" Liam clears his throat and I hope he can't see me blush. "I will kiss thy lips," he says.

"That's my line," I say, even though it would be much easier if the roles were reversed.

"Then go ahead—you say it."

"I will kiss thy lips," I say, hoping my voice doesn't sound as shaky as it feels. But his knees are touching my knees, and it's like there's literal electricity coursing through our bodies. "Haply some poison yet doth hang on them."

This is the part where I'm supposed to lean down and kiss Romeo, hoping to die because life isn't worth living without him. I didn't understand that before, how the thought of living without someone could be worse than the thought of being dead. But I understand now. My chest feels tight and it's getting hard to breathe.

"I'm waiting for my kiss, fair Juliet," Liam says. He's right beside me, but his voice sounds far away. I want to say something back, but I can't. I can't breathe. I can hear my heart beating in my ears and suddenly my breath is the loudest thing in the room.

"CeCe?" Liam's voice sounds a thousand miles away. "It's okay, we don't have to. Just breathe." He takes my hand in his, running his thumb over the back of my hand. He inhales and exhales slowly.

I focus on his face in the dim light and imitate his breathing pattern, in slowly, then out slowly. In, then out. A few more times, and my breathing is back to normal so I can die of total embarrassment instead.

"You okay?" He squeezes my hand and I realize he's sitting even closer now, his knee wedged between mine.

"Yeah," I say. "Sorry, I was just thinking about the scene."

"The kiss?"

I shake my head. "The idea of loving someone so much that you'd rather die than live without them." I turn my face away as if that could stop him from seeing me. I didn't mean to be this honest with him, but the truth is much less weird than what he's probably thinking.

"I can't imagine," he says. I turn back toward him. His breath smells like onion rings and barbecue sauce. "To love someone like that and then lose them." I know he's talking about the play—to him, the emotion is just pretend. I wish I could just pretend again, too.

I close my eyes and try to forget that the one person I really do love that much actually is dying. I try to forget that my so-called best friend betrayed me and told everyone all about everything like I was just the latest piece of gossip. I try to forget that we could get in trouble just by being here. I try to forget that he's Liam and I'm Cecelia. Instead, in this moment, he's Romeo and I'm Juliet.

As Romeo reaches up and runs his hand down Juliet's face, she starts to relax. And as Romeo gets closer, she tilts her head up ever so slightly like they do in the movies. She waits for Romeo to make the first move, and when his lips brush against hers, it's like she comes to life.

I am Juliet and he is Romeo.

His tongue pushes against my lips and I open my mouth, letting him slip inside. His tongue tangles with mine before darting in and out of my mouth. I'm outside of my head and then I'm back in it, suddenly nervous and wondering if I'm doing it right and if kissing is supposed to feel this strange. If it's supposed to be this noisy.

"Cecelia," Liam moans into my mouth.

He said my name, not "Juliet." I'm trying not to think too much about what it means, if anything. As soon as I stop thinking about how I'm supposed to be kissing him, it feels more normal to actually be kissing him. I turn my head and we naturally fall into rhythm. It's not all that different from dancing.

I pull away but he quickly closes the gap, his lips back on mine. Feeling a little bolder, I try slipping my tongue inside his mouth.

Holy shit. I'm kissing Liam Donnelly. And we're not acting. He reaches for my hand and I let him hold it as we keep kissing. He slowly brings my hand to his knee and I let go. I'm not sure what I'm supposed to do, so I give it a little squeeze, which must be a good thing, because he moans into my mouth again.

He laces his fingers between mine, pulling my hand closer, guiding it toward his lap. I realize what he's doing just in time to pull away.

The bell sounds, signaling the end of the lunch hour.

Liam sighs, as disappointed as I am relieved. "Parting is such sweet sorrow," he says.

"That's my line, too." I smile and tilt my head up toward his, hoping he'll kiss me again, but he doesn't.

"You can go out first," he says. "I need a minute."

I stand and make my way back up the aisle, stumbling out the door and into the harsh light. The hallway is crowded, and no one seems to notice me slipping out of the theater. I bring my hand to my lips; they feel like rubber, like they don't belong to me anymore.

The moment is only slightly dampened when I realize I can't tell Sofia what happened since I'm still so mad at her, although not telling her is probably the best revenge. I smile and open the door to English, holding my head high as I walk past the desk where I usually sit next to Sofia, and take a seat in the back row instead.

Chapter Ten

Alexis

It just started," Tommy whispers as I slide into the aisle seat beside him.

"I stopped to get flowers," I tell him, holding up the bouquet of red roses I grabbed at Publix on my way to the high school. I don't mention the fact that I was also twenty minutes late leaving the office thanks to more last-minute changes that came in from the client.

"Me, too," Tommy says softly, nodding toward a beautiful bouquet of purple wildflowers wrapped in burlap. I should have thought to get something purple.

"Shh," someone behind us loud-whispers.

I shrug an apology and focus on the stage, where the set is more elaborate and professional-looking than I remember high school productions being.

The stage has been transformed into the streets of Verona, where two servants from the House of Capulet are talking with disgust about the House of Montague. Before I can fully grasp what's happening, a brawl breaks out between the Capulet and Montague servants. *I think?* I should have paid more attention in my literature classes.

In the next scene, the young boy who plays Juliet's father is discussing his daughter's, my daughter's, hand in marriage. He asks the young man playing Paris to wait two years until Juliet is sixteen.

I steal a look at Tommy. His eyes are riveted on the stage, and I wonder if he's thinking what I am: that giving his blessing to the young man that will one day want to marry CeCe is just one in a lifetime of things he won't be here to do.

I take a deep breath and blink away the tears just in time to see CeCe take the stage. I hope she can see okay without her glasses. Even dressed in a nightgown, she looks beautiful as Lady Capulet tries to convince her she should accept the courtship of Paris, the young man selected by her father.

Thanks to the magic of a few stealthy stagehands dressed in black, the stage transforms again into the Capulet ball.

My attention darts between the stage and watching Tommy take it all in. He must feel my stare, because he reaches down and takes my hand, his eyes never leaving the stage.

CeCe takes my breath away when she walks onto the balcony for the play's most famous scene. I can see the emotion on her face, I can hear it in her voice.

"O Romeo, Romeo! Wherefore art thou Romeo?" she says.

Before Romeo can respond, Tommy coughs. I can tell he's trying to hold it in, but the cancer is rearing its ugly head, letting us all know it won't be controlled. The cough is deep, its sound rattling his lungs and my heart. I put my hand gently on his back, but he brushes me away.

Onstage, CeCe flinches. It's subtle, but I know she recognizes the sound that's become all too familiar in our house. She recovers beautifully and continues her line. "Deny thy father and refuse thy name; or, if thou wilt not, be but sworn my love, and I'll no longer be a Capulet."

I hold Tommy's hand and watch the story unfold onstage, not wanting it to come to its tragic end. But just like life, I know it's inevitable.

As Romeo gets the false news of Juliet's death, his heartbreak doesn't just look real—it feels real. I watch as Liam drinks the poison, collapsing just as CeCe wakes from her coma.

"I will kiss thy lips," CeCe says, her voice shaking with grief. "Haply some poison yet doth hang on them." I hold my breath as she leans down and lays a kiss on Liam's lips. Not for the first time? I wonder.

Before the curtain closes, I hear someone offstage recite the final line of the play: "For never was a story of more woe, than this of Juliet and her Romeo."

Tommy is the first one on his feet. My eyes well up as I watch him, applauding like he's the proudest man in the room, which he is, no doubt.

The love between Romeo and Juliet may be legendary, but it's got nothing on the love my Romeo has for his little girl.

Tommy looks down at me, his eyes shining with tears, and suddenly, I know all my reasons why not to hold a candle to the one reason why we should. If Tommy wants to go to Destin, if that's where he wants to spend the last precious months we have together, then we have to go.

Chapter Eleven

CeCe

Dad is the first one I see as I come out from backstage, finally able to make out more than blurry shapes with my glasses back on. "There's my girl."

He wraps his arms around me so tight that for a second it feels like he's going to squeeze the air out of my lungs.

"I am so proud of you." He kisses the top of my head. "You were brilliant, just brilliant."

"You really think so?" I ask so he'll say it again.

"I know so." He pulls his arm back to hand me the most perfect bouquet of purple flowers I've ever seen.

"They're beautiful—thank you, Daddy!"

I lower my head to smell them, and when I look back up, Mom is standing next to him with a pretty, but generic, bouquet of red roses.

"You were great up there." Her voice goes up an octave, and I can tell she wasn't expecting me to be that good. Maybe now she'll ease up on her stupid "no auditions outside school sanctioned activities" rule.

"You don't have to sound so surprised."

"I'm not," she says, handing me the flowers. "Just really proud."

"Thanks." I decide not to mention that I was standing in the wings and still had my glasses on, so I saw her walk in late. "I can still go to the party, right?"

Mom and Dad exchange a look and I'm fully prepared to go into a soliloquy of all the reasons why I should be allowed to go—starting with the fact that Liam's parents will be there this time—but before I say a single word, Mom says, "Absolutely."

Dad nods. "Do you need a ride?"

"Liam said I could go with him," I say, preparing to make a quick exit. As much as I would love to hang around and let them keep telling me how great I was, I don't want to risk them changing their minds. "Would you mind taking these home?"

"It would be my pleasure." Dad bows before taking the bouquets from me.

"Juliet," Liam calls from the stage. "Your chariot awaits!"

"Don't be home too late," Mom says. "And you really were great tonight."

I smile, even though she should know that saying things more than once doesn't matter as much as acting like you meant it the first time. Still, when she takes an awkward step toward me, I let her give me a quick hug before I run up the steps to find Liam.

"See you guys later." I wave as I duck behind the curtain,

ready for what has the potential to be the best night of my whole, entire life.

THE PARTY IS already in full swing by the time we get back to Liam's house. His sister's friends, who are all home from college, have clearly gotten a head start. Liam said his parents weren't going to be home for a while since they went out to dinner after the play, and that it wouldn't be a big deal when they did get home.

As far as parents go, his were supposedly cool about everyone drinking as long as no one would be driving. Which I wouldn't be, since I'm not even old enough yet.

"Where's the beer?" I ask, ready to get things started.

"In the fridge." Liam stops to high-five a really tall guy with a bushy beard. "Grab me one, too?"

I head to the kitchen as though it's the most natural thing in the world. Like I'm just a girl getting a beer for her guy. *Her guy*. I couldn't wipe the smile off my face if I tried. Not only did we kill the performance, but the play is over. So tonight, there will be no question that Liam is interested in me because of me, and not just because he's getting into character.

After that day in the theater, we only kissed offstage one other time. It was after dress rehearsal and Mom was late picking me up. Usually I'd be annoyed, but Liam offered to wait with me.

Once everyone else was gone, he grabbed my hand and led me around the corner, behind the theater. No one could see us there, so I let him back me up against the brick wall and kiss me again. It didn't feel as weird the second time, and I think I'm getting better at it.

I smile, happy that I'm no longer in the "never been kissed" club. Now that I know how great it is, I wish I hadn't waited so long to do it. I wet my lips in anticipation, hoping the new Chapstick I bought at Dox made my lips as soft and kissable as the label promised.

My phone buzzes so I fish it out of my pocket and see a text from Beau. I put it back without reading it. I'll text him back tomorrow when I have something really good to tell him.

"There she is," Bella says as I walk into the kitchen. She gives me a big hug even though we're not close friends. "You were so good tonight."

"Thanks." I squeeze behind her to open the fridge. I'm not sure why she's there since she wasn't in the cast or the crew.

"Did you guys really kiss? Onstage in front of everyone?" Bella whispers. "Or did you fake it?"

"There was nothing fake about it," I say, not bothering to whisper. I grab two beers and close the refrigerator door with my hip. "I've got to bring these to Liam."

Before I go, I crack one can open and take a big sip as if it were just a Diet Dr Pepper. It doesn't taste as bad as I remember, and I swear I can feel a buzz the second it flows past my lips. I finish it quickly and grab one more before going back to Liam.

I find him in the hallway, still talking to the bearded guy.

"How long did it take you to grow that beard?" I ask, trying to join the conversation.

The bearded guy gives me a look as if it's the strangest question anyone has ever asked him, but I don't care because

I'm drinking beer in Liam's house with Liam, and so far, everything is going according to plan.

Tonight, I'm going to get a do-over. My stomach does a little flip in anticipation as I pop the top of my second beer, because this time, Liam and I will be the ones slow dancing and making out like we're the only ones in the room. Maybe it's a good thing that Bella's here so she can see it all happen and report back to Sofia.

Liam "cheers" his beer against mine, then walks into the living room, leaving me alone with the bearded giant. I don't have anything else to say about his beard, so I take another big sip. And another. I love the way it makes me feel, a little woozy and light-headed, kind of like how I felt when Liam was kissing me.

The thought of his lips is enough to make me smile again. I tilt the can up to take another sip, but it's almost empty, so I head back to the kitchen.

"Baby girl!" Jen, who played my mom, calls out as soon as I walk through the door.

"Hey, Mama." I stumble into her outstretched arms.

"You got a head start, huh?" She laughs.

"Why'd you say that?"

"Someone get this girl another beer," her boyfriend, one of the stagehands, says.

Bella is closest to the refrigerator, so she opens the door and hands me a beer without taking one for herself.

"Aren't you drinking?"

"Nah," Bella says. "I don't like the taste."

"I didn't, either," I whisper. "But you get used to it."

She scrunches her nose as if that would be impossible. I shrug. More for the rest of us.

Back in the living room, someone has finally turned on the music and people are starting to dance. This is my opportunity. But Liam isn't there. I spot him back in the hallway talking to his sister and some of her college friends. They look beautiful with their tight dresses, big boobs, and perfect makeup, smiling and laughing like they just stepped off the pages of a sorority catalog.

I move close and slip my arm around his waist. "Let's dance." The sorority girls laugh, so I laugh, too, even though I'm not sure what's so funny.

"I'll be back," Liam tells them before following me to the dance floor. The song isn't a slow one, but that doesn't stop me from throwing my arms around his neck like it's where they belong.

My arms and my shoulders and my hips feel loose, and I'm ready to pick up where we left off at the last party. I rest my head on his shoulder and for one wonderful moment, it feels like everything is right with the world.

The fast song ends and a slow one starts. I lift my head up so I can look him in the eyes, but he isn't looking at me. He's looking over my shoulder, back at the pretty college girls.

"Hey," I say, calling his attention back toward me. He looks down as if he's expecting me to say something else, but it's not words I want. I tilt my head and stand up on my toes so my mouth is lined up with his. He doesn't make the move, so I go for it. My lips lock onto his like a magnet, but when I open my mouth, his stays closed.

"Easy, tiger," he says, pulling away from me. I frown, waiting for him to explain what's wrong. The room is still swaying a little even though we stopped dancing.

"You want another beer?" I ask. Maybe he just needs

another drink before he's feeling as good as I am, the way we both were at his last party. Then we can get back to the dancing and the kissing.

"Sure."

In the kitchen, I go to open the refrigerator door but it's stuck. I laugh and try again, but no matter how hard I pull, it doesn't open.

"I got it," Bella says. "It opens on the other side." She opens the door and takes a bottle out but doesn't hand it over. "Are you sure you need another one?"

"Are you sure you're supposed to be here? This is a cast and crew party."

"My house is next door," she says. "Liam invites me to all his parties; I think his parents make him." She hands me the beer, and I don't know whether to say thank you or I'm sorry. This night is not turning out how I planned.

I twist the bottle cap, but it doesn't budge. I try again, same results. I look down at my palm and see a bunch of little red marks from the cap.

"Baby girl, you need an opener!" Jen says. Her boyfriend takes the beer from my hands and uses his key chain to open it before handing it back to me. I hold it up and air "cheers" toward Bella before going back to the living room.

"Hey, CeCe?" Bella says. I turn around. "I just wanted to say I'm sorry about your dad. If you ever need to talk—"

"I don't want to talk about it," I snap. "I just want to dance."

I take a defiant swig and turn back toward the dance floor. I stop in the open doorway. Liam isn't where I left him and I forgot his beer. I'm about to turn around when I see him in front of the fireplace, slow dancing with one of his sister's friends. Their bodies are pressed together like they're one person, swaying back and forth in perfect rhythm. I watch as he lowers his head to whisper something in her ear, not mine.

He looks up for a second and sees me see him. I smile, hoping he'll stop dancing with her and come back to dance with me. But he doesn't. He just smiles and whispers something else in her ear. She laughs and the butterflies in my stomach turn to stone.

I want to go home, but the room is spinning and I'm afraid to move.

"CeCe." Bella is standing next to me, holding my arm so I don't fall. "Come on, let's get out of here."

Chapter Twelve

Alexis

Tommy and I are half watching the eleven o'clock news when my phone vibrates with a text. "CeCe wants to sleep over at Bella's," I tell Tommy. It's strange that she texted instead of called. And even stranger that she reached out to me, not her dad. "Should we be worried?"

"About CeCe?"

Tommy's right. I text back a quick reply, letting her know to call in the morning and one of us will pick her up. CeCe's a good kid. As far as teenagers go, we've got it pretty easy. Unlike Jill, one of our closest friends back in Destin. She has her hands full with Beau, her son, who's a year older than CeCe. From the look of his Instagram account, that kid is his father's son in more ways than just his playboy good looks. He's posing with a different scantily clad girl in almost every photo—the one I saw today was wearing shorts that were more revealing than my underwear.

I wonder if Jill can look at him without thinking of all the ways Adam hurt her, cheating when he wasn't at home, and practically ignoring her and the kids when he was. At least Abigail is a good kid; she takes after her mom. I don't know how Jill manages to be everything to everyone all alone.

Alone, like I'll be.

The hole in my stomach stretches, growing aggressively fast like Tommy's tumor. I think I'm going to be sick.

"Hey," Tommy says, sliding closer. "It's going to be okay."

"Easy for you to say" I wipe a tear from my eye before it has a chance to fall down my cheek. "You don't have to live without you."

And there it is, the thought that's been on the tip of my tongue, the words I've been holding back because I know how selfish it sounds. But it's true. I don't know how I'm going to do any of this without him.

"We still have time," Tommy says. "In fact, we should probably make the most of it."

I sniffle. "What'd you have in mind?"

Tommy rubs his hands together and there's a mischievous spark in his eye. "Let's get married."

I laugh in spite of myself. "I said yes to Destin, isn't that enough for one night?"

"Thank you again for that." He reaches for my hand, tracing a line down my palm. I'm not sure if it's the love or the life line.

"You're welcome." I hope he doesn't hear the regret in my voice. When he closes my hand and brings it up to his lips, I lose all the resolve to keep the truth from him.

"I lied," I say before I can change my mind again.

"About what?" Tommy asks. "You do want to get married?" His face lights up at the thought and I hate having to tell him no almost as much as what I really do have to tell him.

"Not that," I say. "I lied about the real reason I don't want to go down to Destin for the summer."

It's Tommy's turn to look confused.

"You don't know, do you?"

"Know what?" he asks, furrowing his eyebrows.

"About Monica."

"Monica, my ex Monica?" he asks, surprised.

What happened between the two of them is the one thing we never talk about—with the exception of one time when I was hugely pregnant with CeCe. I had been tired and miserable and knew I was acting like a total bitch, but I couldn't help it. I asked Tommy how he could bear being around me. And that's when he told me.

Hearing the story in his own words was like hearing it for the first time, even though I had already gotten most of the details from Jill over a year earlier.

That night, I held his hand as he told me how he'd found a positive pregnancy test in their bathroom. He said he'd been beyond excited, but he didn't let Monica know he knew in case she had planned something special to reveal the news. So he waited. And he waited. He even bought a silver baby rattle at Tiffany's so he could surprise her back when she finally told him.

But one night a few weeks later, Monica came home drunk. Tommy lost it—as much as I can imagine Tommy losing it on anyone. He demanded to know how she could go out drinking when she was carrying their baby. That's when she told him that she wasn't.

He paused for a moment and I braced myself for the part I knew was coming: that Monica wasn't carrying the baby anymore. She'd gotten it "taken care of." She'd told him that she had her career to think about, and a baby would ruin that. Their baby. Tommy's baby. The half brother or sister CeCe never had.

I have marched for women's right to choose, but this woman's choice affected the man I love. It was his baby, too. He should have been part of the decision. They were married, for god's sake.

When he finished telling me the story that night, I perched on the edge of his lap and kissed him. His tears mixed with mine and he told me that nothing in the world would keep him from experiencing every single moment of this miracle that had been given to us. The good ones, and the less than good ones.

He asked me if I would mind if he gave our baby the silver rattle I already knew was hidden in the bottom of his sock drawer. I nodded and kissed him, trying to take away what was left of his pain.

But now Tommy's past was rearing her beautiful head and I had to do something to protect my family.

"She's going to be in Destin," I tell him. "All summer—shooting a stupid series for Netflix. She's playing a mom." I scoff at the irony.

"Is that all?" Tommy asks. "You had me worried for a second."

I stand and turn around, looking down at him with a nonplussed look on his face. "Is that all? Isn't that enough? Your movie-star ex-wife is going to be in Destin. All summer."

"She's more of a TV star than a movie star," Tommy says with a smile that fades as soon as he sees my reaction. He reaches for my hand but I pull it away, resting it firmly on my hip instead. "Babe, Monica is part of my past, and that's it. She could be in Beverly Hills or sitting in our living room and it's all the same to me."

"That's exactly the point," I tell him. He looks confused, so I continue. "I don't want her anywhere near our living room, or you, or our daughter."

"Okay," Tommy says.

"What do you mean, okay?" I yell, shaking my hands in frustration.

"I mean okay-okay. We'll keep her out of our living room."

I drop my hands to my sides, not sure what to do now that he's agreed so easily. "And away from CeCe."

"Away from me and from CeCe." Tommy reaches for me, and I let him pull me back down on the couch beside him.

"I'm not crazy," I tell him, which I'm sure doesn't help my case.

"Well, that's too bad," Tommy says, nuzzling my neck. "Because I'm crazy about you. Are you sure you didn't lie about wanting to marry me?"

"I'm sure," I say.

"Why not?" he asks, kissing the curve of my neck.

"For the same reasons I've told you why not for the last fifteen years."

A marriage license didn't stop Tommy's dad from running out on his mom, but somehow Tommy's response to growing up in a dysfunctional home was the exact opposite of mine. Then again, my dad stayed. If he had left—or better yet, if my mom had left him—then maybe I wouldn't have such a strong bias against the institution.

"But things are different now," Tommy says, as if he has to remind me that our happiness has an expiration date.

His mouth finds mine, but only for a moment before pulling away to continue his case. "If we aren't married, you may not be able to come see me at the hospital."

"You said you didn't want to go to the hospital."

"If we're married, you can inherit my estate without being taxed."

"That might be your most romantic proposal yet, Tommy Whistler."

He sighs in defeat and leans back against the couch. I should probably just say yes, but he's the one who told me to stay real. And it wouldn't be real if I suddenly changed my mind after all these years of saying no.

He knows better than anyone else how deep my resentment goes. And I know this is about us now, not my parents, but it's hard to let go of a belief you've held on to for most of your life. I can't remember a time I didn't believe blue was the best color, broccoli was the worst vegetable, and marriage was a joke.

How could I respect an institution that my parents so blatantly disrespected? Maybe if I didn't know my dad cheated, that my mom knew and did nothing. Keeping up appearances was more important to them than the actual relationship. And if that was what marriage was about, I'd decided, I didn't want anything to do with it.

I wanted what Tommy and I have. A relationship that isn't defined by anything but our love for each other, that pays no attention to appearances. We've stayed together because we'd be lost without each other, because we wouldn't dream of being anywhere else or with anyone else—not because we're bound by a stupid piece of parchment paper.

If we change that now, it would be like I'm doing it because he's sick, not because we want to spend the rest of our lives together. The rest of his life.

"How about we skip the wedding and go straight to the honeymoon?" Tommy asks, the sparkle back in his eyes. "We've got the house to ourselves tonight, and there are still a few rooms we haven't christened yet."

"I'm Jewish," I remind him.

"There are a few rooms we haven't Jewished yet," he tries again.

"That's not a thing."

"Let's make it a thing." His lips are back on my neck and I tilt my head, encouraging him to keep going.

"I thought those pills were supposed to decrease your libido?"

"They're supposed to," he says, working his way to my lips. I pull away from his kiss. As much as I want to pretend that everything is okay, it's not. "Maybe they're not working?"

Tommy brushes a loose strand of hair behind my ear. "The pills aren't going to fix me. If they're making me feel better, they're doing their job." He pulls me into his arms and starts kissing the other side of my neck. "You make me feel better. You're my medicine."

He moves from the nape of my neck back to my lips and I'm a hopeless case. "What room should we Jewish first?" I ask.

His lips curve into a smile, and for one brief moment, I'm just a woman in the arms of the man she loves. Until the next time life reminds us otherwise.

Chapter Thirteen

Alexis

The music coming from CeCe's room is loud enough that I can almost make out the lyrics from behind my own closed door across the hall. I wonder if this would be any easier if we could be sad together instead of alone.

It's been like this all week. Her postperformance glow faded as soon as we broke the news about our change of summer plans. Even the flowers we'd given her had wilted, like they, too, had caught her sorrow.

I knock softly at first, afraid to bother her.

I'm not sure when this power shift between us happened, but I don't like it one bit. I'm not the enemy here; cancer is. And she can resent me all she wants for working hard, but one day, she'll appreciate the fact that I was providing a good example for her. Not to mention a roof over her head.

I knock a little louder. Still no answer. I lift my hand, prepared to knock again, when she opens the door. I start to say something but stop at the sight of her looking so small and helpless, swimming in one of her dad's old T-shirts. Behind her, I notice that her suitcase is sitting empty on the floor; she doesn't want to go tomorrow, either.

"What?" CeCe glares at me. The sudden movement causes her thick black glasses to slip down her nose. When she lifts her hand to push them back up, I notice the purple polish has almost chipped off her nails, the edges ragged where she's apparently started biting them again.

I smile in spite of myself, happy to have one problem I can actually solve.

CeCe takes the salon chair next to mine and hands a bottle of polish to the manicurist. I don't have to look to know that it's a shade of purple.

It hadn't been as hard as I thought to convince her that a little pampering would do us both some good. And I'm sure she was as grateful as I was to have a reason to get out of the house.

"Daughter?" the manicurist asks, nodding toward CeCe.

I nod and smile in response, and again, I don't have to look to know CeCe is scowling. I used to take offense at how much she hated the fact that we look so much alike, but Tommy was almost able to convince me that it wasn't so much about our looks as it was wanting to establish her own identity, or some other shrink talk.

I glance over at CeCe, admiring her posture. I square my shoulders and sit up a little straighter myself. She looks over and gives me a small smile, an unexpected gift I wish I could tuck in my pocket to save for later.

Afraid to spoil the moment, I rack my brain for a safe

topic. School is over and anything acting-related will come back around to the fact that she had to drop out of theater camp. I have a feeling she and Sofia had a falling-out, and I don't think either of us is ready to talk about whatever is going on between her and Liam. I'm about to make a comment about the weather when her manicurist asks her a question about her favorite subject in school.

There's something carefree and easy about the way CeCe answers the woman's question. I close my eyes and relax, half listening to their friendly banter. CeCe is charming, something I'd like to think she got from me, and thoughtful in the questions she asks in return, something I know she got from Tommy.

"Right, Mom?" CeCe asks.

I open my eyes, surprised to see the manicurist is applying the last layer of my OPI Cajun Shrimp nail polish.

"What's that?" I ask, not sure how long I'd zoned out.

"Grandma and Grandpa are in Thailand?"

I nod and CeCe goes back to their conversation, something about street food and curry. Since my dad retired last fall, he and my mom have been traveling the world, adding stamps to their passports as if they were frequent-diners cards. Based on the pictures they post on Facebook, it looks like they're enjoying their golden years together—but I know they barely smile at, much less talk to, each other when the camera isn't out and no one else is around. They're both just using each other to get what they want, or what they want other people to think they have.

They were in Cambodia when I finally got up the nerve to tell them what was going on with Tommy. I used the thirteen-hour time difference as an excuse, but the truth is, I didn't want to have to explain that Tommy had given up. I knew they would respond the way they responded to almost everything, throwing money at the problem. Which they did.

My dad offered to pay whatever it took, hire the best doctor, find the best specialist; they would fly us to the moon if that's what they needed to do to make sure I could keep my family of three intact.

In the end, I thanked them and said I would let them know if there was anything they could do, but there wasn't.

"Ten minutes over here," the manicurist says as she pulls out a chair at the nail drying station. I take a seat and close my eyes as she steps behind me for the complimentary shoulder massage.

"A lot of tension," she says as she digs her palm into my right shoulder.

"You have no idea," I tell her. It hurts in a good way and I drop my head, letting the tension leave my body. I consider asking her to keep going for an extra tip when CeCe pulls out the chair beside me.

"How do they look?" I ask.

She holds up her predictably purple nails, a soft shade somewhere in the lavender family.

"Beautiful." My compliment brings a quick smile to CeCe's face. "Perfeçt beach-nails for Destin."

Her face falls and I curse myself for bringing up one of the very things we're here to forget. I wish I could tell her that I don't want to go, either, but I know that won't help anything.

Since we're already on the topic, I figure it can't hurt to keep talking about it. Maybe it will even help, since avoiding the subject won't change the fact that we're leaving first thing in the morning.

"Have you started packing yet?" I ask, even though I know she hasn't.

CeCe shakes her head.

"I can help you when we get home," I offer.

"I'm not a baby," she snaps. I sit back abruptly, wishing I could rewind the clock and never bring up the D-word. It's just as bad as the C-word.

"I'm just trying to help," I say, fully aware that I'm doing anything but.

"If you really want to help," she says, "you can convince Dad we should stay here this summer."

"You used to love spending summers in Destin," I remind her.

"I was a baby then," CeCe says, her tone getting snarkier with each syllable. "How I spend my summers matters now that I'm in high school. Don't you want me to get into a good college?"

How anyone spends the summer between freshman and sophomore year is about as important to colleges as the grade they get in gym class. But I know better than to tell her that—especially in a public place where I'd like to be able to show my face again.

"We'll talk about this later," I say, lowering my voice.

"You don't get it," CeCe says, not bothering to be quiet. I can feel the eyes of everyone in the salon staring, ears perked, listening to what should be a private conversation. "You don't understand how important acting is to me."

"Is it more important than your dad?"

CeCe leans as far away from me as she can get without taking her hands out from under the dryer. "Of course not," she hisses.

"Theater camp will be here next year," I tell her. And before I can stop myself, I add, "Your father won't be."

I watch my daughter's eyes, which look like my eyes, get wide and shiny behind her glasses. She opens her mouth but closes it without saying anything, which is exactly what I should have done.

"I'm sorry." I pull my hands from under the dryer and reach out to touch her arm, but she is out of her chair before I can stop her. The chime on the front door rings loud, breaking the awkward silence left in her wake.

I quickly pay at the front desk, leaving a larger tip than necessary, before I follow CeCe outside. So much for mother-daughter bonding.

Chapter Fourteen

CeCe

Four hours into the drive, I have to pee so badly my bladder feels like it might explode. It wasn't exactly a good idea to drink a giant bottle of water before we left, and it doesn't help that the trip is taking even longer than normal since Mom is the one driving.

I pull my headphones off my ears, which are a little sore. I probably shouldn't have been listening to my music that loud, but I just couldn't handle hearing Mom, trying to act like everything is happy and normal.

"I have to go to the bathroom," I say.

"Can you wait till the next rest stop?" Mom asks. It's a stupid question, because really, what are my options? Squatting on the side of the road?

"Obviously," I say, realizing too late that I accidentally broke the silent treatment. Until now, I haven't spoken a single word to her since we left the salon yesterday. I look down at my imperfect pinky nail, where the polish smeared since I didn't leave it under the dryer long enough. Also her fault.

"Next rest stop, twelve miles," Dad reads off a sign. "Think you can hold it?"

"I'll be fine—I'm not a little girl."

"You'll always be my little girl," Dad says, slipping his hand behind the front seat to grab my knee. I raise my feet so he can't reach.

He and Mom smile at each other in that dopey way parents do, like they're in on some big secret the rest of the world doesn't know about.

"Eyes on the road," I remind Mom.

She looks back at me before turning her attention where it belongs. "Got it," she says. "And my hands are at ten and two in case you were wondering."

"I wasn't," I say, mostly to myself. I don't think she heard me anyway, because "Happy Together," our family song, starts playing and she can't not sing along.

"Imagine me and you," she sings.

Dad turns up the volume and answers back with the next line. If we have to have a family song, would it be too much to ask for one that came from this century?

Usually, I'd chime in at the chorus, but I keep my mouth shut in silent protest.

Dad either doesn't notice or doesn't care, because he just keeps going, singing his modified version of the lyrics about the "girls" he loves, me and Mom.

He reaches behind him again and I bring my knees back in grabbing distance so he knows he's not the one I'm mad at. He turns back and smiles at me, and he looks so happy that

I'm considering joining in at the next chorus to sing about how happy we are together, but then he starts coughing.

"Dad?" I ask at the same time Mom says, "Tommy?"

There's more coughing. It's loud and it sounds like it hurts, and it's the worst noise I've ever heard. It makes my own chest ache. He keeps coughing and then he's wheezing and I'm worried he isn't able to breathe. What if he stops breathing?

I look over at Mom, who's looking at Dad and not at the road ahead, where cars are slowing down in front of us.

"Mom, stop!"

She looks up and hits the brakes just in time. Her arm flies across to the passenger seat as if she could protect Dad. He leans into her arm and stays slumped forward.

"Daddy?"

The coughing fit is over, but he's breathing slow and low. There's a raspy rattle in his breaths. "I'm okay," he says.

My eyes meet Mom's in the rearview mirror. Neither of us says anything, but I know we're both thinking the same thing: that we're not ready to lose him.

"You can go now," Dad says.

"What?" Mom's voice is shaky and I can tell she's trying not to cry.

"Go," he says, louder this time. He sounds angry, and I hope it's not at me.

Mom stares at him a moment longer, then looks back at the highway, where all the other cars are moving again. Someone behind us honks, and Mom hits the gas.

Chapter Fifteen

Alexis

Shit," I say as we zoom past the exit where I was supposed to get off. "Sorry." I bring my eyes up to the rearview mirror, hoping to find CeCe looking back at me. There was a moment when Tommy was coughing that it seemed like she knew we were going to need each other to get through this.

"What?" she asks with snark in her voice, as if she forgot that just moments ago she had to go to the bathroom so badly that she broke her resolve not to talk to me.

I know she's scared, that she's sad and angry. I know because I'm feeling all of those things, too. I wish I could tell her that, but I'm supposed to be the grown-up. I'm supposed to comfort her, to reassure her. But I have no idea how I can do that for her when I need someone to do the same exact things for me.

In different circumstances, I would have talked to Tommy about it. But I can't tell him how I'm really feeling—how my heart practically stopped when he started coughing like that.

I was so scared that we waited too long, that I screwed it up by not saying yes sooner. He couldn't die before we even got to Destin, before he got to do any of the things he wants to do this summer. His last.

"The exit, I missed it," I say.

"Whatever," CeCe says from the backseat. "We're almost there, anyway."

Tommy clears his throat and my eyes dart over to him. "I'm okay," he says.

I wish I could believe him. I know he hates seeing what this is doing to us, and I'm trying to keep things as normal as possible. I was actually happy that CeCe was being a monster earlier. If she had been sweet and agreeable, it wouldn't have been real.

"There's another exit in a few miles," I say.

Tommy nods and turns the music back up. I didn't realize I had turned it down. One of my goals for this summer is to work on being more present and in the moment, especially since our moments are running out.

"Tell me the story about our first kiss," Tommy says.

"You were there," I remind him. "And you've heard me tell that story a hundred times."

"I wouldn't mind hearing it a hundred more." He puts his hand on my leg, letting it slide down to my knee.

My eyes drift up to the rearview mirror to see if CeCe is listening, but she's got her headphones back on and is staring at her phone again.

"You were quiet and shy," I say.

"And you were beautiful."

I laugh. Only through the eyes of love could I be considered beautiful at that awkward twelve-year-old stage. My hair was frizzy, I was at least twenty pounds too heavy, and the style of the clothes we all wore in the eighties was anything but flattering.

"We were standing in the closet on a dare," I tell him. "You were on one side, I was on the other."

"I made the first move," he says proudly.

"But you missed and rammed my nose with your chin."

"It was my first kiss," he says, moving his hand up and down my thigh. I don't remind him it wasn't my first. Now, I wish it had been.

"You were embarrassed and went back to your side of the closet. Then our time was up, they opened the door, and I walked out."

"But you came back."

"I came back." I smile. For years, my memory of the night stopped when I walked out of the closet. It wasn't until years later when I finally came back to Destin that Tommy reminded me what happened next.

I remember now, looking back toward the closet where Tommy hadn't moved. His chubby cheeks were flushed in embarrassment, and he looked sad. Even back then, I never wanted to disappoint him. So I walked back to the closet, leaned forward, and let my lips briefly brush against his. It had been a flutter of a kiss, but it made him smile again.

"I didn't wash my lips for the rest of that summer." Tommy leans over and gives me a quick kiss. He looks in the backseat before giving me one more. "We've lived a good life."

"We're still living it," I insist.

"We are," he agrees. "I know it's not ideal to spend the whole summer down here—"

"CeCe didn't mean what she said."

"I meant for you."

Ouch. I've tried to keep a smile on my face about Destin ever since our conversation about Monica, but of course he can see right through it. "There are worse places we could be," I tell him.

"Like a hospital," he says.

I nod, even though if we were at a hospital, there might be a fighting chance we'd have more summers to spend together. "Or the DMV," I say, in an attempt to change the subject.

It works, according to the smile on Tommy's face. "Or at the mall with a dozen teenage girls."

"In the middle seat of an airplane," I say. "Next to someone gassy."

"In a principal's office," Tommy says with a sly smile.

"You have never seen the inside of a principal's office," I remind him. "You were always a perfect student."

"That's what you think," he says. I steal a glance in his direction and find him looking at me with a smug look on his face. "You don't know all my secrets."

"I know about the time you opened your Christmas presents and rewrapped them all so your mom wouldn't know."

"That, I did."

"And I know you cheated on your driver's test."

"That was you, my love."

Damn, he's right. "Sometimes it's like you know me better than I know myself."

"I wouldn't have it any other way."

Tommy reaches for my hand and gives it a sweet kiss, letting his lips linger long enough that it would garner a comment from CeCe if she were paying attention.

I glance up to the rearview mirror again, where our

daughter is curled up, completely unaware that we're heading toward the only skeleton in her dad's closet.

"Eleven-eleven," Tommy says, nodding toward the dashboard clock.

My eyes find CeCe again. While most of my wishes these days are for more time with Tommy, this wish is that Tommy's past stays in the past. And that CeCe never has to find out about Monica. But there's a sinking feeling in my stomach that Tommy's not the only one I have to worry about losing this summer.

Chapter Sixteen

CeCe

Crossing over the Mid-Bay Bridge toward Destin, I feel like I'm entering the second act of a play. Except this play is my life, and like all tragedies, the end is inevitable.

"It's even prettier than I remember," Dad says, as if it's been years since we've been down here instead of the few months since spring break.

But he's right—it is beautiful. Water as far as I can see to the left and water as far as I can see to the right. The view usually feels like a reward for making it through the long drive, a promise of things to come.

Except this time I know what's coming and I don't want anything to do with it.

Dad seems to have forgotten why we're here, because he's acting like it's just another summer. He lowers his windows all the way and the car fills with a rush of salty air. The wind is so loud that I can't hear what he's saying, but I know him well enough to know he's making a joke about the wind running through his nonexistent hair.

Unbuckling my seatbelt, I lower my window and pull the rubber band out of my hair. Before Mom can tell me to stop, I tilt my head outside.

The wind is strong, but I'm stronger. I close my eyes and turn my face up to the sun. I resist the pressure, letting my head move back and forth like I'm dancing with the wind. My hair whips around, stinging as stray strands slap my face, but I don't care. This is what being alive feels like.

The pressure fades and I slip back inside as Mom slows the car down for the tollbooth.

I lift the armrest back up and slide to the other side so I can get a good look at the painted whales. When I was little, I thought they were real, jumping out of the water to welcome me back to Destin, wondering why I'd stayed away so long.

Of course, I know better now. It's just a mural painted on the side of a warehouse off the road. If you look closely, you can see places where the paint is starting to chip away. Still, there's some small part of me that feels like it's just my old friends saying hello.

"It'll feel good to stretch our legs," Mom says.

I don't bother answering—she always says the most obvious things that don't need to be said. It's like she's just talking to fill space. Dad's more like me; he knows that sometimes there's no need to ruin the quiet with words.

My toes start tapping as we get closer to Highway 98. I've been coming down to Destin since before I was born, so it's like my body has a natural response to this place. Like it's in my genes or something.

As Mom turns onto 98, I look for Bruster's, making sure

my favorite ice cream place is still there. But before my eyes reach the red benches where Dad and I used to sit, eating our ice cream in a race against the sun, a billboard catches my eyes.

"Holy shit," I say before I can stop myself.

"Language," Dad says.

I usually try not to curse around him even though Mom does it all the time. But holy shit! I blink a few times quickly, but sure enough, the billboard still says what it did the first time I read it. DESTIN WELCOMES THE CAST AND CREW OF *THE SEASIDERS*. I read they were shooting the new Netflix series on a beach in a small Florida town, but I didn't realize it was *my* small Florida town.

We stop at a red light directly in front of the billboard, so I snap a picture out the open window. Maybe this summer isn't going to be so bad after all.

My smile fades when I realize Mom is watching me in the rearview mirror. I can see her eyes growing wide as she looks between me and the billboard. It's like she knows I'm imagining the day I'll casually run into one of the show's casting agents on the beach.

I can picture it—he'll say he's got an eye for natural talent, and when I introduce myself as Cecelia Whistler, he'll ask if I'm related to Monica. I'll tell him that no, unfortunately there's no relation between myself and one of the show's stars. My dad's an only child, so I don't have any aunts or cousins or anything. But still, it would be great to play Monica's daughter or something on the show. I mean, who am I kidding, I'd settle for a walk-on role!

"Babe," Dad says, as cars behind us start honking.

Mom takes her eyes off me and back to the road, where the light has already changed. It's pathetic how obvious she is. I really wish she would focus on her own life instead of trying to ruin mine. If she didn't want me to fall in love with acting, then she shouldn't have cast me in one of her stupid commercials when I was a kid. And if she really believes in my talent like she said after the play, then she shouldn't worry about how hard rejection might be because I won't get rejected.

Once I start talking to her again, I'll tell her that's how she can make it up to me—getting me an audition. She could call her commercial casting people in L.A. to see if they know the casting people down here. It's worth a shot, and it's the least she can do after making me spend the whole summer down here.

I post my photo of the billboard to Instagram with a caption: *I'm ready for my audition #ComeFindMe #AStarIsBorn #ActingIsMyJam #TwoWhistlersAreBetterThanOne.*

I text the picture to Liam. I've wanted to text him a million times over the past two weeks, but I didn't want to seem desperate. Now at least I have something interesting to share.

I look back up just as we turn onto Crystal Beach Drive. The familiar two-story houses stand tall in a row, lined up like a box of pastel crayons: pinks and blues and yellows and greens. The palm trees in the front yards make me think of Hollywood. Maybe when I'm a famous actress living there, the palm trees will remind me of Destin, the place where I was first discovered.

Mom turns left on Luke, past Stingray Street, past Cobia—which reminds me I want Dad to take me down to the fish market—and then right before Pompano, there's our beach house with the front porch swing, identical to the one we have back home. It's one of my favorite places to sit when Mom's not hogging it.

"We're here," she says, stating the obvious again.

Chapter Seventeen

Alexis

My heart swells at the sight of my grandmother's house. My house now, since she left it to me. But I still think of the two-story yellow beach house as hers.

After all these years, I still miss her so much it hurts. But even if she won't be walking outside to greet me with a hug and an ice-cold glass of her famous Arnold Palmers, I can feel her down here, where we shared so many summers together, just the two of us. I hope it will be like that with Tommy, that I'll be able to feel him with me. But I'm not ready to think about that. Not now. Not yet.

CeCe has the door open before the car comes to a full and complete stop. I watch as she takes the porch steps in one giant leap, finding the spare key where it's always been hidden, underneath the ceramic bullfrog Gran bought at the dollar store back when it was a five-and-dime.

If Tommy had his way, we'd have moved down here full-time. He says that his home is wherever I am, but his heart is always happier here, where the ocean is blocks, not hundreds of miles, away.

Every year, we say we're going to try to come down more often, but life keeps getting in the way. My work, mostly. But I thought we had plenty of time; this was going to be our retirement home. Tommy would take up golf, I'd try my hand at pickle ball, and we'd spend our sunset years holding hands and walking the beach, reminiscing about the good old days. We had a plan. We're supposed to have more time.

I push the ignition button to turn the engine off, but I don't open the door. As ready as I am to get out of the car, I'm not ready to start this farewell tour. While it might seem like any of the hundreds of times we've made this same drive before, it's not. And I can't ignore the fact that while three of us are arriving, only two of us will be going home.

Tommy gives my leg a squeeze. "Ready?"

"Or not," I say, putting my hand on top of his. "Here goes nothing."

I get out of the car and pop the trunk, ignoring the oxygen he thankfully hasn't had to start using yet—a big tank for the house and a portable oxygen concentrator that looks like a cross between a briefcase and a purse. His doctor back home put us in touch with a specialist here to help with his "comfort care." Tommy told me to stop before I even suggested that maybe he should try to get a third opinion from this doctor.

As much as I'm trying not to get my hopes up, I do hope being down here will remind Tommy how good life can be, that he'll realize we're worth fighting for before it's too late.

"I've got it," Tommy says, bringing me back to the moment. He reaches for my oversize suitcase, weighed down with anything and everything I might need over the next few months.

I watch as he lifts it out of the trunk before grabbing his suitcase, which is just as big and probably just as heavy. With a suitcase in each hand, he heads for the house, trying so hard to maintain the picture of strength.

He doesn't know I've noticed that his appetite is barely there these days. That his face has already hollowed out, that his shirts are starting to hang on his frame and he's wearing his belt a few notches tighter.

We don't talk about those things.

There's a cardboard box in the trunk I don't remember seeing when we packed everything, but I leave it for now, grabbing CeCe's suitcase in one hand and the oxygen tank in the other. I shut the trunk without bothering to lock the doors because this is Destin, and bad things don't happen here. At least, they didn't before this summer.

INSIDE, I HALF expect to find things the way they used to be, with Gran's furniture from her house in Atlanta that always felt a little out of place here. I walk into the only room that escaped our redecorating—the "piano room" with Gran's beloved Steinway holding court in the corner. I used to love listening to her sing as she played everything from Broadway hits to Billie Holiday and the Andrews Sisters while I sat at the card table, drawing or playing Solitaire.

Back when Tommy and CeCe spent whole summers down here, they'd use the table to work on a gigantic jigsaw puzzle. Every time I came down to spend a long weekend, it was a little more complete. Somehow, the timing always worked out so the last piece was in place just before it was time to pack up and head home.

"Babe," Tommy calls from the kitchen.

I walk down the hall toward him, stopping to straighten a framed photo that Jill's daughter, Abigail, snapped of the three of us last summer on the beach.

"Looks like Jill was here," Tommy says, holding up a pitcher of Arnold Palmers—the half iced tea and half lemonade drink she knows my grandmother always kept in the fridge. My eyes well up with tears of gratitude, but I blink them away.

"Did she leave anything else?" I ask, hoping there's a sweet treat from her bakery café to go along with the drink.

"Just a note for you to come by The Broken Crown after we get settled."

I nod, wishing I could leave the unpacking and adulting for later. But rules are rules, and I know if I put it off, I'll end up using my suitcase as a drawer for the rest of the summer.

"Go ahead," Tommy says. "I'll get everything put away."

"I'll go later," I tell him. "We have to go to the grocery store."

Tommy smiles. "I can handle that, too. I do it at home, don't I?"

He's not wrong. "Are you sure?"

Tommy grabs my waist and pulls me closer, answering with a kiss. "Just bring me back something from Jill's?"

"Deal."

I give him one more kiss before walking down the street to get the hug my heart's been aching for since this nightmare began.

Chapter Eighteen

CeCe

I hear the front door close and look out the window just in time to see Mom walking down the street. We barely got here and she's already leaving. It's like she'd rather be anywhere than where we are.

"Dad?" I call as I head down the stairs.

"In here," he yells from the kitchen. "Want an Arnold Palmer?"

"Sure." I walk straight for the cabinet where we keep the glasses. "You want one, too?"

"I thought you'd never ask," he teases.

I reach for a second glass and hand them both to him. "In or out?"

"Always out," he says, filling our glasses before putting the pitcher back in the fridge.

I follow him outside to our usual spot on the front porch swing, him on the left and me on the right with my feet resting in his lap.

"Ahh," he says, taking a sip. "This is the life."

"It's not so bad." The Arnold Palmer tastes fresh, the perfect combination of sweet and tangy. Aunt Jill must have used real lemonade, not the artificial stuff Mom uses.

"Thank you," Dad says, giving my foot a squeeze.

"For what?"

"I know you didn't want to come down here this summer."

"Not for the *whole* summer, but it's not like I had much say, anyway."

"Well, thank you nonetheless."

"You're welcome more the less."

It's easy to pretend that nothing's wrong when everything is normal like this. It's only when Dad starts coughing, or when he stands to the side and I can see how thin he's getting, that I remember. I mean, it's not like I ever forget. It's always lingering in the back of my mind; I just try to keep it as far back as I can. Because thinking about it, it's just too much.

"Penny for your thoughts," Dad says, but I can't tell him what I was thinking. It would make him too sad if he knew what I really thought about, when I let myself think about what's going on with him.

"They're worth at least a dollar," I say with a smile, trying to keep things light.

"Add it to my tab," he says. "I want to know what's going on in that pretty little head of yours."

"Nothing, really."

"Nothing is always something. Are you thinking about Liam?" He raises his eyebrow as if he thinks he knows.

"Who?"

"I get it, not something you want to talk to your old man about."

"It's not that."

He gives me one of his shrink looks, like he's waiting for me to keep talking.

"I mean, I like him," I admit. "And I thought he liked me, but I think it was just an acting thing, like he was getting into character. Whatever it was, it's over now." I shrug, trying to make it seem like it's not a big deal, like I haven't been checking my phone every few minutes to see if he responded to the billboard picture I texted him. Which he hasn't.

"I'm sorry, love bug."

"Whatever," I say again. "I think he's going out with one of his sister's friends. It's hard to compete with a pretty college girl when you're just a high school freshman."

"Just you wait," Dad says. "It won't be long until you're that pretty college girl breaking hearts and taking names."

"It's not a big deal," I say, even though it is.

"I'm sure it feels like it is now, but it's part of growing up," he says. "And if it helps, boys like Liam who are all that now, well, sometimes that's as good as they get."

I roll my eyes. "They tell you to say that in the parenting manual, don't they?"

Dad laughs, which makes me smile. "I wish there was a manual, but it's true. You know, I wasn't always this good-looking."

"You're not that good-looking now," I tease.

"Oh, Cecelia," he sings. "You're breaking my heart."

"And I'm shaking your confidence daily." I say the words since my heart isn't in a singing mood.

"Seriously, though," Dad says, "I was the boy in school that everyone teased."

"I've seen pictures, you were cute."

103

"That's because you love me. I was pretty chubby, and I stuttered when I talked."

"You did?"

"I d-d-did."

"Huh." It's hard to picture my dad as a little kid, much less a little kid who stuttered. I wonder if I would have been nice to him if I'd met him back then. I'm not sure I would've. "Why didn't you ever tell me that?"

"It wasn't important, and I'm only saying it now so you don't worry too much about the boys who are stud muffins in high school."

I flinch at the phrase "stud muffins." "No one says that anymore."

"Well, whatever you want to call it—forget about Liam and look for that frog who's going to turn into a handsome prince like your old man."

"They do say you have to kiss a lot of frogs."

"Not too many," Dad says, nudging his shoulder against mine. "Speaking of kisses . . ."

I sigh louder than necessary.

"Onstage with Liam, was that . . . ?"

"All fake," I lie. "We were just acting."

"Really?" He sounds equally impressed and relieved.

"I told you I'm a good actress."

"You don't have to tell me that," he says. "I saw it with my own eyes."

I blush because I love getting compliments. Especially ones that are well deserved.

My phone vibrates in my pocket and I lean forward so I can get it out. I know it probably isn't Liam, but that doesn't stop me from wishing it were. My face falls a bit when I see it's just Beau.

Mom must have gone to the café. My friendship with Beau would be much less complicated if our moms weren't besties.

"Anyone special?" Dad asks.

"Just a frog."

He reaches for my hand and gives it a kiss.

I put my phone back in my pocket and look at my dad, trying to memorize his face. "So, what now?"

"Now, we sit and talk and drink." He raises his glass to clink against mine. "We relax."

"Not now-now." I hate when I say the wrong words. "I mean, like, now that we're here. What do you want to do?"

I can't read the expression on Dad's face, but I know enough to know it isn't good. I look away, wishing I had never opened my big mouth.

When I finally get the nerve to look again, his smile is back, but it feels painted on, like it isn't real. "I have something in the trunk. A box, will you go get it?"

I nod, happy for the distraction, and head over to the car. Inside the trunk, I find a cardboard box that's like those document boxes Mom keeps in the garage, as if she's ever going to need her old work notebooks and papers again.

It isn't heavy, so I easily carry it to the porch swing. I hand it to Dad, who sets it on his lap. He raises an eyebrow and opens the box slowly, as if there's something dangerous inside. When he realizes I'm not playing along, he takes the lid off and sets it down.

I lean over to see what appears to be a bunch of junk. I try not to look disappointed, but I had hoped it would be something cool. But he looks excited about it, so I pretend, which isn't much different from acting.

"What is all this stuff?" I ask, trying to make my voice sound like it's full of wonder instead of boredom.

"Just a few things to help me with my list." He pats his shirt, where I see a little notebook sticking out of the pocket.

"What list?" I ask, reaching for the notebook. He stops me and shakes his head.

"A list of things I want to do this summer."

I reach into the box and pull out the first thing my fingers wrap around. "A yoyo?"

Dad nods and watches me as I slip my finger into the white loop of string. I hold it in my hand before dropping it to the ground, where it lands with a clunk.

"Here, let me." Dad takes the yoyo, winds the white string back around it and stands up. He drops the yoyo, just like I did, but when he does it, the little blue circle stops before it reaches the ground. I watch in amazement, not having to pretend this time, as my dad makes the yoyo do all sorts of tricks. With a flick of his wrist, the string disappears, getting pulled back into the yoyo, back into my dad's seemingly expert hands.

"Wow."

"Before the end of the summer, I want to teach you how to do that."

I nod, even though I'm pretty sure there aren't enough hours in the summer for me to get as good with the old toy as he is.

"What else do you have in there?" I start digging through what seems like a random collection of junk. A few books and DVDs, a deck of cards, and underneath it all—no, he didn't.

I smile and pull a giant puzzle box out from the bottom.

"Ten thousand pieces?" I ask. The biggest one we've tried before was five thousand, and that had taken us until the morning we left the beach at the end of the summer.

The picture on the front of the box looks like it could have been taken down at our beach, with dunes in the foreground, and pure white sand stretching all the way to the emerald-green water, which blends into the clear blue sky.

"Whaddya think?" Dad says, the smile back in his eyes.

"I think the first one who finds all four corners gets to pick where we start."

"Deal," Dad says, following me back inside. He opens the sliding glass doors so we can feel the breeze while I turn the card table back into a puzzle table, the way it used to be years ago, before everything changed for the worse.

Chapter Nineteen

Alexis

My feet feel heavy, planted like one of the palm trees outside The Broken Crown, the bakery café Jill opened last year. I'm so proud of her for going after her dream, for picking herself up and thriving after Adam left her and the kids for a woman closer to their age than his. I knew he had a wandering eye, and I always suspected he did more than look. But for her sake, I wish I hadn't been right.

One of those friends who's more like family, Jill has been there since before the beginning, back when we were kids without a care in the world building sandcastles and chasing waves at the beach. She was there when Tommy and I first crossed the line from friendship to something more, and she was the first one I called when I found out I was pregnant—before I even told Tommy.

I cried on the phone, telling her how I wanted to be happy about the news, but I was terrified. I lived in Atlanta and Tommy was still living in Destin. A relationship could work long-distance, but I knew that was no way to raise a kid. I didn't want to give up the career I had already sacrificed so much for, and Tommy had his practice in Destin. She let me talk until my voice was worn out, then she reminded me what I knew all along—that Tommy would move heaven and earth to have a family with me.

And she was right. I barely got the words "I'm pregnant" out before he said he was moving up to Atlanta. That was the first time he asked me to marry him. I can still picture him pulling into my driveway. He was so excited, he tried to get out of the car before unbuckling his seatbelt. He dropped to one knee, right there on the blacktop.

I took his hands in mine and pulled him back to his feet. Tommy knew how I felt about marriage—but he still looked disappointed when I told him no. His expression changed back to joy when I brought his hands to my belly. The baby was our future, and I wasn't going anywhere.

Jill was there for me through all of it, and now, she's going to be here for me, with me, through the end. I'm more grateful for that than anything, so I should be running up the stairs to see her. But I can't make myself move.

The bell on the front door jingles a welcoming chime and I look up to see a woman with rusty-red hair and a face full of freckles holding the door open for me. Her smile takes me back to all of the summers when we were kids, younger than our kids are now.

"Are you just going to stand out there all day?"

The sound of Jill's voice brings tears to my eyes. I shake my head and slowly walk up the steps to where she's waiting.

"Your shoes," I say, looking down to the bright pink Crocs on her feet, "are hideous."

Jill laughs and folds me into her arms. I rest my head on her shoulder, and the moment I let myself relax, everything that's been building up is released in a tidal wave of tears.

"Shhh," she says, smoothing my hair the way I used to do with CeCe back when she still let me comfort her. Jill breaks out of our embrace but doesn't let go of my hand as she leads me inside, past the crowded tables, behind the counter, and through the swinging double doors where a petite woman wearing a flour-covered apron is clearly in the middle of something. "Can you give us a minute, Lou?"

"But the tortes . . . ," the woman says.

"They'll be fine, I've got them," Jill assures her.

The woman's eyes avoid mine as she looks around the room, as though she's not sure where else to go. "They need to come out of the oven in thirteen minutes. And then the glaze—"

"I said I've got it, Lou," Jill says, her voice more assertive.

Lou smiles awkwardly, her eyes briefly meeting mine before she pushes through the doors toward the restaurant part of the café.

"Sit," Jill says, pulling a wooden stool up to the industrial island.

"I'm sorry," I manage to say between tears. "I've been so good at holding myself together." I stop talking to wipe my nose, which is running as much as my eyes.

"Here." Jill hands me a clean dishrag. "And you have nothing to be sorry about." Her brown eyes are shining with tears of her own.

Jill pulls another stool up next to mine. "I want to ask how you're doing, but I know it's probably the dumbest question in the world."

"It's not," I say, wiping away what's hopefully the last of my tears. "And in spite of how it looks at the moment, I'm actually doing kind of okay."

"Looks like you're doing better than I would be."

I shake my head. Jill is already doing better than I am. The how, the what, and the why of our current situations are different, but the end result is the same. Of all the things I imagined for Jill and me to be doing together as we grew older, raising kids on our own was not one of them.

As hard as it might be now, I know Abigail and Beau are better off without Adam being such a big presence in their lives. Even when we were kids, Adam acted like the world was his, and we were just along for the ride. If he wanted something, he took it, and he didn't give a damn about the wreck he left in his wake.

When Jill first told me about their friendship-to-love story, she romanticized the slow dance she and Adam shared to "Satellite" by Dave Matthews. They were both at the senior prom with other dates, but the night ended with the two of them in the back of Adam's pickup truck. By the end of summer, Jill had traded her dreams of culinary school for a shotgun wedding. They lost the baby, but the marriage unfortunately stuck.

I like to think that if I had been there, I could have helped Jill see that she had other options. Even if she had the baby, she didn't have to marry him. Because even at his best, Adam Carter was a one-night-stand kind of guy.

He was nothing like Tommy. Who even now is at home, unpacking our suitcases before going to the grocery store. I am the worst caregiver in the history of caregivers. It's so pathetic I have to laugh.

Jill raises an eyebrow. "What's so funny?"

"Nothing," I say, but I can't stop laughing. "Everything."

Jill looks at me like I'm a crazy person, and I'm afraid she may be right. I bend over and focus on my breathing to slow the laughter down. I know all too well that laughter is just one step removed from tears, and I've cried all that I care to for one day.

Once the laughter has faded and my breathing is back to normal, I gather the courage to ask the question that I've been dying to ask, especially since I noticed the production trailers lined up down the street from the café.

"Have you seen her?" I ask, raising an eyebrow so Jill knows which "her" I'm talking about. As if there could be any other.

"She's been in a few times," Jill admits. I try to hide the disappointment on my face, but Jill sees right through me. "It's not like I can turn customers away. They're shooting right down the street. But she only comes in one day a week—I don't think her part is that big."

"Can you believe she's playing a *mother*?" I try to keep my tone light so Jill knows I'm not upset with her. And I'm not, not really. I'm just surprised because Jill is supposed to hate Monica even more than I do.

Back then, almost sixteen years ago, Destin was just a blip on my memory. Whenever I thought about the place I spent so many summers, Tommy and Jill were frozen in time, still twelve-year-olds on the beach where I'd left them. Not adults dealing with unfaithful husbands and evil, deceitful wives.

But Jill had a front-row seat to the destruction when Monica left Tommy with a broken heart—from both the sudden end of their marriage and the child that would never be. To hear Jill tell the story, she didn't care much for Monica even before their relationship turned sour. I can't imagine a world where all of that would be forgotten, much less forgiven.

"If you tell anyone I'll deny it," Jill says. "But I spit in her coffee. Hocked a good loogie in there."

"You didn't!"

"No." Jill shakes her head. "I didn't. I just gave her a quick smile and hid in the back. Mature, right?"

"More mature than I would be." I've thought about what I would do if I ran into her. In my mind, it would play out in different ways depending on whether I was with Tommy or on my own. I'd have an advantage if it was just me since she'd have no idea who I was or how I was even peripherally connected to her life. One good thing about the fact that I wasn't there back then.

Of course, like Jill, I don't know if I'd have the nerve to do any of the things I imagined, but it was therapeutic to think about.

I'm about to tell Jill one of the scenarios that involves my car and a parking lot when I notice an unpleasant smell overpowering the sweet notes that filled the room just moments ago. "Is something burning?" I ask.

"The tortes!" we say at the same time. I move out of the way as she runs around the island and opens the industrial oven, letting black smoke billow out. *Oops.*

Lou rushes back into the kitchen, taking charge. "I've got it," she says, stepping in front of Jill.

If I didn't know any better, I might think Lou was the boss. She grabs the towel hanging from her side and reaches into the oven, pulling out the tray of ruined tortes. She sets the hot pan down and one by one dumps the burned shells into the trash can.

"I am so sorry." It seems like trouble is following me everywhere I go these days.

"It's my fault," Jill says. "I forgot."

"Because I was distracting you."

"Nonsense, it's fine. We'll make another batch."

"We will, will we?" Lou says, giving her a look that lets me know their relationship goes beyond boss and employee.

"Lou will," Jill admits. "Lou will make everything better like she always does."

Lou blushes, humbly turning her face down, and I decide instantly that I like her. "I'm Lexie," I say, slipping into my childhood nickname like I always do when I'm back in Destin. I extend my hand, but Lou hesitates before shaking it, pausing to wipe her hands on her apron first.

Jill shakes her head. "I didn't introduce you?"

"I didn't give you much of a chance," I say.

"It's nice to meet you," Lou mumbles, stringing her words together. Her cheeks are still flushed and she won't quite meet my eye.

"I'd be lost without Lou," Jill says. "She's my head chef and manager and sometimes my therapist."

"We make a good team," Lou agrees, still not making eye contact. The way she's fidgeting, it's obvious she wants us to clear out so she can get back to work.

"The best," Jill says. "And Lexie is one of my oldest, closest friends. She's the one who came up with the name The Broken Crown."

"Jill talks about you all the time, how talented you are,"

Lou says as she goes back to dumping the last of the torte shells. "How'd you come up with the name?"

"I knew it had to be something in the nursery rhyme world because of the whole Jack and Jill thing."

Jill shakes her head. She's always hated the fact that her parents named her and her twin brother after a nursery rhyme, but one of my favorite childhood pastimes was making bad jokes, like asking her or Jack to go fetch me a pail of water.

"I looked up the actual rhyme and it jumped out at me in the first stanza: 'Jack and Jill went up the hill to fetch a pail of water/Jack fell down and broke his crown . . .'"

"'And Jill came tumbling after,'" she says, curtsying.

"I always thought it had to do with that story about you at homecoming," Lou says.

"What story about you at homecoming?" I thought I knew all of Jill's stories.

"It's nothing." But by the shade of red her cheeks are turning, I can tell it's anything but nothing.

"Spill," I demand.

"It's not a big deal." She turns and heads to the pantry to get ingredients for the replacement tortes. "I was nominated homecoming queen senior year."

"You never told me that!" I hated these reminders that life went on in all the years I was gone.

"Because it's embarrassing." She starts to weigh out the ingredients, but Lou shoos her away and takes over.

"I want to see pictures!"

"Never." Jill shakes her head. "Besides, there aren't any. I lost the title before pictures were even taken."

"You were dethroned?" I ask. "How did I not know this?"

"It's hardly something I brag about."

"But you told Lou!"

"Lou and I spend about a thousand hours a week together."

"There aren't that many hours in a week," I say, not bothering to do the actual math.

"I've told Lou a lot of stories about you," she says, trying unsuccessfully to change the subject.

"You leave me out of this," Lou tells Jill.

I laugh, feeling more normal than I have since Tommy got sick. And just like that, it's back on my mind, a shadow over everything.

Jill must notice the shift in my demeanor, because she's instantly back by my side. "We should let Lou get back to work."

"Of course." I stand up. "I'm sorry, again."

"Nonsense, accidents happen."

"It was really nice to meet you."

"Don't be a stranger," Lou says, finally meeting my eyes. Her gray eyes sparkle, and I would compliment them if I didn't think it would make her even more uncomfortable.

"You made quite the impression," Jill says as we walk back into the front room.

"With Lou? She was probably scared I'd start crying again."

"She liked you," Jill says.

"Aunt Lexie?" I hear a soft voice behind me.

I turn around, my arms open, greedy for more love. Abigail hesitates before timidly stepping in for the hug. I pull back from the embrace to get a better look at her.

Almost eighteen, Abigail is timid, but beautiful in a quiet, unassuming way. The ice-blue eyes she inherited from Adam are striking and her strawberry-blond hair hangs past her elbows. She's got her mom's fair complexion and the perfect amount of freckles across the bridge of her nose.

I bring her back in for another hug. "It is so good to see you."

"How's Uncle Tommy?" she asks, stepping back toward the counter.

I glance back at Jill, not sure how much she's told the kids. Her sad smile tells me all I need to know. "He's doing okay, sweetie. He's going to be so excited to see you."

Abigail looks down, her long hair falling in front of her face. She pushes it back, looking toward her mom. "Can I go see him?"

Jill shakes her head. "Not now, Ab. Let's let them get settled first."

Abigail looks disappointed but doesn't push.

"I should probably get back," I say.

"Dinner tomorrow?" Jill asks, sounding as eager to see Tommy as Abigail.

"Yes, please."

"I'll make something special," Jill says.

"No, let's go out," I say. "Camille's for old times' sake?"

"Can I come?" Abigail asks, looking back and forth between us.

"Of course you can," I answer for Jill. "Everyone's invited, even your brother."

Abigail rolls her eyes, and this time, I don't hold back my smile at the apparent sibling rivalry Jill said had gotten even worse since Adam left.

I wonder sometimes how different things would be if

CeCe had a brother or sister. If he or she would be another person for CeCe to bicker with, or if the two of them would pair up against me.

We thought about it, Tommy more than I did. As two only children, we agreed it would be nice for CeCe to have someone else, but the timing was never right.

And now, we're all out of time.

Chapter Twenty

CeCe

I still haven't texted Beau back.

It's not that I don't want to see him. I just don't want to talk about everything that's going on, which I'm sure will be all he wants to talk about.

To my friends back home, my dad is just another dad. He's the man they see for a second when he picks me up or drops me off at school, the guy who takes us to the mall and knows to stand just far enough behind us that we have our space, the one who makes his famous cream-cheese eggs in the mornings after they sleep over.

But Beau's different. He knows my dad has a theory for pretty much everything. And that it's not the best idea to laugh at one of his lame jokes unless you want to keep hearing more of them. Beau knows that my dad's the best listener in the whole world and that sometimes his advice isn't terrible. He knows that he says "interesting" about almost everything—even when it's not. And he knows that my dad gives the best hugs and is never the first to let go. Or maybe that's just with me.

I reach over to grab my phone off the nightstand, staring at it for the seven-hundredth time today, even though it's only 10:03 A.M. and I know that if Liam hasn't texted back by now, he's not going to.

I look down at the textless screen again. It isn't even 10:04 yet. I sigh even though no one is around to hear me. Time moves so slowly down here; this summer is going to feel like a million years. Although that might not be the worst thing if it'll feel like I have more time with Dad.

Mom's words keep running circles in my mind—*Theater camp will be here next summer, but your dad won't be.* I can't believe she said that to me, as if I don't know he's dying. I'm not stupid, but I hadn't really thought about the fact that he won't be here next summer. Or the summer after that. Or the rest of the summers for the rest of my life.

Puppies. Rainbows. Kittens. Unicorns. Ice cream. Puppies. Rainbows. Kittens. Unicorns. Ice cream. I cycle through the list of things that should make me smile, just thinking about them. If I can fill my head with enough happy thoughts, maybe the sad ones will go away. *Puppies. Rainbows. Kittens. Unicorns. Ice cream.* It isn't working.

I think of more things to add to the list—a curtain opening to the thunderous applause of an audience, the first bite of a perfectly cooked meal, Liam's lips, my feet sinking into the sand, the beach. *The beach.* That's what I'll do.

Swinging my legs off the bed, I open the bottom dresser drawer to consider my bathing suit options. The one-piece, no. The tankini, maybe. The bikini, no way.

I shouldn't have let Sofia talk me into buying it. Of course, that was before I was mad at her. I haven't put it on since that day in the dressing room. It's cute and it looks okay on me, but it feels too much like a bra and underwear to wear in public. In front of actual people.

The tankini, it is.

I put the suit on, pick out a cover-up, and throw my hair in a ponytail before heading downstairs. Hopefully I can get out of the house without an interrogation from Mom. She's always so awkward when we first get down here, like she doesn't know what to do with herself. Or me.

I pause at the bottom of the stairs, looking around. The coast is clear. "I'm heading to the beach," I call out so I won't be lying when I say I told them where I was going. I slip out the front door, closing it behind me. *Freedom.*

"Where are you off to?" Mom says from the porch swing. I didn't notice her sitting there, but I shouldn't have been surprised. She's always out here.

"The beach," I answer, even though it should be obvious since I'm carrying a beach towel and a beach bag.

"Is Beau going with you?" she asks.

"No, why?" I ask. She's never cared who I hung out with before.

"I just want you to be careful."

"Around Beau?" I laugh. His mom is her best friend, and he's like a brother to me.

"When boys are teenagers, things can just change. And his dad—" She stops herself even though I already know his dad is a scumbag who left his mom for a younger woman. But that has nothing to do with Beau. If anything, he hates his dad more than his mom does. "Just be careful."

"Sure, whatever."

I take the porch steps in one giant leap and head down Luke Avenue. I resist the urge to look back because I know she'll be watching.

Switching my bag to my other shoulder, I decide to take Barracuda down to Old Highway 98 since there's public beach access at the end of the road. And not because I'll have to pass Beau's house on the way.

The house across from his has a For Sale sign in the yard. I've met the McKeens, the family who lives there, a few times. The kids, William and Madeline, are a little older than Beau, who's a little older than me, but we've all hung out before. I wonder where they're moving.

"Take a picture, it will last longer."

I turn around and see Beau sticking his head out of his bedroom window, his white-blond hair sticking up, looking like he just woke up.

"Hey," I say, trying not to sound like I care. But it is good to see him.

"I'm coming down," he says, assuming I'll wait for him. Which, of course, I do.

While I'm standing there, getting sweatier by the minute, I take a good look at the front of the house that I know almost as well as my own. It's funny how you can look at things so many times your entire life without really seeing them.

The picket fence is more off-white than the bright white it usually is, and the outside of the house looks like a paler shade of pink. The grass is too long and the bushes are growing wild with some branches sticking out farther than others. My stomach does a somersault. This must be what a house without a dad looks like.

"Hey," Beau says, jumping over the fence instead of opening the door like a normal human.

"Sorry I didn't text you back."

"S'okay."

I shift my beach bag back to the other shoulder, not sure what else to say.

"You going to the beach?" he asks.

"No, thought I'd hitch a ride back to Atlanta."

Beau looks confused. "But you just got here?"

"I'm kidding," I say. "Yes, I'm going to the beach."

"Want a good-looking guy to join you?"

"Know any?" I tease.

Beau smiles and starts walking toward the beach, but I don't move because I know he's not ready to go yet, even if he thinks he is. Sometimes it's painfully obvious that I'm the smarter one, even though he's a year older.

"Aren't you forgetting something?" I ask.

"Like what?"

Boys. "I don't know, like, maybe a beach towel? Or sunscreen?"

"I'll share your towel."

"Will you?" I raise my eyebrows.

"And you probably have sunscreen, so I don't need anything else."

I shake my head and take the few steps to catch up with him.

"So how's your boyfriend?" Beau asks, not wasting any time. He texted me the day after the first party at Liam's house and I told him everything—including how I was convinced that I was going to be the last girl in high school to be kissed. He told me he'd help me change that, but I'm sure he was just joking. He thinks of me as a sister, not like a real girl. And besides, if the stories he's told me are true, he's got plenty of girls chasing after him.

"He's not my boyfriend." I try not to sound as disappointed or embarrassed as I feel. It's a lot easier to talk about this stuff when there are hundreds of miles between us and he isn't standing right in front of me, looking cuter than I remembered.

"So you never got that kiss?"

"I didn't say that." I give him a wry smile, but he's not going to get any more details out of me. Maybe if we were talking online, but no way am I going to tell him in person when he can see me blush.

I start to cross Old 98 to get to the beach side of the road, but Beau grabs my hand and pulls me back just in time to avoid an old man riding a bike.

"Watch out," the old man shouts as he speeds past us.

"I just saved your life," Beau says, looking proud of himself.

"Maybe you shouldn't have bothered."

I look both ways and cross the street now that it's clear. At the top of the wooden steps that lead to the beach, I stop to take a quick picture to post on Instagram. Just because I don't want to be here doesn't mean I can't make it look like I'm having the most amazing summer for my friends back home.

The beach is so beautiful I don't even need a filter. The white sand is glistening under the sun and the water looks like it has a reverse ombré—going from a lighter shade of green to darker shades of blue where the water gets deep.

Beau slides past me, practically flying down the wooden stairs. "What are you waiting for?"

I sigh and take the steps one at a time, just to prove that I'm more mature than he is.

THE BEACH IS pretty crowded, which I assumed it would be. Beau waves me over to the spot he found, halfway between the water and the sand dunes. I make my way toward him through the maze of towels, where a mix of tourists and locals are enjoying the beach before the afternoon sun gets too hot.

"How's this?" Beau asks.

"Perfect." I drop my bag in the sand and hold up the top two corners of my towel, passing the other two to Beau. If he's going to share, he can help spread it out.

He sits down, claiming the bottom half of the towel, and motions with his hand, inviting me to join him. As if it's his towel, not mine.

I sit down and pull my knees up to my chest, looking at the couples and families around us. Sometimes I like to pretend I'm in a scene of someone else's play—that we're all characters acting out our own stories.

The young family coming in from the water, I decide, are just here for a week. The mom wants to buy a little vacation house, but the dad doesn't think they can afford it if they want to send their kids to college. The older couple in the folding chairs are retired. They used to live somewhere in the Midwest, maybe, and moved down here when he stopped working. They wish their kids would visit more often.

The older woman smiles in my direction and I quickly divert my eyes, embarrassed to be caught staring. I wonder what she thinks of us—Beau and me. We're clearly not related. Maybe she thinks we're a couple, which is just as weird.

"Get my back?"

I look up at Beau, who has his shirt off and my sunscreen in his hand. "Help yourself."

"I already did." He smiles, missing the point. "But I need help with my back. Don't worry, I'll return the favor."

I haven't decided if I'm going to take off my cover-up or not yet, but I take the sunscreen from his hand and scoot closer to his side of my towel.

He flexes his back a little and I notice he's filled out since the last time we came down here. I'd ask if he's been working out, but I don't think his ego needs to be boosted any more than it already is.

I squeeze the lotion directly onto his skin. His back tenses up as soon as my hands make contact, and I hear him take a deep breath. I make wide circles, going as quickly as I can. The white lotion disappears into his skin and I slide back to my side of the blanket, rubbing my hands over my arms to get rid of the excess sunscreen.

"Your turn," Beau says, turning around to face me.

"I'm okay."

"Amateur."

"Am not," I say in my defense. "I might not live here, but I have been coming down at least twice a year for my entire life."

"And every time you get burned the first day and have to spend the next few days hiding from the sun."

I slip my cover-up over my head, refusing to say he's right even though he is. I hand the sunscreen over and turn around so my back is facing him.

Beau squeezes the lotion on his hands before rubbing it

into my back. He starts at my shoulders and works his way down, kneading my skin like he's giving me a massage instead of just helping me put sunscreen on. I think about saying something but it feels good, so I let it go.

"Thank you," I say, reaching for the bottle when he's finished.

"You don't want help with the other side?" he asks, straight-faced.

I reach for the sunscreen again, not justifying that with a response. He pulls his hand away, teasing, but I know better than to play this game. I lean back and put my arms behind me, propping myself up. I'm not the one who wanted me to put sunscreen on in the first place.

Beau waves the sunscreen closer to me, ready to snap it away the instant I reach for it. His face falls when I don't respond. "You're no fun."

"You don't have to stay if you don't want to," I tell him.

"You want me to go?" he asks, a shadow of disappointment crossing his face. It's so much harder talking in person, without having an arsenal of emojis to let someone know when you're kidding.

"I didn't say that." I hope he doesn't go, and not just because I forgot to bring a book to read. "Just hand me the sunscreen. *My* sunscreen."

Beau smiles and tosses it over. "Only so you don't get burned."

I squeeze the lotion onto my hands and apply it evenly over my skin. Beau's eyes follow my hands as I rub it in, and I try to ignore the queasy feeling in my stomach.

Beau is like a brother to me, I remind myself.

But Liam doesn't know that.

"Let's take a selfie." I pull my iPhone out of my beach bag and Beau slides over so we're sitting side by side. I hold it up to get the best angle and pout my lips a bit. Not bad.

Before I can post the picture, a commotion down by the water distracts me. "Is there a shark?" I ask. My biggest fear is already coming true this summer, so nothing else would surprise me.

"More like guppies." Beau rolls his eyes and leans back on the towel.

"Guppies?"

"Or groupies, whatever you want to call them. I don't get what the big deal is about this stupid show."

"*The Seasiders?*"

"Don't tell me you're one of them, too."

The question is so offensive that I don't bother answering him. Of course I'm not a groupie. I'm an actress, waiting to be discovered. I pull my brush out of my bag and quickly pull it through my tangled ponytail so I don't blow it if this ends up being my one chance.

"Who is it?" I ask Beau, even though I'm sure I know more about the cast than he does. Since I saw the billboard, I have been googling every single one of them.

"Does it matter? They're all nobodies. Except for Monica Whistler and she—"

"It's Victoria and Peter!" I interrupt, recognizing the actors who play the twins as soon as they clear the crowd of immature fans clamoring for their attention.

I decide right then and there that I'm going to come down for a walk on the beach every day until I run into the two of them again. I'll impress them from the start, acting professional and polished so they know to take me seriously as the mature actress I am.

I smile, leaning back onto the towel; this plan might just be crazy enough to actually work. If the worst can happen, who's to say the best can't happen, too?

Chapter Twenty-One
Alexis

CeCe isn't coming?" I ask as Tommy gets into the passenger seat. My driving everywhere is just one of the things that has changed in this new normal.

"She says she's not hungry," Tommy says, buckling his seatbelt.

"Jill said Beau didn't want to come, either," I say. "You don't think . . ."

"Beau and CeCe?" Tommy asks.

"No way." I shut the idea down before it has a chance to fester in my mind. "They're like brother and sister—and she's still hung up on Liam."

"It wouldn't be the worst thing," Tommy says. "Beau's a good kid."

"He *was* a good kid," I say, putting the emphasis on "was." It's both endearing and annoying how much Tommy tries to see the good in people. "But he's a teenager now. You should see the pictures he posts on Instagram—he treats women the same way his father did."

"Women?"

"Girls, whatever. He's like a mini Adam. And he's a fifteen-year-old boy," I add, which should be a scary enough thought on its own.

The realization of what I'm saying settles across Tommy's face. "Should we make her go with us?"

I hesitate. The part of me who tries to be a good parent thinks that yes, we should absolutely make her go. We should be assertive and show her that we are in charge. But the selfish part of me knows that if we make her go, she'll be a pain in the ass and ruin what could otherwise be a very nice evening.

"If you want." I shrug, hoping he doesn't.

"Forget about it," Tommy says. "If she's miserable then we'll all be miserable."

"Isn't that the truth." I back out of the driveway before he can change his mind.

PULLING INTO THE parking lot of Camille's, I can't help but think back to the first time Tommy took me here. We were on a double date of sorts with Adam and Jill, although we were still firmly in the friend zone—which is why I was so confused when he pulled his car into a motel parking lot. Part of me may have been a little disappointed when I realized the restaurant was on the second floor.

"First full day here, and I'm already checking something off my Kick the Bucket list," Tommy says, getting out of the car.

I frown. I'm trying to be supportive, but his making light of everything has the opposite effect on me than it does on him. If it didn't have such a strong reference to death, I might have appreciated his twist on a summer bucket list. But I could do without all the reminders of what the end of this summer holds.

"Uncle Tommy?" Abigail says.

I hadn't noticed Jill's car pull in, but Abigail is standing there looking so timid and lovely. Tommy gives her a smile that lights up his face, and with the permission that it's okay, she lunges into his open arms.

My eyes well up at the sight of them. Tommy and Abigail have always had a special bond, and it hasn't diminished over time. If anything, it's even stronger now that Abigail doesn't have another reliable father figure in her life.

It shouldn't surprise me that Adam has gone MIA since he ran off to play house with his new girl-toy, but it still makes me angry. Even now, Jill tries to make excuses for him, saying that Adam's tried, but the kids refused to talk to him. But he's the dad. It's his job to keep trying. To show that he loves them, even half as much as Tommy does.

"Who is this stunning creature?" Tommy asks Jill over Abigail's shoulder.

"Uncle Tommy, you know it's me." Abigail plays along even though she knows he's teasing.

Tommy holds her an arm's length away. "Abigail Jane?" Tommy looks over at me, the smile on his face stretching from ear to ear. "Lex, look how much our girl has grown."

Suddenly shy again, Abigail drops her head, letting her silky straight hair fall in front of her face. Tommy pushes it back behind her shoulder and gives her a kiss on the cheek. He leans closer to whisper something in her ear.

I catch Jill's eye as she wipes away a tear, and I reach my hand toward hers. Her fingers lace through mine and she clears her throat. "We should get upstairs before they give our table away."

"They wouldn't dare," Tommy says. He gives Jill a hug before walking over to the bottom of the staircase that leads up to both the restaurant and the second floor of the motel, allowing us all to go before him. I try not to notice how he stops to rest halfway up the stairs, or how out of breath he is as we walk through the door to one of our favorite restaurants in Destin.

"TomTom!" Brit, the longtime hostess, calls as she walks toward us. One of Monica's best friends back in the day, she's still beautiful, but less intimidating than she was all those years ago. She gives Tommy a kiss on the lips like she always does, then moves to kiss my cheek—which she didn't always do.

"Did you know Monica is back in town?" she asks Tommy.

My stomach tightens into a knot and I am grateful CeCe isn't around to hear this conversation.

"I heard something about that," he says, putting his arm around my waist. I see right through his gesture, but I appreciate it.

Brit smiles and launches into the story about how Monica landed this great Netflix project and it was just a coincidence that they were filming in Destin, how it's just like the old days and that they should all get together sometime.

Over my dead body.

Brit waits for Tommy to agree, as if she doesn't remember how badly things between them had ended. When he doesn't, she picks up the menus and leads us to our usual spot by the windows in back of the dining room.

As we take our seats, I try to push thoughts of Monica out of my mind and focus instead on the people gathered around our table. We've had so many good meals and good times here, the three of us. I'm grateful that Abigail is completing our foursome tonight instead of her cheating jerk of a father.

That night we first came here, the four of us, was the first time I suspected that Adam might not be as wonderful and doting as Jill claimed. I remember watching him watch Brit as she bent down to pick up a napkin, putting on a little show.

Not only is Jill better off without Adam, but it seems like she's finally coming into the person she was always meant to be. She looks ten years younger and so much more carefree than the last time I saw her. "You look great," I tell her, interrupting whatever conversation I hadn't been paying attention to.

Jill brings her fingers up to her mouth self-consciously. "I can't remember the last time I put on lipstick."

"I keep telling her she should get back out there," Abigail says.

"There is no 'there' here," Jill says. "Trust me."

"You wouldn't know," Abigail says with a little sass in her voice.

"Have you tried the apps?" I ask.

"The appetizers?" Jill teases.

I laugh, but Abigail just rolls her eyes.

"You know I'm talking about the dating apps—I should set up a profile for you, return the favor."

"Don't even think about it," Jill threatens through a smile.

"You know," I tell Abigail, "before your uncle Tommy and

I started dating, your mom made me sign up for a dating site. But she checked the wrong box."

"Lex," Jill warns.

I smile. She doesn't have to worry about my telling her young, impressionable daughter that she clicked the "casual sex" box on the dating profile. The emails I had gotten—and the pictures. Once I'd realized what had happened, I went online and canceled my account.

"Let's just say that there were no love connections," I tell her.

"I beg to differ," Tommy says, leaning in to give me a quick kiss.

Abigail clearly isn't ready to close the topic. "Even if you got her on the apps—"

"Never going to happen," Jill says, interrupting her daughter.

"Even if you got her on the apps," Abigail repeats, "Mom wouldn't have any time to go on a date. She's at the café every day before we wake up, and some days, she's still there after we go to sleep."

"Oh, stop," Jill says, looking flustered.

Even though they're bickering, I'm a little jealous of their relationship. I can't imagine CeCe and me teasing each other that easily.

"You make it sound like I'm never there for you guys," Jill says to Abigail. "I promise, I'm not a terrible mother," she tells us even though we both know she's anything but.

"That's not what I meant," Abigail says, getting defensive.

"You're one of the best parents I know," I tell Jill. "Look how well your daughter turned out!" I hope no one notices that I left Beau out of the equation, but his issues have nothing to do with Jill.

A waitress I don't recognize approaches our table with a

bottle of white wine in one hand, and a plate of Camille's famous fried green tomatoes topped with lump crabmeat in the other. My mouth waters in anticipation. "Compliments of Brit," she says.

The waitress opens the bottle and pours a little taste in my glass, since I always seem to be the nominated taster. I swirl it around, smelling it before I take a sip. "It's perfect, thanks."

She smiles and fills Jill's glass, then Tommy's before hesitating by the empty glass in front of Abigail, who looks at her mom with pleading eyes.

"Not a chance," Jill says.

The waitress nods, skipping Abigail's glass before filling mine. She leaves the bottle in a bucket of ice on a tall stand between my chair and Tommy's.

"I don't see what the big deal is," Abigail says. "You let me have a drink at—" Jill gives Abigail a conversation-stopping look and it actually works. I'm going to have to get Jill to teach me how to do that.

"We're trying to show them I'm not a terrible mother, remember?" Jill says.

"That's enough of that talk," Tommy says. "Now if I may, I'd like to make a toast, and I'd like my goddaughter to join us. Just a sip?"

Abigail sits a little higher in her chair, smiling at her mom as she slowly inches her empty wineglass toward Tommy.

"Just a sip," Jill concedes.

Tommy takes the bottle and pours a few fingers of wine in Abigail's glass, which she holds delicately with both hands. Tommy looks around the table slowly, like he's taking inventory of each of us before lifting his glass.

"Now that we're all here together, well, most of us," he

says, noting the absence of CeCe and Beau, "I want to say a few words."

I close my eyes and take a deep breath, preparing myself to hold it together. I may be the writer of the family, but Tommy is the master of the spoken word.

He clears his throat and Jill and I make eye contact. I can tell she's bracing herself as well, not wanting to break down in front of her daughter and a roomful of strangers.

"Here's to cheating, lying, stealing, and drinking," Tommy says, catching us all off guard.

"Tommy." I look over at Abigail and then back to him.

"It's okay," he says, before continuing. "'If you're going to cheat, cheat death.'" He turns slightly in his chair to face Jill. "'If you're going to lie, lie for a friend.'" He turns back toward me, his eyes locking onto mine. "'If you're going to steal, steal a heart.'" His gaze drifts over to Abigail, who meets his stare. "'If you're going to drink, drink with me.'"

He lifts his glass a little higher and brings his hand toward the center of the table, where we clink our glasses against his.

"Cheers," we say together.

I watch Jill watching Abigail as she takes a sip, and I suddenly wish CeCe were here.

"You thought I was going to get all sentimental, didn't you?" Tommy starts laughing, the kind of laugh that starts low and soft but builds into a deep, gut-wrenching, body-shaking sound.

His laugh has always been contagious, and Abigail is the first one to join in. She's even more beautiful when she lets herself relax. Jill's the next one down, and I finally succumb—unable to resist the circle of people I hold so dear, all laughing as though everything is right with the world.

Of course fate takes that moment to remind us that, no, things aren't all right.

The transition from laughter to coughing is so subtle and seamless that it takes me a second to realize what's happening. But Tommy's coughing again. It's deep and it's raw and it breaks my heart.

I put my hand on his back, rubbing gentle circles. I don't know if it helps him at all, but it makes me feel better than sitting there doing nothing. I look over at Abigail, who has gone pale, her eyes wide and frightened. Jill looks like she's holding her breath, waiting for the moment to pass. I notice Brit standing in the middle of the dining room, staring as if she forgot her manners.

Tommy coughs again, a little quieter this time. I hate that I'm starting to recognize the pattern of these attacks, but it seems like this one is coming to an end. It leaves him breathless, and I let him steady himself before handing him a glass of water.

He thanks me with his eyes as he takes a small sip.

"Why the long faces?" Tommy asks, his voice sounding scratchy. "I know that's the punch line of a pretty good joke, I just can't remember the first part. Something about a horse?"

He looks around the table, but none of us is ready to laugh.

"It's okay," I tell Jill and Abigail. "He's okay."

Tommy takes another sip of water to buy more time, and I know that if I really want to help him feel better, I'll get things as back to normal as they can be.

"So, Abigail," I say, trying to make my voice as bright as I can. "Your mom tells me you've become quite the artist."

"I'm not very good," Abigail says. "But I draw a lot."

"She's being humble," Jill says. "The ones she lets me see

are fantastic. She has a whole collection of people she's drawn while they sit in the café."

"Would you draw me sometime?" Tommy asks.

Abigail smiles shyly and nods.

"You're lucky," Jill says. "She won't draw me."

"You've never asked." Abigail defiantly takes another sip of her wine and I smile, thankful to see my daughter isn't the only one who can deliver a punch with just a few words.

Jill looks hurt but recovers beautifully, shifting the conversation like a pro. "So what are your plans this summer, now that you're here?"

"He's got a list," I tell her, trying not to sound too smug.

"I like lists," Jill says. "What's on it?"

"A little bit of everything," Tommy says. Beyond telling me that there is one, he hasn't divulged any of the details. In due time, he says, even though he knows I'm probably the least patient person on the planet. "Little stuff, like spending time with the three of you, watching some of my favorite old movies again, and some bigger things like getting matching tattoos with Lexie."

"Not a chance," I tell him. "It's against my religion, and you know that pain and I are not friends."

"Speaking of pain," Jill says. "How hard has it been not working? Think you'll really be able to let it go?"

I shrug and take a sip of wine. Normally, the question wouldn't bother me, but I can't help recalling the sting I felt when Jill sounded so surprised after I told her I'd decided to take the summer off rather than try to work remotely. I had hoped now that Jill had her own business she would understand that work isn't a chore for everyone, that I really love what I do.

"It's definitely an adjustment," I tell her. "I think it will be easier next week when I'm not so aware of the day-to-day things going on, the schedules that have to be kept. I mean, I trust Becky to handle everything, it's just a lot."

"I can relate," Jill says. "Lou is the best, but if I'm not there, I don't know, maybe I just like to think I'm more necessary than I am."

I nod a little too eagerly in agreement, relieved to see that she does get it.

"You're a lucky girl, Ab," Tommy says. "You can learn a lot from these two strong, successful women right here."

Jill and I look at each other, and then at Tommy, who is smiling like he doesn't have a care in the world.

We stick to safe subjects for the rest of the evening—a lot of reminiscing and talking about the past, maybe so we don't have to think too much about the bleak future that lies ahead of us. Abigail mostly listens, and Jill doesn't protest when Tommy pours a little more wine in her glass.

On our way out of the restaurant, Brit stops Jill. "Do you have a minute?"

"Sure?" Jill says uncertainly.

"Go ahead," I say, giving her a big hug. "We'll talk tomorrow."

Brit smiles in our direction before leaning in close to talk to Jill.

It could be something about the café. Jill mentioned trying to get her pastries into some local restaurants. But then Brit looks over her shoulder in our direction, and I see the concern in her eyes.

It was impossible not to notice the coughing earlier, and

she's known Tommy long and well enough to notice the changes in his physique.

I send a silent thank-you toward Jill, hoping she knows how much I appreciate her. One of the worst parts of this whole thing has been telling people what's going on. If it had been any other type of cancer, it may have been different, but with lung cancer people put the blame on the victim. Even if they don't ask, you can see the thought cross their mind, wondering if the person was a smoker. As if getting sick was their fault.

"What do you think?" Tommy says as we reach the bottom of the stairs.

"Sorry, I wasn't listening."

"I asked if you wanted to see if there was a room at the inn." There's just enough light in the dark parking lot that I can see the sparkle in Tommy's eyes.

"That inn?" I point toward the motel behind him.

"Babe." I close the distance between us and wrap my arms around his waist. "I love you, but you've clearly lost your mind."

"It could be a little staycation."

"As lovely as that sounds, you know I'm more of a hotel girl."

"This is a hotel."

"It's a motel. And we have a lovely house just a few blocks away."

The beep of the car as he presses the unlock button lets me know I've won this conversation. I hold my hands out for the keys and climb into the driver's seat.

"What's the difference between a hotel and a motel, anyway?" Tommy asks, buckling his seatbelt.

"One letter," I tease. "And about three stars."

"Smart and beautiful," Tommy says. "How in the world did a guy like me get a girl like you."

I reach over and rest my hand on his cheek. He puts his hand on top of mine and I almost consider changing my mind.

"Let's go home," he says.

And I couldn't agree more.

Chapter Twenty-Two

CeCe

@**BeauBo:** HEY
@**WhistlerGurl:** Hey
@**BeauBo:** WHAT R U DOING?
@**WhistlerGurl:** Nothing. And stop using all caps
@**BeauBo:** Want to go to the beach?
@**WhistlerGurl:** Not really
@**BeauBo:** Ur no fun

I don't reply because he's right. I'm not very much fun right now.

@**BeauBo:** Text me if u change ur mind
@**WhistlerGurl:** I won't
@**WhistlerGurl:** But thx
@**BeauBo:** L8r

It's a nice day out. I should go with Beau—but my heart can't take another day on the beach without running into any of the *Seasiders* cast.

It was stupid to think I could casually bump my way into an opportunity of a lifetime. Kind of like it was stupid of me to think I wouldn't be upset to see the cast announcement for the summer camp production of *The Sound of Music* this morning. It hurts knowing my name should have been on the list, and what I saw on Instagram hadn't helped, either.

Liam posted a picture of himself looking as cute as ever, standing by the wall next to the cast list, with his arm around my former best friend. I had to beg Sofia to do theater camp with me; she should have dropped out as soon as I had to.

The text was a little blurry, but I could see enough to tell that Liam was playing Captain von Trapp, which I knew he would be. But I hadn't been expecting to see that Sofia would be playing the role of Maria.

I'd taken some solace in the fact that the Captain and Maria weren't star-crossed lovers like Liam and I had played, but then I googled and found out there is a scene when they kiss. I haven't been able to get the thought of them together out of my head since. It probably doesn't help that I keep looking at their stupid picture.

I close my laptop and decide to at least get some fresh air. I can sit out on the porch swing and read if Mom isn't already out there. She's been spending a lot of time at the café with Aunt Jill, so hopefully she's there. Anywhere but here.

Downstairs, the living room door is closed, which means Dad is probably talking to one of his head cases. I glance out the front window, and it looks like the coast is clear. My spirits pick up as I head into the kitchen to pour a glass of the Arnold Palmers that are always in the fridge. I don't really see what the big deal is about them—it's just iced tea mixed with lemonade, but Mom loves them.

I would understand the fascination a little more if Mom didn't use the granulated lemonade that comes in a canister. She uses the same thing for the iced tea, not even a real tea bag. They'd taste so much better with natural lemonade and sun tea. Maybe some fresh mint.

That's not a bad idea, actually.

I scrawl a quick note that I'm going on a bike ride and grab $20 from the coffee mug on the second shelf of the cabinet by the sink where Mom keeps a little emergency cash.

The Whole Foods is on the other side of 98, and Mom would flip if she knew I rode my bike across the busy six-lane highway—but what she doesn't know won't hurt her.

I grab my helmet and start off. I hesitate at the edge of the highway, almost second-guessing myself, but at least there's a traffic light at this intersection. I wait at the red light, my foot on the brake and my heart beating in my throat.

The light turns green and I pedal as fast as I can until I'm on the right side of the highway. Cars in both directions are stopped at red lights, so it's not really a big deal. But it feels exhilarating, kind of like the day I snuck into the theater at school. I've wasted so much of my life following the rules.

I consider turning left into the Commons to buy a little something for myself. That $20 in my pocket could easily turn into a few new lip glosses at Sephora. But I took the money to buy something for Mom, to do something nice for her so she knows I'm not the worst person in the world.

But lip gloss.

I ignore the urge and turn right toward Whole Foods. Now that I know it's not a big deal to ride across the highway, I'll come back and go to the Commons another time.

There's a bike rack outside Whole Foods, so I lock my bike

up and take off my helmet, trying to fluff a little life back into my matted-down hair. I grab a cart even though I'm just getting a few things and toss my helmet in the basket.

This Whole Foods isn't as big as the one Dad and I go to back in Atlanta, but I'm not looking for anything that fancy today, and I assume they'll have the basics.

My first stop is the produce department, where I ignore the prebagged bunch of lemons and grab an empty bag to fill with the juiciest ones I can find. My eyes are drawn to the brightest ones that don't have any wrinkling on their skin, just the way I learned on the Food Network.

I take two lemons in my hands. They both smell good and feel heavy for their size, but the first one doesn't give when I squeeze it, which I know means it won't yield much juice. The second one has the perfect amount of give, so I drop it in the bag and continue looking for six more that are just as ripe.

Next, I roll my cart over to the fresh herbs. Mint had been my first thought, but now that I'm here, I'm thinking basil or rosemary might be better. I reach for all three containers even though I can't afford to get them all. I smell them one at a time, imagining how each one would taste mixed with freshly squeezed lemons and sun tea.

I put the rosemary back and try to decide between the mint and the basil. On one hand, the whole point of this was to elevate Mom's palate and show off mine, and basil is much more creative. But I know mint will be good, and maybe it's better to take baby steps with Mom.

Holding the two herbs in my hand, I think back to how great it was when I stopped playing it safe and flew across the highway, so I put the mint back and drop the basil in my cart.

I find everything else I need quickly, then make my way to the register. I don't understand why most people, including Mom, complain about going to the grocery store. It's so much fun, picking out different ingredients and imagining how they'll come together. After the thing I don't want to think about happens, maybe I'll take over the grocery shopping. As long as Mom pays for it and lets me decide what to buy.

"Find everything you need?" the cashier, a woman with blond dreadlocks, asks.

"Yes, thank you." I try to make my voice sound as mature as I can. She hands me my change as if it's not weird for a fourteen-year-old to be grocery shopping for herself.

Maybe this will work . . . Pushing the cart back toward the front of the store, I consider the logistics of it all. While there is no doubt in my mind I could do a better job at the grocery shopping than Mom would, I don't know if I'd be able to pull it off. Especially since I won't even have my learner's permit for another year.

As I set the grocery bag into the basket of my bike, the realization of what I'd been thinking makes me sick to my stomach. Something must be seriously wrong with me, making plans for when Dad's gone as if it's not a big deal. And it's the biggest deal. It's the worst thing in the entire world and I'm worried about who's going to go grocery shopping? Maybe Mom's right—maybe I am a horrible, selfish person.

I put my helmet back on. It hurts a little going over my ears, but the hurt feels good. I deserve that, and a lot worse.

Riding back over to the intersection of Highway 98 and

147

Crystal Beach, it doesn't seem like as big of a deal anymore. Instead of butterflies in my stomach, it just feels like there's a big, empty hole.

The light turns green and I pedal across at a normal speed, back down Crystal Beach and back down Luke to the house where my dad is dying.

Chapter Twenty-Three
Alexis

W hat's this?" I ask out loud, even though no one is around to answer me. A big glass jar is sitting on the edge of the front porch with four tea bags floating inside. One of CeCe's cooking experiments, no doubt.

Inside, the sliding doors to the living room are closed, which means Tommy must be talking to a patient, even though he was supposed to stop working before we left Atlanta. He says it makes him feel good to be needed, and I resist the urge to make a joke about clearly not being the only workaholic in the family.

I push the thought of what's happening back at the agency out of my mind and head toward the kitchen to put the canapés Jill insisted I bring home in the refrigerator. I pause in the doorway, surprised to find CeCe sitting at the kitchen table.

"What are you doing inside on such a beautiful day?" I assumed she would be down at the beach.

"Isn't it obvious?"

I look at the Whole Foods bag sitting on the chair beside her and the pile of lemons on the table in front of her.

"Did Dad take you to Whole Foods?" He's not supposed to be driving anymore, but at least it's close by.

"I just got a few things," she says, flickering her eyes between me and the cutting board. "I'm actually making something for you."

I must have heard her wrong. "For me?"

"Is that so hard to believe?" she snaps.

"What? No? I mean, of course not." I pull a chair out and sit down across the table from her. "What are you making?"

"An elevated Arnold Palmer. The powder stuff you use is all chemicals, it's gross."

"That's the way Gran used to make it," I say, which clearly is the wrong thing to say because CeCe's shoulders shoot up and any ounce of softness she was showing me is gone.

"I shouldn't have bothered," she says, picking up the knife.

"No, no, I'm glad you did." I reach for a lemon. "I'm sure it will be much better. Are you following a recipe?"

"It's my recipe," she says, her voice brimming with pride.

I watch as she holds a lemon vertically on the cutting board, slicing off one side. She rotates the lemon and does the same thing with the other three sides. Her hands move so swiftly; I envy the confidence she has in the kitchen. The paint on her nails is chipped again; maybe later this afternoon we can go for another manicure. I could probably use a pedicure, too.

CeCe takes the remaining core of the lemon and squeezes it into the bowl in front of her. She shifts the lemon in her hand and squeezes again, getting every last drop of juice from it.

"How'd you learn to do that?" I ask, impressed.

"Food Network." She tosses the empty skins in the Whole Foods bag before reaching for the next lemon.

I keep watching as she works her way through the stack of lemons. We don't talk much so she can concentrate on what she's doing, but it's nice, sitting together and watching her work. Making something for me.

"What's wrong with you?" she asks.

"Nothing, why?"

"Your face," she says. "It looks funny."

"Hmm." I bring a hand up to my face and slide it down, as though I could wipe away whatever expression CeCe reacted to. I never did have a poker face. "Can I do anything to help?"

"Grab the sugar?"

"Splenda okay?"

"I bought the real stuff, it's over there."

I follow her gaze to the counter, where a growing number of orange prescription bottles have been stacking up. I know it's called comfort care, but it feels more like giving up to me. One of the websites I signed up for weeks ago emailed me an update about a new drug trial the other day, but Tommy shut me down before I even finished the sentence.

My face falls a little and I notice CeCe's does, too. We haven't talked much about what's happening to her dad. I know Tommy has talked to her about it, but I've been afraid to broach the subject since I royally blew it at the nail salon.

"Hard to pretend everything is normal when there are reminders all over the place, huh?"

"Tell me about it," she says. And then she smiles at me. It's just there for a second, but for one beautiful moment, it's like we're in this together.

I'm afraid to say anything to ruin the moment, so I stand

up and get the bag of sugar from next to all the prescription bottles. Maybe I'll talk to Tommy about keeping them in the cabinet so they aren't always in our faces.

"This?" I ask, handing her the sugar.

"Yeah, and can you hand me the measuring cup?"

I get the measuring cup from the drawer to the left of the sink and set it on the table before wordlessly taking my seat. CeCe opens the bag of sugar, using the measuring cup like a scoop. She slides her pointer finger across the top, getting rid of excess granules before pouring it into a second bowl. I resist the urge to comment about how much sugar is in this recipe and smile instead.

She picks up a container of fresh herbs and pops the lid open, releasing a familiar scent. I recognize the minty flavor, but there's something else there, too.

"Is that mint?"

Judging by CeCe's smile, I know I'm not right. But she's so happy to correct me that I'd take being wrong all day if every interaction between us could be like this.

"Nope." CeCe rips a leaf from the stem and hands it to me. "Smell."

As soon as the fuzzy green leaf is beneath my nose, I recognize it as basil, but I'm not going to let her know that I know. At least not yet. "It's on the tip of my tongue."

"It's basil," CeCe says, beaming with pride.

"Basil?" I give it one more deep smell. "Of course. And you're putting it in the lemonade?" I smile to let her know I'm not being critical.

"Yeah, I almost went with mint, but I thought this would be better."

"I can't wait to try it."

She smiles again and I can't remember the last time I was on the receiving end of so many smiles.

I fold my hands on the table and watch as she continues to work. I don't have to pretend to be impressed, because I genuinely am. My idea of making lemonade has always been scooping powder into a pitcher of water and mixing it up. Sometimes it amazes me that this beautiful creature not only grew inside of me, but that she has half of my DNA.

CeCe's fingers move swiftly as she rips the leaves from the stems, leaving a few fully intact. She adds the torn leaves to the bowl of sugar and starts moving a wooden spoon around, more in a stabbing motion than stirring. She stops to push her glasses up her nose and laughs, clearly reading the confusion on my face.

"I'm bruising the basil leaves," she says as though that makes sense.

"Food Network?"

She nods and continues her assault of the basil.

When the leaves are adequately bruised, she pours the mixture into a glass pitcher, followed by the bowl of freshly squeezed lemon juice and water from the faucet.

She angles her body so I can watch as she works, stirring the mixture with the wooden spoon. I can picture her cooking on a set, playing to a camera as she dazzles the audience at home.

"Maybe I should be filming this," I say, pulling my phone out. "Could be worth something someday—early shots of celebrity chef!"

CeCe flashes a smile so pure it makes my heart melt. It's been so long since I've seen her genuinely happy. I start filming.

"What are you making?" I ask.

"Today I'm making lemonade from scratch with fresh basil," she says, looking directly at the camera. "For my mom."

Oh, my heart. It takes everything I have to keep my focus on filming her. "How long do you have to do that?" I ask; she's been stirring for a while.

"Until the sugar is dissolved."

I nod, wishing I didn't know how much sugar was in there.

"And then I'll pour it in the sun tea that's brewing outside to make an elevated Arnold Palmer." She smiles to the camera and I stop recording, but I don't want her to stop talking.

"What kind of tea is it?" I ask.

"It's normal tea," she says. "Well, normal tea bags—not the stuff you usually use. It's called sun tea because you leave it out in the sun for a few hours and it brews naturally."

"Food Network," we say at the same time.

"How long till I can try it?" I ask.

"Maybe after dinner? I want to give the flavors time to meld together, and the tea will have to cool down since it'll be warm from the sun."

I lick my lips in anticipation. "Can I have a little sneak taste before that?"

"Patience is a virtue, Mom."

"Not one of mine." I laugh, and she joins in.

I'm enjoying the moment so much that I don't notice Tommy walking in.

"Everything okay in here?" he asks, leaning against the doorframe with a suspicious look on his face.

"Of course," CeCe responds as if it's a crazy question.

"Of course," I mimic her, giving Tommy a look that I hope says *I don't have any idea, either, but let's go with it.*

He smiles and looks back and forth between the two of us, his eyes resting on the pitcher of lemonade and the grocery bag on the chair between us. "Did you guys go to Whole Foods?"

"I thought you . . ." I look from him to CeCe, who has suddenly stopped laughing. And just like that, the magic of the moment is gone.

Being a parent really sucks sometimes.

Chapter Twenty-Four

Alexis

Tommy, as usual, is the first one up. I find him in the piano room, working on the puzzle. They started from the top, CeCe's choice, and the sky is beginning to come together. I can't remember if the thin and wispy clouds are cumulous or whatever the other kind is, but it looks beautiful.

"Morning." I give him a quick kiss before heading into the kitchen to get us both coffee.

"So what's on tap for today?" I ask. We've been trying to tackle at least one item from his list every day, and as much as I resisted the idea at first, it's been nice giving every day its own purpose.

"I was thinking maybe Big Kahuna's," Tommy says.

The mention of the water park down the street sends waves of worry through me. I shiver at the thought of Tommy there, carrying the portable oxygen concentrator he started bringing everywhere two days ago.

It's almost to the point where even the walk up our stairs leaves him breathless, and I don't see how he could manage to climb to the top of those towering slides. And knowing him, he wouldn't be able to sit back and watch others have all the fun without him.

I bite my lip, trying to figure out how to be a voice of reason without crushing his spirit.

"The mini-golf part," he says.

I exhale a sigh of relief. Mini golf we can handle.

"Are we going to make an exception on the grounding?" I ask.

"About that," Tommy says.

"Were we too hard on her?" I ask.

"Probably not," Tommy says. "But maybe we can let it slide this once? It might be selfish of me, but I don't want to waste a day of the time we have left with CeCe being punished."

"You are the least selfish person I know, Tommy Whistler." I give him a kiss and watch as he focuses his attention on finding a puzzle piece that has a bird's left wing on it.

Once he finds it and snaps the wing into place, he looks up with an expression I can't quite read. "Speaking of being less selfish and more selfless, Monica called me this morning."

The coffee I'd been drinking goes down the wrong way and I start coughing.

"Monica-Monica?" I ask, just to be sure.

"That Monica."

My stomach turns at the thought of my worst fears being realized. I assumed there would be a run-in at some point, but I thought it would be more accidental, and I didn't think it would happen this soon.

"What did she say?" I ask, trying and failing to sound casual.

"That it's been a while."

I snort. "That's an understatement."

"She heard what's going on, from Brit, I'd guess," he says. "She wants to come see me. To talk."

"To talk?" I raise my eyebrow suspiciously. For what reason, I have no idea. Tommy has made it clear I have nothing to be worried about—but that's easy to say when his ex is just an idea. But when he sees her again, with her jet-black hair, olive skin and almost translucent green eyes, making you wonder what cultures collided to create her, then it might be a different story.

I shiver at the thought. Monica would be a hard act to follow even for a woman who had high self-esteem and a positive body image.

"Of course, just to talk," Tommy says. "If you aren't comfortable with it, I'll tell her not to come. I know I promised."

I take another sip of my now cold coffee. He did promise. But I know I can't and won't stop him from talking to her. If nothing else, he deserves closure. There was a moment when she mattered to him, and if he can forgive her, then he's a better person than I am. Which, of course, he is.

"No, you should talk to her if you want to."

"I knew you'd understand," Tommy says. Clearly, he has more faith in me than I do.

"But I don't want CeCe to be here."

Tommy nods, and I search his eyes for a clue to how he's feeling about all of this.

"Do you forgive her?" I ask.

"I did, a long time ago."

I nod, trying to gather enough courage to ask the question I wasn't quite brave enough to ask the last time we talked about her. And I can't unhear the answer if it's what I've been afraid of all these years.

"Have you kept in touch? With her?" I ask.

"With Monica? No." I exhale, relieved. "The last time we spoke was when the divorce was final. But I did tweet her to say congratulations after you told me her Netflix news."

I try to hide my surprise. "You did?"

"Of course not." He laughs. "You know I don't tweet."

"But if you did?" I ask, relaxing into our natural banter.

"Then my tweets would only be for you, my love." He takes my hand and brings it to his lips.

"Oh, stop," I say, pulling my hand away. "But keep going."

"I would sing your praises a hundred forty characters at a time."

"You can have two hundred eighty characters now," I tell him.

"Even better." He smiles and wraps his hand around mine. "Just one more thing about Monica?"

I nod.

"She doesn't hold a candle to you."

"You don't have to." I avert my eyes down to the puzzle, which is starting to take shape.

"I want to." He reaches over and gently turns my head toward his so I have no choice but to look at him. "I wouldn't change a thing—well, maybe a few things. But everything I went through and everything I did before you is what I needed to go through to be ready for you. So what good would it do to be upset with her? I ended up with everything I ever wanted."

I slide my chair closer to his and rest my head on his shoulder, my thoughts bouncing between how I got so lucky to find a man like Tommy, and how in the world I can find a way to keep CeCe out of the house when Monica comes knocking on our door.

Chapter Twenty-Five

Alexis

It doesn't feel like we're still in Destin," CeCe says as we walk out of a cave in the middle of Big Kahuna's tropical miniature golf course.

The transformation in CeCe was automatic, her foul mood disappearing as soon as we told her that we were lifting her punishment, and that we were going to Big Kahuna's for the morning. She was disappointed at first that we wouldn't be able to do any of the crazy waterslides, but she understood. And she even did a little investigating into the park's attractions and found a wave pool that she thought might not be too much for Tommy.

So after the next hole, when Tommy will likely show off his mad mini-golf skills with another hole in one, or at least a hole in three, we're going to cool off with a ride around the wave pool.

"It is pretty magical," I have to admit. It's been years since I let them convince me to come along to the water park, one of the biggest tourist attractions in Destin. The landscaping really is impressive, with trees providing shade overhead and wooden bridges that go over a streaming "river" and under a canopy of tropical flowers. The gigantic tiki heads are a little too much for my taste, but I forgive them as part of the shtick.

"The water's going to feel so good," Tommy says. The breaths between his words sound labored; he's going to need oxygen soon.

"The best," CeCe agrees.

She gives her dad a smile bigger than I've seen, not just since all of this happened, but since she officially made the change from tween to teen. It's almost as if the little girl she used to be has come out to play for the day, and I have to admit it's a nice change.

Maybe Tommy was on to something with this list of his. So far it seems like it's as much for us as it is for him. Like he's leaving us the gift of new memories we'll have to treasure.

I blink back the tears that are threatening to fall because I don't want to put even the slightest blemish on this perfect day.

"You're up first, Mom," CeCe says as we walk up to what we all decided would be our last hole of the day. I drop my blue ball on the starting line and get into position as if I know what I'm doing. I stand with my legs apart and square my shoulders like Tommy told me to, and bring the putter back before swinging it to make contact with the ball.

It flies, getting pretty good distance until it bounces off a windmill, which sends it rolling back almost halfway to where it started.

I shrug and move out of the way so CeCe can take her turn, trying to get her purple ball through the windmill and into the tiny hole on the other side.

Beside me, Tommy leans back against the heavy trunk of a tree, breathing slow and shallow.

"You okay?" I ask, afraid to hear the answer, terrified I cursed us by thinking about the perfection of this day before it's ended.

"I'm fine," Tommy snaps. He tries to soften the sting with a smile, but the pain on his face makes it look more like a grimace.

He slips the oxygen tubes into place before walking over to the green. He drops his red ball onto the fake turf and CeCe moves it into place so Tommy doesn't have to bend down. He ruffles her hair in appreciation as she steps back to watch him in action.

I watch as he gets himself in position as if it's the most natural thing in the world. He brings the putter back and swings. It makes contact, but instead of flying through the opening of the windmill like I expected it to, Tommy's ball makes a similar trajectory to mine, and ends up almost back at the beginning.

"It's okay, Daddy," CeCe says, quickly by his side. He huffs and walks, oxygen bag in hand, up to the ball. We both watch with bated breath as he swings the putter again. This time, the ball hits just to the left of the windmill's opening. It bounces back a few inches, lined up perfectly with the opening.

"Now it's just messing with me," Tommy says, an unfamiliar gruffness to his voice. CeCe looks over at me, unsure. I give her a small smile, hoping that this is just a fleeting moment. Tommy isn't used to being physically challenged, especially at something that should be as carefree and fun as mini golf.

Tommy hits the ball a little harder than necessary, and it glides toward the windmill's entrance at the exact time the spinning arms cross in front of it. The ball bounces back again, but Tommy stops it with his putter, moving it in one fluid motion so it finally rolls through. I exhale the breath I've been holding, and I imagine CeCe doing the same. Tommy's posture immediately changes; he looks exhausted but satisfied.

"The windmills are always the hardest," he says, flipping the putter so it's resting on his shoulder. "What do you say we get out of here?"

I expect CeCe to protest—I know she's been looking forward to the wave pool—but she nods, agreeing with her dad.

"Yeah, let's get out of here," she says. "Up for some ice cream at Bruster's?"

"That sounds good, kiddo," Tommy says.

CeCe rewards him with a smile before running around to the other side of the windmill to collect our balls.

As soon as we're in the car with the AC blasting, Tommy shuts his eyes. He's asleep before we're even out of the parking lot. I turn and look at CeCe in the backseat. It's amazing how quickly she can go back and forth between a little girl and a young woman.

"Thanks for being a good sport today," I tell her, keeping my voice down even though I know it would take more than that to wake Tommy from his slumber.

"It's not a big deal," she mumbles.

"It is," I tell her. "And I appreciate it."

She shrugs and I put the car in drive. I slow down when we get close to Bruster's in case CeCe still wants to stop.

YOU AND ME AND US

"Do you want ice cream?" I ask.

She shakes her head, and I keep going. I'll find a way to make it up to her. We'll pick a day soon and I'll take her back to the water park so she can go on all the slides, not just in the wave pool. And afterward, we'll stop for ice cream and compare notes about which slides we thought were the best.

I sigh, letting reality sink back in. Because even if that day comes true and it's perfect in every other way, it won't make up for the one thing that would make it complete. Because after today, there's no denying that the things we've been trying not to think about are starting to happen.

Back home, CeCe opens the car door to let herself out, and I hate the idea of the day ending on such a sad note. There may be nothing I can do to slow down time as far as Tommy is concerned, but I can do something to make this day a little less awful for CeCe.

"Hey, Ceese?"

She turns and looks back at me, her tired face void of any emotion. Its blankness scares me, and for a moment I forget what I was going to say. But then she brings her hand up to her mouth and starts to bite the edge of her nail.

"What do you say we go for a mani-pedi after we get your dad settled inside?"

"Okay," she says with a shrug.

Not quite the reaction I was hoping for, but at least it isn't a no.

JILL RECOMMENDED A nail salon in a strip mall down on 98, tucked between the Best Buy and Office Depot. Once we get settled into the chairs for our pedicures, the old CeCe starts to come back to life. It may have helped that I let her pick out the color for my toes.

When CeCe was younger, before she started to resent the fact that we look so much alike, she loved it when we got matching colors. It made for some interesting meetings at work when I would show up with a rainbow of sparkling colors on my nails.

I expect her to hand me something purple, but instead she picks a pale, pastel pink. It's a more subtle shade than the orangey pink that's become my summer go-to, but I like the way it looks against my tan skin.

"If you want, we can go for ice cream after," I say. She gives me a look that warns me not to push my luck. "Or we can just go back home."

"Let's go back home unless Dad is up and wants us to bring him some."

I nod. "Hopefully he'll have some energy back after a good nap. We wore him out today, but he's really looking forward to the movie tonight."

CeCe's eyes light up at this. So far she's really enjoyed the movies that have been on Tommy's list for us to watch together, but what's been even more special are the discussions they've inspired. Tommy and CeCe talk about everything from cinema styles to performance techniques, while I watch and listen, enjoying the way they connect over a mutual love.

Tonight, we're supposed to watch *Blues Brothers,* and I'd promised to get some cheddar and caramel popcorn to make the classic Chicago mix.

When the manicurist taps my leg to bring my foot out of the water, I comply, not even thinking that the "hate" part of my love-hate relationship with pedicures might be coming. I realize too late that she's about to start scrubbing the very ticklish bottom of my foot and I let out a little yelp.

CeCe rolls her eyes and I hold on to the edge of the seat, focusing all my energy on not laughing and not pulling my foot away from the manicurist.

"Are you ticklish like your mom?" CeCe's manicurist asks.

"Not that bad," CeCe says, smiling.

"She may look like me," I tell the woman, "but she's got tough skin like her dad."

CeCe's face lights up at the compliment. She settles back into her seat as her manicurist, a step behind mine, takes out the loofah bar.

Never one to turn down a challenge, CeCe keeps her eyes on mine, stoic as the manicurist scrubs her feet. They both watch me, and I cringe as if it's the soles of my feet that are getting attacked with the exfoliator.

I hear the commotion outside before I see it. CeCe notices it, too. Our heads turn at the same time, our jaws drop— but for very different reasons. Because standing outside, on the other side of the glass pane, is none other than Monica Whistler.

CeCe lunges forward, but her feet are thankfully occupied by the manicurist, who has now moved on to painting the first layer on CeCe's third toe. I thank God for tiny miracles and keep looking between my daughter and the semistar outside, as girls her age—and their mothers—pose for selfies with Monica.

"OMG." CeCe says each letter as if it's a word. "Mom— that's Monica Whistler!"

"Is it?" I ask, playing dumb.

"Can I?" CeCe looks desperately between her unpainted toes and Monica taking selfies with the modest crowd that's gathered around her.

"CeCe." I say her name in the lecture tone I've been trying to copy from the way Jill says her kids' names. "They're filming here all summer, I'm sure you'll have other opportunities to meet her."

"Do you think you could call one of your casting connections in L.A. and see if they can get me in for an audition?"

"I'll see what I can do," I lie.

CeCe gives me a smile that I don't deserve, because I'm never going to make that phone call. It's too dangerous—if CeCe gets the chance to meet Monica, she's all but guaranteed to find out who she is. It's hard enough playing second fiddle to Tommy, but there's no way I could compete with Monica.

Chapter Twenty-Six

Alexis

I can't remember the last time I worried so much about an outfit. Everything I tried on this morning feels wrong, like it did when I was an awkward high school girl at least one size too big for all my clothes. Before I figured out which styles were more flattering for "curves."

It's not that I care what Monica Whistler thinks. No matter how good or bad I look, she'll still be judging me—the much-less-beautiful one who came after her. I just want to make a good impression for Tommy's sake. To look and play the part of a good, supportive wife—even though Monica is the only one who's held that title in Tommy's life. Which I know is no one's fault but my own.

He's kept his distance this morning, knowing how I get when I work myself up like this. But he did leave a note next to my pillow for me to find when I woke up. We've been spending so much time together he's gotten out of the habit of leaving me daily love letters. I hadn't realized how much I missed them until I saw his scrawled handwriting this morning, written on the back of an envelope. It said, *In a sea full of people, my eyes will always search for you.*

That man really makes it hard to be mad at him. Of course, I'm not really mad. I understand, I just hate the situation. At least it's just one day—I can do one day. It's not even a full day; she'll only be here for an hour.

Jill was a saint and agreed to invite CeCe to spend the day with them. They're going to the beach in the afternoon, but this morning, CeCe is getting real-kitchen experience working at The Broken Crown. At first, I worried Monica might come in the café before or after, but Jill realized that she only ever sees her on Wednesdays, which must be the day they shoot her scenes. At least I don't have to worry about that anymore.

My phone sounds with my second-to-last "you'd better finish getting ready" alarm, which I haven't had to set in months. I've never been a morning person, and I get distracted so easily that I'd be late to work every day without a few reminders. Kind of like I was late getting home every night, I realize with a sinking feeling.

I take a deep breath and focus on being the positive force Tommy needs me to be. That I need me to be, at least until Monica is out of my house. I put my hair straightener back in the drawer, where it's been collecting dust since we got down here, and steal one more glance in the mirror. I know my critical eyes are looking for problems, but it's hard to ignore the pudgy middle that's only kind of hidden by the pale pink A-line dress I ended up going with.

There isn't enough time to change again, and even if there were, this outfit beat out every other one in my closet. It's a pretty color, it's flattering-ish, and most important, it doesn't make me look like I'm trying too hard. Because trying too hard is even worse than not trying at all.

The doorbell rings, and I look back at the alarm clock next to Tommy's side of the bed. Ten to eleven. Who doesn't have the decency to wait in the car until the time they're expected? Although since she has arrived earlier, hopefully she'll leave earlier, then we can get back to normal and it will be like this morning never happened.

"Coming," I yell as I run down the stairs—loud enough that she can hear, but not so loud that I sound mean or angry. Again, it's all about the balance.

I smile at Tommy, who is sitting on the couch in the living room, where we agreed they should sit and talk. I knew he wouldn't want to start their conversation out of breath, so I told him I would get the door and bring her in to see him.

Standing there now, I take a deep breath and straighten out my dress one last time before opening the door and putting on one of my best fake smiles, a talent I haven't had to use in quite some time.

"You must be Monica," I say, as if she could be anyone else. Her skin is flawless and smooth, her translucent green eyes are so bright they're practically sparkling, and her hair looks so silky soft I have to resist the urge to reach out and touch it. She looks even more beautiful up close than she does in all the paparazzi shots from the celebrity gossip magazines.

"And you're Lexie," she says with a perfect on-camera smile, revealing teeth so white she could star as the "after" model in a Crest 3D Whitestrips commercial. "These are for you." She hands me a gorgeous bouquet of flowers that makes it a little less easy to hate her.

The flowers, like her, are exotic and stunning. They look

so fresh I wouldn't be surprised if they'd bloomed just moments before she rang the bell. These clearly came from a fancy florist, not Publix, where I usually go.

"They're beautiful, thank you." I lower my head into the bouquet and breathe in, enjoying the symphony of smells. I smile before looking back up, caught off guard by the confusion on her face. "I'm sorry, please come in."

I step aside and hold the door open for Monica Whistler. I watch as she looks around and I try to see the house through her eyes. It's small and it's certainly not fancy like her place in L.A. probably is.

"Your home is lovely," she says.

At first, I take offense at her patronizing tone, but then I remember her taste in interior design. And based on the furniture she left behind at the condo she and Tommy used to share—the hard leather couch with absolutely no give, the shaggy white rug and hideous painting—I'd be more concerned if she did like it.

"We're only down here for the summer," I explain. "We live most of the year in Atlanta. I'm from there and Tommy moved up for me." I try to throw that last part in there naturally, but I'm not sure it worked.

"How long have you guys been married?" she asks.

I cover the naked ring finger on my left hand before awkwardly not-answering her question. "Our daughter, CeCe, is fourteen, almost fifteen."

If she realizes I didn't exactly answer her question, she doesn't let it show. She just smiles and nods the way any woman would when meeting the current "wife" of her ex.

"Hey, Mon." Tommy stands up from the couch and I try not to cringe at his use of a nickname I never knew he had for her. There's something so intimate about it, I can't stop myself from picturing them curled up together in bed as he strokes her silky hair, calling her Mon. I shiver at the thought.

Monica makes a noise that might have been his name, but it sounds like the word got caught in her throat.

As much as I try not to see it, I know Tommy looks sick. His normally full face is hollow and he's swimming in his clothes, all too big for his now thin frame.

"It's okay," Tommy says, opening his arms for her to step in.

Monica hesitates for a moment before falling into his embrace. I notice she has to bend a little to rest her head on his shoulder, and I'm relieved to see they don't fit as well together as he and I do.

From the rise and fall of her shoulders, I can tell she's crying. As much as I want to stick around and see if her mascara is running, I decide to give them some privacy. I reach for the sliding door but hesitate. They don't need that much privacy.

I consider sitting just out of sight on the staircase, but I know that would be rude and hard to explain if they caught me. Instead, I head back to the kitchen, trying not to strain to hear too much of what's going on in the living room. It's not like I don't trust Tommy; I do. I trust him with my heart, with my whole life. I just want to know what they're talking about.

I look around for something to occupy my hands and my mind. I could wash the dirty dishes CeCe left in the sink, but the running water would definitely drown out their voices. I could text Becky to see how things are going back at the office, but I know she'll just say everything's fine and not to worry. I wish people would realize that telling someone not to worry just makes them worry more. It's like telling a woman to calm down. Never a good idea.

The sound of Monica's laughter comes wafting in from the other room like a warm summer breeze. I don't sound that pretty when I laugh. *Stop it.* Nothing good will come from comparing myself to her.

More laughter.

Tommy's not *that* funny.

I stand and open the refrigerator. We're running desperately low on everything now that shopping has become my responsibility. Maybe I'll see if CeCe wants to go with me later. If she doesn't, I'll just point out the premade cookie dough that she was so offended I bought the last time I went alone. I clearly can't be trusted.

The cookie dough. That's something I can do. If I pop them in the oven now, they'll be ready before Monica's hour is up, and I can walk in there to offer her fresh, out-of-the-oven cookies. She doesn't have to know they were premade.

Sometimes I surprise myself with how smart I am. I reach for the roll of cookie dough, and for a few minutes, I forget that I'm supposed to be trying to hear what they're saying.

After setting the oven to 350 degrees like the package says, I try to open it. Easier said than done. Both sides are closed with a metal twist-tie thing, but there's no twisting this sucker off. I give up quickly and open the junk drawer, where the scissors are supposed to be. Of course, they aren't there.

Improvising, I grab a small knife and slice down the top of the plastic tube before peeling both sides down. The dough is conveniently cut in perfectly proportioned cookies, but I know homemade cookies never look perfect, so I call an audible and pinch a chunk of cookie dough from the rest of the roll.

Shit, the pan.

I open the oven and sure enough, the cookie sheet is sitting on the top rack. The pot holders are luckily where they're supposed to be, so I grab them and drop the hot cookie sheet on top of the stove.

"Damn it," I curse as it clangs loudly against the stove.

"Everything okay in there, babe?" Tommy calls out.

"Of course, everything's just fine," I answer back. Who knew baking could be so stressful? I have no idea how Jill and CeCe seem to find so much joy in making all this stuff from scratch.

My cooking confidence returns as I spray a thin layer of olive oil to grease the cookie sheet before going back to forming perfectly imperfect cookies. The instructions say to place them about two inches apart, but these are half the size of the ones they precut, so I figure an inch will do.

Once they are all on the cookie sheet, I pop them in the oven and set the timer on my phone for thirteen minutes. I throw the wrapper in the trash can so there's no premade evidence and check the timer. I sigh, seeing less than thirty seconds have passed. Being patient has never been one of my strengths.

I glance back at the table, but I've got too much nervous energy to sit. I open the refrigerator again, this time checking out our beverage situation. Cookies go best with milk, but all we have is almond. We also have soda, and of course the latest batch of fancy Arnold Palmers that CeCe made, but I'm not sure how well basil and lemon go with chocolate chip cookies.

I know I'm acting crazy, but I can't help it. I could bring them drinks now, before the cookies. That would be a nice and normal thing to do.

I open the kitchen cabinet where we keep the fancy glasses

we never use and take two down. I consider reaching for a third, but that would be presumptuous. I fill the glasses with a few ice cubes each then pour the Arnold Palmers. I consider adding a leaf of basil, but that might make it taste too strong. Plus, garnish probably crosses that "trying too hard" line.

My cell phone rings, and I look down to see Jill's smiling face on the screen. I'll call her back later. It's not like I can talk about how it's going while Monica's still here—my voice is too loud, and sound carries in this old house.

I silence my phone, then apply another quick layer of lip gloss, and I'm ready to play the role of domestic semigoddess. Monica's not the only one who can put on a performance.

With a glass in each hand, I walk down the hallway toward the living room.

I'm halfway there when I notice the handle of the front door turning.

Oh, shit.

Chapter Twenty-Seven

CeCe

Forgot my towel," I say as I push through the front door.

Mom is standing there with two glasses of my new and improved Arnold Palmer recipe. I'm trying to be happy she likes it instead of being annoyed that I have to keep making so many batches.

"What?"

The expression on Mom's face is weird, even for her. She doesn't say anything, but her eyes keep darting to the living room. My heart drops. *Dad?*

My eyes follow hers and—*what the hell?* I blink a few times, but I still see the same thing. My dad. Sitting and talking to Monica freaking Whistler.

I smile a stupidly big smile and wave hello before pushing Mom back toward the kitchen. I have been walking the beach for weeks trying to run into someone from the show and I come home to find one of the biggest stars in my house?

"What is Monica Whistler doing in the living room? Oh my god—did you get me an audition?"

"Ceese," Dad says.

I look at Mom, waiting for her to say something, but her mouth is hanging open as if she's a cartoon character.

"Mom?"

"It's a long story," she finally says.

"Cecelia?"

Dad never uses my full name except when he's singing our song. I look down at my outfit—clothes perfect for a morning working at the café and then going to the beach, not so perfect for meeting an actress who could potentially be the key to my big break.

I consider running up to change, but it would be too obvious since she's already seen me. I run my fingers through my hair and take a deep breath, steadying myself the way I do before stepping onstage.

Mom follows behind me like some weird stagehand. She's still holding those two fancy glasses—trying too hard like she always does.

"Hi, Daddy," I say, standing casually in the doorway, acting as though nothing is out of the ordinary.

"Monica, this is my daughter, Cecelia."

"Everyone calls me CeCe," I say, attempting to act like I'm confident, and not like I'm freaking out, which I totally am. I take a few steps closer and extend my hand to shake hers, nice and firm the way Dad taught me.

"Hi, CeCe. I'm—"

"Monica Whistler," I finish her sentence. "Everyone with a TV knows who you are." She blushes and brushes her perfect hair behind her ear. I don't know how it's possible, but she's even more beautiful in person. "But I don't know what you're doing in my house."

She and Dad look at each other in the annoying way grown-ups do, like they're daring each other to be the one to speak first.

"Are we related?" I gasp. "Is she, like, your long-lost sister or something?"

"Or something." Monica laughs and it sounds like flowers and birds and rainbows all rolled into one.

Dad looks over my shoulder at Mom. I almost forgot she's still here. He looks back at me, but I can't read the look on his face.

"Someone tell me."

"Go ahead," Mom says. Her voice sounds small and strange.

"Dad?" I look to him for the answer.

"Monica and I used to be married," he says as casually as he would say we're going out to dinner.

"Shut. Up." I can't decide if I'm excited or horrified at this news. "You were married? Before Mom?" I look back at Mom, who is still standing there, holding those two stupid glasses.

"It was a long time ago," Dad says.

For once in my life, I'm literally speechless.

"She looks like you," Monica says, as if she could change the subject that easily. And she's not even right. No one has ever said I look like my dad. Even strangers have commented before about how much Mom and I look alike.

"Why didn't you tell me?" I ask.

"It didn't seem relevant," Dad says, even though I can't imagine a scenario where it wouldn't be. "I can't tell you how to feel, but—"

"Don't try to shrink me."

Behind me, Mom laughs. I turn and give her the meanest look I can muster.

"Sorry," she says.

I look back and forth between both of my parents. "You lied," I accuse Dad before turning back to Mom. "You were never going to call about an audition, were you?"

"Don't blame your dad," Monica says.

"It's okay, Mon."

"No, let me," Monica Whistler says. "I wasn't very good to your dad. I left him, and this town, because I was selfish and thought my dreams were the only thing that mattered. They weren't. And I regret how I acted. I'm sorry." She says the last part to Dad, and they're both looking at each other as if they're the only ones in the room.

"Hello?" I say. Clearly, they both forgot we're talking about me here.

"Cecelia," Dad says again. I can tell his patience is wearing thin and he's starting to look tired. He's always tired. "I'm sorry if your feelings are hurt, but some things are private."

"But you're my dad."

"I'm also my own person."

I stop and roll that thought around in my head. He's got a point—but so do I. "*And* you're my dad."

"Your dad tells me you want to be an actress?" Monica says. Someone really has to teach her there's a right and a wrong way to change the subject.

"Mon." Dad shakes his head. This is so weird.

"I'm just saying, we're casting for a girl who's just in town for the weekend. It's a bit part, but I can pull a few strings."

"Shut up!" I say.

"Cecelia," Dad says sternly.

"I mean, that would be the most amazing thing ever!"

"I'll give your dad a call later to confirm details," she says.

Behind me, I hear the front door open.

"You coming?" Beau asks, probably wondering why it's taking so long to get a stupid towel.

"Now's not a good time, Beau," Mom says, like it's him she's mad at.

Beau looks at me, clearly confused. And then he looks in the living room and sees what I saw. "Whoa."

"Monica, this is Beau," Dad says.

She tilts her head, almost like she's studying his face. "He looks just like Adam."

"He's Adam and Jill's son."

"Now's not a good time, Beau," Mom says again, like a robot who's only programmed to say one phrase.

Beau shrugs and opens the door but pauses before leaving. "Is something burning?"

"Shit," Mom says. "The cookies."

"Cookies?" This day keeps getting weirder. "Who are you? I don't know either of you!"

I storm up the stairs, wanting to get as far away from them both as I can. Halfway up, I realize I might not get an opportunity like this again, so I quickly retrace my steps and pop my head back into the living room. "It was really nice to meet you," I tell Monica Whistler.

I don't have the courage to glare at my dad when he's looking so sad and sick, but I stop smiling so he knows I'm not happy. I stomp back up the stairs, and for good measure, slam my bedroom door.

"MONICA FREAKING WHISTLER." I open my laptop and start googling.

Monica + Whistler + Destin. Sure enough, she's from here. She graduated from Crestview High. How did I not know that?

I can't believe I never asked Dad if we were related—I always assumed we didn't have any relatives since he and Mom are both only children. And my parents aren't married to each other, so why in the world would I ever think to ask if they'd married anyone else? I wonder if Mom has a secret husband hidden somewhere that I don't know about . . .

Focus, Cecelia.

I change my search: *Monica + Whistler + Tommy.* Nothing. I change Tommy to Thomas and add the word "wedding," and sure enough, there's a link to an article from the *Northwest Florida Daily News.*

The headline reads: CELEBRATIONS: VESELOVSKY AND WHISTLER TO WED.

No wonder she kept my dad's name. I scroll down more and see a picture of them, standing in a prom pose on the beach. Dad still looks like Dad, just a younger, nonsick version with a head almost full of chestnut-brown hair. Monica looks younger, but not really prettier. Her boobs are smaller and her hair isn't as perfect. She looks pretty, just not as drop-dead gorgeous as she is now.

I keep scrolling and read the article:

Boris and Irene Veselovsky of Crestview proudly announce the engagement of their daughter, Monica, to Thomas Whistler, son of Dorothy and the late Richard Whistler of Destin.

The two got engaged in October and are planning a June wedding.

Thomas is a graduate of the University of Georgia and runs a thriving therapy practice in Destin, where the couple live. Monica is an aspiring model who has been featured in the pages of *Coastal Living* magazine and the Everything But Water swimsuit catalog.

They're telling the truth. Not that my parents would lie about having lied to me all these years.

My phone buzzes with a text. Probably from Beau, wondering what the hell he just walked into. I don't know how to even begin explaining what I don't understand myself. And even if I did, he isn't the one I'd want to talk to.

I wish I were talking to Sofia, but ever since she started posting pictures of her and stupid Liam hanging all over each other, there's no way. She knows that I know, and she didn't even say anything to me. *Whatever.*

Maybe I should send this link to TMZ. I can see the headline—PRESURGERY TV STAR! A SECRET WEDDING FROM HER PAST!

Sofia would see it, and she'd come crawling to find out more. Not that I would tell her anything. It would be pretty amazing, but Dad would be furious.

I can't believe I didn't think to ask Monica for a selfie. Now no one will ever know I'm the girl whose dad was married to Monica Whistler. They'll keep thinking of me the way they do now. The girl whose dad is dying.

Chapter Twenty-Eight

Alexis

What do you think?" Tommy asks as he snaps a piece of a palm tree into place. The puzzle is really coming along, probably since we've been sitting around the house a little more than normal. After the failed mini-golf excursion, we've been trying to limit the extraneous activities.

"Sorry?"

"Do you think I should use Alexis or Lexie?" he asks.

For the life of me, I have no idea what he's talking about. My mind has been scattered since the run-in between CeCe and Monica last week. I keep replaying the look on her face, the fact that I just stood there, saying nothing.

CeCe's acting like she's not sure what to make of it all. On one hand, she's ecstatic that her dream is finally coming true. She's been practicing her character techniques, whatever that means, nonstop. But on the other hand, she's furious. More so with me than with Tommy. Logically it doesn't make sense since I wasn't even around in those early days, but I get that it's easier to be mad at me.

She went from giving us both the silent treatment to peppering Tommy nonstop with questions about Monica and their life together. She wanted to know everything from the way he proposed to how Monica took her coffee in the morning. I didn't think it was possible to hate that woman any more than I did, but every new detail gave me a new reason to loathe her. Luckily Tommy tired of it, too, eventually telling CeCe that if she had any more questions, she could ask Google.

"Where were you?" Tommy asks. He can always tell when I'm not fully there.

"Sorry," I say again. "What are you talking about?"

"My tattoo," he says. "Think I should get Alexis or Lexie?"

I narrow my eyes at him, but he keeps going.

"I'm thinking it would look good right across my bicep." He tries to make a muscle with his arms, which were never really that muscular to begin with, but that have never been this thin. "You'll get Tommy, of course."

"Babe." I put my hand tenderly on his shoulder. "I love you, but you've lost your mind."

"You can't blame a guy for trying." Tommy gives me the smile that used to make my heart swell, but now it's tinged with sadness. His face is so thin that his cheeks look sunken and the dimples I've loved my whole life have all but disappeared. "How about a day trip over to Seaside instead?"

I nod, trying to look interested. There's nothing wrong with any of the things we're doing, it just seems false. Like we're in a rush to create all these memories, which, of course, we are.

And I don't need any more reminders that the time we have left is dwindling.

"What day is it, again?" he asks.

Every day down here feels like a Saturday, so I have to glance at my phone to check. "Wednesday."

"Then maybe we'll go tomorrow, so we can avoid the weekend crowd. We can have lunch at one of the food trucks, see the post office and walk through the Modica Market. Ceese will love to see where they filmed *The Truman Show*."

"Mmm hmm," I agree.

"And tonight we're going to watch *Rocky III*," he says, flipping through the little notebook he still hasn't let me see. "Making good progress."

Progress, yes. But I wouldn't call it good. Because the closer we get to the end of Tommy's Kick the Bucket list, the closer to the end it will be.

I try to give him a smile, but my heart just isn't in it. I don't want to bring his mood down, and I have a feeling my blues aren't going anywhere anytime soon. My chest tightens and I can feel my heart drumming faster as the panic rises. It feels like the walls are closing in on me. I have to get out of here. Fast.

"I've got to run an errand," I say, getting up more quickly than necessary.

Tommy gives me a questioning look that softens as soon as he sees my face. He has always been able to see right through me.

I give him a quick kiss before heading out. "I'll be back soon."

Outside, I close the door behind me and lean back against it. I close my eyes and wait for my breathing and my heart rate to slow down.

I breathe in slowly and out even slower, the way Tommy

taught me back when I had my first panic attack when I was pregnant with CeCe, but it doesn't help. A bag, I need a bag. I walk as quickly as I can, my hand over my chest as if it can help calm my heart. I pop the trunk of the car and grab the first bag I see, then bring it up to my mouth, breathing slowly in and out. In and out.

Leaning against the car for support, I drop my head down and continue breathing into what I now see is ironically a Dox Pharmacy bag. In and out, in and out. I drop the bag as my heart rate slows back to normal. I exhale one last time, looking back toward the house. Luckily there's no sign of Tommy or CeCe; neither of them needs an extra thing to worry about, and I'm fine. I'm fine.

But I'd be a lot more fine with an iced vanilla latte and a hug from Jill.

It's too hot to walk, so I drive the short distance to The Broken Crown. As I pass Jill's house, the home she used to share with Adam, I wonder if there was ever a time when a hug from me helped her feel better.

Things were complicated when she and Adam finally split. I didn't say I told you so, but I'm sure she knew what I was thinking. The first time I'd said something to her about his infidelity was back when she was hugely pregnant with Abigail, and Adam got wasted and tried to grope me on the dance floor.

I thought I was being a good friend when I told her the truth, but she wasn't ready to hear it. In hindsight, I know that wasn't the right time; it wasn't what she needed to hear when she was less than a month away from starting a family with the man.

Jill stopped talking to me after that—she blamed me for

sticking my nose in their business, and I blamed Tommy for not stopping me from telling her in the first place. I was a mess, wishing I'd never come back to Destin.

The next morning, my bags were packed and I was more than ready to get back to work when Tommy came knocking on my door. I refused to answer, but he came around to the back door and caught me so off guard I accidentally let him in.

I remember as clearly as if it were yesterday, sitting at the kitchen table with my arms crossed as he talked me into listening to him. He made me see what I'd been too stubborn to realize: that I had a pattern of running away when things got tough. I'd done it when I was a kid, I was doing it then, and as much as I hate to admit it, it's what I'm doing now.

Things got tough this morning, and I ran out of the house as fast as I could. I hate that he's still so right about me. Maybe I'll get the latte to go and bring a treat back for him. Something with a lot of calories to add a little meat back to his bones.

The parking lot is crowded, but I luck into a spot just as someone is backing out. I take it as a sign that this day is starting to turn around, that leaving was exactly what I was meant to do. Sometimes, you just need to step away to get a new perspective, and a box of Jill's cheese Danish. *Or is it Danishes?*

Taking the porch steps one by one, I wonder if the salty-sweet treats are really Tommy's favorites, or if he always picks them because he knows they're mine. Maybe I'll get an assorted box and have him do a taste test. Too bad today is CeCe's day off; it would be even better if we were sampling things she helped make.

What started as a tactic to get CeCe out of the house has

turned into a part-time job helping Lou in the kitchen four days a week—every day but Wednesday. CeCe has been really enjoying it, and it's been nice not having to worry about her running into Monica or getting into trouble with Beau, at least for a few hours of the day.

The door to the café opens, and a gaggle of giggling girls come rushing out. They're so busy looking at whatever is on their phones, squealing about who knows what, that one of them literally bumps into me.

The girl smiles in lieu of an apology and I decide not to care. I don't want anything to bring me or this day back down. Good things only, that's what I'm going to surround myself with, so I can bring positivity and good vibes back into the house. Along with the Danish, of course.

My eyes find Jill right away, sitting at a table in the corner, talking to a customer. The easy smile that almost always greets me falters, and I glance behind me to see what she could possibly be staring at.

And then, as if it's all happening in slow motion, the customer sharing Jill's table turns toward me. Her jet-black hair cascades like a waterfall, her olive skin looks dewy and soft, and the smile on her face is sickeningly sweet. I stop in my tracks, too shocked to say or do anything but stand there like an idiot.

Jill is supposed to hate Monica even more than I do, so what in the world is she doing sitting and smiling and drinking coffee with the devil herself? The legs of the chair screech as Jill pushes back from the table. The offensive noise is so loud I consider bringing my hands up to my ears to block it out. I wish I could cover my eyes, too. Forget the picture I'm afraid I won't be able to erase from my mind.

"Lex," Jill says, standing with one arm on the back of the chair as if she isn't sure whether she should stay or go.

That's one decision I can easily make for her.

I spread my fakest fake smile across my face and somehow manage to say, "Be right back, forgot something in the car," before turning to leave.

I wait until the door closes behind me to make a mad dash for my car, where I can appropriately melt down behind locked doors. It's even worse than my worst fears. I knew that CeCe would easily fall for Monica's charm, but Jill? She's supposed to be mine.

The café door opens and Jill steps out, tentatively looking for me. Not wanting to be found, I turn on the car and get the hell out of there. Where I'm going, I have no idea. If it weren't for Tommy, I might just get back on the highway and head straight for Atlanta. I could be at the office by seven tonight, worrying about problems I can actually solve.

My phone buzzes with a text. I'm not ready to hear Jill's excuses or apologies so I almost don't check. But curiosity gets the best of me, and I look down to see a message from CeCe, breaking the silent treatment long enough to ask me to pick up some popcorn—the raw kernels, not the microwave kind—and fresh butter, not margarine, so she can make snacks for the movie tonight. We've been making good progress; there are only a few more films on the list Tommy wants to see one last time.

I sigh and make a U-turn, wondering why I bother when literally everything is a reminder of the things I'm trying to forget.

Chapter Twenty-Nine

CeCe

@WhistlerGurl: I'm going for a walk on the beach
@BeauBo: k

I stare at the screen, waiting for him to ask if he can join me like he usually does. He's acting like such a girl, like his feelings are hurt that I didn't text him back after the whole thing with Monica. I'm sorry, but I had more important things on my mind, like trying to unravel the lies my parents have been telling me my whole entire life.

@WhistlerGurl: Don't make me ask
@BeauBo: Wut?
@WhistlerGurl: Do you want to go with me
@BeauBo: Only if u want me 2
@WhistlerGurl: Shut up
@BeauBo: Meet u @ my house?
@WhistlerGurl: ok

I close my laptop and consider grabbing a towel, but I'm in the mood for walking, not sitting. All we do down here is sit—in the sun, on the porch, in the living room. Sit, sit, sit, sit. I am sick of sitting.

From the top of the steps, I can't tell if the door to the living room is open or closed, but I take the steps down quietly just in case Dad is talking with one of his nutcases. The doors are open, but Dad is asleep on the couch, so it's a good thing I was quiet.

He's been doing that a lot lately, taking naps in the afternoon like a toddler. It's like he's aging in reverse, on his way back to zero. I don't want to think about zero.

Outside, Mom is sitting on the front porch with a book in her lap, but she's staring out in the distance, not at the pages.

"I'm going for a walk on the beach with Beau."

The blank expression on her face doesn't change—not even at the mention of Beau's name like she's been doing lately. I asked Dad about it when we were working on the puzzle last week, what her problem is with Beau. He just gave me a nonanswer about the past sometimes finding a way into the present, and something about displacement, where people take their issues out on the wrong people.

"Have fun," Mom says, suddenly breaking out into a fake smile as if she just realized I was there. If I weren't still so mad, I might feel a little bad for her. But fourteen years of lies can't just be forgiven.

"I THOUGHT I was meeting you at your house?" I ask Beau as he reaches the intersection where our two streets meet.

"You were walking too slow."

I shrug and keep walking past him. He waits for a minute as if he expects me to stop and wait for him, which I don't.

"So what's new?" he asks, catching up. "Any more skeletons come out of the closet?"

I stop just long enough to give him a dirty look. "You wouldn't think it was so funny if it was your parents who had lied to you."

Beau shrugs and I move past him, down the old wooden stairs that lead to the beach. At the bottom, I step out of my flip-flops so I can feel the sand between my toes.

"It wasn't really a lie," Beau says as he steps out of his own shoes.

"What do you mean, it wasn't a lie?"

"Did you ever ask them if they were married before?"

"I, well . . ." I can feel my face getting red. Beau is supposed to be my friend, he should be on my side. "I shouldn't have had to."

Beau shrugs and starts walking toward Henderson State Park. This time, I'm the one who has to catch up to him. "You would understand if your parents had lied to you."

"You really want to go there?" Beau asks and I quickly back down, remembering all the spilled secrets and broken promises he had to deal with when the truth about his dad's affair came out.

"It's different," I say, still trying to defend the severity of my current situation.

Beau's laugh is short and sarcastic. "You're telling me. It would have been much easier if my dad had told me about an ex-wife instead of a future one."

"Do you ever see him?" I ask, figuring it is okay to talk

about since he was the one who brought his dad up in the first place.

"My father?" Beau makes it sound like a dirty word. "He's dead to me." I stop in my tracks, not sure how he could even joke about something like that in front of me. "Sorry," he says. "That was stupid, but I don't want anything to do with him. When he walked out on my mom, he walked out on us, too."

"But you still talk to him and stuff?"

Beau shakes his head. "He called and texted for a while, but he eventually stopped when he realized I wasn't going to answer."

"When was the last time you heard from him?"

Beau shrugs. He's trying to play it cool, but I can tell he's hurting, too. "A few months ago? Maybe Christmas?"

"Whoa." I start walking again but can't stop thinking about his dad. How he's still here, but not there. How unfair it is, that this is happening to my dad, and not his.

We stop talking as we pass the restaurant 790, looking at all the happy couples and families eating and drinking, enjoying the view as if all is right with the world.

"When I get married, I'm going to do everything differently," Beau says. "I won't cheat, I won't leave. I'll be there for my kids."

"I'm never getting married," I tell him.

"Why not?"

I shrug. "My parents never got married; my mom says it's old-fashioned."

"Some old-fashioned things are good."

"Why do you want to get married so bad?" It's weird for a guy to think about this kind of stuff.

"It's what you're supposed to do. Isn't that the point of everything? To find that one person you belong to."

"I don't want to belong to anyone," I say. "I'm going to be a famous actress and run a food blog in my spare time, which I probably won't have a lot of."

"You're going to be famous?" he asks, mocking me.

I stop and stare, daring him with my eyes to tell me that I can't. "You don't believe me?"

"Oh, I believe you."

"Hey, Beau!" We both look up to see a girl with long blond hair and a tiny bikini waving at him. I never realized a wave could be so overtly sexual before.

Beau smiles and nods in her direction before turning back to me.

"Who's that?" I ask, wondering if she was one of the girls he's always posing with on Instagram.

"Why? You jealous?" he asks, bumping my shoulder with his.

"Of her?" I scoff. "Hardly."

He smiles, clearly thinking he's right when he couldn't be more wrong. "Are you still going out with that Romeo?"

"Liam," I tell him. "And no."

Not wanting to get upset all over again, I leave Beau and walk down toward the edge of the water, watching the waves wash over my feet before rushing back out to the ocean. I should have worn my bathing suit.

"That guy's an idiot if he let you go," Beau says, walking up beside me.

"He never had me," I tell him. "We just made out a few times, it's not a big deal."

"You say that a lot."

"What?"

195

"Big deal."

"Well, some things are, and some things aren't."

"And Romeo's not?"

"Not anymore."

"So you're saying I have a chance?" Beau looks over at me with a mischievous smile and I can't tell if he's joking. I kick water in his direction to splash him in case he isn't.

I shake my head. "That could never happen."

"Why not?" he asks.

"Because you're my godbrother."

"That's not a thing." His tone is suddenly serious. "If you don't think I'm attractive, you can just say so." He strikes a pose, showing off the muscles I've already noticed. There's no denying Beau is cute. "You're blushing, Whistler."

He's never called me by my last name before, but I kind of like it.

"Am not." I kick the water again before turning to walk back up the beach. I sit down on the sand and brush my feet off, even though they'll just get sandy again.

Beau falls down beside me, propping himself up on one arm. His white-blond hair is pointing in all directions and I resist the urge to reach over and smooth it down.

"It's nice having you down here for the whole summer again," he says.

I don't agree with him, but I don't disagree, either. I just sit there, listening to the soundtrack of the beach: waves making contact with the shore, seagulls squawking, children laughing. With the sun shining down on us, I know that most people would call this a perfect day.

It's definitely perfect for the cute little girl walking past us with her dad. Her blond hair is tied in uneven pigtails that her dad probably did. I can relate to that.

I watch as the girl grabs her dad's hand, dragging him toward the water for an adventure she doesn't realize is a big deal. Because she probably thinks her life will be full of adventures with her dad. Why wouldn't she? Life hasn't proved her wrong yet.

"Do you want to know the real reason I know I won't get married?" I ask Beau once the father and his daughter are out of sight.

"Why?"

"Because." I say the word slowly, building up the guts to tell him what I've only admitted to myself. "My dad won't be there to walk me down the aisle."

Beau looks at me as though he's considering his next words carefully. "Heavy," he finally says.

"Tell me about it." If only he could see how dark my thoughts are, if he could know the things I'm embarrassed to even be thinking. Selfish things that probably make me the worst daughter in the history of daughters.

"I know it's stupid and selfish, but him being sick, it's ruining my life."

"It's okay to be mad about it," Beau says. His voice is different now than it was before. He's not joking or flirting.

"I am mad. I'm mad at him for being sick, and that he's not even trying to get better. I'm mad that he won't be there to take pictures before I go to prom, that he won't be there to see me graduate from high school or take me to college."

The tears that have been building up for the past month finally break free and I couldn't stop them if I tried. "I'm mad that he won't be there to give me advice, I'm mad that he can't give me any advice now on how to deal with this. I'm even mad that he won't be here to teach me how to drive. How selfish is that? And I'm really mad at myself for making this about me. I know it's not about me."

"I'll teach you how to drive," Beau says, which gets me laughing even though I don't want to be laughing.

"You can't drive yet, either."

"Not now," he says. "But I'll be sixteen before you, so by the time you're ready, I'll know how."

"Thanks, but it's not the same." I wipe my tears away, but new ones keep falling. This is so embarrassing. I take my glasses off and wipe them on the hem of my shirt. "I hate crying."

Beau pushes himself up so he's sitting on his knees, right in front of me. "Your eyes are pretty when you cry."

I blush and look down at my glasses, folded in my hands.

"It's true," he insists. "Most girls have ugly crying faces. But yours . . ."

I lift my head and my eyes meet his. I want to look away, but I don't. He doesn't, either. And then Beau, my god-brother, leans forward and kisses me.

His lips are softer than Liam's, his kiss gentler. Sweeter. I don't want to like it, but I do. And we're not really related, our moms are just best friends. There's nothing wrong with that.

Beau pulls away and looks at me; there's a little disbelief on his face and a whole lot of happiness. Life is too short to overthink things, so I lean forward and kiss him back. I open my mouth a little and Beau follows my lead.

"Wow," he says, when we stop to take a breath.

"Yeah, wow."

He runs a finger gently down my jaw, making me shiver. "I've been wanting to do that for the last two years."

"Gross, I was twelve." I shove him on the shoulder.

He catches my hand and laces our fingers together. It feels nice; his hands are bigger and stronger than mine. "So what? I was thirteen."

"Pedophile."

He silences me with another kiss, and I can't help but think that this feels right. I was so self-conscious when I was kissing Liam, trying to impress him. But Beau's impressed no matter what I do. I relax, enjoying the way my skin tingles when it touches his, the way his heart thumps beneath my palm when I place it on his chest. He stops before I want him to and leans back, taking his phone out of his pocket.

"What are you doing?" I ask.

"What does it look like?"

He holds his phone up in front of his face, and I can tell he's taking a picture of me.

"My eyes are all red and puffy," I say through a forced picture smile.

"It's okay, I won't show this to anyone."

"Then why take it?"

A blush creeps up the back of his neck and he gives me a small smile. "So I'll never forget how you look right now."

"Can I see?" I reach for his phone, but he shakes his head and puts it back in his pocket.

"It's just for me."

I shake my head and look up at him. He's a little blurry so I put my glasses back on. He still looks like the same Beau I've known my entire life. I wonder if I look any different to him. "You know we can't tell anyone about this, right?"

199

He looks disappointed. "Why not?"

"So many reasons," I say. "First of all—if they know, they'll never let us be alone together."

"Good point," Beau agrees. "It can be our secret."

"Shake on it?" I stick my hand out.

"I'd rather kiss on it," he says, leaning toward me again. I push him away, but my eyes keep drifting down to his lips and I change my mind. I have a feeling those lips are going to get me in a lot of trouble.

"We should get going," I tell him after we've been kissing for a while. I don't really want to stop, but the image of my mom staring out at nothing comes creeping back in my mind. If something's wrong, I should find out sooner rather than later.

Beau stands up and gives me his hand. I take it and let him help me up, but when he tries to keep holding it as we start the long walk back, I pull away. It's strange to feel uncomfortable around someone you've always been so comfortable with. The dynamic between us has totally changed. In a good way, I think. But still.

"This is kind of weird."

"Good weird?" he asks.

I nod. "But I still don't want to hold your hand."

"Fair enough." He smiles and sticks his hands in his pockets.

We stop at the bottom of the stairs so I can put my shoes back on, and so he can kiss me one more time. "It's going to be hard not doing that every time I see you."

I blush, wishing that I'd never kissed Liam so Beau could have been my first. Oh well. I sigh, remembering the old rhyme we used to sing as kids. *First is the worst, second is the best.*

Chapter Thirty
Alexis

Cecelia," I call upstairs. "We're leaving!"

"Coming," she yells back down.

She smiles at me as she comes down the stairs, looking cute in a pale blue sundress that makes her tan skin glow. Her hair is down. It looks like she straightened it and did a little braid with a red ribbon woven through it down one side.

"You're dressed awfully nice for a barbecue," I say.

"It's the Fourth of July—and it's just a dress." There's a defensive edge to her voice, and I'm about to explain that I meant it as a compliment when she tosses a zinger toward me. "It wouldn't hurt you to put a little more effort in."

I don't have to look in the mirror to know she isn't wrong. Dark circles have taken up permanent residence under my eyes, my hair is in its natural half-wavy state, and I haven't put an ounce of makeup on other than the day Monica was here and ruined everything.

"You're right," I say.

CeCe looks confused. "I'm what?"

"You're right. Go keep your dad company in the car, I'm going to freshen up."

"He's in the car? We're just going around the corner."

"We're driving tonight," I say, hoping she lets it go. I don't want to explain how even that short distance is too far a walk for her dad. Just making it up the stairs has become such a struggle that we talked last night about setting up a bed down in the living room. But I don't want to bring that up and risk ruining what has the potential to be a lovely night.

"Whatever," she says with a shrug, heading toward the door.

"Tell him I'll just be a few minutes."

She gives a half salute in response, and I rush upstairs. I plug in my hair straightener for the second time all summer and let it heat up while I find something better to wear.

I grab the first thing I see that will work, a long, dark blue sundress with white and beige flowers. It has two out of the three patriotic colors and a flattering cut. I slip my feet into a pair of tan sandals and go back to the bathroom.

The horn honks, but I ignore it, digging through my makeup drawer for an eye shadow palette Becky gave me. I pick a pale shade of gray and sweep it over my eyes, then add a quick stroke of blush, thankful my skin is tan enough that I don't need foundation. A swipe of mascara and another of lip gloss and I'm almost ready.

I run the straightener quickly through my hair—not the way it's supposed to be done, according to CeCe. She saw me once and cringed, taking the straightener from my hands and showing me the "right" way to do it, slowly, in small chunks.

The horn honks again and I yell, "I'm coming!" even

though I know they can't hear me. I look in the mirror and shrug; it's as good as it's going to get tonight.

"Wow," Tommy says as I open the driver's door.

In the backseat, CeCe rolls her eyes.

"I feel underdressed," Tommy says, looking down at his light blue button-down shirt and the khaki shorts that used to be a little tight on him. Now they hang on his shrinking frame.

"Not at all." I pat his hand reassuringly. "CeCe just reminded me that I should put a little more effort in."

"I think your beauty is effortless," he says.

"You have to say that," CeCe pipes in.

"Seatbelt on," I say, ignoring her jab.

"We're going, like, ten feet. I could probably beat you there if I walked."

"Be my guest." I wait to back up, but she stays put and reluctantly fastens her seatbelt. She's right that we're practically crawling distance from Jill's house, but sometimes it feels good to assert my parental power.

"Seatbelt," she parrots and I fasten mine as well, deciding this one is pretty much a draw.

THE DRIVE OVER to Jill's house is shorter than the chorus of a song on the radio. CeCe is out the door before the next verse starts and I shake my head, watching her run through the picket fence and inside without knocking.

"She's your daughter," I tell Tommy.

"She's a mini version of you." He hands me the bottle of

rosé he was smart enough to grab from the fridge and slings the portable oxygen concentrator over his shoulder. "It's no wonder you drive each other crazy."

I furrow my brow. "I liked it better when you said it was just a stage."

Tommy turns to let himself out of the car and I try to ignore the fact that even his smallest movements look like they take a great amount of effort. This is all happening too fast.

"And just so you know, I was an angel compared to her," I say, walking around to join him.

"Don't forget I knew you when you were just about her age."

"Hey, you're supposed to be on my side."

"Always," he says, taking my hand in his.

I open the door and we let ourselves in. The house smells even more amazing than usual.

"Hello?" I call out, but there's no reply.

"They're probably out back," Tommy says.

We walk through the kitchen, where the oven is on and the island is filled with a medley of salads and various delicacies. Jill outdid herself like she always does.

The back door opens and Jill and Lou walk in. "You're just in time, we're about to fire up the grill."

I hold up the bottle of wine. "We brought this."

"Thank you," Jill says. "And about the other day . . ."

"It's fine." I stop her. "It's bad for business if you aren't polite to the customers—even the heart-crushing, devil-incarnate ones, right?"

"Right," she says, relief clear on her face. "I don't know about you, but I could use a drink."

I smile and walk around the island to the drawer where I know she keeps her fancy corkscrew and grab four glasses from the cabinet above the sink. I love that I feel just as comfortable in Jill's house as my own.

I'm pouring the third glass when Abigail walks in, her sketchpad in hand. Her eyes go straight to the wine bottle.

"Don't even think about it," Jill says, following her eyes.

"I didn't say anything," Abigail says, not so innocently. "You look nice, Aunt Lexie."

Jill turns around and looks at me purposefully. "You do, I'm sorry I didn't notice. It's like I don't really see you anymore. No offense."

"None taken. I think?"

We laugh and clink glasses before taking a sip of the crisp wine that tastes like summer.

Outside, CeCe and Beau are sitting around the centerpiece of Jill's backyard, a beautiful table made of reclaimed wood. The sky is just starting to darken, and the lantern lights hanging around the fence make it look like a scene from a home and garden magazine.

Beau gets up from his seat and holds the chair out at the head of the table for Tommy, who gratefully sits down.

"Can I help?" CeCe asks, standing up as well.

"Be my guest," Jill says, handing over the tongs.

One by one, CeCe takes the chicken breasts from the container where they were marinating and lays them on the hot grill. The sizzle is music to my taste buds and my mouth waters in anticipation.

If CeCe learns how to grill, maybe we can become one of those families who barbecues instead of one of those families who relies on getting invited to other people's barbecues.

"These are pretty thick," CeCe says. "About six minutes per side?"

"That sounds right," Jill says. "Want to set your timer?"

CeCe pulls her phone out of her pocket to set the timer. "I'll go wash the tongs off since they touched raw chicken."

"I'll help," Beau says, following CeCe inside.

Jill sits back down and takes a long sip of her wine, clearly happy to have a helper who shares her passion for cooking. "We're going to miss having CeCe at the café once she has to start on the *Seasiders* set."

"That didn't work out," Tommy says. His voice is low and serious, and he gives Jill and me a conversation-ending look. Not that I want to get into it all again, either.

"I'll tell you later," I tell Jill under my breath.

Last night was the first real fight we've had all summer thanks to this mess. I didn't think it was possible to hate Monica any more than I did for what she did to Tommy, but it's even more despicable to break a little girl's heart. She never should have promised CeCe a role in the show before she knew if it was actually possible.

This was exactly why I didn't want CeCe to get her heart set on acting—being a teenager is hard enough without all the rejection and scrutiny of your appearance. Of course, not getting the part had nothing to do with her talent or her looks. Tommy said the daughter of the executive producer's neighbor had already claimed the role. But still.

I made Tommy tell her since it was his fault we were in this mess in the first place. She took it surprisingly well. Tommy thinks it's because she's more mature than I give her credit for, but I think there's something else going on that's captured her interest. Maybe she's realizing she likes cooking even more than acting?

The alarm on CeCe's phone goes off, startling Abigail,

who's had her head buried in her sketchbook since we sat down. CeCe comes back out with the clean tongs; her face looks a little flushed as she steps back in front of the grill.

She lifts the lid and turns each chicken breast over before resetting the timer. I'm impressed by the way she moves with such confidence; she really knows what she's doing.

"Mom, do you want all this stuff outside?" Beau asks through the screen door.

"That would be great. Ab, will you get the plates and silverware?"

"Fine," Abigail says, clearly not happy that she has to stop drawing to help her brother.

"I can get it," Lou says, starting to stand up.

"Absolutely not." Jill puts her hand on Lou's shoulder, gently pushing her back down. "You're off the clock tonight."

Lou looks embarrassed but stays seated.

"Beau?" Jill calls out as if she's suddenly remembering something. "Will you get the potatoes out of the oven and put them in the MacKenzie-Childs bowl? And the pita needs to be warmed up—never mind, I'm coming."

I reach over and take Tommy's hand in mine, startling him a bit. "Everything okay?" I ask, a little nervous to hear the answer.

"Never better," he says. "Except for this whole cancer thing."

I open my mouth to say something about how we talked about taking it easy on the jokes, but I stop myself. I don't want to make Lou any more uncomfortable than she already seems, and I'm trying to understand that if this is the way Tommy needs to deal with his cancer, I have to try to let him.

Abigail is back outside before I can think of something pithy and light to say in response, so I force a smile and take a big sip of my wine.

"Who's hungry?" Jill asks as she sets a black-and-white-checkered bowl filled with roasted potatoes on the table. I reach over to grab one, ignoring her warning that it's too hot.

CeCe's timer sounds again just as the last dish is being set on the table, and I watch as she transfers the grilled chicken to a clean tray that matches the potato bowl, only pausing once to push up her glasses, which have fogged up from the hot air.

"How do I turn it off?" she asks.

"I've got it." Beau is out of his chair before Jill can say anything. In an exaggerated, heroic move, he pushes the giant off button on the grill. CeCe rolls her eyes.

If I didn't know any better, I'd think Beau might have a little crush on my girl. But according to all the photos on his Instagram feed, he prefers girls with beach-blond hair and bodies to match, just like his dad did. Thank goodness CeCe is still hung up on Liam—I have enough things to worry about this summer without adding a junior Adam to the list.

Adam was always girl-crazy, even when we were kids and "dating" meant holding hands and sharing a sno-cone on the beach. The local girls didn't take him seriously, but he had a way of charming the vacation girls. The rest of us made a joke of it, tracking the different girls he was with every week, using it as a way to mark the passing of time.

"We haven't been to the Donut Hole since Krissie!" or "Remember the movie we watched during the Libby weekend? Or was that D.J.?"

It was funny at the time, not so much looking back. I would have no sooner thought Jill and Adam would get together than I would've imagined a world where I'd end up with Tommy.

Tommy.

I look over at him and take a mental picture of this moment. He looks proud as he spears a chicken breast from the plate Jill is holding out for him. He sets the breast on my plate before getting one for himself.

The smile he gives me when he catches me staring makes my heart swell. I know I should be grateful to have experienced the kind of love they write fairy tales about, but I want more. He coughs and slips the oxygen cannula back in place, a reminder that we won't be getting our happily ever after.

Chapter Thirty-One

CeCe

Aunt Jill keeps giving me funny looks. Beau shouldn't have followed me inside when I went in to wash the tongs. I told him to go back out, but he wouldn't listen. He was so cute about staying that when he went to kiss me, I couldn't bring myself to push him away. Even though his mom, his sister, Lou, and both of my parents were just on the other side of the screen door.

Dad keeps raving about how good the chicken is, and it is really good. But I can't take credit for it. Aunt Jill's the one who made the marinade, which I think is olive oil, lemon, thyme, and rosemary. There's probably a little garlic and black pepper in there, too. All I did was grill it.

"I couldn't eat another bite," Dad says, even though it wouldn't hurt him to eat several more bites. If he gained a little weight, maybe he wouldn't look so sick.

"You'll have to give me the recipe," Mom says, and I have

to hold back a laugh. There's no way she could make a dinner like this, even if she had step-by-step instructions.

"Or maybe she can give it to CeCe?" Dad says, cementing his place as my favorite.

"Whose turn is it to do the dishes?" Aunt Jill asks. She looks at Lou. "Don't you even think about it."

"Let me," Mom volunteers. "It's the least I can do."

"That's not necessary," Aunt Jill says. "But if you insist, Beau will help you."

"He will?" Beau says, trying to be funny. Which he is. And also kind of adorable.

"He will," his mom says, pouring the adults another glass of wine.

Mom and Beau both stand up, and my stomach drops. The two of them in there, talking. What if he says something about us? What if she says something embarrassing about me?

"I'll help," I say a little too eagerly.

"I've got it," Mom says. "Both of you, sit down and let me take care of it. Is the dishwasher clean or dirty?"

"Dirty," Aunt Jill says. "We'll supervise and keep you company. C'mon, Lou."

Lou stands up, grateful for the escape. She's barely said more than ten words tonight; it's like she's a totally different person when it's just us at the café. She's actually kind of funny, she's crazy smart, and she knows literally everything there is to know about baking. I bet the kitchen is her comfort zone, kind of like the stage is mine.

"Hey, Beau Bo," Dad says, using the nickname he gave Beau when he was a baby. "Did I see a guitar in the living room?"

"Yeah, I'm just starting to play—but I'm not very good yet."

"Mind if I take it for a spin?"

"Sure." Beau smiles and heads inside to grab his guitar.

Dad folds his hands behind his head and leans back in his chair. Abigail keeps looking at him, then down at her sketchpad. I lean back to try to see what she's drawing, but she pulls the notebook close to her chest. She's so weird that it's hard to imagine she and Beau came from the same two parents.

Beau is back minutes later, and the second he hands over the guitar, Dad's whole face lights up like he's about to get reacquainted with an old friend. It's been too long since he played; we should bring his guitar downstairs and maybe he'll play it more. Who knows, maybe playing music is as therapeutic as listening to it can be.

"Any requests?" Dad asks as he fiddles around with the strings, tuning it up.

"'More Than Words,'" Abigail says. Her taste in music is so ancient; she likes all the stuff that our parents listen to. I bet her favorite Spotify playlist is *Oldies but Still Goodies* or something equally lame.

Dad starts strumming the intro and I can't stop my toes from tapping along with the beat.

"Ceese, will you sing with me?" Dad asks.

I look at Beau, who has a stupid smile on his face. I don't want to sing in front of him, and I'm a little embarrassed that I know the words, but it's impossible to grow up hearing these songs a million times and not pick up the lyrics.

"Please?"

Before I can answer, he starts to sing. *"Saying I love you . . ."* His voice sounds raspier than normal.

I join in at the next line and Dad smiles so big that he loses his place in the song. I keep going and he just plays the guitar.

He comes back in, singing the chorus with me, and I make the mistake of looking over at Beau, who has a strange expression on his face. He's heard me sing before, so I don't know what the big deal is.

We finish the song just as the fireworks start, lighting up the sky with flashes of blue, red, purple, and green. We all stop and stare up at the show in the sky, and I push the thought away that next year, Dad will have the best view of us all.

Mom, Jill, and Lou come back outside just in time to see four of my favorite, white sparkly ones explode one after another. I look over at Dad, who is watching with an expression that looks happy and sad at the same time.

After the last burst of color fades from the dark sky, leaving clouds of gray smoke that start to disappear, Aunt Jill starts passing out small plates for dessert and Dad picks up the guitar again. He starts to play the "Happy Birthday" song even though it's nobody but America's birthday.

"Whose birthday is it?" Abigail asks, confused.

"No one's," Mom says. She looks sad even though she's smiling.

Aunt Jill and Mom start singing along with Dad, first with Aunt Jill's name in the song, then again with Mom's. I look over at Beau, but he looks just as confused as I am. Old people are so weird.

They sing Dad's name next, then start going around to us kids' and then to Lou. When they've made it through all of our names, Dad stops playing. Aunt Jill wipes her eyes and Mom looks like she's getting weepy, too.

"What was that about?" I ask.

"That," Dad says, "was the first song I learned to play on the guitar."

"So?" I ask. He's clearly learned how to play a lot more since.

"So one night when we were kids, around your age, we had a little bonfire at Jack and Jill's house, and that was the only song I knew how to play. So I played it over and over again all night."

"With all of our names," Mom says.

"And then the names of everyone we knew," Aunt Jill adds.

It's weird to think about our parents being our age, hanging out and being friends and playing guitar like they are tonight. Dad keeps strumming little nothings. "Everyone I love, full and happy, singing, laughing and watching fireworks," he says. "This is what I want my funeral to be like."

Funeral? My fingers stop working and my fork falls from my hand, crashing onto the plate and making a noise louder than the fireworks. Everyone turns and stares at me.

All of the sound is suddenly gone. It's like someone pushed the mute button on the world and I can't hear and I can't breathe and I can't think and I have to get out of here.

"Tommy." My mom is whispering, but it sounds like she's screaming. "Now's not the time."

Of course now isn't the time. Never is the time. There never is and there never will be a time. I look over at my dad, who doesn't even look like my dad anymore.

He reaches for me, this hollowed-out shell of the dad he used to be. The only part of him that looks the same is his eyes, except right now, the blue one and the brown one both look scared. And that's something I've never seen before— not even when we lied to Mom and said we weren't going to watch scary movies on Halloween but we did anyway.

The empty feeling is back in the pit of my stomach and I scoot my chair away from his outstretched hand.

"I need to get some air."

"We're already outside," Beau says. I know he's trying to be funny, but I don't need funny right now. I need my dad to be okay.

Dad reaches for his oxygen bag and slips the little tubes back in place, breathing slow and steady. I can't look at him like this, and I don't want to see the concerned looks on everyone else's faces.

"I'm going for a walk."

"CeCe," Mom says.

I turn and give her a look, daring her to try to stop me.

"Let her go," Dad says.

Everyone looks at him and then at me, and now I don't want to go. I don't want to leave him, but I already said I was going, so I run around the side of the house and push through the white picket fence, letting the gate slam closed behind me.

"I'll go with her," I hear Beau say.

But I don't want that, either. I want to be alone—not with him, not with anyone. Standing on the street, I look in both directions. He probably thinks I'll go left toward the beach. Or maybe he thinks I'll head right toward my house. I look up, knowing my time is running out.

Then I see it. The McKeens' house. The For Sale sign is still out front, so I bet no one's there. I run across the street and crouch in a corner of their front porch where it's dark. Just in time, too, because I see Beau standing in front of his house.

He looks to the right and then to the left, just like I had done moments before. He looks straight ahead and I think he might see me. But then he looks toward the left again and starts walking toward the beach.

He's right. That's where I would have gone.

I could still go. I could run after him and let him help me forget. But that would be too easy, and this shouldn't be easy. I have to be brave and strong and feel every feeling. Even when it hurts.

And right now, it really hurts.

Chapter Thirty-Two
Alexis

It used to be I was the one who fell asleep first. But lately, Tommy can barely keep his eyes open by the time we crawl into bed. Tonight, he had to stop and catch his breath three times on his way up the stairs. Between that and all the excitement at dinner, he was asleep before I turned off the lights.

After CeCe and Beau ran off, Lou excused herself, saying she had to get up early for work the next morning. She couldn't get out of there fast enough. Not that I could blame her. I couldn't wait to escape all the sad faces and uncomfortable glances, either.

It's hard enough to hear Tommy making light of everything that's happening, but when he said the word "funeral." It was like I could see her heart shattering in a million pieces, right before my eyes.

Thank goodness Tommy said he'd talk to her in the morning. I wouldn't know where to start, but he's always had a special way with CeCe. Even when she was a baby, he was the one who knew the difference between her cries—when she was hungry or tired or needed to be changed. He was the one who knew how to hold her just right, rocking her to sleep in his arms. Tommy made everything seem effortless. When I tried, she would scream and scream until her face turned red, as if I were a stranger. Which I guess I was.

I blamed myself for going back to work a few weeks before my maternity leave was up. I'd been itching to go back, not because I didn't love being with CeCe, but because I was desperate to feel like me again. And I felt more like myself when I was surrounded by deadlines and creative briefs than dirty diapers and baby talk.

By the time she grew up into an adorable little person with opinions and stories and a personality all her own, I had already become the third wheel of our family. I never stopped trying, though.

I almost always called to say "sweet dreams" back when Tommy still tucked her in at night, and as she got older I made an effort to read the same books and listen to the same music so we'd have something real to talk about, to bond over. It didn't always work, but at least she saw me trying. I hope she noticed that.

It was more than my mother did—and she didn't even have a good excuse. She stopped working when I was born and still didn't have time for me. Of course, she had more than enough time for all the committees she chaired, the charity balls she planned, and her six-year streak as the president of the PTA. The irony isn't lost on me. Neither is the fact that my dad worked even longer hours than I do now, yet he never felt the need to justify his time.

Eventually, I stopped craving my parents' time and attention. I was proud of my independence, the fact that I didn't need anyone else. Except there was someone who needed me.

I can't believe I didn't realize before that I was repeating the same mistakes my parents made with me. I told myself CeCe was fine because she had Tommy—he was better than both of my parents combined. And all of him was better than half of me.

What in the world are we going to do without him?

I look down at Tommy, his chest moving up and down in haggard breaths that make it seem like even sleeping is too strenuous. The glowing numbers of the clock on his night-stand catch my eye as the number changes to 11:11. For the first time since all of this happened, my wish isn't for Tommy. It's for CeCe. That somehow I can find a way to be enough for her.

Tommy makes a noise and I hold my breath. A second later his breathing is back to normal. This new normal, at least. I sigh and lie back down, willing myself to sleep. It's been harder and harder to come by lately. It seems the more Tommy sleeps, the more awake I get. Like my body is aware that the clock on our time together is running out, and I don't want to miss a single minute.

I try to soothe my mind by thinking about the good times. There are so many of them, it's hard to choose just one. Flipping through the memories like pictures in an old photo album, I stop at a mental image of Tommy and CeCe playing together on the beach. She must have been five or six, squealing as Tommy chased her. Running through the shallow waves, she splashed him before running back to the folding chair where I was holding down the fort.

"Come play, Mommy!" I remember her saying.

"In a minute," I told her, reaching for my cell phone instead of her outstretched hand. We were in the middle of a big new business pitch at work—it was a big deal, I told Tommy.

He probably told me that this, playing on the beach with our daughter, was an even bigger deal, but I wouldn't have listened. I was so focused on proving my boss wrong, showing him that Becky and I, a team of two women, could be just as smart, creative, and clever as any of the guys he threw on the brief.

I was so hyperfocused that I don't think I realized I was chasing success at the price of being present for my daughter's childhood. How many of her memories am I absent in, or just out of reach? God, I really was the worst.

It hurts too much to remember, so I try counting sheep instead. Even though I've never met an actual person that technique has worked for. I'm about to give up and go downstairs to find something mindless on TV when I hear the front door open.

CeCe.

I listen to her footsteps as she climbs the stairs, tiptoeing into her room. I hear a soft click as she closes her door. I stare at my own closed bedroom door like it's a bridge I have to cross.

Who knows where my sudden sense of bravery comes from, maybe from Tommy lying beside me, but I slowly sit up and climb out of bed, careful not to shift the mattress.

I hesitate for a brief moment outside her room, the glow of moonlight shining under the door, but a calm confidence comes over me and I lift my hand, knocking softly. She doesn't say not to come in, so I open the door.

She looks up, surprised, as she tucks herself into her double bed. "What?" She sounds more exhausted than annoyed.

Since "I don't know" doesn't seem like the right answer, I say, "Slide over."

She looks at me like I'm crazy, but after a second, she slides over against the wall and I climb in beside her. I look up to the ceiling at the dull stars that used to glow in the dark a million years ago when this was my bedroom.

"Am I in trouble?"

"No, of course not." I shift so I'm sitting up, leaning against the wall. I stare at her mousy-brown hair, splayed across the pale pink pillow. My hands are itching to reach for it, to run my fingers through the way I did when she was a little girl. "Do you want to talk about it?"

"No."

"Do you mind if I talk?"

She shrugs and I take a deep breath. I rest my hand on top of her head, smoothing her hair over and over in a repetitive motion that I hope is as comforting to her as it is to me.

"From the time your dad and I were kids, he's been taking care of me." I can tell that's not what she was expecting me to say, and it wasn't what I expected, either. But I keep talking, letting the words tumble out. "It was just little things when we were young—he stayed back to walk with me once when my bike got a flat tire and he always made sure I got a grape Popsicle since he knew they were my favorite—but when I got older . . . did I ever tell you about the first time I came back down to Destin? As an adult?"

CeCe shakes her head and I try to decide which details I should leave out, since she is my daughter and she's only fourteen. I don't mind her thinking poorly of Adam, but I don't want her to think worse of me than she already does.

"My heart had just been broken by the man I dated before

your dad, and I came down here to get away. I used to do that a lot when things got tough. And I was about to do it again, to leave Destin and go back to Atlanta after I had a big fight with Aunt Jill and Uncle Adam."

She didn't need to know that the fight was over Adam drunkenly kissing me while Jill was weeks away from giving birth to their first child. "But your dad was there, telling me not to leave. I remember he told me that some things in life were worth sticking around for, and that things would be hard wherever I went. So he told me I should stay and work through the tough parts to get to the good ones."

"Did you stay?" CeCe asks.

"Not then," I tell her, disappointed in my younger self. "But I came back eventually. And when we found out we were having you, he left everything and everyone he knew, he moved his practice and followed me up to Atlanta. It was his idea to stay home with you so I could keep working—he knew that I loved it, and he believed I was good enough that I deserved a shot to be one of the best. Everything he's done, every day of his life, has been for you and me. So now . . ." I pause to gather myself and swallow the tears that are forming. "So now I've got to do everything I can to return the favor and be there for him. Even if that means biting my tongue and letting him make those awful jokes about dying."

I feel CeCe inhale deeply next to me. I should have avoided that word, but we can't pretend it isn't happening.

"He knows there's nothing funny about it—I think that's just how he has to deal with it. To try to lighten the mood. I know it's hard, and I'm so sorry you had to hear him talk like that tonight. But just know, he didn't mean to hurt you."

"Why do you care so much about work anyway?" CeCe

asks. She rolls over on her side and tilts her head up to look at me. That's not exactly what I meant for her to take out of the story.

"It's hard to explain," I say, even though I know it's a cop-out.

"Let me guess, I'll understand when I'm older?" She leans her head back against the wall.

"I hope you will," I say. "If you have a job that you love, then it won't feel so much like work, but it's not just that." She looks up at me, waiting for an answer that will make all the missed moments make sense. "What if I told you I didn't believe you could make a soufflé that wouldn't fall?"

"I'd prove you wrong."

"Exactly." I manage to hold back a laugh, but I can't stop a smile. She is my daughter more than she knows.

"So who said you couldn't do something?"

"My old boss, when I was pregnant with you. He pretty much said my career was over. That I couldn't be a good mom and a good employee. I wanted to prove him wrong."

CeCe nods and I hold my breath, hoping that she doesn't say what I already know. That I wasn't a good mom. But I'm trying now, and hopefully that counts for something.

"I know that's not an excuse, and it doesn't make everything okay. But every time I wasn't there for you, I knew your dad was. And I thought that would be enough, that he would be enough."

"He was," CeCe says. "He is."

The silence hangs between us, heavy with the words neither of us wants to say. But I'm the mom, and I've got to start acting like it.

"I promise you I'm going to try harder. Not just try, I'm

going to do better. I know I'm not your dad." A tear slides down my cheek before I can stop it. "But I love you so much it hurts. And if you need to talk, or if you need me to listen, or if you need me to leave you alone or be there by your side, I promise you I'm not going anywhere."

CeCe hiccups back a sob and then launches into my arms, letting the tears go. I don't tell her to stop, I just hold her, letting her cry until she falls asleep in my arms.

Chapter Thirty-Three

CeCe

Table for one?" the hostess at 790 asks.

"For two," I say, trying to sound as grown-up as I can.

Monica and I have been texting for a few weeks, ever since I "accidentally" found her number in Dad's cell phone—but it was her idea to meet for lunch before filming started up again after the Fourth of July break.

I was going to tell Aunt Jill that I wasn't feeling well so I had to leave the café early—but Beau pointed out that she might call and ask my mom if I was feeling better, and then I'd be busted. He has a lot more experience breaking the rules, and he told me that when you're lying, less is more. So I just told Aunt Jill I needed to leave work a little early. She didn't ask why, so I didn't tell her. And if she mentions my leaving early to Mom, I'll just say that I needed some time to be alone. After our heart-to-heart the other night, I know she won't push or question me.

The restaurant I picked is just a few blocks down the beach

from the café, so I got here in plenty of time to change into clothes that aren't covered in flour.

The hostess grabs two menus and walks outside to the patio, which Dad says is the prettiest hidden gem in Destin. It isn't touristy and it's right on the beach with a view of the sand dunes and the water, which is like every shade of blue and green rolled into one. She pauses by a small table right along the edge of the patio, overlooking the beach. "This okay?"

"Perfect." I take the seat facing the door so I'll be able to see the moment Monica arrives.

I glance down at my phone: 12:05. She's late. I guess that's what you're supposed to do when you're kind of famous. It's hard to make an entrance if you're the first one there. I make a mental note to start showing up just a little late to things. Except for class. Maybe I'll get there right as the bell rings so I can have the effect without getting detention.

I'm already learning so much and she isn't even here yet.

"Expecting one more?" the waiter asks. Usually, I'd be a little annoyed at the obvious question. I mean, there are two menus on the table. But today, I don't mind.

"My stepmom," I say as he sets down two glasses of water.

I've been thinking of Monica as my stepmom since I found out about her and Dad, because that's really the best way to describe her. Plus, if she'd been married to my dad after I was born instead of before, that's what she'd be. I shouldn't be punished just because I was born inconveniently late.

Today is the first time I've actually said it out loud, and it's pretty freaking awesome.

"My name is Gary," he says. "Would you like anything besides water while you wait?"

"I'm okay, thank you."

If I were casting the role of the waiter for the first of what I hope will be many lunches together, this guy would totally get the part. He's older than my parents, but you can tell he was a catch in his day, with his tanned, dark skin, and light blue eyes. His hair is gray, but not the bad kind. It makes him look distinguished, not old.

I'm looking at Gary when Monica walks in, but I can sense her arrival. The whole patio goes quiet except for some woman talking loudly about how she'd asked for no tomatoes. It's like people are doing the Wave, but instead of standing and lifting their arms, they turn and stare.

Who can blame them—it's Monica Whistler. Even if they didn't know who she was before *The Seasiders* started filming in Destin, they know now. And anybody can clearly see that she's somebody: it's obvious in the way she walks, the way she holds her head up high, the way her white linen pants and flowery off-the-shoulder top look like they were literally made for her.

"CeCe!" She sounds almost as excited to see me as I am to see her. Now the heads turn and stare at me, wondering who the lucky girl having lunch with a celebrity is. And it's me. I'm the lucky girl.

I stand up the way Dad does when someone he knows comes up to our table. I smooth out my outfit, a black and white sundress that I hoped would look nice but not too fancy.

"You look gorge." Monica leans in to give me a kiss on the cheek.

"Thank you." I can feel my face turning red. "You do, too," I remember to add as I sit back at the table, where I am about to have lunch with Monica freaking Whistler!

227

"You're sweet, but I know I look exhausted," Monica says as she sits down. "I took the red-eye back from L.A. last night, my agent insisted I go to this silly little party."

I try to cross my legs the way I notice she does, but my knee bumps into the table, making it shake and send water splashing out of my glass. I'll have to practice that move at the kitchen table when Mom and Dad aren't around.

"Thanks for inviting me to lunch," I say, after we order our drinks.

"Oh, please. I was tickled you said yes." There I go, blushing again. I'm going to have to figure out a way to stop doing that. I take a sip of water, hoping that will help calm my face down. "I can't tell you how bad I feel about the part not working out—I had no idea they already promised it to someone else."

"It's okay," I tell her.

"It's not," Monica says. "But I'll make it up to you. Your dad says you're really good."

"He has to say that." I look down for just a second, but it's enough for my glasses to fall down my nose. I push them up quickly, hoping Monica didn't notice.

"Tom wouldn't lie. Not to me."

"You and my dad," I say. "I still can't believe he never told me."

Monica leans forward and looks me in the eye. I resist the urge to break her stare and push my glasses up even though they haven't slipped again. "It wasn't his fault; it was all mine. And it's one of the biggest regrets in my life."

Before I can decide whether or not it would be appropriate of me to ask what happened, Gary the waiter comes back with our drinks.

Monica's whole face changes as she lifts her glass of champagne, and I can tell the opportunity is over. "To the beginning of a very long friendship," she says.

I clink my glass against hers and take a sip of my Arnold Palmer.

"I brought you something." Monica reaches into her giant black purse and hands me a hardcover book. The author's name is in bright yellow letters along the top: Stella Adler. And at the bottom in the same bright letters it says: *The Art of Acting*.

"Thank you." I hug the book to my chest before looking down at the cover again.

"Have you ever heard of Stella Adler?" Monica asks.

"She wrote this book," I say, hoping the obvious answer is the right one.

Monica smiles, but not in a way that makes me feel stupid. "She was one of the most important and highly respected acting teachers in the country."

"Did she teach you?"

"Not directly, no. But I took classes at a studio where they teach her method."

"Wow." I open the book to the table of contents and scan the names of the chapters: The World of the Stage Isn't Your World; Acting Is Doing; Instant and Inner Justifications; Learning a Character's Rhythm. "There's so much to learn."

"This is only the beginning, but it's a good start."

"Thank you." I wish there were better words to show just how much I mean it. "This is the best present anyone has ever given me."

Monica smiles and I smile and we're smiling together, and I wish I could freeze this moment, where things feel so good I can almost forget how bad everything really is.

When Gary the waiter comes back to take our lunch orders, Monica asks for the Tropical Chicken Salad with the dressing on the side and I get the same thing because as much as I love their crab cakes, I love saying, "I'll have what she's having," even more.

While we wait for our salads, Monica tells me about all kinds of things—like the fact that she left Florida and moved to New York with just two suitcases to follow her dreams. That winter, she moved out to L.A. when it got too cold for her Florida blood. She said it wasn't easy and it wasn't always pretty, but she did it thanks to her stick-to-itiveness.

"There are some parts I'm still sad about not getting," Monica tells me.

"Which ones?" I ask.

She lifts her chin and looks down at me, as if she's trying to decide whether or not I'm worthy of hearing her deepest, darkest secrets. She smiles and glances around to make sure no one is listening, then she brings her voice down just above a whisper. "Let's just say I would have been starring in a major motion picture opposite George Clooney."

Monica lifts her hand and waves it like a fan in front of her face.

"Wow," I say, trying to think through all the movies George Clooney has been in. Maybe one of the Ocean movies?

"It's not all about talent, you know," Monica says. "A lot of it has to do with hard work, and a little luck from being in the right place at the right time."

"I know all about that," I say. "If I hadn't forgotten my towel at home that day, I never would have known you were my stepmom."

I wish I could stuff the words back in my mouth, but I obviously can't, so I take a giant sip of water instead. I wait for Monica to say something, to correct me. When she doesn't, I look up and see her smiling, her eyes a little misty. Maybe she likes thinking of me as her stepdaughter, too.

Before I can say anything else stupid, our salads arrive. The conversation shifts back to the book, and Monica tells me more about Stella Adler and how her acting method teaches you to make your connection with a character more intense by emotionally recalling moments in your life when you had a feeling similar to the character's. She says you can use your imagination, but it's the connection to something real in your life that can push you from good to great.

While listening to her every word and trying to remember everything she says, I'm also studying everything she does. The way she cuts her lettuce into tiny, bite-size pieces, how she sets her fork down between each bite, dabbing the corner of her lips every so often with a napkin. Mom doesn't look that ladylike when she eats a salad. And even though she orders her dressing on the side, she ends up dumping it all on, which makes it just as bad for you as a cheeseburger.

Monica only eats half of her salad, so I only eat half of mine, even though I'm still hungry. And when Gary asks if she wants a box for the rest, she says no. So I do, too.

After lunch, I say we should do it again sometime, and Monica says, "Absolutely," before giving me another kiss on the cheek. "Next time, maybe you can come down to the set first?"

"Oh my god, really?" I say, trying not to squeal.

"It would be fun."

But she's wrong. Lunch was fun. Going to the set would be epic. The only thing that could make this day any better is if one of the people here who I could totally tell was sneaking a picture of us sent it in to TMZ. That way I wouldn't have to brag for everyone to know that I'm someone important now.

I know that probably won't happen, but a girl can dream.

Chapter Thirty-Four

Alexis

Tommy and I are sitting around the puzzle table when CeCe walks in the house wearing a cute black-and-white sundress. Her cheeks flush when she sees us, and I wonder if she's up to something. Whatever it is can't be that bad since Liam is three hundred miles away and Monica is even farther, according to the Google Alert I got last night that showed her out on the town in Beverly Hills. The show must be on break for the holiday.

"Hey," CeCe says, giving me a bright smile. I glance behind my shoulder to make sure it's me her sunshine is directed toward. Things have gotten a bit better between us since our chat a few nights ago, but this is new.

She sits down at the table and admires the puzzle. Tommy made quite a bit of progress while she was at work this morning. The sky with all its clouds is complete and so are the palm trees on the left side. All that's missing is the right side and the bottom, where the water meets the sand.

CeCe picks up a piece and rubs it between her fingers like it's a lucky charm. "Remember when I used to hide pieces around the house?" she asks.

"I'd find them everywhere." I smile at the memory. "Why'd you do that?"

"So we'd never finish," she says, as if it's the most logical explanation, but I can't fathom why anyone would want to work so hard on a project without finishing it.

She smiles again, clearly reading the confusion on my face. "When we finished the puzzle, summer was over."

"And if we never finished," Tommy says with a smile in return, appreciating her childlike logic, "summer would never end."

"And we'd never have to go home."

I watch the sad smile settle over CeCe's face as she looks at just how close they are to finishing this puzzle. She looks at the piece in her hand and sets it back down on the table.

"You know, I think we have pictures of some of the finished puzzles in here." I open the piano bench and start digging through all the old five-by-seven photographs that have found their way here over the years.

CeCe kneels beside me and we look through memories tracing back to before either of us was born. My eye is drawn to a copy of a photo that used to hang on the wall by the stairs, of Gran and Gramps standing in front of the house the day they bought it. I trace her face with my finger, missing her fiercely.

"Is that Great-Gran?" CeCe asks. "She was beautiful."

I nod and hand her the photo, and one I spot behind it. "Here's one of her holding you when you were little."

"I wish I remembered her," CeCe says, looking longingly at the photo.

"She was crazy about you," I tell her. "I think she must have known that you inherited her acting chops."

A flash of confusion crosses CeCe's face. "She was an actress?"

"I told you that." I can't imagine never mentioning her great-grandmother's acting legacy. "Didn't I?"

"And you said there were no more family secrets," CeCe teases.

"It's not a secret." I turn back toward the piano bench and keep digging until I find what I'm looking for. "Here, look."

I hand CeCe a bundle of theater programs, bound together with a thick rubber band that falls apart when she tries to take it off.

A shiver runs down my spine, and I hope it's a sign that Gran is here, seeing this. CeCe looks back up, her eyes shimmering with tears, and I know that she feels it, too.

"Can I keep these?" she asks, clutching them to her chest.

"Of course," I tell her. "Gran would have loved that."

CeCe smiles and gets up, still holding on to the old programs. "I'm going to go sit outside and look through them—how cool would it be if we were both in the same play?"

"The coolest," I agree.

I close the piano bench and use it for support to stand up. Tommy pats the chair next to him, and I sit back down, looking over the puzzle. I run my hands over the blue sky, feeling the contrast between the smooth pieces and the jagged parts where they fit together.

"You picked a good one this year," I tell Tommy. "It's beautiful."

"Looks like heaven," he says.

Before I can stop it, my smile turns into a frown. "I don't want to talk about heaven."

"What should we talk about instead?" Tommy asks, fitting a piece with the whitecap of a wave into place.

I shrug. "I can't remember what we used to talk about."

"We talked about all sorts of things," Tommy says.

"Name some," I challenge.

"We talked about making more time to come down here," he says.

"Which we finally did."

"We talked about reality TV and what it is about those shows that makes people forget everything their mothers taught them," he says.

I smile. "And why people like us can't get enough of watching them."

"People like you," Tommy corrects me.

"Hush, you watch, too."

"Only so I can spend more time with you, my love." He leans over to kiss me.

"Oh, stop," I say. "But keep going."

Tommy laughs, the sound I once loved. But now it's laced with the rattling in his chest that used to be there only when he coughed. It's creeping into everything.

"This sucks." I lean into his shoulder, and just like that, we're back on the subject I don't want to think about. The thing I can't get away from, no matter how hard I try.

I close my eyes and try to picture Tommy the way he looked six weeks ago, but I can't erase the image of him looking sick, with the oxygen tubes from the cannula going up his nose and tucked behind his ears.

It's getting harder and harder to pretend it's not happening. And even though I'm not ready, it might be time to start talking about it, or at least letting him talk. Like I told CeCe a few nights ago, he's been so strong for me—it's time I start being strong for him.

"So how are you feeling? Really?"

From the look on his face, I can tell the question surprises, and maybe even relieves, him. "I feel okay. I just wish I had more energy, and that I didn't get out of breath so easily. I hate that."

"I hate that, too," I say. "For you, I mean."

"That's probably the worst part, other than the coughing. And the dry mouth, my mouth is always dry."

"Did you tell the doctor about that?"

Tommy shakes his head. "Seems a little like complaining about a paint chip on a totaled car."

I frown. "And how are you feeling, you know, emotionally?" I hope I don't sound as uncertain as I feel. This is his territory, not mine.

"Those feelings aren't so easy to explain," he says.

"Try."

Tommy takes a deep breath, coughing a little as he exhales. "I feel like I don't want to take a single second for granted, I want to make the most of the time I have left."

"Your Kick the Bucket list," I say.

"Exactly." He smiles. "It's like I want to live as many moments as I can, like I'm filling my heart and my mind with all the memories I can get, so I can take them with me." He reaches over and caresses my cheek. I roll my head back, moving with his touch like a cat, begging for more. "I want to remember the way you bite your lip when you're thinking hard about something. The way your face lights up when you get a good idea. The way you sing when you don't think I'm listening."

"I always know you're listening."

He takes my hands in his. "I want to remember how soft your hands are, and how there's always at least one chipped nail." I pull my hands away self-consciously, but Tommy reaches for them again. "I want to remember the way you look right before you fall asleep at night and when you wake up first thing in the morning. I want to remember the taste of your lips." He leans forward to give me a kiss. "And this spot right here." He kisses the curve of my neck and I can't stop myself from laughing. I'm not used to this much attention, even from Tommy.

"CeCe's right outside," I tell him, but I don't pull away and he doesn't stop. "I love you, Tommy Whistler."

"I don't need to try to remember that," he says. "That, I know."

Chapter Thirty-Five

CeCe

"Hold your hands at ten and two o'clock," Dad says.

I bring my hands up to where I think they should be. Someone should really come up with a more modern reference—who even uses clocks with hands anymore?

"A little higher." He guides my right hand up a bit and I bring my left one up so they're even. Now if I could just figure out what to do with my feet.

We went over the different pedals and what they are for earlier, but now that I'm actually sitting in the car, I'm a little scared to touch them. The car's not on yet, but still.

"Put your foot on the brake pedal," Dad says.

The brake, I remember, is the one on the left, so I bring my left foot up and hold the pedal down.

"Your other foot," Dad says. "Always your right foot."

"Always," Mom says from the backseat.

I shoot her a dirty look in the mirror. This was supposed to be one of the things on Dad's list for us to do together, just the two of us. Except he can't really drive anymore, and I obviously can't drive yet, so Mom had to drive us over to the Belk parking lot behind the Commons.

"Okay, now focus," Dad says. "Remember, slow and subtle movements. You don't have to turn the wheel a lot to make it move."

"Got it." I open up my hands to stretch my fingers out before wrapping them around the wheel, holding on tight.

"Foot on the brake?"

I nod.

"Now slowly bring your foot over to the gas and apply a little pressure. Not a lot, just a little."

I move my foot to the right and rest it on the gas pedal.

"A little more than that, but slowly. Remember, everything slowly." I put a little more pressure on the gas. "Now back to the brake," he says.

I move my foot back to the brake and press down.

"Good, you've got it. Ready?"

"I think so," I say, even though this is all happening two years before it's supposed to.

"Keep your foot on the brake," Dad says, and I push down even harder. "Now push the start button."

I reach for the button to the right of the steering wheel, letting my finger hover over it for a second. *I'm about to drive a car!* I push the button and the engine roars to life, the wheel shaking beneath my hands.

From the backseat, I hear Mom gasp. I shoot her a look in the rearview mirror and she shrugs an apology.

"Now push the button on top of the gear shift and move it into *D* for drive."

I push the button and move the lever to the right, then

down two notches. It feels like the controller to one of Beau's games. "It's like a video game."

"It is not a game." Dad sounds mad.

"I know, I was just saying."

"Driving is a privilege and a responsibility. Do you understand that?"

"I understand." I keep my eyes straight ahead, hoping I didn't ruin this moment that I'm supposed to remember fondly for the rest of my life.

"Okay, now ease your foot off the brake. Slowly," he says, back in his normal voice.

Slowly, like Dad said, I lift my foot up. It's not even all the way off the brake when the car starts to move. It freaks me out, so I push back down, a little too hard, apparently, because we all jerk forward along with the car.

"And that's why we always wear our seatbelts." Mom can't pass up the opportunity for one of her stupid teaching moments.

"Lex," Dad says. "Don't make me make you wait outside."

Another reason he's my favorite. I turn around and watch as Mom brings her hand up to her mouth, pretending she's zipping her lips shut.

"Eyes on the road," Dad says, back in his mean voice.

"Sorry," I mumble, turning back around.

"Okay, now let's try that again," Dad says. "Gently off the brake, the car is going to move, but that's okay." This time, I take my foot all the way off the brake. It's not as scary now that I know what's going to happen. "Now, gently on the gas. Just a little tap."

I tap my foot on the gas, but nothing happens.

"Good, a little more pressure."

"Oof!" The car lurches forward as I hit the gas.

"Now ease up," he says.

I lift my foot a little and we slow down. "I'm driving!" I look over at Dad, and even though he's smiling, his eyes look sad.

And then it hits me, harder than the jerk when I hit the brake too hard, why we're doing this in the first place.

"You okay?" Dad asks.

"What? Oh yeah." I shake it off, because the last thing I want is to make him even sadder than he already is.

"Put your blinker on," he says as we approach the end of the parking lot.

"No one else is around," I say.

"Put your blinker on," Dad repeats and I do what he says.

"Now turn the wheel to the left, harder, harder, good." The blinker shuts itself off on its own as I straighten the wheel out. I had no idea it did that.

"Hit the gas a little more," Dad says. "You can see how fast you're going right there." He points to one of the little circles on the dashboard.

"Five?" It didn't feel like I was going that slow.

"You can go a little faster," he says.

I put more pressure on the pedal and watch as the lever goes higher, first to eight, then to twelve before jumping to fifteen.

"Eyes on the road," Dad reminds me. I look back up, seeing the other end of the parking lot getting closer and closer.

"How do I slow down?" I ask, trying not to sound as panicked as I feel.

"Ease your foot off the gas and onto the brake, press down slow but firm."

I follow his instructions and the car slows down smoothly before coming to a stop. "How'd I do?"

"You were great, baby."

Since my foot is on the brake, I figure it's okay to take my eyes off the road for a second, and I quickly look up in the rearview mirror. Mom's eyes are a little misty, but she's smiling. I smile back, because I feel the same way.

"Want to go around the full circle?" Dad asks.

"Can I?"

"You tell me," he says.

"I can do it." I take my foot off the brake and slowly move it over to the gas. I turn the wheel to the left, hoping Dad didn't notice that I forgot to put the blinker on.

At the next end of the big square parking lot, I remember to put my blinker on before turning left. I do the same thing for the other three sides until we're back where we started.

"Think you're ready to drive us home?" he asks.

"No way," Mom says from the backseat.

I don't mind this time since I know Dad was just joking. I'm not ready for the real roads, but when I am, I hope I'll be able to remember everything he taught me.

Chapter Thirty-Six
Alexis

The second week of July, Tommy took a turn for the worse and I couldn't deny that it was too much for me to handle on my own. He would stop breathing for what felt like a minute at a time, gasping for air like a fish out of water. I was afraid to leave his side long enough to go to the bathroom, and CeCe was so scared she wouldn't get closer than our bedroom door.

I probably would have put off calling hospice for another few weeks, but Jill convinced me that having their help would be good for all of us. I thought it would bother me, having strangers in my house. But from the first day they came to set up a bed down in the living room, I knew they weren't strangers. They were angels.

And now, walking into Dox Pharmacy armed with a shopping list from Dolly, one of the hospice nurses, I'm relieved not to feel so helpless for once. I drop the new prescriptions off at the pharmacy before going up and down the aisles in search of everything she thought might help. They've already helped, just by being there.

I glance down at the list, looking for the one thing I know isn't there. I asked Dolly three times, but she kept saying I didn't need to get any snacks for the nurses, but she's wrong. I need to do something nice for them, so I detour down the snack aisle, grabbing anything they might like.

My cart filled with a variety of chips and candy, I head over to the freezer aisle for a box of the Fla-Vor-Ice pops Dolly said would be both easy to eat and soothing for Tommy's throat. Next, I grab a few packs of bendy straws—another ordinary thing I never would have thought of. They are going to make it so much easier for Tommy to have a sip of water when the bed is reclined.

This is the kind of stuff Dox should be sharing with their customers. Not the hogwash they have us put in their brochures and emails, empty lines about how much they care about your family's health, with obvious tips like washing your hands during cold and flu season. If they really cared about their customers, they would share tips like this.

Rolling my cart down the over-the-counter-medicine aisle, I grab a pack of ZzzQuil, which I assume is for me, since sleeping is not something Tommy has trouble with anymore. I wonder how they knew I've been up all night, almost every night. Afraid to go to sleep in case Tommy needs me. I make a mental note to pick up some more under-eye concealer in case the dark circles gave me away.

Next on the list is the one thing I don't want to buy. I hesitate in front of the aisle, staring at the shelves stocked full of diapers, formula and pacifiers. I'm flooded with memories of the first time I bought Tampax, the first time I bought a pack of condoms. This isn't the first time I've had to buy a baby monitor, but it is the most depressing.

The process of death is so damn patronizing. I understand the logistics of having a monitor so I can keep an eye on Tommy down in his bed while I'm upstairs in mine—but would it kill someone to package a baby monitor a little differently so it's easier for a wife to buy for her dying husband, a grown man?

I take a deep breath, trying to calm myself down. The last thing I need is to have another panic attack right here in the goddamn baby aisle. I rest my hand over my heart and breathe in and out slowly. I close my eyes and continue to breathe, counting my breaths.

"It gets easier," a woman says as she walks by. "And it gets harder; just wait till they can talk!"

I cringe and exhale with purpose. The universe, it seems, has the same sense of humor that Tommy does.

My phone buzzes with a text from the pharmacy that the prescriptions are ready—a service we advertised with a "fill your cart while we fill your script" messaging. At least this is one thing that has proven to be useful.

"Lexie?"

I turn at the sound of my name, a fake smile plastered on my face to make polite conversation with someone who may or may not have heard about what's going on with us. It's a small town, and bad news seems to spread.

When I see the face that the voice belongs to, my lips tighten back into a disapproving line. Like a living page of the "stars are just like us" magazine spread, Monica Whistler is standing in front of me, a prescription bag in her hand.

If there is any justice in the world, her Rx is for something painful like hemorrhoids.

"I thought that was you," Monica says. She walks closer to me and puts her hand on my arm. I pull away and step to the other side of my cart so there's a buffer between us. "I have been meaning to give you a call and apologize. I am so sorry about the little mix-up with CeCe."

"Little mix-up?" I say, not believing the audacity of this woman.

"What are the odds the producer had promised the same role to a different girl the very same day?" Monica laughs and it takes everything in my being not to slap her across the face. "But I promise, I'll make it up to CeCe. If another part doesn't come up, I'll find a different way to help her out. Tom said she's got a lot of talent."

I bite my lip to stop myself from telling her that he goes by Tommy now, evidence of the time that's passed, proof that he's mine now, not hers.

"I could make some introductions." Monica is still talking. "It's the least I can do."

"No," I say, a little too abruptly by the look on her face. "You've done enough."

Before she can say anything else, I push my cart back down the stupid baby aisle and away from the pharmacy counter, where Tommy's prescriptions are waiting. I'll go through the drive-through or come back for them later.

There's a line at the register, so I stand there with my foot tapping, looking behind me every few seconds to make sure Monica isn't standing there. The woman checking out is making small talk with the cashier, and I'm considering just walking out and leaving everything there when another register opens.

"Did you find everything okay?" the cashier, an older woman with blue-gray hair and too much red lipstick, says.

I give her a curt nod and continue to empty the cart, hoping she will get the sign that I'm not in the mood to talk. I don't want to be rude, but I don't want to make idle chitchat even more.

"Looks like you're having a party," the cashier says, scanning bag after bag of the chips. She picks up the baby monitor next. "A baby shower?"

I can't bring myself to answer so I just stare past her at a poster we worked on last year for the refresh of their loyalty card program.

Once the last item has been scanned and bagged, the woman makes eye contact and smiles so wide I can see a spot of lipstick on her front tooth. "Would you like to donate a dollar for cancer research?" she asks.

All of the rage that has been building inside of me bubbles up and I snap. "Why in the hell would I want to do that?"

The cashier takes a step back, shocked. I know I should say I'm sorry and leave, but now that I've started, I can't stop.

"Do you know how much money I've donated over the years to cancer research? And what have they been doing with it? I can tell you what they haven't been doing—they haven't been finding a cure for small-cell lung cancer. So why would I give them another fucking dollar when they can't give me more time? Is that too much to ask?"

"I'm sorry, ma'am," the cashier says. Her chin quivers and I feel like the most heartless person in the world.

Behind me, someone sets a hand on my shoulder, and I

turn to see Monica staring at me with sad eyes. Make that the second most heartless person in the world.

"I can't." I slide my card through the credit card machine and stand there for what feels like an eternity before I can sign my name and roll my cart out the door.

Somehow, I manage to keep myself together until I'm in the car, the door locked behind me. Of course Kleenex wasn't on the shopping list. I find a brown paper napkin in the armrest and wipe my eyes. The rough paper scratches, but the physical pain can stop, it will heal. My heart is a different story.

I drop my head into my hands and let myself cry, sobs shaking my shoulders. I let it all go, getting it out of my system before I head home to put on a smiling face for my family.

The knock on the window is so soft I almost think I'm imagining things. But I look up, and Monica is standing there, her face looking even more forlorn than before. The woman really can't take a hint.

I shake my head and turn the car on, hoping she's smart enough to get out of the way before I start backing up. Because if she doesn't, Tommy won't be the only one who needs end-of-life care.

Chapter Thirty-Seven

CeCe

Y ou don't want to talk about it?" Beau asks.

I shake my head and slide my feet underneath me, try-ing to find comfort in the gentle swaying of the front porch swing outside my house. No matter how many puppies or unicorns I try to think about, nothing can erase the image of my dad crying earlier this morning. He stopped when he saw me and pretended like everything was okay, but we both know it wasn't. It isn't, and it won't be.

Beau tries to hold my hand, but I'm not in the mood to be comforted. I know he's trying, but nothing can change the fact that nurses have invaded our house. Dolly and Sandra, with cheery smiles on their faces like false advertising.

At first, I thought it was a good thing, that they were here to help Dad feel better, but then I heard Mom talking to Aunt Jill. She said something about hospice nurses—I didn't know what that word meant so I googled it. And now I can't unknow that they are the ones who come in at the end of a patient's life when there's no hope left.

"Want to tell me more about Monica?"

I look at him and frown, knowing there's no way I heard him right. "Don't be mean."

"How is that mean?" Beau laughs. "I just want to see you smile." He reaches for my hand again, and this time I let him. He brings it to his mouth, kissing it gently. It's sweet and I don't want him to leave, so I give him a little smile.

"That's better," he says, putting his arm around me. I lean into his shoulder, letting myself relax. "You can tell me about the lunch again if you want, or that you're going to the set soon, right?"

I nod, but I'm too sad to think about how excited I was when Monica texted, inviting me to come down to the set on Wednesday—which couldn't have been more perfect since it's my day off. I know Beau is sick of hearing about it, and I think I hurt his feelings when I said that meeting Monica was the one good thing that happened to me this summer.

Beau knows he's a good thing, too. I look up and give him another smile, this one meant to thank him for being there for me. But he clearly interprets it as an invitation to kiss me, which it totally isn't.

"Not here," I tell him, sliding farther away from him.

"Isn't your dad sleeping?"

"So?" I ask, a little annoyed he brought it up. Now that Dad's bed is down in the living room, it seems like he's always sleeping, just waking up, or just about to fall asleep.

"And your mom is out running errands." Beau tries again.

I elbow him in the side to let him know that I mean it.

"Oh, Cecelia," he sings. *"You're breaking my heart."*

I'm on my feet in less than a second. "Don't say that." I cross my arms and glare at him so he knows I'm serious. "My dad, that's our thing, you can't say that."

"I'm sorry." Beau reaches for me and I can tell he means it. "I really am. Come sit back down."

I stay put. This is a big deal, not just something he can brush away with two little words.

"Let me show you how sorry I am." He reaches for my hand again. "Please?" I sigh and sit back down, but only because if I stay mad at him, I won't have anyone else to talk to. "You sure you don't want to tell me about what you're going to wear on Wednesday?"

"Not really." This time, I let Beau take my hand. I appreciate him, but I need to find some girlfriends I can talk with about this stuff. It's not worth trying to make him understand how good it feels to finally have someone who's willing to help me make my acting dreams come true.

"Want to talk about something else?"

"Not really," I say again, resting my head on my favorite spot, just below his shoulder.

When Beau kisses the top of my head, I let him. I close my eyes and focus on the rise and fall of his chest as he slides his arm around my shoulder again. He means well, even if he doesn't always say the right thing. I pull back so I can look at him. He really is cute. He could have his pick of girls on the beach, but he's here with me, even though I won't let him get any further than kissing.

I smile, and he takes it as a sign it's okay to try again, which I guess it is.

He kisses me, just a little peck. And then I kiss him back. He kisses me again and I forget everything else that isn't the two of us.

In the distance, I hear something that sounds like the slamming of a car door.

Chapter Thirty-Eight

Alexis

My first thought is that something must be wrong.

CeCe and Beau are sitting on the porch swing and he has his arms around her, their heads bent together. If he's comforting her—I jump out of the car. Tommy was fine when I left an hour ago. The hospice nurse said he was doing okay. CeCe should have called me. Tommy was tired, but he was fine. He was going to take a nap, and then he said he'd feel better.

He said—wait one damn second. Beau is not comforting her.

I slam the car door and they don't even hear me. "Get your hands off my daughter," I scream, louder than I mean to. They pull away from each other and CeCe's face is bright red. "Cecelia, get in the house. Adam, go home."

"I'm not Adam." He stands, still holding my daughter's hand. "I'm not my dad."

"I said go home."

He may not be his dad, but he's got the same white-blond hair, the same ice-cold blue eyes, and I'm willing to bet he's got the same streak of trouble and destruction and disregard for the people who care about him.

CeCe and Beau look at each other, and I can't believe I missed this. All the girls on his Instagram. I haven't checked either of their accounts in the last few weeks. I didn't think I needed to, they were both here or with Jill or—oh, God. Who knows where they could have been, what they could have done. Right under my nose, and I didn't see it.

"We weren't doing anything wrong," CeCe says.

"Go inside, Cecelia."

The front door opens and Tommy stands there looking like a ghost of himself. I'm too angry to be embarrassed that Dolly is standing there beside him, hearing everything.

"Everything okay?" Tommy asks in his shrink voice, slow and careful.

"Nothing is okay." CeCe's voice is strong but quivering. I can tell she's on the verge of tears. "I hate you," she says before running inside. Beau follows her and I don't stop him even though I want to.

"You handle this," I tell Tommy before turning and walking away. I'm not sure where I'm going, and I don't care that the groceries are still in the back of the car. Let them go bad. Everything else around here has.

Out of habit, I turn down Barracuda, but I don't stop at Jill's house. I keep walking toward the beach, hoping the calming energy of the water will help me relax. At the bottom of the old, wooden steps, I slip my shoes off and step into the sand.

I walk closer to the water and take a deep breath, letting the salty air fill my lungs. My footprints get washed away as

255

soon as I pick my feet up, as if I were never there. I stop and let the water rush over my toes as I sink deeper into the cold, hard sand.

When they hand you the baby at the hospital and send you on your way, they make sure you know how to change their diaper, how to feed and bathe and swaddle them. But after that, you're on your own.

It's like I blinked and CeCe went from a baby to a toddler. I blinked again and she was double digits. And now, she's a teenager, trying so hard to be a woman. Tommy can handle this. That's what he does, he handles the hard things.

"Beautiful day, isn't it?" a woman says, walking toward me. She looks like she doesn't have a care in the world, but she's got to. Everyone has something difficult they're facing. I want to know what hers is, but I stop myself from asking because I know that's not a normal thing to say or do.

Instead, I smile and let her pass me by. But I'm tired of smiling and pretending everything is okay. Why do people do that, anyway? It's not like it's a secret that life is hard, that it isn't fair. They say you should be kind to strangers because you don't know what they're going through. So why don't we tell each other what we're going through?

The next time someone asks how I'm doing, I'm going to be honest. I'm going to tell them that I'm sad and I'm scared and I'm trying to be brave, but it's hard when you don't recognize your own life anymore.

I know what Tommy would say. He would tell me that all I have to do is be there. To stay. You'd think I would have learned the lesson by now, but things got tough and off I went again.

The first time Tommy called me out on my habit of running away when things got too hard, he said I should stay and face the music. He told me that some things are worth fighting for.

Of course he was right. He still is.

If there's one thing I know, it's that Tommy is worth fighting for. So is CeCe. I kick the sand, mad at myself for doing the same damn thing again. I need to find a way to let him know that I'm not going anywhere; even when it gets harder than it is now, I'm going to stay.

There's got to be something I can do. I twirl the Art Deco ring on my finger, wishing an idea would come to me the way it did when I was at work, trying to solve a stupid marketing problem that in the end didn't really matter.

What really matters is waiting for me at home; Tommy and CeCe matter more than anything. I glance down at the ring, and suddenly, I know what I have to do. But I can't do it alone.

JILL'S CAR IS in her driveway, so I let myself in the gate and walk up to the front door. Normally I'd just walk inside, but normally she knows I'm coming.

I knock and Jill opens the door with a dishrag thrown over her shoulder and splatters of something sugary and sweet on her apron.

"Hey," I say, trying to contain my excitement. But instead of moving aside to let me in, Jill steps outside and closes the door behind her. She puts her hands on her hips and leans against the doorframe. There's an expression on her face I've never seen before. "What's wrong?"

"Beau told me what happened," she says in the stern-mom voice I've been unsuccessfully trying to replicate for the last fourteen years.

"Oh, that."

Jill laughs in a way that makes it clear that she finds it to be anything but funny.

"What would you have done if you'd caught them making out?" I ask in my defense. This is not going the way I thought it would.

"I'd be okay with it—they're teenagers, and they're our kids."

"Boys are different than girls." I hate that I can't explain how terrifying it felt, seeing my little girl in the arms of her son. Maybe it wouldn't have been quite as bad if he didn't look so much like his father.

"I've got one of each," Jill reminds me. Poor Abigail is awfully forgettable.

"Abigail is different, you don't have to worry about her. CeCe—she's . . . I don't even know what she is. And Beau is his father's son."

I'm waiting for Jill to tell me she understands. She was married to the man, surely she can see all the ways her son is just like him—but she's still standing there, glaring at me with an icy expression I've never been on the receiving end of before. "He's also his mother's son."

"You're really mad about this?"

"I'm madder than mad!" She spits the words out and crosses her arms over her chest to make the point. Her eyes turn cold and her lips stretch into a disappointed line. It's like her whole face shuts down.

I'm speechless, which I've never been with Jill. Not ever.

"You insulted my son—twice now," she says. "He's up-stairs hurting, by the way."

"I'm sorry."

"You know, I don't think you are." We stand there for a second, and I'm not sure what else to say. "I think I heard the timer go off," Jill says.

I didn't hear anything, but I let her go.

Chapter Thirty-Nine

Alexis

The next afternoon, I get my coffee from Starbucks at the Commons instead of The Broken Crown. The vanilla syrup in my iced latte isn't as sweet as the pure vanilla Jill uses, and it didn't come with a hug.

I find a seat at a table outside and try to get comfortable, but the air is thick with humidity and beads of sweat are already dripping down the sides of my glass. What I wouldn't give to be sitting on the Crown's porch enjoying the slow whirl of the fan overhead and the breeze drifting up from the ocean.

This is ridiculous.

She has to forgive me—she must know it wasn't personal. At least, I didn't mean it to be. The irony of it all is that she's the one person I wish I could call and talk to about how upset and hurt I am.

I sigh and look at the people seated around me, reminders

that I'm alone. A sweet elderly couple are bickering in the corner about who's going to take the last bite of their pound cake. At the table next to them, two women around my age have their heads bent together, gossiping.

The last table is occupied with a woman older than me and her daughter, who looks at least six years younger than CeCe. I notice the mother doesn't have a wedding ring on her finger, and I wish I were brave enough to ask her for advice. In return, I would tell her not to blink because before she knows it, her daughter will be grown up. It will be too late.

I glance down at my phone, disappointed to see it's only been about five minutes since I sat down. Dolly is at the house giving Tommy a sponge bath. She practically shooed me away, told me to stay gone for at least an hour. It would be good for me, she said.

As much as I was dreading having hospice nurses in the house, it really has been nice. I know Tommy is their patient, but they've made me feel better, too.

I look back down at my phone.

This has got to stop—if I've learned anything from this whole experience, it's that life is too damn short to stay mad at the people we love. And Jill may not realize it right now, but she loves me.

I'm a little surprised to see her number still at the top of my "recently called" list. It's only been a day, but it feels like weeks. I push her number and the phone rings.

Once. Twice. Three times.

I squint at the screen to see if I accidentally hit the wrong number. But it's hers.

Four rings.

Five.

Six.

I hang up before her voicemail picks up, feeling more rejected than I have since Lionel Chavez took me to the eighth grade dance and spent the whole time dancing with another girl.

Even if Jill does calls back, I'm not sure I'd answer. It's not like I'm desperate. I have other friends. I have Becky.

Becky.

I have to find her name in the contacts app, proof that it's been too long since we've talked. She answers on the first ring. "Buttercup, how are you?"

"Not great," I admit. She inhales a quick breath that echoes in my ear. "It's not Tommy, he's fine. Well, as fine as he can be."

"Thank goodness," she says. "Hold on a sec." In the background, I hear the murmur of conversation. I didn't think about the fact she'd be at work, holding down the fort since I left her to deal with everything alone. Just another in the long line of people I'm letting down these days.

"Sorry, I'm back. Tell me what's going on?"

"My life is falling apart."

"Oh, sweet pea," she says. "I wish I could do something. What can I do?"

"Nothing."

"Do you want to talk about it?"

"Not really."

Becky sighs, and I can imagine what she's thinking: *Then why the hell did you call me?*

"You'll feel better if you do," she suggests. Normally, she'd be right. But this isn't like the things we usually talk about.

I'm not stressed because of a client or feeling guilty for missing another important event in CeCe's life. "Try me."

"Tommy's ex is everywhere I go—she looks even more beautiful in person, and CeCe found out about her, she knows everything. And Monica said she could get her a part in *The Seasiders,* but then backed out."

"Whoa," Becky says when I stop to take a breath.

"But that's not the worst part. I came home the other day and found CeCe making out with Jill's son, Beau."

"Hot damn!" Becky laughs. "Way to go, Ceese."

"Way to go?" I should have known better than to think Becky would understand. "She's fourteen."

"I was eleven when I had my first kiss—and didn't she already smooch that Romeo?"

"You don't get it."

"Believe it or not, I do, lovey. Everything is changing with Tommy, and I'm sure you're wishing at least one thing could stay the same, or at least be easy."

My shoulders drop as some of the tension I've been carrying around dissipates. "When'd you get to be so smart?"

"I may not have raised a teenage girl, but some people—present company included—have said that I still act like one at times."

"Touché." I smile, realizing Becky should have been my first call from the start.

"Did Jill freak out, too?"

My smile fades. "Not exactly."

"What did you do?" I can hear the hint of a laugh in Becky's voice through the phone.

"What makes you think I did something?" One of the

gossiping ladies shoots daggers in my direction before whispering something to her friend. I didn't mean for my voice to get that loud, but we're outside—not in a damn library. Still, I hush my voice. "I mean, I did, but why'd you think that?"

Becky laughs. "I miss you."

"I miss you, too, but that's beside the point."

"I remember reading something once—if you have a boy, you only have to worry about one penis. If you have a girl, you have to worry about all the penises."

"See? I'm right."

"Yes and no," Becky says. From her tone, I can tell she's treading carefully. "It's not just any boy, it's Beau."

"You've never met him," I remind her. I've been trying to get Becky to come down with us for years, but she always has an excuse—usually some guy she just started dating. "You should see all the girls on his Instagram."

"What if they're his friends? In my dating experience—and you know, I've had a lot of it—some of the best guys have more girl friends than guy friends."

"These aren't the friend kind of girls. The bathing suits they wear barely cover anything."

Becky laughs. "They're teenage girls who live on the beach. And it probably says more about them than him."

"If it were anyone else, I might see your point," I tell her. "But he's a player, just like his dad."

"He's a fifteen-year-old boy," Becky says. "And he can't be that bad if he's got some Jill in him, too."

"That's pretty much what she said," I tell Becky, remembering the cold, hard look on Jill's face. "But—"

Becky cuts me off. "No buts, buttercup. CeCe's her own person, and she's going to make a lot of choices in her life.

Some that you're really not going to like. In the long run, this isn't that big of a deal. Plus . . . never mind."

"What? You can say it." I take a sip of my watered-down latte and try to brace myself.

"It's just that, I know you're losing the love of your life, but she's losing her dad." My eyes well up and I nod, even though she can't see me. "Life is hard enough when you're an awkward teenager without all this going on. So let her have a little fun. I'm sure she can use the distraction."

I nod again.

"You still there?"

"Yeah." I wipe my eyes with the back of my hand and shift the phone to my other ear.

"Aren't you going to ask me how I got so smart again?"

I laugh. "I really do miss you."

"Duh," Becky says. "Now go make things right with Jill."

"Yes, boss."

"I love you," she says, which starts the waterworks again.

"I love you, too."

I hang up feeling better than I have since I had my big idea yesterday. I didn't even think to tell Becky about it. I'll call her back and fill her in soon, provided I can pull it off alone since Jill clearly won't be helping me.

She still hasn't called me back, not that I can blame her. I'm the one who owes her the apology; I should be doing the calling. I tap her name to call again. My breath catches when I hear her voice.

"Hi," she says.

"I am so—"

"It's Jill, and I can't get to the phone right now, so leave a message. Or better yet, send me a text."

My face falls and I hang up without leaving a message. I won't send her a text in case that feels too pushy or needy. Even though I really do need her.

I rest my head in my hands and focus on my breathing. It helps, but not as much as a conversation with Jill would.

I look up as the older couple walk by, holding hands on their way out. The woman stops by my table and reaches into her purse, handing me a Kleenex. She doesn't say anything, just smiles and keeps walking.

After using the tissue to wipe my eyes, I make a quick stop in Sephora to fix my makeup so Tommy won't be able to tell I've been crying.

He's got enough on his plate without having to worry about me.

Chapter Forty

CeCe

A security guard stops me at the front gate where I'm supposed to be meeting Monica. The pale blue house is at least twice as big as ours, but it's got the same beachy vibe all the houses in this neighborhood have. I wonder if anyone actually lives here when they aren't filming.

"Badge," the man says, unsmiling.

"I, I don't have one," I stutter. "I'm here to see—"

"She's with me."

Monica appears in the doorway of the house, leaning against the frame like she's straight off the pages of a magazine spread. She was beautiful the last time I saw her, but now, with her hair and makeup done, she looks like a movie star. I blush as the security guy steps aside to let me in. He still doesn't smile, but I'm smiling enough for both of us.

"I'm so glad you could make it," Monica says. She gives me a hug and I notice she smells as pretty as she looks, like a field of fresh flowers sprinkled with lemon and sunshine.

"I'm so glad you invited me," I tell her.

It couldn't have been more perfect; the day she's on set every week is the same day I'm off work from the café, like it was meant to be.

"So this is where the magic happens," Monica says, holding her hand out like she's setting the whole world at my feet. Which, if you think about it, she kind of is. "Cool, huh?"

"The coolest," I say, even though it doesn't look that different from the few commercial sets I've been on with my mom.

"Want to see the kitchen?" she asks. "It's kind of like the hub of the house; we have a lot of scenes in there."

I nod, more excited about how excited she is to show me everything than I am about seeing the set.

Heads turn as we walk down the hallway and I wonder if people are thinking, *There go the Whistler girls.* No one would ever say that about me and Mom. It never really bothered me that her last name was different from mine—but it is pretty cool to share a name with someone. It's like you're bonded together with them in a way that's just yours.

"Here it is," Monica says. We turn a corner into the open kitchen just as two men are carrying some camera gear out. I step back to get out of their way, but Monica pulls me back toward her. "The crew can go around us."

I stay put like Monica instructed, but smile an apology as the two men pass by. Every time Mom lets me tag along to a commercial set or photoshoot with her, she always makes sure to be extra nice to the crew since they're the ones who are really working hard. But I guess it's different when you're a movie star.

"Here, give me your phone and I'll take a picture. Stand over there, by the counter." Monica points toward the kitchen island. "That's the exact spot where I stand and talk to my TV kids about their days and give them all kinds of great life advice."

"Right here?" I ask as I step into place.

She nods and holds my phone up. I can feel my cheeks turning red as she snaps a few pictures. Just past her, the real cameras are set up and for a minute, it feels like all my dreams are coming true.

"Would you mind?" Monica says, handing my phone to another guy on the crew. He shrugs and takes it, as if he could tell the star of the show no.

Monica walks behind me and puts her arm around my shoulder, her face just inches from my own. I turn and look at her, then she turns and looks at me, and I have this crazy thought that this could have been my life.

If Monica were my mom, I might already be a famous actress. She would have never held her child back from achieving her dream, especially since it was the same dream she'd had as a little girl. Monica would have let me audition for real parts, helping me succeed instead of trying to protect me from rejection that might not even happen anyway.

"We're shooting in five, people," a man with a British accent yells. I hear him before I see him, but the way people scatter at the sound of his voice tells me he's someone important. Monica, however, doesn't move.

"Richard, darling," Monica says. "This is the young actress I was telling you about."

I hold my hand out to shake, but he just stands there, looking me up and down. I put my hand back by my side and smile, grateful Monica is still there next to me.

"Casey, right?" Richard asks.

I'm willing to nod and claim my new name, but Monica corrects him. "Close, it's CeCe."

Richard nods, and then turns, his attention clearly needed elsewhere. "Where the hell is Victoria? We haven't got all day, people!"

Monica drops her arm from my shoulder and takes my hand, leading me out of the room. "They'll be a while, let's go wait in my trailer."

I follow Monica out the back door toward the trailers that are lined up on the side of Old 98. The trailers I used to walk by, hoping that someone from the cast would stop and notice me.

As we climb the stairs to the middle trailer, I notice her last name, and mine, written on a white sheet of paper taped to the door.

"Would you take a picture of me here, too?" I ask.

Monica looks up at our last name on the door and smiles. We trade places on the steps, and I pose, perfectly framing my name. Hopefully it looks like I'm just casually walking into my personal trailer. One day when I'm on the *Tonight Show,* maybe they'll show this photo and I'll tell them the story about the first day my stepmom took me with her to the set.

Inside, the trailer isn't nearly as fancy as I thought it would be. There's an old couch with a little table at one end, and a vanity set up with more hair and makeup products than I've ever seen outside of Sephora.

Monica notices me staring and nods permission for me to go look closer. I sit down on the chair in front of the vanity mirror and she reaches over me to flip a switch that makes all the lights around the mirror turn on. I smile at our side-by-side reflections, wishing I didn't look so much like my mom.

All of Monica's makeup is organized by type and by color. Her lipstick is lined up like crayons in a box, almost every shade from the palest pink to a red so deep it almost looks black.

"I think you'd look fab in this one," Monica says, reaching for a soft, pastel pink. I'm about to take it from her hands when I realize she already has the lid off and is twisting it up. She reaches down to lift my chin and shows me how to pout my lips just so.

Not smiling in that moment is one of the hardest things I've ever done, but when she's finished, we both turn to look in the mirror. I raise an eyebrow, not sure about the color. Luckily, Monica shares my opinion. She hands me a tissue to wipe it off and reaches for a rich red shade instead.

"This was always your dad's favorite," Monica says. She smiles a little and I wonder how many other things she knows about Dad that I don't. That Mom doesn't even know— she barely ever wears makeup.

I pout my lips and look back up at Monica as she concentrates, applying the lipstick to my bottom lip and then my top. I rub my lips together and watch as she does the same, applying the red shade on top of the lipstick she's already wearing.

"It's called Lady Bug," Monica says. I try to memorize the name so I can buy it when I get home, but Monica hands it to me. "You can keep it, it looks good on you."

I smile at my reflection in the mirror, wondering if I can get Monica to tell me more stories about when she and my dad were married. Before I can ask anything, the trailer door flies open and a woman with a walkie-talkie sticks her head inside.

"Richard's looking for you," the woman says.

"You don't say, Kate," Monica says, looking like she's anything but concerned.

"It's Laura." The woman doesn't look happy. "And he's going to come and get you himself if you're not there in sixty seconds."

Monica sighs as if going on set to act is a chore instead of the coolest thing ever. I wonder if they have a place with chairs and monitors where I can watch like they do on my mom's commercial sets. But when we get outside, Monica leans down and presses her cheek to mine, doing a fancy French air kiss like they do in the movies. It's all so Hollywood.

"Until next time, my dear."

I smile and watch her go. Sad, but excited there will be a next time.

Chapter Forty-One
Alexis

My walk home from the beach is longer than normal since I'm avoiding Jill's house. Seven days. It's been seven whole days since I've talked to Jill. We've never gone that long without talking before.

CeCe's still mad at me, too. But I'm used to her not talking to me, to the angry looks she throws in my direction. I did get her to listen to me for a minute when she was in the middle of some cooking experiment. I knew she wouldn't walk away, so I took the opportunity to get all my words out.

I apologized for the way I acted and told her to tell Beau that I wanted to apologize to him, too. I told her that it hadn't been fair of me to jump to conclusions about Beau, and that I was okay if they still hung out—as long as they weren't alone at either house, or behind any closed doors. I'd hoped the message would make its way to Jill, but no such luck.

At this point, I'm not even sure I want to talk to Jill anymore. I've officially gone from sad to mad—I get what I did was insensitive, but her shutting me out during one of the toughest times in my life, that's worse.

I thought about texting her to say that I wasn't going to try anymore, but that kind of defeats the purpose. I'm so lost in my thoughts that I don't realize anyone is sitting out on the front porch until I'm standing on the top step.

"Hi," Jill says.

I look from her to Tommy, who is smiling a *don't be mad at me* smile. "Hey, babe."

"Don't 'hey, babe' me." I turn to Jill. "If you're not talking to me, you can't talk to him, either."

"Lex," Tommy says in his shrink voice. The glare I shoot him makes him stop before he starts. They look at each other then back at me.

Dolly breaks the silence, humming as she walks out the front door with a small paper cup holding Tommy's afternoon pills. She smiles at me, and when I don't smile back, she follows my gaze to where Jill looks equally upset.

"I'll just come back in a bit," she says, disappearing into the house.

As soon as the door closes behind her, I look back at the two traitors. "Aren't you going to say anything? Either of you?" I know I told them not to say anything, but since when do either of them do what I say?

"I asked Jill to come over," Tommy says. "So you both could talk."

"I'm listening," I say. I'm done trying to talk.

"I'm ready to hear your apology," Jill says.

"Ha!" The laugh that comes from my mouth doesn't sound

like my own. "My apology window has passed, sister. It's your turn to say you're sorry."

"Me? You're the one who insulted my son."

"And I told you I was sorry—but you abandoned me when I needed you. When I didn't have anyone else."

"You have someone else," Tommy says. "I'm still here."

"You know it's not the same," I tell him. I turn back to Jill. "I needed you." I brush a tear from my eye before it has a chance to fall. I don't want her to know how much she hurt me.

"I needed you, too," Jill says.

We both stand there, looking at each other. I wonder if she's thinking what I am, that our friendship is almost as old as we are.

"We don't fight," Jill says. "So I don't know how we're supposed to make up."

I'm not sure, either, but I'm also not that mad anymore. I'm the one who started this whole thing, and I know I should be the one to make it right.

"Truce?" I ask.

Her bottom lip quivers and she nods before lunging toward me with her arms wide open.

Jill wraps me in the hug I've been craving all week, and there would be no stopping the tears now even if I wanted to. Over her shoulder, I see Tommy smile, proud of himself for a job well done.

He pushes the swing back to get enough momentum so he can stand on his own. I drop my arms from around Jill to help Tommy back inside but he shakes his head.

I watch his slow, careful steps as he makes his way into the house, which makes me cry even harder. He pauses at the door, smiling again before going inside.

ALISON HAMMER

"Promise me we'll never go that long without talking again?" Jill says.

"You're the one who wasn't answering my calls."

"I hated being mad at you," she says.

"You should never do it again." I take her hand and we both walk toward the swing. "I told CeCe I wanted to talk to Beau myself, to tell him I'm sorry."

"He told me."

"And you were still mad?"

"No," she admits.

"Then why didn't you call me back?"

Jill sighs. "I don't know, I was scared."

"Of me?"

Jill nods.

"Look at me," I tell her. "I am the same girl who busted her knee on your front sidewalk when I was seven because I couldn't run fast enough to see you even though I'm the clumsiest human alive."

She smiles, but I still don't think she gets it. Luckily, I have a life full of memories I can remind her about.

"When we were twelve, it was me, sitting on the bathroom counter with you, putting ridiculous amounts of makeup on because we thought it would make us look older."

"We looked ridiculous," she says with a hint of a smile. "That was the night you kissed Jack."

"And if he wasn't gay, I would have married him just so I could be your sister."

She laughs at that one.

"We've been through so much together," I remind her. "You're the one who made me see a future with Tommy was possible."

"And you were the first one who tried to make me see that my future might be better off without Adam."

"I'm still sorry about that," I tell her.

"I'm not," she says. Her eyes are brimming with tears and I wrap her in a hug.

"Don't ever be mad at me again," I tell her. I pull back so I can look her in the eye to ask the next question that's been on my mind all week. "You were lying about the timer going off, weren't you?"

Jill laughs. "I missed you." She leans in to give me another hug.

"Yeah, yeah, I'm very missable."

I squeeze her back, ready to tell her the idea that brought me to her doorstep last week. I've been mulling it over for the past few days, and I know I can't pull it off without Jill's help. I need her on my side, now more than ever. And I don't want Tommy to know what I'm planning. Not yet.

"I need your help with something,"

"What?"

"Not here." I look behind me, where I imagine Tommy is sitting by the window, trying to hear the rest of our conversation.

It's what I would do.

Chapter Forty-Two
Alexis

The bell on the door chimes as I walk inside The Broken Crown. Jill is at the counter ringing up a customer. She lifts a finger to let me know she'll be ready in a minute.

I notice Abigail hunkered down at a table in the corner, so focused on whatever she's drawing that she didn't hear me walk in. As much as I would love to sneak a peek at what's on the page, I have to remind myself this isn't a social visit.

"Are you as excited about this as I am?" Jill asks, coming out from behind the counter to give me a hug.

"I think so?"

"CeCe and Lou are in back finishing up the samples."

My mouth waters in anticipation as she leads me toward the kitchen. As I push through the swinging doors, I hear Lou say, "I've never been there, but I heard it's beautiful."

Then CeCe's voice: "I had lunch there a few weeks ago with my stepmom."

Stepmom? Oh, hell no.

"Hey, guys," Jill says, interrupting moments too late.

The smile on CeCe's face vanishes the second she sees me. Her cheeks blush red. Lucky for her, this isn't the time or the place to discuss the fact that she has a warped perception of reality when it comes to her father's ex-wife.

"What are you doing here?" CeCe asks, not bothering to hide her annoyance.

"Hello to you, too. Hi, Lou." I smile toward Lou, who looks like she wishes she could disappear into the background.

"I'm working," CeCe says under her breath. "We have an appointment for a wedding cake tasting."

"I know."

CeCe tilts her head and furrows her eyebrows—the same thing I do when I'm confused.

Jill pulls a stool up to the island. "You can sit here, Lex."

"Wait, what?" I watch as the realization washes over CeCe's face. "You?"

"Me."

"And Dad?"

I nod, anxiously awaiting her reaction. I wasn't going to tell her, I wanted to surprise her along with Tommy, but Jill convinced me it would be better for everyone if I let her know. And better yet, if I let her help.

"You're getting married? Why now?"

"Why not?" I say, even though it's a cop-out. I've been asking myself the same question since I had the idea, and I haven't found the words to quite explain it, other than the fact that I owe it to them both.

CeCe deserves to know she's part of a real family and that

I'm not going anywhere. And Tommy, he deserves to know that he finally cured me from my running-away habit. That even now, I'm in for keeps.

"I can't believe Dad didn't tell me."

"He doesn't know. I'm going to surprise him."

CeCe's lips twitch and I can tell she's trying not to smile. "I'm still going to be a bastard," she says. "Because you weren't married when I was born."

Lou slips away into the pantry, and I don't blame her. CeCe's words are meant to hurt me, but I'm not going to let them. I keep my eyes locked on hers as I smile back and stick with the plan.

"I was hoping you'd be my maid of honor."

"You're really going to do this?"

"I am," I tell her. "And I would love nothing more than to have you standing by my side."

"Do you want to try the cake samples?" CeCe asks, offering a temporary truce.

"First we need some champagne for our bride," Jill says, opening up the industrial fridge.

"And how about a glass for my maid of honor?"

CeCe looks at me, surprised.

"Of course." Jill takes four glasses from a cabinet and sets them on the island. "Lou, will you do the honors?"

She hands the bottle to Lou, who peels the gold foil from the top of the bottle and effortlessly pops the cork.

"A toast?" Jill asks.

"I think that's my job," CeCe says. I try to keep my face stoic because I know better than to push my luck. "Here's to finally making it official." She holds her glass up and we clink ours together. "I'll come up with something better for the actual day."

"That was perfect." I take a sip and raise my glass toward her again.

"Speaking of the actual day," CeCe says. "When exactly is this happening?"

"On Saturday," Jill says, answering for me.

"This Saturday?" CeCe asks, almost choking on her sip of champagne. "As in two days from now?"

"That's the one."

CeCe looks flabbergasted. "You waited this long, what's the rush?" Her face falls as she realizes why, and it takes everything in me to keep a smile on mine.

"Do you want to try the vanilla first?" Lou asks, bless her heart.

"My dad likes chocolate," CeCe says.

She's right, he does. "Can we try the chocolate first?" I ask.

Lou lifts the lid off a tray, revealing four small slices of chocolate cake. One has chocolate icing, another has vanilla, a third looks almost like the second except for crystal specks in the icing, and the fourth has a layer of fresh strawberries in the middle.

I take a fork and bite into the chocolate-on-chocolate one first. "This is amazing." I go in for another bite. "You're so good at what you do," I tell Lou.

"I didn't make that one," she says. "CeCe did."

CeCe glances down at her feet, just long enough for her glasses to slip down her nose. She pushes them back and shrugs as if she's trying to make light of the fact that she has baked a delicious, professional cake that's fit for a wedding.

"I'm really impressed."

"It's not a big deal," she says.

I take a bite of the next sample. "This icing is amazing."

"It's buttercream," CeCe says. "The secret is using unsalted butter."

Jill refills my glass and I'm not sure if this light, airy feeling is from the champagne or the fact that in this moment, I'm just a bride tasting cake with her daughter and her best friend.

"The next one has the same icing but there's salted caramel bits mixed in," CeCe tells me.

"That was her idea," Lou says, clearly proud of her protégé.

I cut a little bite off with my fork and taste it. "This is it," I say. "This is the one." I take another forkful and pass it to Jill so she can taste.

"So good," she agrees.

Lou takes the lids off of two other trays filled with more cake samples. "I guess there's no reason to taste these?"

I laugh and reach to pull the trays closer. "Do you have more forks?"

Lou nods and turns to get three more forks so we can all enjoy the fruits of CeCe's labor together.

I know this is all happening out of order, but I've never been one to follow the conventional path. And if we had gotten married after the first time Tommy asked, our daughter wouldn't have been able to bake our wedding cake.

I'm so swept up in the emotion of the moment that I walk over to CeCe and wrap my arms around her. She resists for a second but gives in and kind of hugs me back.

Chapter Forty-Three
CeCe

Mom?" I knock even though her bedroom door is open.

"Everything okay?" she asks as if something must be wrong if I'm willingly coming into her room. Which I guess I deserve. But this whole me-being-nice-to-her thing is new.

"I can come back if you're busy."

"I'm never too busy for you." She pats the bed next to her and puts the book she was reading down on the nightstand. I hate it when she says corny stuff like that. It sounds fake, like a line she would write for one of her stupid ads. But I can't let that distract me, not now.

"You haven't given me much time to plan something," I tell her. "But as maid of honor, I'm supposed to throw a bachelorette party."

"Oh, sweetie. I don't need a party."

"Good, because you're not getting one." I try to sound more cute than snarky, but I'm not sure it worked. "But I did want to do something."

Mom's eyes get all big and wide and I don't want her to start crying, so I get up and go back to my room for the gift bag full of everything I got at Dox.

I hand her the bag, and she holds it in both of her hands as if it is something really special, and I hope she doesn't have her hopes set too high, because it's not that big of a deal.

She takes the tissue paper out one piece at a time, like she's trying to make this whole thing last as long as humanly possible. The first thing she takes out is the L'Oréal clay face mask.

"I figured we could both use a little beauty treatment before tomorrow."

"It's perfect, thank you."

"There's more." She pulls out the blue nail polish next. I can tell from her face she's trying to figure out how to get out of painting her fingers blue. "It's for your toes, you know, something blue."

"I love it."

She pulls the pink polish out, and then the No Gray Quick Fix touch-up for her hair. Based on the way her lips press together, I probably should have left that one out.

"And I have ice cream downstairs," I say, trying to recover. "Mint chocolate chip." Mom doesn't say anything, and I hope I didn't do something wrong. "It's not much."

Her face relaxes in a smile. "It's just how I wanted to spend my last night as a single woman."

A noise comes from the baby monitor on her nightstand and we both hold our breath. She reaches over and takes it in her hand, watching the video of dad sleeping downstairs.

"He's okay," she says, relief thick in her voice. She sets it back down, then looks at me. "I was going to give this to you tomorrow, but I might as well do it now."

Mom opens the drawer in her nightstand and takes out a wrapped box that's not much bigger than a deck of cards. It feels light in my hands as I peel the paper from its corners, one at a time.

Inside, there's a white box with the green script logo of Emerald Lady Jewelry. I hesitate before lifting the lid. I've never had real jewelry—just the fake stuff from Charming Charlie.

I open the box and my jaw literally drops. "Are you serious?"

Mom nods and looks like she's about to cry again. I take two tiny diamond studs out of the box. Each one isn't bigger than a pea, but they are the sparkliest, most beautiful things I've ever seen.

"Are they real?"

Mom nods. "Tomorrow is as much for you as it is for your dad and me. It's about you and me and us. Our family."

"Can I try them on?"

"Of course." Mom looks so happy you'd think she was the one who just got a pair of amazingly gorgeous diamond earrings.

I take the small silver studs out of my ears one at a time and set them in the box, carefully replacing them with the diamonds. I walk into the bathroom to look in the mirror, turning my head as tiny rainbows dance around the room.

Mom walks up behind me and I look at our reflections, mirror images of each other. I move my head to the left and the right, watching my ears sparkle.

"Beautiful," Mom says, and I have to agree. "Should we do the ice cream first, or the masks?"

"Let's start with the mask and eat the ice cream while it dries?"

"Perfect."

She grabs two cloth headbands from the bathroom drawer and hands one to me. We both sit on her bed as she takes the jar out and hands me the empty box to read the instructions.

"'Apply an even layer to clean, dry skin,'" I read. "We should wash our faces first."

"Okay, meet back here in five?"

I nod and head into my bathroom to wash my face. This is actually more fun than I thought it was going to be. It helps that Mom is acting close to normal, and the earrings definitely didn't hurt, either. I admire them in the mirror again and make sure the backs are on tight before I turn the water on.

Back in Mom's room, I read the rest of the instructions.

"'Avoid the eye and lip area and leave on for ten to fifteen minutes. Remove with warm water in circular motions to exfoliate.'"

Mom twists the lid off and offers it to me first. I dip two fingers in the jar, scooping out a bit of clay before handing it back to her. It feels wet and cool as I spread it over my forehead, then down my cheeks.

I look up at Mom and laugh. "You look ridiculous."

"Well, you don't look much better," she says. I can tell she's trying to smile, but the clay is already starting to dry, making it hard to move her mouth.

"How long did it say to keep it on?" Mom asks. Her voice sounds funny since she can't open her mouth all the way.

"Ten to fifteen minutes." My voice sounds just as strange.

"Set your phone for twelve?"

I reach for my phone to set the timer. "Let's get the ice cream," I say, even though we might not be able to move our mouths enough to eat it.

"Then nails?"

"Perfect." If Mom always acted this cool, maybe it wouldn't be so hard to like her.

We're halfway out the door when we hear it, groaning coming both from downstairs and the baby monitor. "Why don't you stay up here?" Mom says. "I'll check on Dad and bring the ice cream up?"

I nod, afraid to say anything. I know I should go down and help, but it's too hard to see him like this. I hope he'll be okay for the wedding tomorrow, so it won't be too little, too late.

I climb onto the bed and lean back against the headboard, hugging a pillow from what used to be Dad's side of the bed. I can hear Mom's voice through the monitor.

"It's okay," she says. "It's okay."

I know she's comforting Dad, but it feels like she's comforting me, too. I grab the baby monitor and watch the video screen as Mom angles the bed up higher. She helps him put the oxygen tubes in his nose then moves to rub his back.

Once his breathing is back to normal, he looks up and asks, "What's on your face?"

"It's a mud mask—CeCe bought it for us to do together." The picture on the video screen is grainy, but I know my dad well enough to know he's raising an eyebrow. "What?" Mom says.

I can't see her face, but I know she's got a geeky grin as wide as she can stretch her mouth with this stupid mask on.

"Nothing," Dad says. "It's nice, that's all."

"We're eating ice cream next, want some? Might feel good on your throat."

Dad shakes his head. "Just sit with me for another minute?"

"Of course."

He slides over to make room for my mom and I feel a little

weird watching such a private moment. They're my parents, but like Dad said the other day, they're people, too.

The timer on my cell phone goes off, so I set the monitor back on the dresser and go to wash the mask off my face. I consider calling down to Mom, but I figure a few more minutes won't hurt. And those minutes are better spent where she is, anyway.

I know I haven't been making any of this easier on her. But it's not like I can just wipe the slate clean and forget about fourteen years' worth of disappointments. Even if I do forgive her, we can't just snap our fingers and start being close. Although she would love that.

After I wipe the last bit of mud from my cheek, my skin feels soft and new. I consider my face, a carbon copy of hers. Maybe I can start by not hating her so much.

For Dad's sake.

Chapter Forty-Four

Tommy

Sometimes I regret it.

In the quiet moments when it's just me and Lexie. When she laughs, and for a second, it's like everything is back to normal. When she's holding my hand and I see the faraway look in her eyes. When I don't ask what she's thinking because I already know. And I know that if I did ask, she wouldn't tell me the truth.

In the loud moments, too. When CeCe is being her fiercely independent self. When she does something that makes me stop and realize she isn't a little girl anymore, but she's not quite an adult yet, either. She's stuck in that in-between, kind of like I am now.

In those moments, I wonder if I should have fought it. If I should have tried harder, to make my time here with them last longer. More time. I want more time. Even if it's just one day more.

But then I see CeCe laughing or smiling in a carefree

moment before she catches herself and stops. Her poker face is as bad as her mother's. I can see the thoughts fluttering behind her eyes, see her thinking, *I shouldn't be laughing.*

I never wanted to be the reason for her sadness.

And Lexie, my heart. She doesn't believe me, but she's the only woman I ever really loved. Even when we were kids, it was her. It was always her. There's a photo from a summer when we were kids. The two of us are on the beach with Jill and Adam.

We'd just devoured a box of Popsicles; I no doubt had two. Our lips, red and purple and green and blue, are all smiling. Jill is smiling because she has no idea that when she grows up and marries Adam, he'll cheat and leave her alone to put her dreams back together and raise two amazing kids on her own. Adam is smiling because even back then, he acted like he owned the world. Lexie is smiling because she always smiles on the outside. And then there's me—the only one who isn't looking at the camera. But I'm smiling, because I'm looking at Lexie.

She's still the reason I smile. She's the reason I wake up each morning, even when it hurts. I want so badly to be that same thing for her. I used to be. But now . . . I hate being the reason her eyes look sad. I hate hearing her cry from our bedroom upstairs. I hate that I can't climb the damn stairs to crawl in bed with her, to hold her and let her know that she'll be okay. I hate the way she comes downstairs each morning, smiling that smile she thinks is hiding the pain.

It's those moments when I see what it's doing to them, this disease that's killing my body breath by breath. That's when I know I made the right decision. Because even though I'm the one who's sick, it's killing all of us. And it would be selfish of me to hold on, to make them suffer even one more day than they have to. I've been there, where they are.

And I know the longer I'm here, the longer they're hurting, the longer it will take them to heal. I know they'll be okay. CeCe is going to be even more amazing than she already is. She's got enough of her mother's independence and stubbornness to make sure of that. Together with the thoughtfulness and introspective view of the world she got from me, there will be no stopping my baby girl.

And Lexie. If she can make it through this, she can survive anything. I know this has been hard. Staying for her has never been easy, but I now know she'll never run. This summer has changed her, too.

CeCe doesn't know it, but my sweet girl is so lucky. One day she'll realize just how special and amazing her mother is. And hopefully, she'll be able to look back and think her old man wasn't so bad, either.

Of all the things I hope for, I hope these aren't the days she holds on to, the days she remembers when she thinks of me. I hate that it's how I remember my mom most, lying sick in bed. Of course with her, it was sick years, not sick months.

When CeCe is grown-up, maybe with children of her own, I hope she can look back and smile at all of the good times: the way we danced in the kitchen with her tiny feet on mine, the after-school snacks around the kitchen table, driving her to and from ballet and piano and gymnastics and theater. The bedtime stories and Saturday-morning snuggles, watching cartoons in bed between her mom and me.

I hope she remembers how much I loved her. Love her. Even when I'm gone, my love for her will still be here.

Damn, this is hard.

Sometimes I wish I didn't know it was coming. That I didn't have all this time, as short as it is, to think about what I'm leaving behind. It would be easier if I just went to bed one day and never woke up.

But then I wouldn't be able to say goodbye. I wouldn't be able to put this last plan, my last gift, into motion.

Even though it's for Lexie, it's for me, too.

And CeCe.

It's for all of us.

Chapter Forty-Five

Alexis

As I walk down the stairs on my wedding day, I'm happy to see that Dolly is already there. Her smile and her presence are a relief after last night.

"How are you doing this morning, bride?" Dolly asks, whispering the last part.

"Last night was tough," I tell her. "I wasn't sure, I thought—" I look down, not able to say the words, to admit that I worried all of our planning would be for nothing. One minute, my heart was swelling with love from CeCe's unexpected gift, and the next it was in my throat.

Dolly reaches for my hand and tucks it between hers. "We're going to get him there, I promise you that."

"Thank you," I tell her, even though those two words don't come nearly close enough to conveying how much I appreciate her.

"It's nothing," Dolly says, breaking eye contact. Even if she doesn't admit it, I know she feels it, too.

"It's the opposite of nothing," I tell her. "You do know that, don't you?"

Dolly looks back at me, confusion on her face. "I'm just doing my job."

"Your job is to take care of Tommy," I tell her. "But you've been taking such good care of me, too."

"Oh, dear heart." Dolly brushes a tear from her eye and pulls me in for a hug. "You know, I think this wedding is just what the doctor ordered—for both of you."

I nod, giving her one more squeeze before letting her get back to work.

"Now, as much as I'd love to have you sit here and talk with me all day, I think you have somewhere you need to be getting off to," Dolly says, a sparkle in her eye. It's beyond me how someone can be around so much sadness and still exude such happiness. "Enjoy your day today; it's such a beautiful thing you're doing for him."

I blink away the tears and try to focus on the fact that if all goes as planned, I will be a married woman by the end of the day. And I hope with all my heart that I'll get to enjoy being a newlywed before I become a widow.

I throw the two bottles of nail polish we didn't get around to using last night in my purse, hoping I'll have a chance to paint my nails over at Jill's. The schedule is already tight—CeCe is down at The Broken Crown with Lou, putting the finishing touches on the cake. She's coming back soon to sit with Tommy while I walk to Jill's to get ready.

Jack's going to do my hair and makeup—he and Blake said they were driving down before I even got the question out. He offered to do CeCe's hair as well, but she thought that would give it away for her dad. She might be just as excited about this whole thing as I am.

Jill was right. I can't imagine how this would have gone if I hadn't told her. I'm trying not to go overboard, showing CeCe how much everything she's doing means to me, but I've never been good at hiding how I feel.

I'm going to have to hide it now, I remind myself as I walk into the living room, where Tommy's been drifting in and out of sleep. He knows there's something going on, but I don't think he's figured out what. I've been turning his proposals down for the last fifteen years, so I'm sure this is the last thing he'd expect.

"Your skin," he says as I lean closer to kiss him goodbye. "It's glowing."

"What can I say, it was a magic mask. How are you feeling?"

"Don't worry, I'm not going to die today."

I force a smile, even though these comments are getting harder and harder to stomach.

"That's a relief," I try to tease back. "Jill would be very upset if you missed this dinner she's planning. She's making all your favorites, and CeCe's making dessert."

"I can't wait."

"I'm going to go over and help if you think you'll be okay?"

"I'll be fine," he says with a smile. "It's Jill I'm worried about—promise me you won't try to help with the cooking?"

"I'm not that bad in the kitchen," I say in my defense.

"You are the best order-out-er I've ever met."

"And don't you forget it." I give him one more kiss before I go. "You and CeCe should head over around six. Dolly's going to help."

"Got it." Tommy gives me a half salute before putting his oxygen cannula in and closing his eyes. He's been wearing it more and more lately. A simple conversation is enough to wear him out.

WALKING DOWN THE street toward Jill's house, I feel a little lighter with each step. Every breath of salty air is bringing me slowly back to life, filling me with excitement for the day ahead.

This is really happening.

Jack is out the door before I even open the front gate. He and Jill still look like spitting images of each other, although Jack's freckled face looks younger, his skin tighter—probably from all the product he has access to at the salon. But they both have the same smile that lights up their eyes, and the same red hair that's calmed into a rusty shade of brown. "You didn't wash your hair, did you?"

"Good to see you, too." I laugh. "And no, I followed your instructions."

"That's my girl." He folds me into a hug and kisses the top of my head. "I love that you're doing this."

"And I love that you're here; thank you for coming."

"Please, as if you could keep me away."

"Where's Blake?" I ask.

"Out back setting everything up." He smiles and ruffles my hair as we head inside. "Now let's see if I can make a miracle out of this."

Jill greets us at the front door and hugs me tight. "Happy wedding day!"

"There will be time for that later," he tells his twin as he shoos her away and leads me upstairs. "I set everything up in Jill's bathroom."

I sneak a peek as we walk past Abigail's room. Part of me expects it to look the way it did when she was a little girl, but the canopy princess bed is long gone and her giant stuffed animals have been replaced by art supplies. I'm happy to see there is one stuffed animal left. Propped up against the pillows on her bed sits Beary, the white GUND bear Tommy gave her when Beau was born. He looks well loved, like any good teddy bear should.

The door to Beau's room is closed, but I can hear the telltale sounds of video games coming from inside. I hesitate at the door, emotions threatening to overcome me again. Ever since my talk with Becky, I've been able to look at Beau a bit differently. Now, I can see some of Jill in him, too. And if he's as good a friend to CeCe as his mom is to me, then I'm grateful she has him. Although they still aren't allowed in either house alone.

"You coming?" Jack calls from Jill's bedroom at the end of the hall.

"Just a minute."

I raise my hand to knock on Beau's door. He opens it and does a double take, clearly surprised to see me.

"I just wanted to let you know how sorry I am," I say.

"It's okay," Beau says. "You don't have to—"

"It's not okay, and I do have to. I'm sorry and I hope you can forgive me. I know—" Before I can get the rest of my apology out, Beau has his arms around me in a quick hug.

"It's okay, Aunt Lexie," he says. "All this with Uncle Tommy, it's messing everything up. But what you're doing today, it's pretty cool."

"Thanks Beau Bo," I say, using Tommy's nickname for him.

His eyes shimmer with tears and I smile before turning to go. He doesn't want me to see him cry, and I know that if he does, I won't be able to stop from joining him.

I find Jack in Jill's bathroom, where he's created a pop-up salon. I take a seat at the kitchen stool set up in front of the sink, surveying the counter and what looks like every styling product known to woman.

"So how are you really?" Jack asks, running his hands through my hair. I close my eyes and savor the feeling of his fingers massaging my scalp.

"Better now."

"I'm serious."

I open my left eye and see Jack's reflection staring back at me, his forehead wrinkled in concern. "I don't want to be sad today."

"Fair enough." He puts a smile back on his face and squeezes my shoulder before reaching for a bottle of something that comes out white and foamy.

"Aren't you going to ask me what I was thinking about for my hair?" I ask, playing coy.

Jack's fingers don't stop moving. "If you want."

"Would it make a difference if I told you?"

"Boo, please."

I turn to give him a look, but his hands are instantly on both sides of my face, moving my head back in position. I smile and try to keep still so Jack can do his best to transform me into a bride on what's supposed to be the happiest day of her life.

Chapter Forty-Six

CeCe

Usually, it would bum me out that Dad is inside sleeping in the middle of the afternoon, but I know he could use the rest so he'll be able to enjoy tonight. Plus, since he's asleep and I know there's no chance Mom will be coming home, I can sit outside and read *The Art of Acting* out in the open.

I feel like a boy sneaking a peek at dirty magazines every time I read it. I know there's nothing to be ashamed of, it's just not worth their questions. And as long as they don't know that Monica and I are talking, they can't tell me to stop. And if I stop, she won't be able to invite me to come out to L.A. to live with her. She was this close to doing it the other day, I could feel it.

She didn't correct the craft services lady when she called me her daughter, and she was telling me about how lonely it was in her apartment, and that she didn't have any guests to use her guest bedroom.

I sigh and open up the book to where I left off with the

chapter "Instant and Inner Justifications" when a Yellow Cab pulls into the driveway. I close the book and set it beside me. We aren't expecting anyone.

The cab's back door opens and I see a flash of hot pink in the backseat.

"Aunt Becky!" I scream so loud I probably woke Dad, which I totally didn't mean to do. But Aunt Becky!

"Baby cakes!"

I run into her open arms so hard that she stumbles back against the cab. "What are you doing here?" My eyes start to water even though I'm the opposite of sad.

"You don't know?" Becky asks. "Shit."

"I don't know what?" She can't know about the wedding. Mom would have told me if Becky was coming.

"Your dad is planning a little surprise for your mom."

Behind us, the front door opens and Dad stands there, leaning against the doorframe, his oxygen tank beside him. "Our first wedding guest has arrived."

"You know?" I ask Dad. I don't understand what's happening.

"So you do know?" Becky asks before dragging her suitcase toward the house. If she's surprised to see how bad Dad looks, she doesn't let it show. "Hello, groom."

"Hey, Becks." Dad gives her a quick kiss on the cheek.

"I am so confused," I say, still standing in the driveway.

"Come on, sweet girl," Becky says.

I sigh and run up the stairs to join them inside to see if I can figure out what in the world is going on.

"Ceese, why don't you go and get our guest a glass of your fancy Arnold Palmers," Dad says. "And one for your old man."

I nod and walk into the kitchen, still trying to make sense of everything.

When I get back to the living room, Dad and Becky are both sitting on the couch. There's no room for me, so I climb onto Dad's bed. Aunt Becky gives me a smile, but her eyes are glassy and I can tell it's hard for her to see Dad like this, even though she's doing a pretty good job of pretending.

"Now someone talk," I demand.

"Your aunt Jill let it slip about the plan," Dad says. "Maybe on purpose. Or maybe because she's never been good at keeping secrets."

"Mom is going to be so pissed."

"Not as pissed as I'd be if she finally tied the knot and I wasn't here," Becky says. "This is really good, by the way. Your mom told me you've turned into a whiz in the kitchen."

"She did?" I'm surprised and flattered, but I can't let an unexpected compliment derail me. "But I still don't know what you're doing here. No offense."

"None taken, lamb chop. I had to deliver the goods."

Becky unzips her faux–army issue backpack and hands a jewelry box to my dad.

"Is that . . . ?"

"The ring I bought for your mom before you were born, just in case she ever said yes." He hands me the box and I lift the lid. There's one big round diamond surrounded by a bunch of smaller ones in a platinum setting.

"Whoa."

"Do you think she'll like it?" Dad asks.

"Hasn't she seen it before?"

Dad shakes his head, and there's a sparkle in his eye I haven't seen since I can't remember when. "When she said yes, I wanted it to be because of me, and not for a new, shiny ring."

"That's such a shrink thing to say." I take the ring out of the box and slip it on my finger. I hope that's not bad luck, but I figure our luck can't get any worse. "She's going to love it. So how are you going to give it to her?"

"I haven't figured that part out yet."

"It might be cool if you let Alexis propose this time," Becky says.

"Interesting," Dad says.

"The trick is going to be getting her to do it," Becky thinks out loud, resting a finger thoughtfully on her chin. They look at each other, their expressions changing like they're communicating with their eyes. Then they both turn to look at me. "You guys were thinking they'd just start the ceremony right away?"

I shrug. "I think so."

"Maybe you suggest it to her," Dad says.

"Suggest what?" I ask. "Proposing?"

"Why not?" he asks.

"Because." But I can't think of a good reason. I give a little harrumph and stand up. I think better when I'm pacing. I grab the blue yoyo off the coffee table, mindlessly doing the tricks Dad taught me as I walk back and forth at the foot of his bed. How can I pull this off?

"It's like looking at a clone," Becky says. I stop pacing and yank the yoyo back into my palm before shooting her a dirty look. I can't help it if my mom paces, too. "Don't stop on my account," she says.

"I could text her with the idea," I say, walking back and forth again, letting the yoyo drop before flicking my wrist to pull it back up. "Jack's probably still doing her hair."

"Jack's here?" Dad sounds surprised.

"Great, I spoiled the one secret that's left." I stop pacing and sit back down on the bed.

"If I go over there, she'll be worried about you being here alone."

"Say that Dolly got here early," Dad suggests.

"Who's Dolly?" Becky asks.

"One of the hospice nurses," I tell her. "She's really nice."

"When she gets here, can I sing 'Hello, Dolly, well, hello, Dolly!'?" Becky starts doing jazz hands as she sings.

"I'm sure she's never heard that one before," Dad says.

Becky shrugs. "It's better than a Dolly Parton joke."

"Can we get back on track, people?" Sometimes it seems like I'm the only grown-up around here.

"I think this could work," Becky says, back to business. "You can go over early and tell her you realized she missed a step—she can't have a wedding without a proposal, so she needs to propose first."

"But how? And when?"

"Right after your dad gets there, when it's just the two of them."

"But she'll be in her dress—he'll see her."

"That doesn't matter, none of this is traditional." Becky looks at my dad. "No offense."

He smiles. "None taken."

"When she asks you if you'll marry her, you can take the ring out and surprise her right back," Becky says.

Dad runs his hand over his head the way he always does when he's trying to process something. "It could work."

"You think?" I ask him.

Dad shrugs. "It hasn't worked the other seventy-two times

I've asked, but what's one more try?" He laughs but stops himself before it turns into a coughing fit.

"It's a good thing they say the seventy-third time is the charm," Becky says.

I shake my head. "No one says that."

"Well, maybe they'll start now." Dad smiles and I realize this is the happiest I've seen him since before he got sick. Or at least since he taught me how to drive—he did seem pretty happy that day. After we got back home, he slept for, like, thirteen hours. He can't get that tired now.

"We should let you rest, Dad." I give Becky a look that lets her know I'm not messing around.

"Your daughter, the triple threat," Becky says. "Actress, chef, and now, nurse."

"She's the boss," Dad says.

Becky stands and offers Dad a hand. He takes it and lets her help him up.

Before he gets back into his bed, he folds Aunt Becky into a hug and whispers something in her ear. It's probably just something like thank you, but I liked it better when I didn't worry about respecting his privacy.

Chapter Forty-Seven
Alexis

Wow," CeCe says as she walks into the living room at Jill's. I look down at my dress, wishing there were a mirror nearby. "Good wow or bad wow?"

"Good. Great. The best," my daughter, who has never in her life given me a sincere compliment, says. "You look beautiful."

"Thank you," Jack says. I reach back to swat him but miss.

"You don't look like yourself," CeCe says, slightly spoiling the compliment.

"Thank you?"

"You know I didn't mean it like that." CeCe rolls her eyes and perches on the edge of the couch. "Dad's outside—I told him you were going to come help him get into the backyard."

"Okay." I take a deep breath and smooth out my dress even though there isn't a single wrinkle in the off-white fabric. It's not a wedding dress per se, but it's white-ish, it's flattering, and it's the best we could find on such short notice.

It was CeCe's idea that I propose to Tommy before springing the whole wedding on him. I have to admit, there's something perfect about turning the tables on him, and it will give him a chance to catch his breath and wrap his head around the whole thing.

"Hold these for me?" I hand CeCe the bouquet of yellow roses with red tips. The kind of flower Tommy's been bringing me since I told him once upon a time that they symbolize friendship turning into love.

"Break a leg, Mom."

I give CeCe a kiss on the cheek before walking toward the front door where Jill is waiting. She smiles and brushes a tear from her eye.

"Stop," I warn her. "If you cry, I'll cry."

"Don't you dare," Jack says, coming up behind us both. "I didn't spend an hour on your makeup just so you could ruin it."

I nod and try to blink the tears away, although we might want to hurry and snap a few pictures, because I'm not sure how long I'll be able to hold them back.

"Dad's waiting," CeCe says.

I open the door and step outside where my Romeo is waiting in his wheelchair, wearing his old tux, now more than a few sizes too big. I glance behind me at Jill and CeCe, looking as eager and excited as I feel.

"You're a little overdressed for a barbecue," I say, walking toward him.

"What, this old thing?" Tommy's smile still melts my heart. I don't know what I was thinking saying no to this man for all these years.

"So you know?" I ask.

"Know what?" he teases. "You look beautiful, by the way."

"Thank you."

Tommy laughs and I know what he's thinking—I've finally learned how to accept a compliment. I take his hands in mine and bend down so I can look into those beautiful mismatched eyes. They draw me in and all the words I'd planned to say disappear.

"Yes," Tommy says before I have a chance to gather my thoughts enough to ask the question.

"Not yet." I take a deep breath and speak straight from my heart. "All those years ago, you told me to stay, to stop running away. You said life is going to be tough no matter where I went, and that some things were worth sticking around for. And that's you. You're worth sticking around for, and I want to spend the rest of the time we have together as your wife."

"Yes," Tommy says again.

"Not yet." I laugh through the tears that I've given up trying to stop. "Tommy Whistler, will you marry me?"

"Now?" he asks and I nod. "Then yes. The answer has always been yes."

I lean over to kiss him and hear a round of applause coming from our spectators just inside the open door.

"If I knew this was all it took to convince you, I would have gotten cancer years ago."

"Not today," I plead, standing back up. "We've got a wedding to get to."

"Not so fast," Tommy says. He reaches into the pocket of his jacket and pulls out a ring box. "This is a two-way street, baby."

I smile, feeling for a moment like an ordinary bride on the

happiest day of her life. Tommy opens the box to reveal the exact ring I would have picked out for myself. It sparkles in the sun, almost as much as his tired eyes.

"Alexis Gold, will you do me the honor of making me the happiest dying man in the world by becoming my wife?"

"What took you so long?" I tease.

He laughs and slips the ring on my finger. It fits perfectly, just the way we do. I lean in for another kiss, but out of the corner of my eye, I see a flash of hot pink.

"Becky?"

"Hey, buttercup," she says, as casually as if she's walking into our office, not standing in front of Jill's house in Destin. She snaps a flurry of pictures with her fancy camera before coming through the front gate.

"How?" I ask, speechless again.

"Tommy said you needed a photographer," she says. "And you know I couldn't miss this."

"Thank you." I walk over to give her a hug and hold on tight. I didn't realize just how much I missed her. "I'm so happy you're here."

"Me, too, lovey. Now let's get you married before you change your mind."

"Never." I look from her down to my fiancé. "Let's do this."

Jack takes the cue, joining us out front to wheel Tommy around to the backyard, where Blake and Abigail have been hard at work all afternoon.

Tommy blows me a kiss as they disappear around the corner, and I wonder how it's possible to feel so lucky and unlucky at the same time.

"Ready, Mom?" CeCe stands in the open doorway; she's changed into her maid of honor dress and looks more like a woman than my little girl. The dress is a little too short and a little too tight for my taste, but I'm learning to pick my battles.

"You look beautiful." I kiss her cheek as I walk past her into the house. "And nice job getting your dad involved."

"It wasn't me!"

I follow her stare and look at Jill, standing in the kitchen doorway with a guilty grin on her face. "I'm sorry, I couldn't help it."

"I love you." I give her a hug. "Now let's get me married!"

Becky captures a picture of the moment before introducing herself. "You must be Jill."

"And you're the famous Becky." Jill sticks her hand out, but Becky ignores it, pulling her into a hug. Jill laughs and my heart grows even bigger.

I never imagined I would have a wedding, but I'm grateful for every perfectly imperfect detail. CeCe hands me the bouquet before stepping out the back door behind Becky and Jill.

The backyard has been transformed into a perfect little oasis. The lantern lights are glowing overhead and wooden chairs I recognize from The Broken Crown are set up in a half circle with a little part in the middle for us to walk through. Beyond them, they've even managed to put together a makeshift chuppah by draping a white tablecloth over four wooden poles.

After Jill and Becky have taken their seats, CeCe starts walking down the aisle, slow and steady the way she did at Jack and Blake's wedding. I know I'm supposed to follow her, but I can't make my legs move.

CeCe turns back after she realizes I'm not right behind her. "Mom?"

"I'm okay."

I compose myself and take one step forward, then another. I keep moving, toward Tommy, who is standing tall next to Blake. His oxygen bag is beside him, but his wheelchair is off to the side. My eyes scan the faces, all looking at me. Becky and Jill, Abigail and Beau, Lou and Jack.

Somehow, my legs move me forward, and Blake greets me with a kiss on the cheek.

CeCe takes a seat next to Beau, but it doesn't feel right. "Up here." I nod toward my right. She blushes but doesn't protest.

Once she's beside me, Tommy reaches out and takes both my hands in his.

"We are gathered here today," Blake says, "to witness the union of Tommy and Alexis in holy matrimony."

"It's about damn time," Jack calls out.

Jill shushes him, but the rest of us laugh.

"In holy matrimony," Blake continues, "which is an honorable estate that is not to be entered into unadvisedly or lightly, but reverently and soberly."

He looks at us both and we nod in agreement.

"Tommy, repeat after me. 'I, Thomas Jacob Whistler, take you, Alexis Leah Gold, to be my lawful wedded wife.'"

"I, Thomas Jacob Whistler, take you, Alexis Leah Gold, to be my lawful wedded wife."

"'To have and to hold from this day forward, for better or worse, for richer or poorer, in sickness and in health,'" Blake says.

In sickness, yes. But it's too late for health.

"To have and to hold from this day forward," Tommy says. "For better or worse, for richer or poorer, in sickness"—he pauses to take an ironic breath—"and health."

"'To love, honor, and cherish till . . .'" Blake's voice falls

off at the end of the line we all knew was coming. I should
have written vows for us to say.

But when Tommy repeats Blake's words, he doesn't stop.
He keeps me grounded in this moment like he has in all the
other moments since he came back into my life. I love this
man with every fiber of my being.

"Till death do us part," he says firmly.

"Lexie," Blake says. "Repeat after me."

"I think I've got it," I say. I take a deep breath and recite
the words I never thought I'd be saying. "I, Alexis Leah Gold,
take you, Thomas Jacob Whistler, to be my lawful wedded
husband; to have and to hold from this day forward, for better or worse, for richer or poorer, in sickness and in health.
To love, honor, and cherish until I take my last breath."

I hear a cry that I assume is coming from Becky or Jill, but
I don't take my eyes off of Tommy's to find out.

"Do you have rings?" Blake asks me, momentarily breaking out of character. Someone laughs and I'm grateful for the
brief comic relief. This is all so clearly unrehearsed.

"Jill?" I ask.

She steps forward and hands me the two simple white-
gold bands she helped me pick out along with CeCe's earrings. I give my ring to Tommy.

He repeats the words after Blake, but it feels like it's just
the two of us.

"Lexie, I give you this ring as a symbol of our vows; with
all that I am and all that I have—" Tommy's voice breaks and
this time, I'm the strong one. I rub my thumbs over the back
of his hand and wait until he's ready to go on. "I honor you.
With this ring, I thee wed."

He slips the ring on my finger, where it fits perfectly on

top of the one he gave me just moments ago. Now it's my turn.

"Tommy, I give you this ring as a symbol of our vows; with all that I am and all that I have, I honor you. With this ring, I thee wed."

The ring slides on his finger too easily. His hands are so thin now, just like the rest of him. I went down one ring size for him, but I should have gone down two or three.

"Ladies and gentlemen, by the power granted to me by the World Wide Web, I now pronounce you man and wife," Blake says. "And daughter."

Tommy and I both look back toward CeCe, whose glasses are fogged with tears.

"You may kiss the bride."

As Tommy and I kiss, our small group of witnesses applaud. I pull him into my arms and hug him tight.

"Thank you," he whispers in my ear.

"No, thank you." I pull back and kiss him again. My husband.

"Wait, the glass!" Jill says. I swear she pays more attention to the Jewish stuff than I do.

She hands Blake a wineglass wrapped in a cloth napkin that he places on the ground. I hold Tommy's hand as he lifts his foot and brings it down, shattering the glass into a dozen pieces.

"Mazel tov!" everyone shouts.

I remember learning something about this tradition in one of the few Sunday school classes I attended as a kid. It had to do with reminding the happy couple in this moment of joy that life holds sorrow as well.

That's one reminder I don't need.

Chapter Forty-Eight

CeCe

My parents are slow dancing to "It Had to Be You," which has always been their song. They're just swaying back and forth, nothing fancy like the choreographed dances that go viral, but I think it might be the best first dance I've ever seen.

"Is that him?" Becky whispers, her eyes darting toward Beau.

"She told you?" Just when I was starting to think there might be hope for my mom and me to have a semi-normal relationship, she had to blab her big mouth.

"She didn't tell me anything," Becky says. "But he hasn't taken his eyes off you."

I look toward the other end of the table and sure enough, Beau is staring at me with puppy-dog eyes, which would be a little annoying if it weren't so cute. We've had to slow things down more than a little now that our parents know there's something to be looking out for.

He smiles, and I smile before turning back to Becky. "Yeah, well."

"Good for you, girlfriend."

"My mom freaked when she found out."

"Parents," Becky says. "They just don't get what it's like to be young and in love."

"Tell me about it."

I look at Beau, who is still looking at me, then back at my parents, who seem to only have eyes for each other. I wonder if I'll ever feel that way about someone. If I do, I won't wait until it's almost too late to get married.

I can feel Beau's eyes on me.

Maybe we can share one slow dance without it feeling too weird.

Dancing at my parents' wedding with the guy my mom doesn't want me to date—now, that'll be good to have in my emotional arsenal. Since I started reading the book Monica gave me, I'm trying really hard to absorb every moment. Because the more I live, the more experiences I'll have to borrow from.

The song ends, and everyone claps.

"Ceese," Dad says. I get up and grab his wheelchair, but he stops me. "Not yet, just come here."

Aunt Becky seems to know what's going on, because she stands off to the side with her camera taking a video. My stomach drops and I'm suddenly nervous. I walk closer to him and look up into his eyes, one blue and one brown, which are the only part of him that still looks like him. But then I see his smile and I realize no matter what he looks like, he's still my dad.

"May I have this dance?" he asks.

I hiccup back a sob and nod. A song I recognize starts playing. I think it's called "Isn't She Lovely," but I don't remember who sings it. My dad reaches for my hand and pulls me close. With my face buried in his chest, I breathe in his scent and try to memorize this moment so I can think about it on my wedding day.

It hits me then: that's probably what he had in mind the whole time. That's why Becky is filming this. A tear slips from my eye and it's like my dad knows. He kisses the top of my head as we keep swaying back and forth.

When the song is over, he kisses my cheek and thanks me. I move my lips to thank him, too, but no words come out.

ONCE I'VE COLLECTED myself and everyone is sitting back around the table, I raise my glass and clink my fork against it like people do in the movies. Everyone stops talking and looks at me.

"Most kids don't get to be at their parents' wedding, much less be their mom's maid of honor," I say. "But since I'm here, I want to say a few words."

I push my glasses up and take the folded piece of paper out from under my plate, where I tucked it earlier. "My whole life, I wondered why my parents weren't married. It wasn't normal. But then I realized, what they have isn't normal. It's better than that." My voice starts to crack, but I don't stop. "Thank you for loving each other and for loving me and for finally making our family official. To the bride and groom, my mom and dad."

I lift my glass toward them and take a sip of the champagne they let us all have to celebrate.

"Time for the cake!" Aunt Jill says.

Aunt Jill sets the cake down in front of my parents and their eyes get all wide like they can't believe it. I can't blame them—it is pretty amazing. Lou helped me a lot, obviously, but she let me decide what it should look like. Since there weren't that many people going to be here, we used a ten-inch cake as the base. There's an eight-inch cake on top of that, and a four-inch one at the very top.

Lou told me it's tradition for brides and grooms to freeze the top tier so they can eat it again on their one-year anniversary. I know enough to know that won't be happening, but we might save it anyway. In case of a miracle or something.

There's a miniature bride and groom on top of the cake— Lou had a whole collection of them, like a toy box filled with Barbie dolls, in all different styles. I picked a Caucasian bride with brown hair for Mom, and a bald Caucasian guy for Dad.

We decided to keep the icing simple, and I just piped around the edges with a round tip. We used real flowers, yellow-and-red roses to match Mom's bouquet. Lou helped me strategically place three of them on the bottom tier and two on the middle tier to add a little extra *oomph*.

She could have done something fancier, but I wanted to stick with a design I knew I could do an okay job with. It wouldn't have been the same if Lou had done it, and I wanted it to look as close to perfect as possible.

I catch Mom's eye just as she and Dad bring the knife down to make a cut on the first tier. She mouths *thank you,* and I smile.

"Feed your bride," Jack says. "It's tradition."

Dad shoots him a playful look, and for a second, this all feels completely normal. Mom is shaking her head no, but

Dad breaks a piece off and feeds it to her. She looks embarrassed, but I can tell she's loving it.

Dad can tell, too. He laughs, a big, deep laugh that I'm worried will turn into a coughing fit, but luckily it doesn't.

Mom takes advantage of his open mouth and shoves a bite inside. She misses a little, on purpose, I think, and it looks like he has an icing goatee.

"Cecelia," Dad says. "Come here."

I walk over and bend down to his level, expecting a compliment about the cake and maybe a kiss on the cheek. But instead, he smashes a piece of the cake in my face before I even have a chance to open my mouth.

"Hey!" I step back, wiping icing from my lips.

"It's delicious," he says and for one brief moment, all is right with the world.

Chapter Forty-Nine

Alexis

Slide over," I whisper, crawling into the hospital bed that's turned our living room into a dying room.

"What are you doing?" Tommy asks through a yawn.

"It's lonely upstairs."

Tommy lifts his arm and I curl into his side, my head on his chest, the way we've lain for thousands of nights together. My head rises and falls along with his chest, and I try to block out the hollow rattle. His breaths are getting harder and harder to take.

I can't.

I prop my arm up and lean my head against my hand so I can look down at him. My husband.

In the week since the wedding, not much has changed. I don't know what I expected to be different—we have a daughter, a house, a life together. We've practically been married for the last fifteen years. We would have been, if I hadn't been so damn stubborn.

Tommy reaches up and brushes his hand over my cheek. "What are you looking at?"

"My husband." The word feels strange on my lips, but I like it.

"My wife," Tommy says.

"I would hate us if we weren't us," I say. "So cheesy."

"Mmm, cheese."

I laugh. "You want some?"

"Nah, you'd have to get out of bed. And I like having you here with me."

"It'll just take a minute." I pull the blanket back and climb out of the hospital bed that isn't meant for two.

Tiptoeing into the kitchen, I quietly open the fridge. It feels like we're sneaking around, although there's nothing wrong with eating cheese in bed with my husband. *My husband*. I'm too old to swoon, but I can't help myself.

I slide the cheese drawer open and consider the options, grabbing two sticks of string cheese before going back to my husband.

Turning the corner into the living room, I wave the cheese sticks around like they're the glow sticks people dance with at those raves Becky goes to.

"Tommy?" I whisper when he doesn't react. "Babe?" I hold my breath and lean closer until I see his chest rise ever so slightly. He's just asleep. *Thank god.*

I put the string cheese on the coffee table and climb back in bed next to him. I yawn and reluctantly close my eyes.

Sometime later, I feel his hand on my shoulder, his breath in my ear. "I missed the cheese."

"Hmm?" I mumble, not fully awake.

"The cheese. I'm sorry."

I open my eyes and turn to face him. It's not quite morning yet; the room is still dark. "It's still here if you want it." He shakes his head and I reach out to stroke his cheek, the stubble rough against my fingers. "Can I get you something else?"

"All of the papers, everything you'll need is in the top left drawer of my office at home. For the house, insurance, my will."

"We don't have to talk about this now."

"I think we do."

My breath catches in my throat. "I'm not ready."

"What was the quote Gran had embroidered on that pillow?" he asks before taking a labored breath. "'You're braver than you think, stronger than you seem'?"

I smile at his mention of my grandmother. I'm not sure how much of the heaven story I believe, but I hope she'll be there to greet him, wherever he's going.

But he's wrong, I'm not strong. I lean down and kiss his lips. "You're the strong one." I kiss him again. "You're the brave one, the kind one." Another kiss. "You're the calm one, and the patient one."

He lifts his hand, bringing his finger to my lips, stopping me. "I'm also the selfish and the stubborn one," he says. "But I guess love filters the way you see people."

"I'm pretty sure everyone who knows you would agree with me," I tell him. "Then again, to know you is to love you."

"Oh, stop," Tommy says with a smile.

"I believe you told me once that the proper response to a compliment is to say thank you."

"You're welcome." He kisses my forehead and I try to memorize the way it feels, his lips on my skin, his hand on my hip.

"I don't know what I'm going to do without you," I whisper. "It's not fair that I have to go on without you."

"You're right," Tommy says. The softness is gone from his voice and it chills me to the core. "None of this is fair—it's not fair that I won't be able to grow old and gray with you. That I'm going to miss seeing the amazing woman CeCe's on her way to becoming. It's not fair that I won't be here to play with our grandchildren and laugh about how much they remind us of CeCe at their age. None of it's fair."

The tears I've been holding back come crashing down in fits and waves. I give up trying to control them and let my body shake with grief. Tommy pulls me closer, running his hands over my hair, trying to comfort me when I should be comforting him. "Shhh," he says as he rocks me back and forth like a baby. "Shhh, I'm sorry, I'm sorry."

He holds me until my tears run dry and my head hurts as much as my heart does. "I'm sorry," I tell him this time. I wipe snot away from my nose, hoping this isn't the last picture he'll have of me in his mind. "I told you I was the selfish one."

Tommy brushes the tears from my cheeks. "You're the only one. My only one." He kisses my eyes, then both sides of my face before his lips find mine. His kisses are hungry in a way they were when we were young and in love and thought we had forever.

I still want forever.

Chapter Fifty

Alexis

Where're we going?" Tommy asks as Beau helps him into the passenger seat.

"Patience, Dad," CeCe says. She slides over to make room for Beau, who's riding with us. Jill and Abigail are meeting us there since Jill had to stop by the café first.

"Is it something from my list?" he asks, even though he still hasn't let us see what's on it.

"Maybe," I tease.

"We're getting tattoos?" Tommy claps his hands like a little boy who can't wait to open his birthday presents. "I knew it!"

"Keep dreaming, my love." I lean over to give him a kiss before starting the car.

I half expect Tommy to keep making guesses as I drive down 98, but he just stares out the window as we pass through the town where he grew up, where we fell in love and made so many memories with our family.

There's the Publix where we first ran into each other as adults—I was there to buy aloe after falling asleep in the sun, and he was buying flowers to take on a first date. The Donut Hole, where we went for breakfast and ended up talking straight through to lunch. McGuire's, the Irish pub that has a dollar bill up on the wall with our two names on it, and another we added years later with CeCe's name, too.

When I pull into the parking lot of Tailfins, Tommy looks confused. "Are we going to brunch?"

I shake my head. "Not exactly."

"You're going to love it, Dad," CeCe says, getting out of the car. She pops the trunk and takes Tommy's wheelchair out, unfolding it while Beau helps Tommy out of the car.

Jill and Abigail are already there, standing at the edge of the parking lot, with a giant beach bag and a cooler big enough to fit CeCe inside of it.

"Hey, there, handsome," Jill calls.

Tommy smiles and reaches for my hand. Beau pushes the chair as I walk beside him, down the long ramp toward the harbor.

"Did you buy me a boat?" Tommy asks as we get closer. "For a Viking burial at sea?"

I glance behind me, grateful CeCe was out of earshot for the last part, which I choose to ignore. "Just for the day."

"Awesome," he says. "Best day ever."

I give him a kiss and head over to the wooden shed to check in, hoping he's right and that's exactly what it will be.

After filling out all the paperwork, the dockhands help us get everything onto the boat and point out all the safety instructions for Beau, who was nominated to be captain. Jill busies herself getting the drinks and snacks ready, and

I help Tommy get settled into a seat near the back of the pontoon boat.

Beau expertly backs out of the dock and as soon as we're on the open water, a calm settles over Tommy. He closes his eyes and lifts his head to the wind. "This is the life," he says, taking my hand in his. "Where are we heading? Going for pizza at Helen Back?"

"It's not open anymore," Jill says as she hands Tommy one of her famous Bloody Marys. "Tax problems or something."

"But don't worry," Beau says. "We've got something fun planned."

"It's already perfect," Tommy says.

Beau smiles and pushes the throttle, making the boat go faster. I reach for Tommy to make sure he's okay, but he looks better than he's looked in weeks, smiling into the wind, letting the spray of saltwater splash onto him.

"Faster, Beau Bo," Tommy calls.

Beau obliges and pushes the throttle forward even more.

"Faster!" Tommy says again.

Beau takes it up another notch and Tommy looks back at me, smiling as if he doesn't have a care in the world. As if his world, our world, isn't ending.

As Crab Island comes into view, Beau pulls back on the speed until we're idling in the no-wake zone. It's been years since we've been out to the "Island," where boats anchor off one another and people swim and drink, hang out, listen to music, and buy everything from boiled peanuts to hot dogs and margaritas from the vendor boats that put around.

Tommy rests a hand on my leg, and I wonder if he's thinking about what I am—one of our first dates when we came out to Crab Island on his friend Frank's boat.

It was the day after our first night together, and as much as we'd wanted to stay in bed making up for lost time, Tommy had already accepted the invitation. It ended up being an amazing day, lying out in the sun, falling off those silly pad-dleboards, and hurrying back to his apartment as soon as the boat docked again. I'd been so nervous that his friends would compare me to Monica, but the only thing Frank's wife said was that she could tell how happy I made Tommy. How happy we made each other.

"Thank you, guys," Tommy says. He lifts his glass and takes a sip. "This is just what the doctor ordered."

"What up, Beau!"

I look over the edge of the boat and see a kid I don't rec-ognize gliding by on a Jet Ski.

Beau waves and the guy keeps going, probably on the prowl for a young girl who's willing to get on the back of his Jet Ski.

"Who's that?" Tommy asks.

"Parker," Beau says. "A kid in my class."

"Hey, Parker!" Tommy calls out, his voice hoarse but loud.

At the sound of his name, Parker circles back until he's at the side of our boat. "'Sup?"

"Wha'sup," Tommy says, trying to sound cool but failing miserably, "is that I haven't been on one of those rides in more than a decade. Mind if I just sit on it, for a picture?"

Parker looks at Beau, not sure what to make of the situation.

"Do you mind, dude?" Beau asks.

Parker shrugs and pulls around to the back of the boat while Beau helps Tommy up so he can take Parker's place on the Jet Ski.

"How do I look?" Tommy asks.

"Like you belong on the water," I tell him. "Abigail, grab your camera."

Abigail obliges, smiling shyly at Parker before snapping a picture of Tommy. He poses for one, smiling, then takes off like a bat out of hell.

"Hey!" Parker yells.

"He'll be back," I tell him, watching Tommy fly. He drives the Jet Ski to the left, disappearing from view, then he drives to the right, disappearing again. I silence the nagging thought of what this sudden surge of energy likely means and instead try to think of it as a precious gift. He's too far away for me to see his face, but I know Tommy's never looked happier.

Jill walks up beside me and throws her arm around my shoulder. "Are you mad?" she asks.

"At Tommy?"

She nods.

"Not a chance," I tell her. "I don't want to waste a minute we have together being upset, and look at him." We both look up to see Tommy getting smaller in the distance before he whips back around.

"Babe!" Tommy calls as he gets closer. "That was incredible, I got it up to seventy-five."

Parker looks impressed but doesn't move to get up from his seat next to Abigail.

"Mind if I take my bride for a ride?" Tommy asks.

Parker looks at Abigail and then back at Tommy, shrugging in agreement.

"I want a turn, too," CeCe says.

"You can go first," I tell CeCe, who eagerly climbs over the back gate, hopping onto the Jet Ski like a natural, even though she's never been on one before.

"Hold on tight," I call out as the two halves of my heart ride away, creating what I have a feeling is going to be their last truly happy memory together.

TOMMY FELL ASLEEP in the car on the ride home and didn't even wake up when Beau carried him inside. I was a little worried that he hadn't woken up, but Dolly said he's okay, just worn out.

Still, I keep checking in on him, pacing between the living room and the kitchen, where CeCe is biting her lip in concentration as she stirs the batter for her dad's favorite cheesecake brownies.

I open the refrigerator and stare inside at all the containers full of everything CeCe has been making, all of Tommy's favorites. She knows as well as I do that his appetite is practically nonexistent these days, but I know as well as she does that it's better to try than to give up.

We've both been trying to stay positive for each other, but I've heard her crying at night. It's an impossible balance I'm trying to strike, giving her the space she needs while reminding her she isn't alone.

Things have been good since the wedding, and today out on the water, it was just about as perfect as it's been this summer. I'm cautiously optimistic, aware that one wrong move, one wrong look, one wrong word could bring all the anger she's been holding inside raging to the surface.

Neither of us has said the words out loud, but we both know the end is near.

We should be talking about it. No one knows what we're

going through as much as we both do, but of course she's not going to voluntarily open up to me. It's my job to make the first move. I'm the parent.

"What are you doing?" CeCe asks, a hint of annoyance in her voice. "You're going to let all the cold air out."

I close the refrigerator door without taking anything out since the only thing I really want is sitting at the kitchen table. "How are you doing?" I ask, taking a seat across from her.

She raises an eyebrow, clearly suspicious. "Okay?"

"That's not what I meant." I can feel myself getting flustered. "I mean, how are you, really?"

"Fine?"

"Did you have fun today?" I ask.

She nods, still stirring. She looks back up at me looking at her and sighs. "Why don't you just say what you really want to ask me?"

"I . . . I . . ." My words are gone. CeCe rolls her eyes and goes back to stirring. "I really did just want to know how you're doing, with all of this."

"All of what?"

She's going to make me say the words out loud. I look down at the table and steady myself before bringing my eyes up to meet hers. "Your dad, he thought it would be a good idea if we talked."

"We talk every day."

"Really talked, about what's going on."

CeCe laughs, but it sounds like the laugh of a stranger, not my daughter.

"What's so funny?"

"None of it." She stops stirring and puts the spoon down. "All of it."

"Exactly." I sigh, knowing she gets it. I wish she knew that I did, too.

CeCe looks down at the batter she's probably overstirred before looking back at me. "Do you want to talk?"

"I'm not very good at it," I admit, being more honest with her than I probably should be.

"Tell me about it."

"Why don't you? Tell me about it."

"What?"

"Everything, what you're thinking about."

"Penny for your thoughts," she says, dipping the spoon back into the bowl. She swipes her fingers across it, bringing a taste of the chocolate batter to her lips. "That's what Dad says."

She offers the chocolate-covered spoon to me and I follow her lead, twirling my finger around in my mouth as I work up the courage to repeat the phrase back to her.

"Penny for your thoughts?" I say, my voice wavering.

"You know you can't replace him," she says. Her words are honest, not mean.

"No one ever will." I reach across the table and take her hand. Surprisingly, she lets me hold it. "But I can be here for you, with you. If you want to talk, or not talk."

"Not talking is better."

I nod, happy that I was at least able to lay the groundwork for a future conversation. When she's ready to talk, I'll be here to listen.

My chair makes an unfortunate screeching sound against the floor as I push back from the table. CeCe looks at me and I hesitate before standing.

"Will you grab the butter?" she asks. I walk over to the refrigerator door again, opening it with purpose this time.

My eyes go straight for the tub of light margarine I always use, but I know she wants the real thing. "And the baking dish on the counter?"

Handing her both the butter and the dish, I follow her eyes to the empty chair I'd just been sitting in. She looks back up at me and gives me the smallest of smiles, which I take as an invitation to sit together and not talk.

Chapter Fifty-One

CeCe

I can hear Beau's frantic footsteps going back and forth on the porch outside The Broken Crown. He's looking for me like I knew he would. After that performance, how could he not?

The way I looked down at my phone, then stopped midstep—frozen in place before running out the door. It was nothing short of brilliant. Even Abigail looked worried.

"CeCe?" he calls.

His footsteps are getting closer. He'll find me soon, standing in the corner where the porch wraps around toward the back of the café. I pull my hands into tight fists and try to make my stare look vacant to justify my reactions, the way Stella Adler explains in chapter 11.

That's how he finds me, standing like a statue, staring blankly toward the water.

"CeCe?" He sounds really worried; maybe I'm even better at this than I thought. "Ceese?"

I stay in character, resisting the urge to respond. "Is it your dad? Is he okay?"

Of course he's not okay. He's dying. But that's not what this is about.

"Should I get my mom?"

Crap. If Aunt Jill makes me tell her what I'm doing, if she finds out I've been spending time down on the set with Monica, she'll tell my mom. Mom will make me stop, even though working on my acting is the only thing that helps me feel normal these days. She'll make it all about Monica even though it's really about me. It's not worth it.

"End scene," I say, turning toward Beau, my face back to normal.

"Are you okay?"

"Obviously." I push my glasses back up my nose. They'd been slipping for the last minute, but I didn't want to break character. "You really thought I was upset?"

"You were," Beau insists. "The way you ran out, I thought . . ."

"I was acting," I explain.

"Acting?"

"I'm totally fine. Well, I mean, my life still epically sucks, but it sucks a little less if you really thought I was upset."

"So you're okay?" Beau asks again.

I smile and nudge his shoulder with mine, a little proud of myself. I'm about to ask if there was one certain thing that really made him believe my act when he turns and walks back toward the front of the café. Not exactly the review I was hoping for.

"What's the matter?" I lower down next to him on the bench, where he's sitting with his head in his hands.

"I thought something was wrong."

"But everything's fine, so it's all good."

He sits back up and looks at me; his eyes are shining but I can't tell if it's because he's sad or angry. "You don't get it," he says.

"Then tell me."

"I was worried. I thought—" His eyes meet mine for a second, but he quickly looks back down at his fisted hands, sitting in his lap. "I thought he died, okay?"

Beau stands, and so do I. "Not everything is about my dad, you know."

Beau nods, but I can tell he's still mad.

"I'm sorry you were worried, but if I'm going to be a famous actress, I've got to practice."

"Just not on me anymore."

"Fine," I agree reluctantly before sitting back down.

"What are you practicing for anyway?" Beau asks, sitting next to me. "You're not in a play or anything."

"I'm just honing my craft. I'm learning so much from the book Monica gave me, but you don't learn from reading. You learn from doing. Monica says—"

"Monica, Monica, Monica." He says her name like it's an ugly word.

"What's that supposed to mean?"

"Nothing, it's just, you talk about her a lot."

"Sorry, but I'm not going to apologize for being excited that a famous actress decided to take me under her wing."

"She's not that famous," Beau says. "And my mom says she did some pretty bad things to your dad."

My stomach flutters. I hate the idea of him knowing something about my dad that I don't. "Nothing can be more terrible than what's happening to him now," I say, trying not to think about how bad things have gotten. He's almost always sleeping now. Even when he's awake, he looks like he can barely keep his eyes open and the oxygen tubes are in his nose 24/7.

"I thought you didn't want to talk about that?"

"I don't." We're both quiet and I can hear Aunt Jill talking to a customer on the other side of the open window. "None of this would be happening if Monica was my mom."

"Then you wouldn't be you."

"Of course I would."

"How? You look exactly like your mom."

"Then maybe I'd look exactly like Monica. I'd be beautiful."

"You already are."

The compliment rolls off my shoulder. He has to say I'm pretty.

I twirl my hair around my finger. "If my hair was like hers, it would be silky smooth and straight instead of frizzy and wavy. And it would be blacker than midnight—she doesn't dye it, I asked."

"You could dye yours," he says.

Interesting. I hadn't thought about that. "You think I should?"

"No." He folds his arms across his chest and leans back on the bench.

"Then why'd you say it?"

"I don't know why I say half the things I say. But your mom would freak."

"Even better," I say, even though I'm not really mad at her anymore. I stand up for good this time and start walking toward the drugstore around the corner on Old 98.

Beau doesn't move, but I know his only other option is hanging out at the café. And if he does that, Aunt Jill will rope him into helping Lou wash the dishes or clean out the pantry.

"Wait," Beau says, catching up to me like I knew he would.

Chapter Fifty-Two

Alexis

Your daughter." I slide the living room door closed so CeCe can't see how angry she made me.

"What'd she do?" Tommy asks, opening his eyes. I don't think I woke him, but it's getting harder to tell lately if he's sleeping or just resting his eyes. I shake my head and bite my bottom lip, trying to compose myself. I'm too mad to form a complete sentence. "What?"

Dolly stands up from the couch, where I hadn't noticed she was sitting, filling out a chart. She lets herself out without saying a word, sliding the door closed behind her. I'm too upset to be embarrassed. I take her place on the couch and look up at Tommy, sitting propped up in that stupid hospital bed. "She *dyed* her *hair.*" I spit the words out like venom.

"Is that all?" Tommy closes his eyes again.

My right leg is bouncing with the adrenaline pulsing inside me. I can't sit still, so I stand and start walking back and forth at the foot of his bed. Of course he doesn't understand.

"Isn't that what teenage girls do?" Tommy asks in his shrink voice. It's been a while since I've heard that tone and I can't say I've missed being on the receiving end of it. "She's just experimenting and trying to figure out who she wants to be."

"Oh, she knows who she wants to be. That's the problem."

As if on cue, there's a soft knock at the door. "Daddy?"

"Come on in, baby."

The door slides open and CeCe walks in with my face and Monica's jet-black hair.

"Wow," Tommy says, looking at me then back at CeCe.

I give him the biggest *I told you so* look I can muster and sit back down on the couch facing him. I can't look at her right now.

"What do you think?" she says, her voice timid and small.

"It's interesting," Tommy says. "Come closer."

CeCe hesitates at the door. She hasn't been in here much since we set up the hospital bed. I can't blame her for wanting to keep her distance, but since Tommy is hardly getting out of bed these days, she doesn't have much choice.

She walks to the side of the bed, perching herself on the edge, facing her dad.

"Why'd you do that?" he asks in a way that sounds curious and not annoyed or angry like it did when I said almost the exact same thing a few minutes ago.

"You don't like it?"

Tommy brings his hand up and runs his fingers through her new, dark hair. "It's not that I don't like it," he says. "You just don't look like you anymore."

"You mean I don't look like her." She tilts her head in my direction.

"You don't look like you. Sweet girl, you and your mom have a lot in common, but you are very one of a kind."

CeCe nods, quiet for a moment. "I was thinking about getting contacts."

My jaw drops. We'd talked about contacts when she turned ten, but she was grossed out by the idea of putting her finger in her eyes. One guess who changed her mind about that.

"That would be nice," Tommy tells her.

"The only thing," she says. "I just . . ."

She bows her head and a tear falls onto the crisp white sheets and my anger changes its target. I can't be mad at my daughter. But I can definitely be mad at Monica for existing, and at myself for not being the bigger person.

"I just," CeCe says, trying again. "I just want you to know, so that you'll still be able to recognize me. When you . . . after you . . . if you can—" The rest of her words get lost in a sea of tears.

Tommy opens his arms and CeCe falls into them. "Shhh," he whispers, smoothing her hair. "Nothing you ever do will keep me from recognizing you. I know your heart, my beautiful girl. And you can't change that."

Her shoulders are shaking and the sobs coming from my little girl are more than I can bear. I excuse myself to give them time alone, and so neither of them will see me cry.

The tears come faster than I can stop them. I clasp my hand over my mouth, rushing toward the kitchen so they don't hear the wailing that doesn't sound like it's coming from me. I turn the faucet on, hoping the water can drown out the sound of my heart breaking into a million microscopic pieces.

I splash my face, cold water mixing with my tears, until

eventually, there's nothing left. I don't have to see my face to know it's red and splotchy.

The almost empty pitcher of Arnold Palmers is still sitting where I left it on the counter when CeCe walked in the front door an hour ago, looking like a familiar stranger. I pour what's left into a glass and drink it like a shot, which I could honestly use right now. Alcohol makes you numb, it helps you forget. It would be good to forget.

I stare at the empty pitcher, wishing it were full so I could make myself a glass and add a little vodka to it. Instead of standing there, thirsty and helpless, I open the pantry door and get the powdered lemonade and iced tea mixes that Gran always used.

I'm not patient enough to wait for the flavors to blend together like CeCe always insists, so I fill a glass with ice and pour my old-fashioned Arnold Palmer mixture over it and take a big sip.

The taste, one that's always been synonymous with my childhood, is artificial and sweet. CeCe is right: fresh ingredients are so much better.

I take one more sip before emptying the glass and pour the pitcher down the drain.

"Mom?"

I turn to see CeCe standing in the door. She looks so small and fragile with her arms wrapped around herself. As tough as she acts and as mature as she tries to be, it's easy to forget she's still a little girl. "Hey, sweetie."

"Dad wants you."

He may want me, but she needs me. I take the few steps toward her and wrap my arms around her. She doesn't hug me back, but that doesn't stop me from hugging her even harder.

"Dad wants you," she says again.

I give her one more squeeze before letting her go, hoping she can feel how sorry I am. For everything.

TOMMY'S EYES ARE closed when I walk back in the room. I sit down on the couch, watching him breathe. Every breath sounds like a struggle and my heart is so torn. As much as I want him to hold on and stay with me, I don't want him to hurt anymore.

A sob escapes my mouth and Tommy's eyes fly open. He smiles and I fall in love with him all over again.

"Did you have a good talk?" I ask.

"We did," he says. "And the color will wash out, it's not permanent."

"It's not just about the color," I say, even though none of it matters anymore.

"Of course it's not," Tommy says. "Come lie with me."

I crawl on the bed and curl into his side, resting my head on his shoulder. He brushes his fingers through my hair the way he knows I love.

"What'd she say?" I ask.

"That's between us. Father-daughter confidentiality."

I pull back so I can look him in the eye. "That's not a thing."

"Shhh." I concede and put my head back down so he can keep playing with my hair. "We talked about the things I love about her, the things that make her who she is. We talked about my hopes and dreams for her future."

"Like when she was little," I say. "What do you want her to be when she grows up?"

"Happy."

I nod and close my eyes. As long as she's happy, nothing else matters. Tommy bends his head down toward mine and whispers in my ear, "Thank you for making me so happy."

I smile even though those might be the saddest happy words I've ever heard.

Chapter Fifty-Three

Alexis

The second first time I saw you, you were carrying a bouquet of flowers for somebody else," I tell Tommy. His eyes are closed and his breathing is labored, but I know he can hear me. I've been sitting on his bed, talking to him since the sun came up this morning, and I don't plan on stopping even now that it's starting to set. There's a pink cast to the room, and I wish he could open his eyes to appreciate it, but they've been closed since early yesterday.

I keep talking and rubbing circles with my thumb on the back of his hand in time with his breaths, because if I stop, I'm terrified he will, too.

"I was at Publix looking for aloe and you made some comment about tourists and sunscreen. I turned around, ready to defend my local status, but you caught me off guard. I recognized your eyes before I knew they belonged to you."

I laugh at the memory, as clear as if it happened just yesterday. "I was so jealous of whatever lucky woman was going to be getting those daisies."

I hear a noise behind me, and I turn, not letting go of Tommy's hand. It's CeCe, standing as close to the room as she can get without actually coming inside. She looks terrified, with her toes at the edge of the door, hanging on to the wall as if she's standing on unstable ground at the edge of a cliff.

"It's okay," I tell her. "I'm just talking to Dad; want to come sit with us?"

CeCe bites her lip and shakes her head no.

I nod because I understand and don't want to push her. Dolly told me it is best to let CeCe process everything in her own way, in her own time.

"CeCe's here," I tell Tommy, looking back over my shoulder. "She loves you so much."

Tommy inhales sharply and exhales a strange, grumbling noise. "It's okay," I repeat, both to him and to CeCe, but when I look back behind me, she's gone.

"I'm sorry we didn't get a chance to finish everything on your list," I tell Tommy. "I know I gave you a hard time about it, but you knew what you were doing, didn't you? You always do."

I bow my head and close my eyes, trying to think of the stories I have left to tell him. We've lived a lot of good ones, but there are supposed to be more. In the past few days, I've covered them all, some more than once.

"How we doing?" I hear Dolly softly ask.

"He's doing okay," I say without lifting my head.

"I'm talking about you, dear."

I sigh, because the words for how I'm feeling don't exist. Seeing him like this is the hardest thing I've ever done. Every

343

breath he takes is a struggle; the very thing keeping him alive is causing him pain. With his paper-thin skin, hollow cheeks, and suddenly deep-set eyes, he doesn't look like himself. It hurts seeing him like this, but it will hurt even more having to say goodbye. I'm not ready.

I hiccup back a sob and Dolly lays a comforting hand on my shoulder.

"We could use some air in here," she says. "I know Tommy likes the breeze."

As Dolly opens the window, I hear the familiar creaking of the porch swing swaying back and forth on the other side of the wall. CeCe is out there, strumming Tommy's old guitar.

The breeze carries her soft voice to us. *"Saying I love you,"* she sings, her voice wavering.

A tear slides down my cheek and I don't bother wiping it away. I look down at Tommy and let go of his hand just long enough to lie down beside him. I wrap an arm around his chest and bury my face in his side. I try to keep my eyes open because I don't want to miss even a second. But my eyelids are so heavy. I'll just close them for a minute.

"Lexie, Lex."

My eyes fly open; it's dark and I have no idea what time it is.

"Lex," I hear again.

I prop myself up on an arm and look down at Tommy, whose eyes are open. He looks alert and lucid, focused clearly on me for the first time in days.

"Hey, you," I whisper back.

His lips look so dry and chapped, they can't not hurt. I reach for the side table and take an ice cube from the bucket Dolly's made sure has been full all week. The ice is cold on my fingers, but Tommy smiles when I bring it to his lips.

"Thank you," he mumbles.

"Want another?" I ask, my hand already reaching toward the bucket.

"Not for that," he says. "For everything. For marrying me, and making me a dad."

"Not in that order," I tease. My eyes well with tears. I've missed this—our banter and the sound of his voice. He's still here, but I already miss him so much it's hard to breathe.

"Will you tell them for me?" Tommy asks.

"Who?" I whisper.

"We should have danced more," he says.

I nod, grateful that Dolly warned me it might get like this. I remember her advice: just let him talk, don't try to make sense of it all. It might not make sense, and that's okay.

"You made me happy," he says.

My heart swells. "Not as happy as you've made me."

"Monica's not so bad, you know," he says.

I grimace at the mention of her name. She doesn't belong here, not now.

"We don't have to talk about her."

"The baby," he says so quietly I'm not sure if he's talking to me or himself.

"Shhh."

"No," he says with more force than before. "I want to tell you."

"I know," I tell him, kissing his forehead. "You don't have to tell me again."

"Our baby. CeCe."

I take a deep breath, relieved. His lips still look dry, so I bring another ice cube to his lips. Once it's melted, he looks up at me, locking his eyes with mine.

"I know you think I should hate her for hurting me." He pauses to take a rough, shallow breath. "I'd go through it all again because it brought me to you."

He looks at me intently to make sure I'm hearing him, and I am. I'm focused on every word in case this conversation is our last. I don't want it to be our last.

"I'd go through it all again because it brought me to you." Tommy pauses for another moment to catch his breath. "I wouldn't trade our life for anything in the world."

"I know," I tell him. "I know."

"Of the two of us, me and Monica, I'm the one who won." He inhales sharply and I worry this is too much for him, but he presses on. "Her life hasn't been easy, and it's not as perfect as it looks from the outside."

"Shhh," I say, partly because I don't want him to wear himself out, and I don't want him to waste any more energy on that woman.

"I forgave her a long time ago."

"We both know you're a better person than I am," I tell him.

"Let me finish."

I nod and take Tommy's hand in mine, waiting until he's ready to continue. "There's been enough sadness. If she can help CeCe, promise me you won't hold the grudge for me. It was mine, and I let it go."

I nod, relieved that it's CeCe, not Monica, who was so important he woke me to talk about. Still, for him, I'll try not to hate her so much. If he could forgive her, at least I can try.

"I don't know what I did to deserve you, Tommy Whistler, but I'm so glad you married me."

"You know," Tommy says, his voice soft and low, "I used to think you didn't want to marry me so it would be easier to leave if you needed to run."

"Never away from you."

He smiles through the pain of his ragged breaths. "Stay with me tonight?"

"Always," I promise.

Tommy smiles and as his face relaxes, his breathing does, too. He closes his eyes and I kiss them both before giving the love of my life a kiss good night.

Chapter Fifty-Four

CeCe

It happened.

Mom woke me up at 5:23 this morning to tell me. She didn't have to say the words; I knew as soon as I heard the handle on my door turn.

Even though I knew it was coming, it still caught me by surprise.

I already miss him so much it hurts. It's like there's a big dad-shaped hole in my heart and I don't think it will ever be whole again.

Chapter Fifty-Five

Alexis

My closet has so much black in it, but nothing seems quite right for today.

I pull out a short black dress that has lace on the top and an A-line skirt that makes a perfect halo around me when I spin around—too much for a funeral. People would say I was being disrespectful.

I toss the party dress on the bed and pull another black dress out of the closet. This one is long and simple, one of my favorites. With flats or sandals, it's perfect for a day of running errands. With wedges and a statement necklace, it can do the trick for a night out. I wear it all the time.

As perfect as it would be for today, I toss it on the bed with the others. Because I know whatever dress I choose, I'll never be able to wear it again. It will always be the dress I wore to my husband's funeral.

Three more black dresses. One at a time, I hold them up in front of the mirror. The first one is too short, the second is way too fancy, and the third, there's just something about it that doesn't feel right. They all end up in the pile on my bed.

There's a knock at my door. "Lex? You almost ready?"

"Come in," I say, even though I'm standing there in a black bra and underwear. Jill opens the door, slipping inside and closing it behind her after she sees my state of undress. "I don't have anything to wear."

She looks over at the dresses thrown across my bed and her eyes go straight toward the one with lace. She lifts it up. "Tommy loved how you looked in this one."

I smile and nod.

"You should wear it."

"It's too much. People will think—"

"Today isn't for other people. It's for Tommy. For you and for CeCe. Wear the dress."

I nod and wipe a tear from my eye. I take the dress from Jill's outstretched hands and hold her stare, hoping she can feel the gratitude I haven't been able to find the words to express. Without her, none of this would have come together.

Since I'm Jew-ish and Tommy was raised Christian-ish, religion never really played an important part in our lives. So it was hard to figure out how much of a role it should play in his death.

Having a ceremony in a church felt hypocritical. The funeral home was an option, but the room they showed me was ugly and cold.

It was Jill's idea to ask a retired minister who's a regular at the café to help us out. Once they started talking, plans fell into place to have a small ceremony on the beach. And since Tommy wanted some of his ashes spread there, it made sense.

"We're going to be late, Mom," CeCe says, opening the

door without knocking. She's wearing a red dress that's not exactly funeral-appropriate, although mine isn't either. I don't say anything, but I can't stop the look of surprise on my face.

"It's Dad's favorite color," she says, defending her choice.

"You look beautiful," I tell her. "Zip me up?"

I turn and she closes the distance between us. She slides the zipper up and hooks the clasp at the top.

"I just got off the phone with Grandma and Grandpa," she says. "They feel bad they aren't here."

I nod, pretending to seem disappointed that my parents were halfway around the world on a cruise of the Greek Islands when it happened. They offered to catch a flight from Crete, but I told them it was silly. Tommy would want them to enjoy themselves, and even if their flight got them here in time, they'd be so jet-lagged they wouldn't really be here anyway.

Secretly, I was a little relieved not to have a reminder that they're the ones who get to grow old together when they don't even really like each other all that much.

"You ready?" Jill asks, glancing down at her watch.

"As I'll ever be." I take her outstretched hand and follow her out the door, grabbing CeCe's hand with my free one: a chain of love and support that I can feel coursing through me.

I climb into the front passenger seat of Jill's car and CeCe gets into the back, where Abigail and Beau are waiting. We drive the few blocks to Tommy's favorite spot on the beach and walk down to where a modest crowd is waiting.

I'm surprised but happy to see that Becky is there. So are Jack and Blake. Even Brit and a few other people we know from Camille's. Lou is there; she makes eye contact for a second before looking away. I see Dolly and Sandra from hospice, which means so much. I know attending funerals isn't in their job description. There are a few other faces I recognize but don't have the energy to place.

I do a double take when my eyes lock with Adam's. He looks older, and not better. His skin looks rough from years in the sun, his face is ruddy, and I notice he's got an old-man beer belly.

"Lexie," he says, his voice cracking. "I'm so sorry."

I nod and force a smile. As much as I despise the man, I know Tommy would tell me he has a right to be here. There was a time when he was an important part of all our lives.

I glance behind me and see Beau glaring in his dad's direction. In an attempt to set an example and be the bigger person, I give Adam a kiss on the cheek before going to find the retired minister.

I'm grateful he's dressed casually and not in the traditional minister garb. I'm sure he picked up on my resistance to organized religion when we met yesterday to talk. Still, there's something comforting about being in his presence and I'm glad he agreed to do this. He and Tommy would have liked each other if they'd ever met.

I look up at the sun breaking through the clouds and feel the warmth on my face. I don't know what I believe in as far as the afterlife goes, but I hope that wherever Tommy is, he'll be able to give me a sign that he's watching over us.

"We are here to celebrate the life of Thomas Jacob Whistler, Tommy to his friends and family," the minister says. "Tommy wasn't a religious man, but he cherished his wife and their daughter, he was a good friend to all he met, a confidant, a good listener, and according to his treasured daughter, Cecelia, he was the world's best advice-giver."

A few small chuckles come from the crowd and I, too, have to smile. I look over at CeCe and squeeze her hand, but she stays stoic, staring out at the water in the distance.

"I chose a passage from Ecclesiastes that I think Tommy would agree with, and I hope it brings a little comfort to those he has left behind. 'For everything there is a season, and a time for every matter under heaven: a time to be born, a time to die, a time to plant and a time to pluck up what is planted. A time to break down, and a time to build up. A time to weep, and a time to laugh, a time to mourn, and a time to dance. For everything there is a season, and a time for every matter under heaven.'

"Lexie, did you want to say a few words?"

I nod and open the wrinkled sheet of paper that I've been folding and unfolding since I put my scattered thoughts down in the dark hours between late last night and early this morning.

"Over the last decade," I begin, "Tommy left me little love notes, almost every day. I'd find them in a drawer at home, in the visor of my car, tucked into a notebook—once, he left a note that a babysitter found in the refrigerator. That took some explaining."

There are a few laughs and I smile, feeling less and less like I'm giving a eulogy and more like I'm telling a story about the man I love.

"Even though all of those love notes were stolen words from other writers, lyrics from songs, quotes he googled, Tommy never let a second of the day go by without me knowing how much I was loved. And I only hope that he knows, that he knew, how much I loved him, too."

I put the paper down—I don't need help remembering

the rest; it's the story of us. I look down at the inside of my wrist, at the *xx* in his handwriting. It didn't hurt as much as I thought it would, and the look on Tommy's face when I showed him made it all worth it. The skin around it is still red, but seeing those two letters, the ones he used to close all the love notes over the years, gives me the strength to go on.

"I can't remember a time when I didn't know Tommy Whistler. He was the sweet boy with a stutter, and one of the best parts of the summers when I came down here to visit with my grandmother. He was always there with a smile and a kind word that made you feel like you were special.

"Then I grew up, life got in the way, and it took twenty years for me to find my way back here. I remember running into Tommy again for the first time. We were at Publix and I almost didn't recognize him, the man he'd grown up to be.

"It didn't take long for us to fall back into our old friendship. And then it grew into so much more. My story and Tommy's story shouldn't be over. I shouldn't be standing here, talking about him in the past tense. And there won't be a single second for the rest of my life that I won't feel like a piece of my heart is missing.

"But if Tommy taught me one thing, it's that you can't run away from the hard things in life, because you might end up missing the beautiful moments. And every moment I spent with him was beautiful. I love you, Tommy Whistler, now and forever."

I fold the paper back into my hand and walk back to take my spot next to CeCe.

She looks up at me, her eyes brimming with tears.

"Would anyone else like to say a few words?"

"I do," CeCe says.

"You don't have to," I whisper. When we talked about it yesterday, she said she didn't think she'd be able to make it through saying anything without falling apart, which she didn't want to do with people watching.

"I know," she says. "But I want to."

Chapter Fifty-Six

CeCe

I wasn't planning to say anything, but now that I'm here, I can't not say something. I don't have anything written down or prepared, but it's not like I'll ever have this chance again.

"Everyone thinks they have the best dad," I say, pushing my glasses up. "But mine really is the best. Was the best," I correct myself. "I'm a teenager, I'm supposed to hate my parents—most of my friends do. But my dad, he was my best friend. He got me like no one else did. He knew when I needed space, or when I needed a hug. He gave the best hugs."

I look up and Mom is ugly crying. I know I'll lose it, too, if I keep looking at her, so I find Beau's eyes and hold his stare. He smiles and I'm ready to go on.

"He was nice to strangers, he always gave a dollar to the homeless people when he saw them on the street, he was good to animals and the environment and to me and my mom. He taught me to treat others the way I wanted to be treated. I know that sounds like cheesy advice, but when he said it, you just believed it.

"I know there are going to be times in my life when I'll see my friends with their dads and I'll be jealous. But none of their dads are like mine was, and I'd rather have fourteen years as his daughter than a hundred years as someone else's."

My eyes scan all the sad faces standing in front of me and I decide I've said all that I needed to say. But I'm not sure how to end this, so I just stand there like a moron and start to cry. Once the tears start falling, I can't stop them.

Mom holds out her arms, so I walk toward her and let her hug me. She whispers in my ear, her voice loud and fierce, "You'll always be his daughter, and he'll always be your dad."

The minister says some other stupid religious stuff that's supposed to be comforting but is really just annoying. Then he hands my mom the canister that's full of what they claim are my dad's ashes. But for all we know, it's a scam and they just scoop a bunch of dust into a fancy bucket and put a lid on it.

Mom reaches for my hand and I let her take it in case it makes her feel better. But it doesn't help me. None of this is helping me—I just want to be alone.

She told me yesterday that after the service we were going to walk to the edge of the water, just the two of us, to spread a handful of the ashes. I agreed, but I hadn't really been thinking about how strange it would feel.

Mom takes the lid off the canister that looks kind of like the one we keep flour in back home. She reaches inside to take a handful of ashes then offers the open container to me, but I jerk my hand away.

"I know this feels really weird," she says.

357

I look at her, surprised. She was the one who wanted to do this in the first place.

"This wasn't my idea," Mom says. "But it's what your dad wanted, and that's all the reason I need."

I take a deep breath and reach my hand into the pile of ashes. If it's what my dad wanted, then I don't want to let him down. The ashes feel kind of like sand, but softer and finer.

"Think we should say something?" Mom asks.

I shrug. I said all that I wanted to say up there.

Mom smiles at me and then looks down to her hands, holding what's supposed to be my dad. "I love you, babe," she says as she tosses her handful into the water.

I watch the ashes swirl, mixing with the water before disappearing as a wave pulls them back into the surf. Mom looks over at me, her eyes all shiny. She doesn't bother to wipe away the tear that slides down her cheek.

My lips move to say the words "I love you, Daddy," but no sound comes out. I open my fist and let the wind carry the pieces that may or may not be him out into the ocean.

This time, I'm the one who reaches for my mom's hand as we start what feels like the world's longest walk back up to the rest of the group.

"You're all invited to join us back at Lexie and CeCe's house for some light refreshments," Aunt Jill says. "But first, if everyone would please take a balloon."

A balloon? This isn't a birthday party.

Abigail and Lou start walking around with two of the big black trash bags we use at The Broken Crown. They open the bags for each person to take an inflated red balloon, tied at the bottom with a long, white ribbon. This has Pinterest written all over it.

Even though it seems completely stupid, I take one when Abigail walks up to me.

"I have markers if you want them," Aunt Jill explains, "to write a message or a prayer on the balloon, then we'll all send them up together."

Everyone takes a Sharpie and starts writing on the balloons as if it's a totally normal thing to do, like Dad will actually be able to read them. I look back to my own blank balloon.

I pull the Sharpie cap off, feeling empty and out of words. I close the marker back up. This is stupid.

Mom and I make eye contact and I can tell she's thinking the same thing. But then she bows her head and starts scribbling something. I sigh and take the cap back off. I put the tip of the marker on the balloon, hoping words will come to me, but they don't.

I write *I love you, Daddy.* But I need something more, just in case he does see it. I close my eyes and hear a song playing somewhere in the distance, as if the wind is carrying it to me. I know what to write.

I smile and blink to try to stop the tears from falling. I write: *This time, you're the one breaking my heart. I'll love you forever and miss you for always.—Cecelia*

I lift my glasses up to wipe the fresh tears away. When I'm as put back together as I can get, I notice Aunt Jill looking at me as if she understands. I look away because I don't want to cry in front of all these people again.

"It looks like everyone's ready," Aunt Jill says. "On the count of three, let go of your balloon." She looks around the group, and everyone nods in understanding. "One, two, three."

At her signal, everyone lets go of their balloons. I hold on to mine for a second more, giving it a kiss before letting it fly. A chill rushes through me and I wrap my arms around my shoulders, looking up at all the red balloons on their way to heaven.

The group shifts and Aunt Becky is the first one out of the pack. She gives me a quick squeeze and whispers in my ear, "I love you, baby cakes." She moves on to my mom and I'm standing alone for a brief moment, which is more than okay with me.

A little old woman I don't know comes up and gives me a sloppy, wet kiss on the cheek. "He's in a better place, dear."

I force a smile and ball my hands into tight fists, squeezing so hard I feel my nails digging into my palms. "Excuse me," I say before I explode.

I can't handle all these people acting like they know me, like they knew my dad. I scan the faces, looking for Beau, and find him standing off to the side. I see his dad walking up to him at the same time he does.

Beau looks away from his dad and locks his eyes with mine instead. He moves to walk toward me, but I shake my head. He stops, pausing for a moment before turning back to the man who really does look like him. Beau might hate his dad, but he's still alive. And he knows I won't be his excuse for not talking to him. Not today.

It's easy to find Mom. There's a crowd of people circled around her, all waiting their turn to talk. I wouldn't be able to stand it if I were her.

"Mom?" I ask, even though she's clearly in the middle of a conversation.

Under normal circumstances, she'd tell me not to interrupt, but there's nothing normal about these circumstances. "Yeah, sweetie?"

"Can I walk home?"

"You don't want to wait for a ride?" I shake my head. "Okay, we'll be there soon."

I turn and start to walk down the beach, figuring I'll walk by the water until I get closer to the beach access by our house.

"Ceese?" I turn back around. "I love you."

"I love you, too."

Chapter Fifty-Seven

Alexis

It was a nice service," Jill says, clearing the last of the deli platters from the folding table someone set up where Tommy's bed used to be. It's amazing how fast they made everything disappear, how quickly everything changed. It's like I went to sleep one morning and July had somehow turned into August and Tommy was gone.

"Very nice," Becky agrees.

"Nice," I echo with just a bit of sarcasm. It's such a pedestrian word for something so life-alteringly devastating.

If Tommy were here, he'd raise his eyebrows and give me a look that said, *Don't be mean.* Later, in a quiet moment, he would get all shrinky and tell me everyone handles grief differently, and that no one knows the right things to say because sometimes there aren't any.

"I'm going to make some tea," Jill says, moving around the house as if it's hers. "Do you want some?"

"She drinks coffee," Becky says, looking up from the stack

of folding chairs she's refolding. "Well, half coffee and half skim milk with one and a half Splendas. Sometimes two."

They look at each other and then back at me, waiting. As if the choice of a hot beverage I don't even want in the first place could determine which one knows me best. Really, it's just further proof that I'm like two different people—Alexis back in Atlanta and Lexie down here. Tommy was the one common denominator that bridged the gap and held the two pieces of me together.

"Tea's fine," I tell Jill, who smiles and retreats to the kitchen. "Coffee will just keep me awake," I tell Becky.

Becky abandons her task and sits next to me on the love seat where I've been holding court most of the afternoon. "I bet you're ready for this day to be over."

"Yes and no." She looks at me, curious. "I was ready for the funeral. Well, not ready." I hate when I can't find the right words. "I knew it was coming."

"Too soon." Becky sighs.

I nod in agreement, although any time before never would have been too soon. "But after this?" I look around at the aftermath of the shiva-ish thing everyone thought would be nice to have after the service. "I don't know what to do next."

"You'll take it one day at a time," Becky says, laying her hand gently on top of mine.

I can't blame her for the cliché advice—just a few short months ago, before words like "terminal" and "cancer" and "stage 4B" were part of my vocabulary, I probably would have said the same sort of thing. Hell, I've probably written those exact words on any number of letters and pamphlets on behalf of Dox Pharmacy.

I know this isn't the right time to make Becky tell me about what's been happening at the agency, but getting back to work would help take my mind off everything I don't want to be dwelling on. If Tommy were here, he would remind me that I was fine all summer, that I got used to not thinking about work after the first two weeks. He would tell me to be careful, not to use work as a crutch, an excuse to run away. He would tell me to be here, to be present in the moment for myself and for CeCe. Of course, he wouldn't be wrong.

"When do you think you'll come back home to Atlanta?" Becky asks.

"I just said I don't know," I snap. She tightens her grip on my hand, letting me know she knows I don't mean it. "I'm sorry."

"Nothing to be sorry about, lovey." I put my left hand on top of hers and I know we're both staring at the diamond ring that looks so out of place on my finger. "It really is beautiful," she says, lifting my hand for a closer look.

Something falls in the other room, clattering to the floor. "Everything's okay," Jill calls out. "Nothing's broken."

"She's a good friend," Becky says.

"So are you."

"I should have come down sooner." The words catch in her throat and I can tell she's trying not to cry.

"You made it to the wedding, you brought the ring and Tommy's tux, and you kept everything running back at the office so I could be here, where I needed to be," I say, comforting her in an odd twist that makes me feel more normal than I have in weeks.

"And now the funeral." She takes her hand back, wiping away a lone tear. "I've got to tell you: the wedding was much more fun."

We both laugh, stopping as quickly as we started. This isn't a time for laughter.

The silence that follows feels awkward and unnatural, another reminder that I have no clue how to do any of this.

The kettle blows, its sharp whistle a welcome distraction.

"Tea's ready," Jill says, coming down the hall with a dishrag in her hands, looking like she's busy at work in the café. "Do you want a cup?" she asks Becky.

"I'd love one, thanks."

I give Becky a sideways glance. She hates tea, unless it's the Long Island iced variety. "You don't have to," I whisper.

She ignores me, turning her smile up a notch, and I laugh again, appreciating her gesture. If only these two could stay by my side for all the days ahead, then maybe, just maybe I can get through this.

"Where's the love bug?" Becky asks.

"Up in her room, I think?" I'm a terrible mother. "Or maybe she's still out for a walk with Beau."

"Your tea, madam," Jill says, handing me the blue mug that's always been mine. "Careful, it's hot." I notice she took a generic mug from the cupboard for Becky's tea and I'm grateful she didn't use the red one that was Tommy's.

It's too hot to take a sip just yet, so I set it on the coffee table. Before my hand leaves the handle, Jill swoops in with a coaster. I bite my lip to hold back a smile as Becky places her mug on the second coaster Jill made sure was ready and waiting.

"I'm going to run down to my house for a minute," Jill says. "You're out of Saran Wrap and I don't want all this food to go bad."

"We're not out," I tell her. "I don't think we ever had any."

Jill smiles. "I'll just be a second."

I reach for her hand. "Sit down."

"But—" she protests.

"Sit."

"There are a lot of things that still need to be done."

"And there will be just as many things to do in ten minutes. But sit with me first. Please?"

Jill sighs and throws the dishrag over her shoulder before sitting on the arm of the love seat. "I'm sitting," she says. "Better?"

"Almost." I hook my arm around her waist and pull her down beside me. The three of us, squeezed onto the sofa made for two. I link my arm with Becky's and lay my head on Jill's shoulder.

"Now it's better." I close my eyes and take a deep breath, wishing I could hold on to this moment, surrounded by the two people left on this planet who know my flaws but love me anyway.

I hear Jill take a sharp breath and I reach for her hand. "In case I haven't said it enough, I love you girls. Thank you for everything, for being here."

"Of course," Jill says, her voice wavering.

"There's no place I'd rather be, buttercup." Becky leans her head on my shoulder. "Well, that's a lie. I'd rather be in Paris with the hottie I sat next to on the flight down here."

"Wouldn't we all?" Jill agrees.

"We're all single women now," Becky says. "Too soon?"

I laugh in spite of myself. I can no easier picture myself a single woman than I can a widow. I stop when I hear a creak on the front porch step. I wonder if it's Adam. He didn't come to the house after the service. His kids didn't exactly make him feel welcome, which I can't blame them for. Maybe he needed to go for a stiff drink first—that would be like the Adam I used to know. I lift my head, waiting for the knock that should be coming.

"Did you hear something?" I ask when it doesn't.

Becky shakes her head.

We all listen, but don't hear anything other than the air-conditioning kicking in. "Must have been my imagination," I say even though I know it wasn't.

Knock, knock.

Jill sits up; she heard it, too. "Come in," she calls.

The door opens, slowly at first and then all at once as she walks in, sucking all the oxygen out of the room.

"I'm sorry, I didn't want to interrupt. I just . . ." Monica stops midsentence.

The jet-black hair CeCe was trying to emulate falls in soft, frizzless curls in spite of the humidity. Her skin looks flawless as usual and her green eyes have a dewy look about them as if she's been crying. Which she probably has. As long ago as it was and as badly as it ended, Tommy meant something to her once.

Jill's the first one off the couch. "Monica," she says.

"Jill." They hug curtly and I push the memory of the two of them sitting at the café together out of my mind.

"Would you like something to drink?" Becky asks. "We were just having tea."

"Tea would be lovely, thank you."

Jill and Becky make eye contact and both head toward the kitchen, leaving Monica and me alone in the room where, not that long ago, she was reunited with Tommy.

"Do you want to sit?" I offer. I can see her hesitation and I don't blame her. "Actually, I could use some fresh air."

Monica looks relieved. She follows me out the door and

we both take a seat on the front porch swing, as much space between us as the small bench seat allows.

"It was a very nice service," she says, using those words again. I'm surprised I didn't see her there; the crowd wasn't that big, and she has a knack for making an entrance. "I was a ways back, I didn't want to make a scene."

"Thank you."

"I just, I'm just so sorry," Monica says. It's hard to hate her when she sounds so sad and sincere. But it's also hard to forget that she's the woman who broke Tommy's heart before it became mine.

I can hear his voice in my head, echoing one of the last conversations we had. His words about how lonely she is in spite of all the glitz and glamour. About forgiveness, and if he can forgive her, why shouldn't I?

"I have so many regrets about the things I did, the choices I made. I know Tommy was able to forgive me because he ended up where he was supposed to be, with you and CeCe. She really is something, you know."

I narrow my eyes at her; the audacity of this woman continues to amaze me. "Of course I know."

"She's been coming by the set on her days off," Monica says.

I sit up straight, trying not to let the shock show on my face. The whole point of Jill giving CeCe Wednesdays off was so she wouldn't be at the café when Monica showed up, not so CeCe could have the day free to spend with her.

Monica doesn't pick up on my shift in demeanor or she doesn't care, because she keeps talking. "It's hard not to think about what might have been, if things had been different. If I had the baby." My fists tighten as she says the words that confirm my suspicions of her motives with CeCe. "Anyway, my offer, what I told CeCe, to have her come out to L.A. and stay with me for a few weeks, it's still open."

"She is my daughter." I say the words slowly and clearly so there's no mistaking the matter. "You may regret what you did, but you can't undo it. And you can't have my daughter. She is not going to Hollywood or anywhere else with you."

"I hate you!"

I look up. CeCe is standing on the sidewalk, listening to us. Her words shoot straight to my heart.

"Dad would let me go," CeCe says, and I know she isn't wrong. She takes the porch steps in one giant leap, throwing the front door open as if she can't get away from me fast enough.

"CeCe," Monica calls, trying to help. It doesn't.

My lost and sad and angry daughter hesitates at the door, glaring in my direction. "I wish it was you that died."

I stand there, accepting my punishment as I silently count to ten, when I know her bedroom door will slam so hard I'll feel it in my bones.

Monica stands, looking as out of place here as I would in her world. "I'm sorry, I shouldn't have come."

"That's one thing we can agree on."

"Let me just give you my card, in case you change your mind." She reaches into her expensive purse that matches her expensive shoes and pulls out a shiny white business card.

I fold my arms, making it clear I have no interest in having any contact with her, not now or ever. I walk past her and into the house, closing the door on her once and for all.

Chapter Fifty-Eight

CeCe

The last time I stopped talking to my mom, I only lasted a few hours. But that was different because Dad was there. This time, it's easy.

It's already been a few days and I haven't said a word.

She's talked to me plenty. More like talked *at* me. I swear, the title of single parent has already gone to her head and she's making decisions left and right as if she's the only one affected by them.

She decided that we're going back to Atlanta today even though school doesn't start for three more weeks. I know I threw a fit about coming down here in the first place, but it was different then. Everything was different. I was different.

I lie back on my bed and stare up at the collection of dull stars on the ceiling, spinning the blue yoyo around in my hand.

"CeCe?" Mom calls upstairs as if she's expecting an answer. She should be happy I'm not talking to her because if I were, she wouldn't like the things I'd tell her.

To say that I'm mad would be the understatement of the century—she's managed to single-handedly ruin a life that was already pretty ruined. Now, not only am I a girl without a father, but I'm a girl whose mother put her own selfish pride ahead of her only daughter's dream. Monica's not even texting me back now. I wrote her to say I was sorry and that I still wanted to go to L.A. with her. I can tell she read the text, but she hasn't written back. Mom ruined that, too.

I hear footsteps coming up the stairs—too light to be Mom's. They stop outside my door and whoever it is knocks.

"Come in," I say, since I know it isn't her.

"Hey," Beau says.

"What are you doing?" I sit up. "My mom will kill you if she catches you in here."

"She's the one who sent me up," he says. "To help you with your bags." Beau looks down at the floor where my suitcase is lying open and empty. "You haven't packed yet?"

"I don't want to go."

"I don't want you to, either." He reaches for my hand and pulls me off the bed and into his arms. He kisses the top of my head and holds me. He doesn't say anything else because he knows there isn't anything else to say.

"Maybe I can stay with you guys," I say into his shoulder. "I can keep working at the café to help your mom instead of paying rent." I look up into his blue eyes, which seem to have lost their sparkle. He gives me a sad smile before bending down to kiss me. His hands slip under my shirt; they feel warm against my back.

Usually, this is when I'd brush his hands away and tell him to stop.

But this isn't usually.

I pull away from his kiss, only for a second so he can see that I'm smiling, so he knows it's okay.

The smile he gives me back is anything but sad. With his lips on mine, I let his hands drift a little higher. I step closer into his embrace and his hands fall back down to the curve of my waist.

My lips don't leave his, but I take a step back. He closes the gap, not allowing any distance to come between us. I take another step back and he follows, like a dance. I stop when I feel the edge of my bed behind my knees. Bringing my arms up around Beau's shoulders, I pull him with me as I lie down.

He pulls back and stands up. "What are you doing?"

"Isn't it obvious?" I reach for his hand and pull him toward me, but he resists. I frown. He's the one who's been testing the limits since whatever this thing is between us started.

"Shit, you're beautiful," he says, taking a step back. "I want to be with you more than anything."

"I'm right here," I say. "But we're leaving soon."

"I know. We should get you packed."

"That's not what I meant."

"I know." He turns around and opens the door to the closet, where all my dresses are hanging. He starts taking them off the hangers one at a time, folding them into my suitcase.

"Everything okay up here?" Aunt Jill asks, coming around the corner and into my room. I can tell from the expression on her face that she's surprised not to have caught us doing something like what we were doing just a few minutes ago.

"I'm helping CeCe pack."

"You're not packed?" Aunt Jill shakes her head. "Okay, well, hurry up. Your mom's almost ready to hit the road."

I roll my eyes and hope Aunt Jill knows it's directed toward my mom, not her.

"Are you going to help me or what?" Beau asks, once his mom is out of earshot.

"I thought you didn't want me to leave."

"I don't," he says. "But it's not up to us." I get up and walk between him and my suitcase. He leans down and gives me a quick kiss before turning back to the closet to get more clothes. I step behind him and wrap my arms around his waist. "You're not helping," he says. "Look, my mom is already talking about coming to visit. So I'll see you soon, and we can talk and text all the time."

"It won't be the same." I drop my hands and step away, looking down for a second, which is all it takes for my stupid glasses to slip. I'm seriously getting contacts as soon as I get back to Atlanta. I'll call and make an appointment myself, just see if Mom can stop me.

Beau drops the sundress he's folding into my suitcase. It's the blue one I wore to the barbecue on the Fourth of July. It feels like that was a million years ago, not just a month.

I look up and meet his eyes for a second, and I have a feeling he's thinking the same thing. In the time it takes me to look away, his arms are wrapped around me, hugging me tight.

"Ahem." I look up to find Abigail standing in the open doorway with a disapproving look on her face. I bet she's never even hugged a guy who isn't related to her before. "I was sent to supervise."

Beau gives her a dirty look but doesn't let go. I'm grateful for

one more moment in his arms, but know it won't be long before they send a whole army up, so I wiggle out of his embrace.

"If you're going to stand there, you might as well help," I
tell Abigail.

She shrugs and goes to open a dresser drawer, lifting folded
shorts and T-shirts in stacks, setting them carefully into my
suitcase.

I pull a small duffel out from under the bathroom sink and
scoop the contents of the drawers inside it without bothering
to look through it all. Better to take everything than realize
too late that I forgot something.

A few minutes later, Beau is zipping my overstuffed suitcase and telling me to make sure nothing is left behind.

"Go ahead," I tell him. "I'll meet you guys downstairs."

He takes the big suitcase and follows Abigail out the door,
leaving me alone for what feels like the last time in my room,
even though I know we'll be back.

The closet is empty except for all the hangers, and I open
the dresser drawers one at a time just to make sure. They're
all empty, too. I look under the bed in case a shoe or something is hiding under there. My breath catches when I see an
envelope with my name scrawled across the front in my dad's
handwriting. It must have fallen off the nightstand.

I wonder how long it's been there—Dad hasn't been upstairs in weeks, unless he gave it to Mom or one of the nurses.
I close my eyes and wrap my hands around it, the last note
my dad ever wrote to me. My eyes start to well up, but I wipe
the tears away before they fall.

"Cecelia," Mom calls from downstairs.

I roll my eyes and tuck the note into my pocket. I'll read it
later when I have more time. And a little privacy.

The duffel bag in one hand, I switch the light off with the other and head downstairs.

"Oh, good, you're ready," Mom says, coming from the kitchen with a Whole Foods bag full of whatever groceries she decided were worth taking back.

I ignore her and walk past her, into the piano room. I stand in front of the card table, looking down at the puzzle with the white sand beach, the crashing waves, and the clear blue sky. The whole picture is pieced together now, except for one piece that's missing from the blue sky. That's the way it should be. If my dad can't finish the puzzle, it shouldn't be finished. I look back one more time before I go outside, where Beau is lifting my suitcase into the trunk. I put my duffel bag next to it and close the lid.

Aunt Jill has me wrapped in a hug before I even turn all the way around. "I'm going to miss you so much. Thank you for all your help. Lou's going to miss you, too."

"Thanks," I mumble. I hate goodbyes, and I've already had my fair share of them this summer.

Aunt Jill pulls back and looks at me like she's deciding whether or not to say something else. Of course she can't resist. She pulls me in again and whispers in my ear, "Be good to your mom. Please, for me. You both need each other."

"Aunt Lexie?" Abigail says, her voice quiet and mousy like her. For a second, I forgot she was even there.

"Hey, sweetie."

"I have something for you," Abigail says. "It's not much."

I watch as she hands my mom a rolled-up sheet of paper.

My mom's back is facing me and I see her shoulders fall as she unrolls it. Curiosity gets the best of me, and I walk closer. When I see what she's holding, my stomach drops. It's a drawing of my dad and it looks so much like him—the real him, not the sick him—that the hole in my heart grows even bigger and emptier.

"It's beautiful," I tell Abigail.

Mom wipes a tear from her eye and looks at me. She smiles as if I said something to her and not to Abigail.

"I hope you like it," she says.

"Sweet girl," Mom says, pulling Abigail close. "I love it. And I love you. Thank you so much."

Abigail blushes and steps back, behind her mom.

Our moms hug and cry as though we're going across the country and not just five hours away. "I miss you already," Aunt Jill says.

"I couldn't have survived any of this without you," Mom tells her. "I love you so much."

I haven't heard "I love you" come out of her mouth this many times in my entire life.

"Say goodbye, CeCe," she says, climbing into the driver's seat.

"Goodbye, CeCe," I mutter under my breath.

But since this really is goodbye, I give Aunt Jill one more hug and even give Abigail a quick one. Saving the best for last, I turn toward Beau, who is standing there suddenly looking shy, with his hands in his pockets.

I slip my arms through his and squeeze him tight. He doesn't reciprocate and I know it's because my mom is watching us in the rearview mirror.

In spite of that, or maybe because of it, I go up on my tippy toes, giving Beau one last kiss. And not a platonic one, either. I can feel his face getting hot, his cheeks flushing as he steps away.

"Don't forget about me," I whisper before walking around to the passenger side of the car.

Through the window, I see Mom lifting her purse off the passenger seat, putting it on the armrest. If she thinks I'm going to spend five hours sitting next to her, she's crazier than I thought.

I open the door to the backseat and climb in.

She might be the parent, but she's not the boss of me.

Chapter Fifty-Nine
Alexis

Five hours have never felt so long in my entire life. If the government needs a new form of torture, I'd be happy to lend them CeCe. Because a road trip with a sulking teenager refusing to talk even if it's just to answer a simple question like "Are you hungry?" or "Do you have to go to the bathroom?" is just about as bad as it gets.

At least we're almost home. Depending on traffic, we'll be there in somewhere between five and twenty-five minutes. Of all the things I missed about Atlanta, the traffic is not one of them.

I glance in the rearview mirror: CeCe is curled up, looking down at her phone. Texting Beau, I bet.

"Imagine me and you, I do." The familiar song comes drifting through the speakers.

CeCe hears it, too.

She looks up and her eyes meet mine for a millisecond before she looks away and puts her headphones back on. I don't blame her; I'm not ready for this song yet, either.

I turn the volume knob all the way to the left. We *were* happy together.

The silence is even louder than the music had been. I focus on the wind whirring outside the car and not the beating of my heart, echoing in my chest and in my ears. Better listening to that than the doubts that keep circling through my head. *How am I going to do this?* I don't think I can.

Turning onto our street, my heart skips a beat when I see a bunch of red balloons tied to a mailbox outside the Murrays' house. As much as I wish they were a sign from Tommy, I know they're probably just a sign that Dylan or Alex is having a birthday party.

Still, I watch the red balloons wave in the wind until they disappear from my view as I turn into our driveway. Without Tommy, our house feels like it's just a building where three people used to live. Now two.

The willow tree in our front yard seems sadder than normal, its branches bowing in reverence to the man of the house, who didn't come home. We're all in mourning.

I turn the car off but don't move to get out. I'm not quite ready. Neither is CeCe, apparently, because she's still sitting there, so quiet and still that if her eyes weren't open, I'd think she was asleep. It's like we both know that once we open the front door, it will feel like we're moving on. And neither of us is ready for that.

But I have to pretend like I am because I'm the grown-up. I open the door and pop the trunk. I grab my suitcase but leave Tommy's where it is. I'm not sure why I packed all his things to bring home. Maybe because I couldn't bring him home.

I turn the key and push the front door open. The floors are shiny and there's an essence of lemon in the air. Someone must have let Effie know we were coming back. I close my eyes and brace myself.

CeCe's watching me.

I can feel her eyes on my back, so I lift the suitcase and step inside, one foot after the other. That wasn't so bad.

I set it down just inside the door and turn to give CeCe a small smile to let her know it's okay. There's a bouquet of flowers on the hallway table with piles of mail on both sides.

Becky must have been here. I can picture her letting herself in with the spare key she's had for years but until a few months ago never used. The mail looks organized: one stack for the bills Tommy used to take care of, another stack of magazines and catalogs, and finally, a stack of what looks like sympathy cards.

I recognize the Dox Pharmacy logo on an envelope on top of the pile. The address label reads: *To the loved ones of Thomas Whistler.* I slide my finger under the flap and pull out the card. *Our thoughts are with you,* it reads.

When I wrote the copy for this sympathy card, I never expected to be on the receiving end of it. I remember knocking out the project in less than an hour. I didn't think about how it would feel to get this card in the mail. I'll talk to Becky about coming up with something better. Something more heartfelt, more authentic and real.

The front door opens and closes. CeCe walks past me and up the stairs toward her room without saying a word. I know

I should try to get her to talk to me, but she can't stay mad forever.

I wish there was a way I could make her understand that I was trying to protect her, not hurt her. That even though she may not realize it now, it's for her own good.

There's a part of me that knows I'm being selfish. But it's not just about Monica. I've been on the other side of that casting couch at commercial auditions—I know how tough it can be for an actress.

It's not that I don't believe in CeCe, I do. I know she's talented, but the teenage years are tough enough without constantly putting yourself out there for rejection. And when she comes home disappointed like she inevitably will, Tommy won't be here with the words of wisdom to help her get through it all. And I don't have it in me. Even if I knew the right words to say, I won't be able to lift her back up on my own.

Putting the card back down, I'm not sure what to do next.

The house feels like a museum, each room an exhibit, a memory of us. I walk through them, one at a time. Through the den, where we watched movies and played Scrabble. Where we set up the Christmas tree and watched CeCe open way more presents than any one child needed. Where CeCe, always the performer, put on one-girl plays for us. The kitchen, where CeCe cooked and Tommy did the dishes, where I sat drinking wine and watching them work. The dining room, where we dined only on the rare occasion we had people over. Tommy's office.

I walk inside the room where he spent so much of his time. I wonder if anyone let his patients know he's gone. I would if I could, but Tommy would be the first to remind me about doctor-patient confidentiality.

Sitting down in his chair, I close my eyes, trying to feel close to him. But all I feel is the cold leather of the chair sticking to my skin, damp with sweat. I open the left-side drawer and find a folder with my name on it. The papers. He mentioned papers, but it's too soon.

I close the drawer and open the datebook he insists, *insisted,* on keeping even though everyone else on the planet has upgraded to a digital version. I flip to today's date. It's blank. And so are all the pages that come after it, except for the odd reminder to pay recurring bills. Credit cards, cable and electric on the fifteenth. Mortgage and insurance on the first.

My phone vibrates in my pocket. I fish it out to see Becky's face flashing across the screen. "Hey, Becks."

"Hey, yourself. Just wanted to make sure you made it back okay."

"A few minutes ago." In the background, I can hear the bustle of the office. It's good to hear things sounding busy there. I'm anxious to get back, to feel normal again. "I might come in tomorrow."

"Isn't that too soon?" Becky asks. "I mean, you don't have to, if you aren't ready."

"I think it might actually help, to get my mind focused on something else."

"But CeCe—"

"Still isn't talking to me," I say. "I don't think it matters to her if I'm here or not." Becky sighs and I know she's struggling to find the right words to say, so I change the subject for her. I used to be good at that. "But if any projects come up that have to do with cancer or terminal illness . . ."

"We'll have someone else cover them, don't you worry. It'll be good to have you back, it hasn't been the same around here without you."

"It'll be good to be back."

From what Becky finally told me, things at the agency have been going well. The Dox chief marketing officer seems to have had a change of heart. Apparently, he's been acting impressed, even appreciative, of our work, so there hasn't been any more talk about putting the account up for review.

Even if they do, I know we'll be okay. Win or lose. It's funny how differently I see my dad's advice now—the advice I held on to, the advice that influenced so many decisions over the years. I was gone long enough for everyone at the agency to realize they don't need me—but it was also long enough for me to realize they would be okay without me. The world won't stop turning if I go home on time, if I don't go in at all some days. They'll be okay, and so will CeCe and I.

"Alrighty, my dear. I have to go settle a typeface dispute. Call me later if you want a distraction."

"Thanks, Beck. Love you."

She hangs up and I feel a little braver having talked to her. I'll have to remember that the next time things start to feel like they're spinning out of control.

I decide to take advantage of this feeling before it fades and finally open the envelope Jill handed me before we left. The envelope with my name on it, written in Tommy's familiar, scratchy handwriting.

Standing up, I roll the chair back and put the planner down where Tommy left it. I close the door behind me. Maybe I can trick myself into thinking he's in there, busy helping a patient.

The envelope is sticking out of my purse, taunting me. I bring it outside to read. The porch swing looks inviting, but I wonder if it's wrong to sit there. In the place where Tommy first told me he was sick.

I can do this. I take a seat and pull my legs up underneath me, finding comfort in the slight sway of the swing. I hold the closed envelope over my heart for a second until I'm ready. It's sealed so tightly the flap on the back rips a bit when I try to open it, so I stop. I know it's just an envelope, but I don't want to tear it, or God forbid, the letter inside.

I bite my lip in concentration and slowly peel the flap open, one millimeter at a time. I reach inside for the letter. Two pages, the front and back filled with Tommy's handwriting.

To my wife,

> *My wife. How cool is that?*
> *There's that smile, I hope. The one that lights up your beautiful eyes and my world. I think your smile was the first thing that made me fall in love with you all those years ago. How lucky am I that I finally got to marry the girl of my dreams?*
> *You were worth the wait, my love.*
> *I'm not sure what I'm supposed to say from here—words are your forte, not mine. But I wanted to leave you with one last reminder that I love you with all of my heart and my*

soul. That even though I'm not physically there with you, I'm with you.

I know you don't think you're strong enough for this, but Lexie, my love, my life, you are the strongest, bravest, most wonderful woman I have ever met. I only wish that you could see yourself the way that I do. Then you would have no doubt.

Be easy on yourself, my love. This is not an easy hand you have been dealt, but you aren't alone. Don't try to do it all alone. There are so many people around you that love you as much as I do, that want to help. Let them.

I have so many things left I want to say to you, but I know in my heart of hearts that you already know them all.

Thank you for loving me. Thank you for giving me a daughter who is so much like you, and not just in the way she looks. I know you worry about her, but she's strong like her mother. And if she has you in her corner believing in her, there's nothing she won't be able to accomplish or overcome.

I hope that one day you can forgive me for not fighting harder. Believe me, it was the hardest decision I ever had to make, and I'd be lying if I said there weren't days that I regretted it. I never wanted to leave you. You are my everything.

And so, my dear, here is one last stolen line from my heart to yours.

> "Don't cry because it's over,
> smile because it happened."
> —Dr. Seuss

xx, Tommy

I read the letter through two times and then a third. My fingers fumble as I reach into my pocket and pull out the piece of heavenly sky I've been carrying with me since I took it from the puzzle weeks ago. I rub the piece between my fingers, and suddenly, without a doubt, I know what I have to do.

CeCe was right. It's what Tommy would have done.

Chapter Sixty

CeCe

I still haven't read the last note my dad left me. There's just something about knowing there won't be another one that makes me want to save it. Once I read it, there won't be anything else from him for me to read. Ever.

Instead, I've been rereading all the notes he ever wrote me, all the ones he left in my lunch box or my backpack. There must be more than a thousand. A lot of them just say little things like "Have a great day!" or "I love you!" but others have silly advice like "Remember—never look a tiger in the eyes" or "Always say please and thank you when a monkey gives you a banana."

My favorites are the longer ones he wrote every year on my birthday, talking about the things I said or did throughout the year and what he was looking forward to in the year ahead. Thanks to those letters, I know I said my first curse word at three years old, that I rode my bicycle without training wheels at six and baked my first cake at eight.

There's something special about seeing my life through his eyes. I miss him so much it physically hurts.

I'm rereading the letter he wrote on my tenth birthday when my laptop starts ringing with a Skype call.

I set the letter down and click to accept the call.

"Hey," Beau says.

"Hey."

"Hey," he says again and I laugh. He's the only one who can make me smile these days.

Mom's been back at work since the day after we got back. I had to break the silent treatment to convince her I'm old enough to stay in the house on my own without a stupid baby-sitter, but I'm only talking to her on a very limited, need-to basis.

"So how's it being back?" Beau asks. "Because it sucks here without you."

"I'm sure it's not that bad."

"Seriously, how is it?"

"Fine." I shrug. "I haven't been doing much. Watching a lot of TV. Cooking. Lou has been emailing me about new recipe ideas and stuff."

"That's cool."

"Yeah, she is."

"I bet your friends are happy to have you back."

I shrug again. If I felt like a pariah when everyone found out Dad was sick, I don't even know how to describe how weird it is now. I'm like a leper. "I haven't really seen them. The big show for theater camp is next week, so everyone's busy with rehearsals."

"Are you going to the show?"

"Why would I?" I ask. "To support my former best friend? She hasn't reached out to say she's sorry that my dad died.

Probably because she knows that I know she stabbed me in the back by dating the guy that I like. The guy I liked." I correct myself a little too late.

"The guy you like?"

"The guy I liked," I repeat. We haven't talked about whether or not we're going to try to do the whole long-distance thing yet. But he doesn't have anything to be worried about. "It's not even about him. It's about Sofia. She was my best friend."

"I thought I was your best friend?"

"Stop, you know you're different."

"You look pretty," he says. I blush, even though I know he's just trying to change the subject.

"So do you," I tell him.

"I'm trying to convince my mom we should drive up to Atlanta for a weekend before school starts."

"That would be amazing. I miss you."

"I miss you, too." He brings his finger up toward the camera on his laptop and I do the same so it's almost like our hands are touching in spite of the distance. "When I get my license, I'll drive up every weekend."

"That's almost a year away."

"I guess you'll have to make some new friends in the meantime. Girlfriends . . ." His smile fades for just a moment before coming back, a little shyer than before. "You don't need any more guy friends."

"There is one girl, Bella. We were kind of friends before, but she's really quiet and kind of shy."

"What's wrong with quiet people?"

"Nothing, it's just . . . I don't know."

"Is she cool?"

I nod. "She sent me a card with a really sweet note. It turns out her mom is really her stepmom. Her real mom died of cancer when she was five."

"Oh, man."

"I know. We're going to go to the movies or something later this week. It's just cool that she gets it, you know?"

"I know."

I tilt my head and smile at him. He tilts his head and smiles back at me. "You're cute," I tell him.

"And don't you forget it. Are you and your mom talking yet?"

I shrug. "Sometimes."

"I bet it's hard on her, too. You know, missing your dad."

"Whose side are you on?" I don't mean to sound as angry as I do, but I can't help it. I push my chair back, away from my laptop. Away from him. Aunt Jill can say that sort of stuff to me because she's Mom's friend. But Beau is mine.

"Your side," he says. "Come back. I'm always on your side."

The computer dings and an alert pops up on the screen. An email from my mom.

"What the . . . ?" I click to open it. Notes and letters were Dad's thing. If she thinks she can just step in and take over, she's crazier than I thought. "Hold on," I tell Beau.

I read the email:

Subject: Pack Your Bags

My darling daughter,

I know how hard this all has been for you, and I'm sorry that I haven't done a better job at being there for you. I'm sorry that I let myself get lost in my own grief without

being the strong mother that you need. And I'm sorry I let
my fears stand in the way of your dreams.

There's a part of me, I'm ashamed to admit, that was
afraid you would love Monica more than you loved me. I
know I haven't been easy to love, that I let you down so many
times. And I'm sorry, I hope you know how sorry I am.

This summer will always be the worst summer in our
lives, a summer of endings. But I thought that maybe,
we could have a bit of a new beginning as well. I know
you think that I don't want you to pursue acting, but
remember, I was the one who got you your very first
acting gig.

I glance over at the framed picture on my desk, the still
frame from my one and only commercial shoot. It was that
experience that made me catch the acting bug when I was six.

When I cast you to play that role, I had no idea it would
spark a passion inside of you. I was just tired of leaving
you and your dad behind on production trips, and I
wanted to have you both there with me. But you were a
natural, even back then.

And who am I to stand in the way of your destiny?

Your dad reminded me that life is worth living, that
risks are worth taking, and that your dreams are worth
chasing. So, my beautiful, talented, smart, special
daughter, let's go chase your dreams.

For one week—we'll be back before school starts.

I love you more than you know,
Mom

ALISON HAMMER

"Holy shit."

"Ceese?" I hear Beau's voice, but the email is blocking his face. "Is everything okay? CeCe?"

"I've gotta go, I'll call you later."

I close the Skype screen before he has time to say anything else. I read the email a second time. If this is a joke, I'll really never talk to her again.

But if it's real?

Holy shit.

I open the door and Mom is standing there with a goofy grin on her face. That's when I know it's really happening.

Chapter Sixty-One

Alexis

Now boarding first-class passengers," the Delta gate agent announces.

"That's us," I tell CeCe.

It's like she's become a different person in the week since I broke the news, and not just because I'm taking her to L.A. I've become different with her, too, telling her the things I need her to know, that she's not alone. That we've got each other.

"Are your eyes okay?" I ask as we settle into our seats. I've been saving miles for the last ten years, hoping the three of us could take a big European vacation together after CeCe graduated high school. But if this summer taught me one thing, it's that life is too short to wait for anything. So when I cashed in the miles, I went for it.

"They're fine," she says. "A little dry, but I have drops."

CeCe takes the eye drops from her purse and leans back, squeezing a drop into her left eye and then the right. She blinks and turns to look at me, a smile on her face.

It's a little unsettling, seeing her with one brown eye and one blue, thanks to the one colored contact. I wasn't sure at first, but when she said it was in honor of her dad, I couldn't say no.

"Would you ladies like a drink before takeoff?" the flight attendant asks.

"I'd love a glass of champagne."

"Make that two," CeCe says.

The flight attendant looks at me and then back at CeCe. "How about sparkling grape juice?"

"That works, too," CeCe tells the flight attendant before turning back to me. "I still can't believe this is really happening. Thank you so much, Mom."

"You're so welcome, and you can stop saying thank you now. You've said it more than enough."

"Here you go, ladies." The flight attendant hands us both our sparkling beverages.

"Smile, Mom." CeCe puts her phone in selfie mode and snaps a picture of us living the life in first class. Champagne wishes . . .

"Do you have the itinerary Monica sent?" I ask.

After I read Tommy's letter, I reached out to Brit to get Monica's email and wrote her a letter, an apology. I don't think we'll ever be friends, but like Tommy said, if she can help our daughter, who am I to say no?

CeCe nods and pulls it out of her purse. "I've pretty much got it memorized. Lunch at the Ivy, meetings with her agent and a casting director. Walking the real red carpet for a movie premiere!"

"There's one more thing that isn't on her agenda."

"What do you mean?"

"Monica's not the only one with connections in L.A."

"Mom? What did you do?"

"I may have made a call to one of the casting companies I've done a lot of work with."

"Am I auditioning for another commercial?"

"Not exactly."

The captain announces that we're almost ready for take-off, so the flight attendant comes back around to collect our glasses.

"If it's not a commercial, then what is it?"

"One of the casting agents works on another project."

"Just tell me." CeCe's leg is bouncing in anticipation.

MasterChef Junior.

"Shut up!" CeCe screams so loud the other passengers turn and stare.

"Shh." I laugh.

"Are you serious?"

"Couldn't be more serious. But no guarantees—it's just an audition."

"Thank you, Mom." CeCe leans over the wide armrest and gives me a hug. When she pulls back, I notice her eyes are shining with tears.

"You okay?"

She nods. "I just wish Dad were here."

"Me, too, baby."

She leans in for another hug and I kiss the top of her head. I'm so grateful she's letting me love her. As much as I'm trying to live in the present, I can't help but think back to the times I was on the outside looking in, the third wheel of our family. Now there's only two of us.

ALISON HAMMER

I turn back and stare out the window as the plane takes off, trying to blink away the tears. They sneak up on me sometimes. One minute I'm fine, and the next, I'm not.

It feels wrong that he's gone. Like the universe made a mistake and eventually I'll wake up with Tommy beside me, saying it was all a bad dream. The worst dream.

"I'm going to watch a movie," CeCe says once we've reached the cruising altitude.

I nod and mumble something that I hope sounds like "okay." I don't want her to worry about me.

The plane jerks with what I tell myself is just turbulence, but my hand instinctively reaches out for CeCe, as if my arm could protect her. She smiles and shakes her head before turning back to the movie on her laptop. Across the aisle, a woman is rubbing rosary beads.

For the first time in my life, I wish I were religious, that I had something to believe in. That I could feel or know there is a bigger purpose to all of this. That Tommy really is in a better place. I'm not even sure if I believe in heaven—it feels so manufactured, like a story invented to comfort the people left behind.

It would be nice to believe he's somewhere waiting for me, that we'll all be together again. But, I don't know, it's all too much.

CeCe laughs at something in the movie and I wish I could bottle that sound. There has been enough sadness around us to last a lifetime, and I'm going to try my hardest to give her reasons to smile every day, even if it's just saying I love her.

I glance back out the window and for a second, I swear I

see a red balloon floating by. I blink and it's gone, if it was ever there.

As much as I know it's probably impossible because of atmospheric pressure or some other scientific thing, it would be nice to believe it's a sign. To believe that maybe, just maybe, there's a spirit or an angel or whatever you want to call him, watching over us with one brown eye and one blue.

One Year Later

CeCe!" I call upstairs. "It's almost on!"

"Coming!" She runs down the steps wearing her chef's jacket from the show. "Sorry, I was just talking to Beau."

I was surprised she didn't want to have a big party for the finale night, but she said she wanted it to be just the two of us. Other than the gorgeous bouquet of flowers Monica sent, it feels like just another night with us watching TV together after dinner. She sits on the edge of her seat in her spot, and I take the one next to hers. The one that used to be Tommy's.

CeCe can barely sit still as we watch her cook her final menu: three courses, each more impressive than the last. We know the way the show ends, but it still takes my breath away to see her standing up there among the other finalists. And when Gordon Ramsay announces that my sweet girl will be going home, I watch, proud, as she smiles and shakes his hand, thanking him for the experience.

It wasn't easy, taking classes remotely and studying between shoots. Learning new techniques, competing against so many insanely talented kids. Cooking things that I've never heard of, much less tasted. And she did it all while processing her grief and trying to figure out what this new life of ours looked like.

And third place is nothing to scoff at.

While it was my connection that got her the audition, her talent and drive got her onto the show. Her positive attitude, her ability to lead and be a team player all while cooking the hell out of whatever ingredients they threw her way, that's what got her to the top.

At eleven o'clock, the show gives way to the news and CeCe's phone lights up with congratulations texts from her school friends and the other aspiring chefs she met along the journey.

"Sorry, Mom," she says, as she picks up the phone, squealing words I can't make out.

"Nothing to be sorry about, enjoy your moment."

I watch her, nodding with excitement as she talks to one of her friends. Bella, I assume. I love how close the two of them have become. It's not that I didn't like her friends before, but there's something genuine about Bella. She's been a good influence on CeCe, and I think CeCe has helped bring her out of her shell. They've been good for each other.

"Bella, I've gotta call you back." CeCe looks up at me and shakes her head as she switches calls. "I told you he's just a friend."

The winner, a boy named Jason, was CeCe's age and devilishly handsome. No wonder Beau was jealous, but he doesn't need to be. CeCe really does care about him, and I know from experience not to write off your childhood love.

"It was just a hug—he won the whole competition. Everyone hugged him." She sighs and collapses onto the couch.

I head into the kitchen to give her a little privacy and take tonight's special dessert out of the refrigerator, where it's been defrosting.

While I never wanted to spend my first wedding anniversary as a widow, I'm happy I'm not alone. That CeCe and I have really started to figure things out. It's far from perfect and we have our moments, but she knows I'm not going anywhere. And while her dad will always be her number one fan, I'm proud to hold the number two spot.

I set the top tier of the wedding cake CeCe made exactly one year ago today on the kitchen table and wait for her to finish the call with Beau. They'll have to wrap things up soon, because she has a test in algebra tomorrow. And future celebrity chef or not, she needs a good night's sleep.

"Beau, come on!" I hear her yell from the other room. "Stop being ridiculous."

I smile and look behind me to check the time on the microwave. It's 11:11.

I close my eyes and make the same wish I always make, that I could climb in bed one more night with Tommy. I know it's impossible, but isn't that what wishes are for?

Acknowledgments

Writing is not a solo sport, and I have so many people to thank for helping turn this lifelong dream into a reality

First and foremost, none of this would be possible without my amazing agent, Joanna MacKenzie. The $29 I spent for ten minutes with you at the Writing Workshop of Chicago was the best money I've ever spent. Thank you for believing in me, for helping to make this story stronger, and for finding it a wonderful home.

To Tessa Woodward, my editor at William Morrow, thank you for taking a chance on a debut author and bringing Alexis and CeCe's story to the world. I'll forever be grateful.

There aren't enough words to thank Bradeigh Godfrey, the world's best critique partner. Thank you for pushing me when I need to be pushed, encouraging me when I need to be encouraged, and being swoontastic when I need to add a little swoon. I can't wait until the world discovers how amazing you are.

I owe so much to Kristie Cain Raymer for sharing a piece of her and Ian's story with me. Thank you for your friendship and for telling me your stories, even when it wasn't easy. I will always be a #RaymerWarrior.

Thank you times a million to my writing tribe. The Women's Fiction Writers Association (WFWA) transformed my writing life and introduced me to "my people." I am proud and honored to be part of such an incredible organization.

I'm grateful for the subgroups I've found and formed along the way—first and foremost, the Fictionistas, who are always there for a #spitball and support. I was never alone on this journey thanks to the Querying Support group, the Sub Support group, and now, the 2020 Debuts with help and guidance from Mike Chen and the 2019 group and Jennifer Klepper and the 2018 group. I can't wait to pay your kindness forward. And, of course, the Every Damn Day Writers, who keep me inspired and accountable.

Alexis and Tommy have been around for a very long time, so I have to thank my first-ever critique group, Catherine Becker, Shannon Heffernan, Paige Warren, and Whitney Wolf, for helping to shape them both. And my local Slice of Fiction ladies, Mary Chase, Amy Melnicsak, Kasia Manolas, and Nancy Johnson, who I have to thank for many things, including opening my eyes to the unique way people with lung cancer are treated.

So many writers have helped me by looking at my pages, critiquing my query letters, or giving general advice, including: Lainey Cameron (the best writing conference roommate); Sharon Peterson; Julie Carrick Dalton; Orly Konig; Christine Adler; Kathleen West, who has been in step with me on this crazy journey; Sheri Taylor-Emery; Natalia Iwanyckyj; Peggy Finck (with her mad query skills); Michele Montgomery; Lisa Montanaro; Jessica Zimmerman Smith; Meghan Scott Molin;

ACKNOWLEDGMENTS

Suanne Schafer; Jessie Starr; Fern Ronay; Brenda Linskey; Gisèle Lewis; Karen Stensgaard; and everyone in the Women's Fiction Critique Group. An additional thank-you to Abby Saul for the early revision help, and to Esi Sogah and Alicia Clancy.

I have been fortunate to have so many friends who have been through this journey before, and I am beyond grateful for their friendship, support, and advice. Thank you to Barbara Claypole White, Heather Webb, Kristin Rockaway, Kathleen Barber, Kimmery Martin, Julie Clark, Erin Bartles, Liz Fenton, Colleen Oakley, Meg Donohue, Laura Drake, Rea Frey, and Amy Mason Doan. A special thanks to Kristin Harmel for showing me the way early on, telling me how *not* to format a manuscript, and to Camille Pagán for becoming a mentor and a friend.

Thank you to Grant Faulkner for starting National Novel Writing Month (NaNoWriMo)—the main reason I was able to write the first draft of this book in two months, which is fourteen years and ten months faster than I wrote my first manuscript.

I'm never finished learning, and I owe so much to my teachers along the way, including Josh Russell, Jennie Nash, Donald Maass, the Muse and the Marketplace, Writer Unboxed, StoryStudio Chicago, the Marks of the Bestseller Experiment, and my writing teachers at Clayton High, the University of Kansas, and the University of Florida. Go Gators!

There's a reason this book is dedicated to my family. Thank you to my mom, Kathy Hammer—who, for the record, I have a great relationship with—for being one of my best friends and biggest fans from day one. To my dad, Dr. Randy Hammer, who, like Tommy, makes the world's best cream cheese eggs, gives great advice, and is always one of my most enthusiastic readers. And to Elizabeth Murray, my sister by chance and friend by choice. Thank you for your support and excitement, and for giving me one of my favorite job titles: aunt.

Thank you to the Lewin, Berger, Hammer, and Block families. And to my grandparents, Elaine and Joe Berger and Annette and Buddy Hammer, who are always in my heart. Thank you to Nick Murray, Dylan Murray, Alex "Bear-Bear" Murray, and to Carlene Jarrett.

Friends are the family you choose, and I've got some of the best. Thank you, Meg McKeen, for being the best Myrna a girl could ask for. To Jenna Shulman, my BFFAEAE; Christina Williams for always having my back, DJ Johnson and Chardy McEwan, Amy Wallace, Sally MF Bright, Amy Gerhartz and the rest of MyGirls, Libby Love; Krissie Callahan, Jeff and Julie Johnson, Brian and Kristen Fechino, Michelle Dash, Shana Freedman, and Marija McPherson.

To Tom Piazza and the McGee's Sunday Funday crew; Mia Pfifer; Meredith Bailey; Katie Ross; the Sunday Dinner Club; Ken Block and the Rock Boat family; Beth Gosnell and the Rock by the Sea family; the Charleston Place crew; the men of LOVESWEAT: Steve Everett, Paul Pfau, JD Eicher, and Connor Pledger. To Jen Wedick for all the high fives, Will Byington for the friendship and the photos, David Boran for help with the cooking terms, and Dr. Carla Lewin and Lauren Black for the oxygen education. And to Andrea Kate of Great Thoughts' Great Readers.

Thank you to my past and present FCB Chicago family for the support and encouragement. To Stump Mahoney for the music help; Kevin Grady, Jennifer Ludwig, Paige Miller, Kristin Zuccarini, Angela Carlson, and So A Ryu for your

ACKNOWLEDGMENTS

design expertise; Lauren Cabot Altergott for being one of my first readers; my CB team; and Teddy Brown for being a great boss and friend (most of the time). While I'm on the topic of my other career (and Alexis's), thank you to GirlsDay and the Three Percent Conference for making the advertising industry a better place for everyone to work.

Thank you to all the Starbucks I have regulared for providing a great environment to write and having the "Save to Spotify" feature on your app for my writing playlist. And, speaking of music, I'd like to thank some of the artists who inspire me and frequently play before, during, and after my writing sessions: Red Wanting Blue, Will Hoge, The Alternate Routes, Aslyn, Shawn Mullins, Stephen Kellogg, Brandi Carlile, Matt Nathanson, Emerson Hart, and Sister Hazel.

For all the behind-the-scenes work, thank you to Kristin Nelson, Brian Nelson, Tallahj Curry, Samantha Cronin, and Angie Hodapp of the Nelson Literary Agency. Many thanks to Alice Lawson at Gersh and my entire team at Harper-Collins: Elle Keck, Molly Waxman, Rachel Meyers, Robin Barletta, Jennifer Hart, Kelly Rudolph, Karen Richardson, Mumtaz Mustafa, Christina Joell, and Maureen Cole. Also to Crystal Patriarche and the BookSparks team.

Thank you to the booksellers, book reviewers, bloggers, bookstagrammers, and the Tall Poppy Writers, and last but certainly not least, thank you to the readers for choosing to spend time with this story. I'm grateful, and I'd love to hear from you online at AlisonHammer.com or @ThisHammer on Facebook, Twitter, and Instagram.

About the author

About the book

Insights,
Interviews
& More . . .

Meet Alison Hammer

© Will Byington

Founder of the Every Damn Day Writers, Alison Hammer has been spinning words to tell stories since she learned how to talk. A graduate of the University of Florida and the Creative Circus in Atlanta, she lived in nine cities before settling down in Chicago, where she works as a VP creative director at an advertising agency. *You and Me and Us* is her first novel.

Behind the Book Essay

Alexis Gold has been floating around in my head for almost twenty years. Two whole decades. She's like a real person to me, and after reading part of her story, I hope she's a little real for you, too.

The first time I wrote about Alexis, her last name was Hersh. I changed it pretty early on because I thought that if she had the same initials as I did, people would think she was a thinly veiled version of myself. And she is NOT me. Although I do tell people that if they don't like me, they probably won't like her, either.

That first first-draft was a short story called "Her Mom Was Popular with Men" that I workshopped in a fiction class at the University of Florida. I finished the story and turned it in, but I had a feeling that I wasn't finished with Alexis. More accurately, she wasn't finished with me.

Over the next fifteen years, I took that short story about a woman who had returned to a place from her past and suddenly remembered a traumatic event she'd witnessed as a child, and I turned it into a way-too-long novel. (I eventually cut 30,000 words—but that's a story for another day.)

In the novel version, renamed *Face the Music*, Alexis Gold was a ▶

3

thirtysomething woman who worked in advertising and had been recently dumped by her boyfriend of ten years. She and Peter hadn't been married— if you've read *You and Me and Us*, you know Alexis doesn't believe in marriage. At least she didn't back then.

Reeling from the breakup, Alexis needed to get out of the Atlanta house she and Peter had shared, so she packed her bags and headed out on a road trip for Destin, Florida. Alexis hadn't been back to the small beach town where she spent summers growing up in more than twenty years, but she had nowhere else to go.

A few days into her stay, Alexis was on an emergency aloe trip to Publix after falling asleep on the beach, when she ran into a familiar stranger with one brown eye and one blue: Tommy.

I don't want to give too much of that story away because I hope that one day a version of it will find its way into the world, but there are two things I can share.

The first is that throughout the book, there are flashbacks and memories of the summer Alexis was twelve: the last summer she spent on the beach with her childhood friends Tommy, Jill, Jack, and Adam.

The second, which isn't a spoiler if you've read *You and Me and Us*, is that eventually, Tommy and Alexis cross the line from friendship to something more. Alexis didn't know it at the time, but in one of the last chapters, she and Tommy, as she later puts it, "had the oops that turned into CeCe."

When I finally reached the last page of the manuscript that had been fifteen years in the making, I didn't just write "The End." Instead, I wrote: "The End, For Now." I knew there was more to Tommy and Alexis's story. I just wasn't sure what it was yet.

I did have one idea—that it would be interesting to show Alexis with a daughter the same age as she had been during the flashbacks in *Face the Music*. I knew their daughter's name would be CeCe, based on a scene where Tommy and Alexis sang and danced to several "name songs," including Simon & Garfunkel's "Cecelia."

But that was it.

I had no idea what the story would be "about."

It was the end of September 2016, less than two months away from November, or as I now call it, NaNoWriMo.

National Novel Writing Month is an international writing event where writers around the world are challenged to write 50,000 words in the thirty days of November. I first heard of NaNoWriMo in 2006, when I was five years into the writing process of *Face the Music* and thought the idea ▶

Behind the Book Essay *(continued)*

of writing a book that quickly was insane. Still, I was curious, and the timing was right, so I decided to give it a shot.

For a few weeks, I tried to think of what story I could tell about Alexis, Tommy, and their twelve-year-old daughter, CeCe. (I aged CeCe up to fourteen after a few early readers told me what a big deal it would be for a twelve-year-old girl to drink beer and kiss boys. What can I say, it's been a long time since I was twelve.)

One day, I was sitting out on the community porch of the building where I lived at the time in Pittsburgh, thinking about how NaNo was coming up and I still didn't have an idea for the story. And then it came to me, just like that. Tommy was sick.

I don't do much research in the early stages of my writing (I have a very strong "Finish First" philosophy), but that afternoon, I did a lot of googling about different terminal illnesses, their symptoms, and the reality of someone passing away a few months after diagnosis.

My first thought was pancreatic cancer, after losing a friend, Tattoo Dave, to the horrible disease a few years earlier. But after looking into the symptoms, it didn't seem right for the story. A few Google searches later, and I found out there were different kinds of lung cancer—one of them, small-cell cancer, was harder to beat, and its symptoms were things that I could picture happening to Tommy. The cough, the weight loss, and the shortness of breath. Once I knew what Tommy would have, I started writing a very loose outline of the story.

In the writing world, people say that they are plotters, who plot a story out, or pantsers, who fly by the seat of their pants. I like to say I'm a plotser, a combination of the two. There are a lot of scenes that are still around from that first outline—but some of my favorites weren't planned at all. Like the wedding scene, or even the idea that Tommy and Alexis would eventually get married. I know I wrote the words, but every time I read that scene, it makes me cry.

I wrote the first line of *You and Me and Us* at midnight on Halloween in 2016, with a glass of champagne as soon as it officially became November 1.

Thanks to NaNoWriMo, I got in the habit of writing every day. My day job is in advertising, so I'm used to writing on a deadline—I actually prefer it. I'm an expert procrastinator, so having a deadline helps kick my creativity into action. I'm also pretty competitive, so I didn't just complete NaNo. I WON IT. I crossed the 50,000-word finish line almost a week ahead of schedule, and then I kept going, writing every day ▶

until I reached the end of that first draft
the third week of December.

At the time, I thought I had written
a story about what happened to Tommy.
But then a few very wise writer friends
informed me otherwise. They helped me
see that the story wasn't "about" Tommy
getting sick. That's what happens in
the story. The story itself was about the
relationship between Alexis and CeCe.
(For the record, my mom and I have a
great relationship—she wants to make
sure everyone knows that!)

Four years after that first spark of an
idea, I'm still heartbroken over the loss
of Tommy. I wish his story didn't have
to end that way, but I've got a feeling
that Alexis's story still isn't finished.
And neither is CeCe's.

In the meantime, I've got other stories
I'm excited to tell, but I can't wait for the
day when CeCe and Alexis pop back up
and fill me in on what's next.

Reading Group Guide

1. Do you think Tommy made the right decision choosing not to get treatment? How would you approach weighing the factors he had to consider—quality of life versus quantity of life—if you were in his shoes? And what about his choice to spend his last weeks at the beach? Where would you spend your last days?

2. A lot of parents and teenagers have tough relationships. Do you think the way CeCe and Alexis saw each other was fair? Without Tommy's illness, do you think they would have been able to repair their relationship?

3. Alexis didn't want to get married because she equates the legal bond of marriage with her parents' relationship, which was nothing like hers and Tommy's. Why do you think she changed her mind in the end? How do you think this will affect CeCe's future views on marriage and relationships? ▶

4. Alexis has two best friends—Jill and Becky. Her friendships with each woman fill very different purposes in her life. What are those purposes? Do you have more than one best friend? If life has ever brought you all together, did everyone get along?

5. CeCe has a moment when she realizes that Tommy isn't just her dad, but that he's also his own person. At what moment in your life did you realize that your parents were more than just your parents?

6. What did you think of Tommy's decision to see and forgive Monica? If you were Alexis, would you have been okay with having his ex over to your house?

7. Do you think Alexis made the right decision taking CeCe to California? Why or why not?

8. Where do you think Alexis and CeCe will be in five years? Ten years? ᴄᴧ

Discover great authors, exclusive offers, and more at hc.com.